BIG GREEN COUNTRY

A NOVEL

FRANCES RIVETTI

ISBN 978-0-9904921-2-2

Author photo by Dominic Rivetti

Book design by ebooklaunch.com

This book is for my sisters, Kerry and Lindsey
and my brother, Stuart

"Family, like branches on a tree, we all grow in different directions, yet our roots remain as one"

— unknown.

CHAPTER 1

MAGGIE

At first sight, the ranch appeared deserted. In drawing closer, an amber porch light glowed in the blue funk of the afternoon gloom, a suggestion that Bridget, my sister, or someone at least, was home. It was February and not yet the tail end of another interminably long, wet winter, especially for the renegades, the social outcasts, the misfits among us who live on the coastal edge.

As the last of the endangered species of my family's weathered, salt-water tribe, Bridget, her daughter, Mia and me, we were hardly what you'd call tight, despite our limited ranks. My sister always said I would wash up again one day, like a sleeper wave sneaking up on these wild, uncivilized shores. And, as a special reward for her patience, now here I was, as predicted, belly up, gasping for breath. How well I'd marked her words with a spectacular series of personal failures that led to her prophecy of my return.

I readied myself for the look, the smug and judging silent sting she'd had about her since we were kids. It was Bridget's way of warning me against my tendency toward lofty aspirations, the dangers of rising above my station in the order of mediocre, the mantra of the McCleery lot. Maybe, I hoped, my sister had grown a little kinder with time when it came to tolerating my airs and graces; more forgiving, somehow. In my defense, all I really had in mind that dreary afternoon was a low-key reentry, no drama, to simply be a part of it all, like I'd never left.

I would not have come anywhere near the place but for the fact that my bright, shiny life, one that had been so far removed from this mud-splattered expanse had unceremoniously imploded into a million toxic components of its own. I was trespassing on hostile territory, this desolate place with its miserable winter microclimate I'd fought so long to ditch.

It was hardly a death sentence, I consoled myself — my coming back — merely proof that, after all, I am who I am and who I've always been. Ranch-born and raised. That and the fact that the grandiose city apartment I could no longer afford was gone, along with more or less everything else I possessed. That same morning I'd cut all but one of a slew of credit cards into a pile of small, ragged, triangular shards that I subsequently distributed out of habit into four different trash bags. Oh, what pure, unadulterated glee I'd experienced in the previous day's act of stripping my closet of its shameless jumble of casual luxury brands, the swearing of an end to the corporate ethos, my former existence.

I'd pulled the plug on the last of my shallow connections. My plan was to spend what was left of the wet winter months curled up in a blanket, licking my wounds, lounging away the last of the season's short, dark, damp and dreary days on my sister's sad excuse of a couch. The volume of internal toxicity that built up in my last months in San Francisco had proved a ticking time bomb. And there was only ever one direction this was bound for — upward in a painful and messy explosion of my letting go. Anxiety and mood swings further fueled my long-winded, overdue metamorphosis. It wasn't pretty and if I've learned anything over the past few months, it's that it's best to embrace failure, call it out, move on and start showing up sooner rather than later in the next chapter and one of your own design. There are no prizes for champions in procrastination and self-pity.

The stormy weather pattern made its appearance in early fall. By February, continuing heavy rainfall slammed the Bay Area and beyond. October's lumbering first drops that had escalated into a seemingly endless downpour, served to wash away what little was left of my grip on reality, the false world of the same tech titan I'd so desperately clung to for fifteen ridiculously long years. A barrage of winter storms battered the saturated coastline from central California and up to the Oregon border as I'd panicked, then reconciled and later, felt strangely soothed by my wasteful and contorted past steadily siphoning itself down the drain.

An irritatingly chirpy Bay Area news meteorologist in her slim, figure-hugging, cool-hued rotation of the same form-fitting dress, nightly hailed it a rare, one-hundred-year winter, with downpours intense and unforgiving, entire coastal communities being cut off for days, weeks at a time. Big Sur, to the south, for one, was sealed off for several months by mudslides that submerged the shoreline highway in and out.

That afternoon's rain-slicked return plays on in my mind — an intense and primitive tableau of densely painted scenes, made all the more dramatic by my indulgent sense of personal doom. It was in fact, a perfect prelude, a portent of more violent things to come. Earlier, as I was waiting on the shiny city sidewalk for my ride out of the city, I recall being struck by the sight of a small bird emerging from its narrow shelter, a crack in the siding of my closed-up apartment building. I'd watched, mesmerized, as the little feathered creature flew to the top of a metal stop sign, narrowly missing her wings being clipped by an electric Muni trolley bus powered by a set of potentially lethal overhead wires. I tracked the bird's flight path back to the crevice behind the one dry spot on the sidewalk where I'd positioned my bags. Slowly, so as not to startle her, I crouched down to take a closer look at her tiny nest. An open-beaked, fluffy-downed nestling huddled inside in hopeful anticipation of its mother's haul. She, in turn, apologetically ruffled her baby's whispery fluff and took off a second time in search of something, anything, even the smallest morsel, I guessed, to satisfy her duty, keep her promise. Bits of paper and plastic poked out of the nesting she'd constructed of dried grass and twigs. I still think of her and how resourceful and determined she'd been to survive the cold, hard city, to brave the perils of the sky above in placing her infant's needs before her own.

I'd observed him with a similar degree of quiet fascination, my clean-cut and clueless, twenty-something Uber driver, as he took in the changing topography of our two-hour journey. Only sixty miles in distance yet light years apart from our primitive destination objective of coastal Point B. We headed north out of the city, matrix of my shame, over the rain-slick surface of the Golden Gate Bridge, through the Robin Williams Tunnel and into Marin County, silently weaving our way northwest, up and out toward the wide-open spaces of storm battered western Sonoma County. Red barns in open fields, black and white bovines heavy with milk, their lumbering bodies in vibrant contrast to the rolling green hills, the last of the proud herds of Holstein dairy cows bracing side by side in tight formation against the onslaught of the constant rain.

I'd made it clear, for his sake more than mine, in giving him a fair and honest heads-up of the formidable, potentially slippery territory ahead, a hard-going route along the Sonoma Coast during the rainy months, even for the most seasoned driver. If you're unfamiliar with this remote and watery border of Northern California, then best take my word, for it's a uniquely foreign, otherworldly place to all except the few of us who were born and raised out here. Geographic distance has little to do with it. No matter how close it looks on a map, reaching the more insular points of the western shoreline is to travel from one microcosm to another, one that exists in a kind of time bubble of its own. By the time we'd made it out to the coast, my unsuspecting agent of change had proved, as I feared he would, woefully inept at motoring this unsung stretch of shoreline, this wolfish terrain, the wild and familiar seascape of my formative years. Not that I was judging him too hard. It wasn't like I had a choice and I really couldn't afford to be picky.

After a while, a swift stab to the heart and there it was again, that old, cold, innate fear of having come too close to the steeper drops, the slicker edges of the coastline with its rows of craggy, wind-tormented Cypress trees masked by a thick, barely transparent cloak of briny, creeping fog. Thinking back, mostly, overwhelmingly so, it is the ever present, nostalgia-triggering, pervasive smell of decomposing grass that transports me back to that winter's afternoon, that and my being engulfed by a second, overlaying odor of a strange and yet compelling blend of home, the salty Pacific mixed with the wet and ghostly aroma of once pervasive cow poop.

Great globs of Neptunian spittle ambushed my view as my eyes were fixed on our waterlogged route from a narrowly framed vantage point — the rain-drenched windshield of a stranger's lemon-scented Honda Civic sedan. Fast flowing streaks of precipitation, a salty blend of tear-shaped raindrops hammered the windshield as we slowly inched our way northwest along the Pacific Ocean and up to the ranch. I couldn't stop my mind from flashing back to the futuristic-looking cartoon-like self-driving cars being tested on the busy streets of San Francisco. I'm sorry, but not sorry in that I find it hard to imagine placing my trust in a supposedly obedient intelligent car ever fully safely delivering someone like me someplace like this and in such lousy conditions.

A greenish-brownish muddy squall was holding my very human driver and me captive under the glassed-in assault of a pair of angry windshield wipers that swung madly, back and forth. My gut still wrenches at the grim memory of having witnessed an innocent pedestrian, minding her own business, struck and killed by one of these self-driving test cars in the drizzle of dusk, shortly before I left the city for good. I've tried and tried to block it out of my mind, but the image of the old woman who hit the windshield and was left like a jagged mannequin in the middle of the road, has taken up permanent residence in my head. There it remains as the ultimate risk of the dangers and risks of artificial intelligence. Humans are arrogant and we've gotten way too far ahead of ourselves. For all of the software, algorithms and radar, it turned out that neither the so-called smart car nor its emergency back up driver so much as saw her coming. I'd prefer to leave my chances to human error thank you very much.

I twisted one of a pair of sizable diamond studs around in my right earlobe. I'd worn these coveted studs consistently since my splurge with a portion of my stock option cash-out, days before Andres talked me into the doomed investment we'd made together. Most startups fail, I'd known that, which makes it all the worse. I rotated its thin, platinum edge around and around with my finger and thumb, mindful not to loosen the clasp. Oh how fast we had trailed back into corporate servitude, Andres and me, our tails firmly between our legs, back to where we started, shamefaced and lightened of the substantial load we should have put into a property in the City if we'd had half a brain between us.

A defect in the rideshare vehicle's internal fan caused it to rattle and clank. It spluttered and struggled in its vain attempt to combat the constant spew of hot air that heaved out of the dashboard vents. Still, we'd pressed on due north along a thick smudge of craggy, water-washed coast, aquaplaning three or four times as small streams pushed over their banks, the two of us encased in condensation and the cloying aroma of a heavy lavender-scented laundry detergent. I'd kept my mouth firmly shut as he gripped the steering wheel with tense, white, knuckles, willing, I assumed, his own safe navigation clear of this strange and storm-lashed, oceanic outer realm of the greater Bay Area.

"What do you think of the new self-driving cars?" I asked, unable to keep silent any longer as I made a futile attempt to shake off the disturbing image of the old woman's demise. "How soon do you suppose they will they put hard working people like you out of business?"

"Faster than most folk realize," he replied. "It's an interesting advancement for science, for sure, though personally, I have plenty of concerns aside from the mechanics."

His accent was unidentifiable, though his English was good, an intermixing of street words with grammar that was better than a lot of kids I'd grown up with.

"Seriously," I said. "It's all about ethics if you ask me. You know, the big questions, such as if you were faced this afternoon with the option of hitting a full-grown stag out here in the middle of the coastal road, or swerving and running the very real risk of going over the edge? If I'd asked a self-driving car to get me here as fast as possible, I'd most certainly have thrown up all over the dashboard by now."

The leaden heavens dumped on the black and roiling frigid waters of the Pacific. He drove on, dodging potholes, random unfortunate roadkill and crumbling asphalt as we cruised at a slow crawl alongside saturated layers of soggy bluff, he, tight-lipped as he navigated switchbacks with a bird's-eye view of the empty beach and angry surf below. The Pacific Ocean is a dramatic landscape painting that begs to be made. One of these days I'll get around to my fulfilling a minor fantasy of mine in setting up an artist's easel and a blank canvas. I can see it now as I slowly and luxuriously drag my thumb through several long layers of thick, dense, acrylic, blending the elements in one extended, shameless smudge of muted indigo topped by a deeper, thicker, darker charcoal color and another, a third, paler, clumpier streak of shimmering silver, in the form of one of the looming, low hanging storm clouds I picture with my eyes closed. A triangular, wooden easel set up in the old dairy pasture in full view of the Pacific, my thumb coated with messy wet paint, sensory and expressive and indulgent, like a kindergartner with nothing to worry about other than creating something base yet meaningful from absolutely nothing.

"Have you ever seen anything so insane, so darn beautiful?" I asked, arranging the elements in my mind. He, thankfully, was concentrating on the road, not in the least inspired by the scenery. A heavy frown deepened, etched into a crevice carved above the bridge of his metal eyeglass frame.

"Gnarly, more like," he replied, a smattering of urban slang unbefitting of his earnest character, I thought. I'd sat alongside and eaten lunch with zealous and purposeful coworkers from practically every country on earth over the years. I looked at him quizzically.

"Foreign student," he said. "UC Berkeley. Engineering, masters." No wonder he'd harbored concerns with regard to the risks of smart technology. It's no longer science fiction, is it? Hawking, Gates, Musk, they've all spoken publicly on the dangers of misaligned intelligence. Is anyone taking notes? The thought crossed my mind to open the door and throw myself out. The future is a scary place. I'd come dangerously close to spilling my guts to an engineering student from Iraq or Afghanistan or Lebanon, wherever. I couldn't have cared less where in the world he was from, we're all here on the same uphill battle as far as I'm concerned. I did care that he thought me an idiot for dragging him out here on such a shitty afternoon. Still, it had felt good to have some company, to speak candidly to someone who had absolutely no reason to judge. I'd been isolated for all intents and purposes, holed up alone for a punishing stretch of miserably dark days and nights and his putting himself out there to get me where I needed to be was significant in my book even if he was about to be paid handsomely for it.

"This, here, mister hard working, ethical, ambitious engineering student with your entire life ahead of you," I said, laying it on the line: "is you assisting me in bailing. Human-to-human. I'm over it, you see, the whole cursed monotone of concrete city life. I can't take any more of it. The homeless masses begging for scraps dropped by passing billionaires. Big tech's evil quest to save the world has lost its allure with me."

He peeled his eyes off the rain-soaked road and shot me a look of genuine concern. I was one of those rides, one of the bunglers, the squandering losers in life guaranteed to share way too much unwanted personal information. Before I blurted out anything else I might have regretted, I rolled the window down a slither and sucked in the first of the chill, dank air, the taste of ozone on my tongue, the smell of musky plant oils and pungent bacteria spores — the damp earth that continues to reignite the more potent memories of my childhood years. He offered me a small bottle of sealed water from the drink holder in the central console.

"I wish you well out there in the world, hon, but, as for me, well, I've jumped ship from all of it — the decadence, the corruption, the lies." I'd started up again, despite myself. "Do us all a favor. Please don't be suckered into engineering anything that has the potential to be smarter than yourself."

We'd reached the end of the potholed mud pit of a single-track lane that led to the ranch, literally the end of the road as far as I was concerned. My heartbeat raced. I braced myself for the possibility of a panic attack, the sort that make me think I'm having a freaking heart attack. To my relief, the stampede of hysteria failed to materialize. Admitting my colossal failures to a stranger had been a revelation of sorts, I guess, a small one, but a start. Anyway, he was the one who had opened the floodgates with his snippets of well-meaning, genial conversation.

He turned toward me, a pair of soft, brown eyes widening and magnified behind his thick eyeglass lenses. I thought at that moment he might have taken pity on me, hung a U-ey — flipped a fast and sudden about-turn in the rising waters of this lower trough of a craggy ranch road. "Life goes on," he said with the slightest of smiles, revealing his small, neat teeth, though he was barely what I'd describe as at ease. I wanted to believe him, this young, smart, hopeful, rational engineer of tomorrow. Everything would be all right in the end and what is it they say — if it's not all right, then it's not the end? If he was tempted to drive me back to my senses, return me, like a wrongly addressed past-prime Amazon package to my well lit upper floor unit with its marble countertops and its twinkling, vintage crystal chandeliers, well, he chose not to act on it. How many times had I avoided this scene? Failed to show up to any of Bridget's half-hearted attempts to gather me back into the fold. I might at least have made an appearance for one or two lousy birthdays, holiday afternoons. I consoled myself that he would make it back over the bridge by dark, time enough to fit in a handful of less demanding rides as the city folk made their way home from San Francisco's almost embarrassing overload of warm and brightly lit restaurants and bars.

"Looks like a good place to visit in the summer months," he shivered, visibly. I figured he must have been aware he was breaking one of the basic rules of the rideshare code with regard to making comment on my questionable destination. He couldn't stop himself as he scanned the dense green stretch of sodden ranch land that circled the blurry silhouette of the house. I narrowed my eyes and looked for the old, familiar mound of trees I'd climbed with Bridget, as kids, a clump of Coast Live Oaks, barely visible through the heavy mist. In stark contrast, two rows of unruly and oppressively large eucalyptus trees shielded our approach, like a foreign militia of giant, unpredictable soldiers, in salute of my return.

After narrowly dodging a deep, wide puddle at the end of the driveway, the spluttering vehicle crawled to a stop by the steps of the ramshackle porch. "Right here?" he asked, thick eyebrows raised, his eyes darting from a flattened portion of picket fence to porch steps almost totally devoid of the last vestiges of peeling white paint. A fierce wind howled as it whipped off the churning Pacific, topping the rocky shore, rolling, madcap and pummeling the once ornate, now decrepit 19th century carvings. Fallen leaves and other debris from the eucalyptus trees smacked against my face and hands.

I was stone cold sober for the first time in weeks and with nothing more than a half-empty water bottle in hand, I was able to thoroughly soak in all these visuals of my homecoming. The thought briefly crossed my mind of a faraway mother somewhere on the other side of the world missing this well-mannered student in his polished leather lace-ups as he made his first tentative move to step out onto a dry patch of ground. He hovered a second or two before braving the muddy mire as he planted my two small bags in a sheltered spot at the foot of the porch. If my sister heard the engine running, she'd chosen to ignore it, hoping, I guess, whomever it was would simply turn around and pass on by. I stood there, wrestling with what I should say as I watched the taillights of the mud splattered sedan bob up and down in a spray of puddles in retreat on the uneven surface of the unpaved road. Poor guy couldn't get out of there fast enough. I fixed my eyes on his vehicle as it skirted a series of muddy potholes and sunk into the steely light of the distant horizon.

I was pumped and primed to ask my sister for shelter, beg a little if need be. After all, it was Bridget who had held the fort since before dad died. On paper, we co-own the property, for what it's worth. In reality, I hadn't had a single iota to do with its maintenance and upkeep and not much more to do with Bridget and later on, my niece, Mia, her kid, since I'd left home more or less at the age that Mia is now. Bridget, for her part, had spent the past twenty-plus years in a perpetual state of being pissed at my lack of interest. And, in turn, honestly, she'd had little choice but to leave me to my own shallow devices. For the longest time, I'd felt like I'd been given a get out of jail free card, a ticket to a new life, far from the more uncomfortable memories of early hardship out on the ranch.

I could've used a drink to settle my nerves, a glass of wine at least to smooth the sharp edges of my pitiless return. Too bad I'd drained the last drop of my soon-to-be ex-husband's favorite wine club subscription — a case of bloated Napa Valley Cab, each bottle topped with a pompous ruby-red wax seal. He'd inadvertently left a blissfully intact case under the stairs and I stand in full, unabashed confession to having savored each and every last sip and swirl of this particularly insane and grossly priced wine shipment that was charged to Andres' credit card quarterly. I know my wine and it was a good one.

I was spent. Despite my foolish intentions to make this the first day of the rest of my life and all that baloney, the near constant melancholy that set in as my situation with Andres had slowly eroded was proving hard to shake. I'd grown comfortable with it, I suppose, a protective layer I'd clung to in a sick sort of way, my hopeless cloak, a security blanket that kept me from any further vulnerability. Damn it, Andres had been the bigger fraud, the cheater and worse, in my mind, the guilty partaker of way more sinister corporate pursuits than I'd been greedy enough to contrive. I'd been the fool for blithely going along with it all, for failing to call it out, for sticking around and indulging his bougie lifestyle.

Even aside from his philandering, his secretive work assignments, the high risk-taking venture capitalism he'd dragged me down with, Andres had been excessively conceited, a disappointing, mediocre partner at best. It was my sister I ought to have been thinking of, not the tail end of the grim shell of my marriage and its doomed investment strategy. Bridget is not well. By then, she'd been sick for several months. Shame on me for I have to admit, I'd known full well all this was true.

I muttered more basic encouragements to myself as I lingered under the dismal glimmer of the porch light. "Be yourself, Maggie. Do not even think of groveling, girl." Despite the desperate measures I'd taken to shed my city skin, at that moment, the only thing I felt like was an imposter and I hated it. Anyway, I'm over it now, for sure, there's no more regret. I've completely lost the stomach for the constant cosmetic upkeep, the mind-numbing flow of posts, tweets, shares, likes, comments, email, texts, chat, blogs, wikis and other such crap and nonsense I'd been required to keep up with to stay relevant. All this babble and complex social code proved way too much for my addled brain, then and now. I want no more of it. Have I made myself clear, my total and enduring distrust of digital technology stems from the inside out? Do I miss it, the glamour of life on the cutting edge, the power of knowing what's next on the bleeding edge of science and technology? Hell no.

11

As for this place, the ranch where I was raised, it might as well be the back of beyond, world's end, a dark hole in the universe for all my soon-to-be ex, my cutthroat, minted former coworkers, the last of my fair-weather friends, in truth, could give a damn. And, the funny thing about this inaccessibility, my newfound splendid isolation, it's become my most valued commodity. I left behind the old me when I patterned the initials of my maiden name in the passenger seat window of the rideshare car. Using the tip of my manicured pointer finger, I outlined M.M. — Maggie McCleery version 3.0. And with that, I was fully unshackled, tossed into the roiling sea, a willing wave rider, a hopeful piece of flotsam in the surf of letting go.

The split with Andres was one thing. I'd grown to detest the stifling, boxed in rules and regulations of a self-imposed downward spiral in the nauseating, thankless world of tech internal communications. In other words, my getting paid to systematically plot the corporate information flow that influenced the attitudes and behaviors of my workmates had constituted, in base terms, my downing the daily poison for years.

I felt the damp wood of the sagging porch sigh under the weight of my feet. I strained my eyes in the dim light, making out a fuzzy silhouette through a small pane of cracked and clouded, turquoise colored glass in the upper portion of the scuffed and weather beaten door. The rusted doorbell damn well jammed in protest at my disturbing the silent house, my unsuspecting sister and whomever else was home with her guy Bobby, maybe — though I'd been hoping for it to be my niece, Mia to be the one to break the proverbial ice. I rapped my knuckles on the glass panel, its fragility mirrored my own.

It was Bridget who came to the door. I'm not sure which of us took a step or two backward, first, she or me. And well, we froze, the both of us. She visibly recoiled. Bridget retreated into the shadows of the entryway as if she'd seen a ghost. My own sister stood there, rail thin, birdlike, staring at me, an unwelcome apparition, my abrupt arrival shrouded by storm clouds and the merciless wind that chased in alongside me and what I'd naively dared to think were the last of my troubles.

Chapter 2

Mia

Last night I dreamed I was back at the ranch. Only it wasn't me as I am now, it was when I was a kid. Before Bobby came into our lives. This is pretty weird, as I don't have a lot of memories of being little, like, you know, before kindergarten. I never went to preschool. There wasn't one out there and who had the money to pay for it even if there was? Not my mom, for sure. Anyway, who the heck, except me, remembers this stuff from early childhood, how things were before we had the words to describe it?

This morning I'm working outside in the garden. I'm proud to say I've been hard at it, planting a whole bunch of tomatoes and corn and eggplant, peppers — summer squash from starters that I grew myself from seed in small plastic pots in the greenhouse. I'm kinda kneeling down, or as best I can on a folded, old newspaper as I dig a series of deep, narrow furrows into the rich, black soil. All I'm thinking of is last night's dream and how totally creepy it was.

I don't like talking about the past. I have gotta believe what's done is done for the most part. That's how I look at it now. "Do you, girl." I tell myself. This time, though, I'm breaking my own rule in forcing myself to circle back to last night's freaky dream. I want to better remember myself as little me, to feel the pull of it as I figure myself out, how I came to be here, where the hell I'm going.

In the dream it was nighttime, winter, cold, wet. I was outside, totally alone in the old dairy pasture, running around in circles in the spooky, pitch-dark rain. My jeans and T-shirt were soaking wet, my feet bare and scratched up under the mud. I was frightened, go figure, shivering like crazy and no matter how hard I tried, I could not find my way back to the house.

All the lights were off. "Mommy," I cried, over and over. "I'm here, where are you?"

Who else was there to take care of me? In real life, my mom went to work part-time at the roadhouse after Bobby came along, soon after I started school. By the time I hit my teens, the both of them were gone most every late afternoon and evening, except for Mondays and Tuesdays when the roadhouse was dark.

Today, as soon as I finish digging these rows, I'm gonna stick a bunch of metal cages into the ground, place them over the tomato plants I've established. The cages are meant to stop the vines from toppling over when they're full with fruit. Be honest, did you know a tomato is a fruit? There were plenty of nights when I'd worked myself up, back when Mom first started working the dinner shifts. I'd made myself sick with worry that she'd never come home, that I'd be left there on that lonely ranch all on my ownsome, forever, like crazy Norman Bates from the Psycho movie she and Bobby watched on the TV one night when they thought I was asleep. I'd snuck down the stairs and witnessed more or less the whole sick, sensation seeking horror of it from my hiding place in the shadows behind the hallway door.

Sticking my hands into the soil is surprisingly satisfying. My nails, farmer's nails, are clipped short and yet they're still full of dirt. Now, here, away from all that went down, I'm finally learning a big lesson in how to enjoy my own company. I like being alone. It's the sense of peace I guess that brings me some relief. When I think about it, maybe my mom was a little too clingy for my own good before she had Bobby to keep her company. She trapped me out there and then she pretty much kinda ignored me for the rest of my growing up, never so much as asking me about school, how my day was, my grades and all, who I was hanging out with. There was never any talk about what I might want for my future. I guess it was enough work for her to get up and face each new day as it dawned, never mind the bother of me. I get it, now.

It's heating up, close to noon. I move on to checking the sprinkler heads on the drip irrigation system that runs from the grey water tank. I've been taught to check for stones and dirt that clog up the sprinklers. I take time to twist them around to make sure they're pointed in the right direction for keeping the veggies well watered during the warmer days ahead.

To think, I was the stupid, lazy little ranch chick who never so much as stuck her hands in the mud — least not 'til now. Whenever I'm outside, I catch myself over and over, checking for a way out, the fear of being penned is hard to shake.

Turkey vultures hover overhead looking for lunch. Some sad critter must have met its end in the garden during the night. I watch them going about their business. They're impressive. I'll give 'em that. Super scavengers. It's crazy that the turkey vulture travels up to 200 miles a day in search of its next meal. Pilots have reported spotting them flying, like as far as 20,000 feet up in the sky. Blows my mind. I wrote a report on turkey vultures one time in high school biology, back when I gave a crap. I was really into it. I hand illustrated it with colored pencils and all.

If you've never seen one, here's another cool thing about turkey vultures. They're bald. The reason they have no feathers on their heads is so as to stop any bits of flesh sticking to them when they nosedive headfirst into a fresh carcass. They're kinda grotesque to look at, what with their massive beaks, hence the sharp sense of smell. I turn to watch them bathe in the sun on the fence posts out back, their huge wings spread six feet wide. Bizarre, but also true, the turkey vulture is known to shit on its own claws to cool itself in the hot, summer months.

Still, I'm fascinated in some sick way by how mean they look, the largest and the ugliest of the birds of prey, at least in this part of the world, which is all I know since I have never been any place that's not in Northern California. I go on watching them at their work a minute or two more. Their flapping around reminds me of the most vivid part of my dream, the part where I found my way back to the house, feeling my way up the porch steps in the pitch dark on my hands and knees like a creature myself, crawling through puddles of cold, wet sand.

I was deathly afraid that vultures and other birds of the night might swoop down on my hands and into my hair, more so the bats and the rats the size of small barn cats that still populate the place, far as I know. A thin sliver of moonlight illuminated the front door. I rattled the handle 'til it creaked open and I grabbed onto the wooden frame as a river of cold, salty seawater gushed out, flooding the porch and submerging the steps. I was marooned.

I waded into the darkened, flooded entryway as jellyfish, dozens of clear, wobbly spaceships floated silently around me in the black water. I pushed on in the direction of muffled voices in the dining room we barely ever used, drawn by the sound of a bunch of people talking at the same time. Four wrinkly old folk were sitting around the table along with Mom, who looked sad, with dark shadows under her eyes. My aunt, Maggie was also there, glowing, in contrast, her long, shiny black hair, like mine used to be, tied back to frame her real-pretty, pink-cheeked face. I'm darker skinned than her and my eyes are more of a hazel brown where hers are green, but we look a lot alike otherwise. They all seemed to know each other around that table. It was like the old ones had stepped straight out of the faded old portrait that hangs on the wall for real. I can see it now, how they were all decked out in old Western-style clothing, the oldies, he in some sort of heavy vest and a collarless shirt, she in a long, blue dress with a delicate floral print. They wore serious expressions on their weather-beaten faces and they spoke my name, like I wasn't there. "Well! What's to be done about Mia?" my mom asked, her eyes sunken. I called out again and again, "I'm here, see for yourself," but nobody heard. I waved my arms and stomped around, wiping tears and snot from my face with the back of my hand. I pulled at my aunt's arm. Milling it around in my mind now, any fool ought to figure I was starving for attention. Still, did they see me? Hell no.

I pinch off small sprigs of white flowers not un-similar to those on the old woman's dress. These sprigs have sprouted from the top of four good-sized basil plants and my fingers at once smell peppery, minty. I'm not sure it's a good idea for me to read too deeply into these night visions, nightmares you might call them. I know what a nightmare is and this was not one of them. Why torture myself by trying too hard to figure it all out?

Mom announced when I was about six or seven, in real life, not in the dream, that Bobby was as close to a dad to me as any. Something along those lines — anyway, turns out she had decided it was time for me to call him Daddy, not Bobby. My real dad was as good as dead, she said. It was the first I'd heard her speak of the man who is my father and it sucked. If I'd ever asked her why I didn't have a dad, I don't remember. Why would I? I knew nothing different. It wasn't like I'd been around a lot of kids with dads when I was little, stuck out there all alone with only my mom for company.

"Maybe my daddy doesn't want me because I'm a girl." That's what I told myself the day she dropped the bombshell that I did, in fact, have a father. I really thought then, for the longest time, if I'd been a boy, he might not have been so disappointed, gone and ditched us and left me there, alone with her. Later, when I was in junior high, she confessed to me the worst of it, in that he never even so much as knew I existed. I was gutted. I don't know what's more hurtful, him turning his back or having no fucking clue? I wanted so badly to find him, write him, phone him, reassure him: "Hey, I'm here, you'd like me." I'd have done anything to talk to my dad, to see him even once, if only for the shortest time, to prove myself worthy. I'm over that shit now. No more playing small and insignificant. At least there's that.

I turn my attention to trimming the native flowering varietals I've planted on the edge of the garden beds. These are the kind of flowers I've discovered, happily, that hummingbirds and honeybees love: purple-blue, bell-shaped Honeywort, blue-tinted, thistlelike, False Sea Holly, spicy smelling, bluish-purple Licorice Mint. My favorite, crazy named Miss Willmott's Ghost —is white tufted, corn on the cob shaped, a big, silvery-green blossom that is taking over the garden. I'm hard pushed to think of anything that has ever once made me smile as much as this dumb flowerbed. I've scribbled the names of the plants on wooden popsicle sticks with permanent markers so I don't forget. I'm told these blooms will be chock-full of nectar as the fog burns off and the warmer weather kicks in. Only thing that would make me happier than a garden full of blooms right now would be to share it with Jazmin. What I would give to lay here, side by side with my BFF, chillin' in the sunshine, the only sound and movement the whisper of her breathing and the breeze in the tall, wild grass.

A cloud passes overhead casting a shadow on my plants. My childhood was nothing to get worked up about, despite what I've said. Boring as hell is all. And I'm in danger of losing the dream sequence if I don't work hard to line up the pictures in the right order. It's sort of like looking at jumbled scenes in a movie. And I'm the star. Who needs that sort of bullshit celebrity?

In the dream, Maggie finally got that I was tugging at her sleeve. She was the only one who caught a clue that I was there, although she, like the rest of them, never saw me in the flesh. I knew it, she knew it, but she never let on, much to my frustration, for some reason, she never told the others that I was there in the room with them.

When I woke up around seven, having tossed and turned as I do through the night hours to ease the discomfort, my PJs were soaked through with sweat. It's gotta mean something that in real life, Maggie made it the hell out of that old ranch and way before me. And if she keep on thinking she wants to be in my life after she's been gone for so long, well, she's gonna have to keep on circling back around big time, build my trust and show me that she sees me, really sees me, for who I am and who I've become.

CHAPTER 3

MAGGIE

They say that time stands still. Well, that's a myth we trick ourselves into believing. Standing there, like a fool, frozen on the doormat, it was evident my sister was much changed, her pale, milky face small and delicate beneath a scarf wrapped around her head like a turban.

"Hello Bridget," I said, holding onto the handles of my bags with a viselike grip. Seeing her face-to-face was a shock to my system and, from any lack of movement to greet me, my sudden appearance was clearly as unsettling for her as it was for me.

I had nowhere else to go. There was no plan B, despite the end-game having been unceremoniously scrawled on the wall in permanent red marker months if not years before. If Bridget had turned me away and I would not have blamed her for doing so, I have no clue where I would have turned.

"Maggie. Jesus. What the fuck?" she snapped. "I sure would've appreciated some advance warning." Her looks may have been diminished but she had no problem giving off a steely, high-voltage charge.

I was bone tired. I'd been up and about since the break of dawn, closing up the last details of the apartment. Despite all my prepping for this moment, I was mentally unprepared for an on the spot showdown with my big sis. I braced against the upset of confronting this pale, new, hairless version of her — frail, yet decidedly hostile. Had she shrunk in height? Maybe. I've been a couple of inches taller than her since I hit my teens; by then it felt like I towered over her. I was little more than a stranger to my only sibling, the sister I'd been way too wrapped up in my foolish ambitions to give a shit about.

"Don't be like this, Bridg'."

"No? How is it you'd like me to be?" she snapped a second time, stepping forward, reaching out and pinching me sharply on the fleshy part above the curve of my hip. "I'd barely recognize you, Maggie, it's been so long," she said. "Packin' on some pounds for the both of us, I see?"

I cringed. Bridget had always been way cruder than me with her use of language. She cut me to the quick in a way that only a sister can. "OK. Thanks for the warm and fuzzy welcome," I said, reigning in the sarcasm. Bridget is way more than her illness, there's no way she's letting it define her. "May I come in?" I asked.

Once inside, it hit me, over and above the heady aroma of damp wood, aside from the stink of old stuff — the familiar, slightly moldy overtone of an aging Victorian structure — a stronger, more benevolent odor of weed infused the very essence of the place. The scent of cannabis clung to the shabby interior fabric of old rugs and peeling wallpaper, an earthy, pungent, skunk-like aroma had absorbed itself deep beneath the surface of the dingy rooms.

"Whatever," Bridget said, catching my eye as it darted about. "Just don't you dare come barging in now, pointlessly stirring up all the old ghosts."

I scanned the scene. Whatever your preferred word for it, good old-fashioned cannabis, marijuana, pot, weed — an unabashed broadcast of its unmistakable overtones is the giveaway with its warm, slightly powdery sandalwood and fig, forest-like aroma with hints of patchouli and pepper. If its scent has a color, its musky overtone is the deepest, darkest shade of its greenest leaves. There's no disguising an active cannabis cache to a Northern California native. One way or another I've been around weed since my early teens. Even my soon-to-be ex considers himself somehow elevated in his status as both wine and weed connoisseur. I'd never known him not to smoke. Andres stashed his cache of designer cannabis in French glass jars he differentiated with decorative labels designed for jams and jellies. These are the type of jars with fancy wire closures and thick, orange colored rubber seals. He would purchase them each fall, by the half dozen in cases from Williams Sonoma on Union Square. He'd gotten a kick out

of convincing the clerks he was an ardent impresario of homemade holiday preserves. "Grandma's recipes," he'd tease, ever flirtatious.

The pervasive aroma hit me then as no surprise, Bridget was a legendary pot smoker, never much of a drinker. Hey, I had my fancy wine fetish and she had her weed. Inside, a repetitive medley of leaking rainwater plip-plopped percussion-like into a series of galvanized buckets and plastic bowls positioned in strategic spots. I shuddered visualizing the creeping black mold I imagined inching its way through the drywall. Aside from her tired, puffy face, Bridget appeared ashen, weak, an anemic version of herself.

"You better be good with all this," she gestured with a small, blue-veined, almost translucent hand at the general state of the place. "I know how you are, neat freak and all."

Bridget is four years my senior. She'd been diagnosed with breast cancer the previous summer — July to be precise and with all that was going on in my life, I'd not bothered to take the time for even the briefest of visits, to see for myself how she was faring. Bridget busied herself in a spurt of rounding up a mess of open boxes of tea, a half-eaten bar of dark chocolate, a handful of scattered garlic cloves, a chunk of shriveled root ginger. A basket of funky-shaped, unidentifiable mushrooms cluttered the countertop alongside a bowl of red pomegranates, green leaves intact. Amongst these scattered remedies sat a tube of unopened topical cannabis analgesic and an open pack of pain relieving patches.

"A smorgasbord of restoratives, Bridget." I ventured.

It wasn't like I didn't know the worst of it. We'd not seen one another in well over a year in part due to my thoughtless lack of consideration and also Bridget being long since inflicted by the inconvenient phobia that makes her scared to death to drive over a bridge. Still, we had spoken at length by phone the evening of her first oncology consultation. She had received the dreaded call back from the one and only mammogram she'd had in her entire life, soon after she'd turned fifty. One thing's for sure, she was damn lucky they'd caught it when they did.

"What do you know, Maggie?" Bridget hissed. "You'd best chill out fast if you're planning on sticking around for the evening."

At first, she'd stuck to her stance that chemo and radiation would do her more harm than good. Hell, who'd blame her for being wary of Big Pharma? Cancer treatment is no walk in the park. And Bridget had lived her life until that point as poster girl for natural remedies. I looked her over, subtly, the brittle, delicate figure before me. She explained how she'd taken the high road as long as she'd been able in her gamble on alternative treatments, her initial tactic having revolved around a super intense raw food diet and herbs, a ton of them, plus the elimination of all sugars and processed foods. Whatever weight she'd had to spare had fallen from her frame like tender meat from a rack of slow cooked ribs.

Bridget was up-front in how she'd smoked a bunch of weed for the pain. "Don't worry, only the good stuff," she confessed, cannabis she'd grown herself, out back. I listened as she told me how she had diligently tested the soil for ph levels, adding an assortment of minerals to nourish plant roots. "I harvested the resinous flower heads at the peak of their power, the same day my plants showed signs of growing cloudy," she said, adding: "I managed to get it together to dry and trim the good stuff, the super stinky, sticky, gluey intoxicants."

After three months of resisting standard treatment, her oncologist found that her tumor marker had increased. Bridget felt she'd been given no choice but to reconsider her options. We'd not progressed in any sisterly support system after I'd left home and I was, by then, suddenly and ashamedly acutely aware of my part in it. I looked down at my left hand. It was shaking, slightly. I was still wearing my thin platinum wedding band and diamond solitaire engagement ring, which flashed as I listened to my sister's updates. I forced myself to think of something other than a bottle opener, the comforting sound of a cork easing its way out of a snug, slim, glass bottleneck and the glug of a generous pour.

Bridget had been in no position to seek a second opinion. The concept of taking a drive down to Stanford for a visit with the super docs, or anywhere else for that matter was as foreign to her as the price tag. If I'd been smarter, more reserved with my finances, I would've comfortably been able to grant her the dignity of a second opinion. Jeez, this is my one and only sibling we're talking about. She'd been a

homebody her whole life, never pushing beyond the borders of her beloved Sonoma County and in that way, I'd always thought of Bridget as the cool, calm, grounded one of the two of us, the one who had never given up on this old place, on our family. I'd figured, in my selfishness, that she'd be fine. She had to be. Bridget is a fighter. She's proved it this far. Boy has she. The alternative is too hard to fathom.

By the time she'd visited her oncologist for a second appointment, the tumor had continued growing and significantly. Evil thing had wormed its way into her lymph nodes. My self-sufficient sis was being forced to swallow her tough, old, pioneer pride.

"Plant-based medicine is totally where it's at as far as simultaneous treatment," Bridget rattled on, even now, as I scanned the numerous lotions and potions and medicines she was intent on shuffling away from my prying eyes. Ultimately, she's been forced to agree to conventional treatment, however hideous it proves to be.

They'd operated on her at the end of the year. Chemo followed soon after and, daunting still: "radiation is next in the cards," she explained, looking like she'd seen the worst that life could dish up and was tough enough yet to deal with whatever came next.

I'd been absent for all of it to that point, the entire nightmarish trajectory of my sister's cancer trauma, while I, in turn, had fallen unceremoniously from the gilded perch of my own making.

"You never asked for help," a weak attempt to justify my stupendously late arrival.

"And you never offered," Bridget shot back, suppressed fury building in her eyes. I could feel it, see it. "Where were you when I was at my worst, Maggie? The days and nights after my surgery — damn it, that's when a decent sister might have made an appearance. Why now?"

A sudden wave of shame washed over me, not guilt — far worse. Christ, she could have died, she may still. To think I'd lain awake, night after night, weeks, months, willing sleep to visit, indulgently revisiting scenes of my own poor decision-making, abandonment and selfish despair. All the while, my sister was fighting for her life. Who was I to complain?

Bridget, seemingly undaunted by what seemed to me the brutal butchering of both her breasts and the physical evidence of her post-chemo fragility, struggled in the low light of dwindling afternoon to maneuver our dear, departed mother's dinosaur of a food processor from its dark lair in a lower cabinet. "One of us has to work in the morning," she announced, more briskly, baiting me to spill the reason of my showing up on a workday. Her thin lips clenched as she shot me a narrowed, sideways glance that swept over to my bags, her line of fire swiveling back in my direction: "I've kept it together without your help, Maggie, thank you very much."

Only no, I beg to differ, clearly, she had not. I'd be walking on eggshells awhile, I'd expected as much.

"It's a little late for a sisterly show of support," Bridget cautioned, as she stood aside and reluctantly submitted to my stepping in and hauling the heavy, antiquated kitchen gadget up and onto the counter.

My labored breath formed a small cloud in the chill of the kitchen as I unloaded the bulky Gigantosaurus of a machine onto the scratched and yellowed surface of the Formica countertop. The kitchen was cold and damp, in need of a clean sweep of what I figured was a good six months of old mail, bags of recycling — cartons, bottles, pill packets and containers — layers of unwashed sweaters and jackets that hung lifelessly from the backs of chairs.

I'm a tad on the obsessive-compulsive side, I'll freely admit, especially when it comes to kitchens. Walking into a cluttered environment makes my eyes twitch. My fingers were itching to work. I love to beautify things. If it were up to me, I'd have happily set to there and then, armed with a box of trash bags. I'd have gladly rolled my sleeves up to make a clean sweep of the place, to clear at least enough space so as to be able to see what we were dealing with. It wasn't that it was outright dirty. I could see that Bridget, Bobby, Mia, even, at least one diligent soul appeared to have been making some effort to keep the countertops, floors and sink wiped clean.

She dealt me a scowl, the first hint it was Bridget herself who was struggling to keep it all together. "Don't fucking go there, Maggie," she warned. We're a stubborn bunch, the McCleerys, always have been. I'd long since thought of Bridget as "The Boss", though I'd jokingly taunted her during our teens that she was never the boss of me, though she had been and we'd both known it. She'd liked it that way, taking charge, or so I'd thought, until I'd left her to it by taking off without so much as a look back.

Bridget set about fiddling obsessively with the close-to-defunct food processor, putting an end to any further uncomfortable dialogue for the moment. I could see its cutting blades were blunt. An unappealing feed tube that funnels food in for shredding, slicing, pureeing and grinding was clouded, yellowed with use and age. I've been around plenty of state of the art kitchen tools and equipment hanging out with the big earners, the new money of the City. It's fair to say I'm a snob when it comes to cookware and utensils, Andres and me, we both are, were — I won't deny it. The bastard commandeered most of what we'd painstakingly picked out together at our favorite Sur La Table in the Ferry Building over the years. Bridget spotted my thinly veiled look of disdain before I managed to check myself. She stormed out of the kitchen, slamming the door behind her so hard the whole house shook as she stomped upstairs equally forcefully and as noisily as her weightless frame would allow.

I'd been a lousy sister. Hell, I was having a hard enough time getting used to the idea of the old/new me. How was I to deal with this frail and sensitive new Bridget? She possessed a natural beauty, my alluring older sister. It makes me cringe to think of how I'd shown up here so clueless — a wine-drenched, used up, high tech chatter slut — newly single and broke, to boot, and oh, yes, rapidly aging out of the upper limits of an extended breeding age. Shoot, let's not forget that.

"Maggie, must it always be about you?" Bridget stormed back downstairs and into the room, minutes later, red faced and agitated. Her patchy, fair colored eyebrows were raised in a pair of sharp triangular attack signals and she held her upward pointed nose into the air. She was primed for the fight that was brewing. I jumped, as I'd always done at the sudden sound and motion of Mom's old automated cuckoo clock, despite it having been the same outdated timekeeper that taunted me each and every hour on the hour since childhood. A hand-carved wooden bird darted out on cue from its dusty lair, breaking the tension with its ridiculous chorale. Brood parasite, the female cuckoo, according to the old man's book of country lore, I recalled. After she finds another unsuspecting bird's nest, the she-bird waits 'til the other one's out and about before she works up the nerve to push one of her rival's eggs out in order to lay one of her own. Life's a bitch however you look at it.

I glanced around for a second relic of the past, the equally sinister ceramic rooster that held court in the center of the kitchen table. Its beady, black, hand-painted eyes confirmed its continued extended residence as they stared back at me in accusatory silence. Why Bridget kept all this worthless junk sitting around was a mystery to me. Was the woman sentimental, lazy, or merely indifferent to change? I haven't figured it out, though I managed to check my sudden impulse to swipe the foul-faced fucker from his perch, launch him on his first and final flight into a heap of shards. That's where he belonged, in my opinion, along with the infuriating cuckoo clock — swept to the bottom of the trash can of our past.

A finer example of a time-warped western country kitchen, way beyond its most chronic need of a makeover, would be hard to find in a still inhabited home, a tawdry dream come true for any television makeover show worth its salt, as close to a lost cause as it gets. We're talking total interior demolition, a complete and thorough renovation. My one sentimental concession to the general kitsch — the salvage of our grandmother's pride, a hulking O'Keefe & Merritt stove and range top in want of a remedy for heavy-duty rust removal but otherwise in good working order. They don't make them like this anymore.

Rainwater dripped teasingly in a musical fashion into the multiple receptacles. A fresh leak was making its debut appearance from a dangerous entry point somewhere within the region of the central overhead light. The metallic, rhythmic dripping sounded like a bunch of dried peas being pelted into a tin can by an invisible tormentor hiding in the rafters. Leaking rainwater splish-splashed onto the ceramic rooster who, in turn, glistened and menaced as he held court in the failing light.

It was a disaster.

"Flashing needs replacing, siding too," Bridget declared, raising her arms above her head as if she'd read my thoughts. My razor sharp sister knew all along all what I was thinking. No fooling the boss. Not then, not now, not ever.

"Whole place is fit for the junkyard for want of anyone around here taking a notion to fix it up," she said.

Even if we had the money, if it floated down from the sky in crisp, green, freshly printed notes, if cash fluttered in through the leaking roof in one hundred dollar bills, neither of us would have had the wherewithal to take it on without some serious offer of help. All I'd done for more than two decades was move my designer-clad ass from one extortionate rental apartment to the next, popping bottles of the priciest wine country bubbly with each new change of address, chasing the best neighborhood, the best kitchen, biggest bathroom, most scenic view for the rent. Sunday brunches by the Bay, weekend city breaks in other overpriced parts of the country, endless happy hours after work, frittering away a small fortune over the years. To be fair, I did call to invite Bridget and Mia to one or two housewarming parties over the years, though I knew full well even if she worked up the courage to brave the drive over the bridge, my sister was way too self-aware to turn up in her jeans and T-shirt, a pair of scuffed old ranch boots on her feet, barefaced, fiercely devoid of mascara or lipstick her whole life long.

Clearly Bobby wasn't particularly handy in the home repair department, either.

"Every goddamn thing needs doing, Maggie," Bridget said, folding her fragile frame into the sunken well of a wobbly chair. "Place is a downright teardown. Wiring, water heater, bathroom, kitchen, porch, steps, roofing . . . the dang barn is the one thing I'm not beside myself worried about right now."

Light was fading fast into the last, desperate throws of a wet and worn-out day. The one kitchen light fixture that appeared still moderately safe to use hung languorously over the countertop, casting its strained, tawny glow across the butt-ugly, pebble brown freckled linoleum floor. Our mood was equally gloomy, hour by hour a reunion more befitting by its miserable design. I registered no sight nor sound of my niece. I figured she must have been out, that she'd likely enrolled in classes at Santa Rosa Junior College, maybe even Sonoma State since graduating high school the previous summer. There wasn't any news of her getting a job or going away for school, though I hadn't thought to ask. An old, innate fear of downed power lines sprang to mind. It was no night for an inexperienced driver to be out on the west-country back roads. Did Mia have her license? I had no idea.

Looking back, my personal and work problems had come to crisis point with the exact same poor timing that Bridget was faced with the knife. While I reeled from rejection and the first throws of early separation, my sister had opted for a double mastectomy. I watched her as she emptied bowls and buckets filled halfway with murky water from the numerous leaking points.

"I want to say, Bridget," I gestured, softening my voice. "You've kept it real. If it was me dealing with all that you've had on your plate, I'd be knee-deep right now in the weirdest damn treatments the world has to offer, all that crazy shit I've read about over the years, scorpion venom, Venus flytraps, deep sea sponges . . . I'd be signing up for it, the whole nine yards — and hell, I'd auction off this old leak-ridden shithole to pay for it."

My sister was a shrunken version of herself, her tufted head wrapped in an uncharacteristic turban of a raw silk-like scarf of olive green that tempered her stark profile with its soft, earthy hue. Bridget's pretty, long and wavy, red hair had been her best feature, her number one source of pride since childhood. She'd worn it loose or else braided at the back.

A pair of camouflage pants was cinched around her tiny waist with an elastic stretch belt. It reminded me of a belt I'd picked out as a teenager when we'd been more than happy to shop for bargain back-to-school gear at the Walmart in Rohnert Park. Come to think, it may well have been that same belt given Bridget's hoarding tendencies. She'd tucked her baggy pants into a pair of sloppy, well-worn sheepskin boot slippers, the same genuine, pricey Australian brand I'd sent both she and Mia for Christmas the year before, ordered from Nordstrom online in a fit of generosity, after I had cashed out the stock options that I would subsequently lose.

Now it was Bridget who was lost — in her clothing — a small bag of sticks under a bulky sweater, at sea, all hard, pointed angles where

I'd been so jealous of her slender, well-proportioned contours. I took a second look at the chunky sweater that only served to emphasize the skin and bones swimming around in it. The Celtic knit was unmistakable, yet another unnerving blast from the past. It was the same old sweater that Mom had knitted me for my fifteenth birthday, the last thing she'd made for me or for any of us for that matter, a physical reminder of the few material, if not practical indulgences she'd afforded her girls when she was alive.

The sight of it brought back a flood of memories of Mom seated by the fireside during the long evening hours of the wet winter months, its classic Irish heather cable-knit she'd favored to fend off the fog and chill. Mom never could get enough of the sentimental old-world Irish stuff. Me, I hadn't bothered to hold on to any such obsessions, except for on St. Patrick's Day, when it felt like half the population of San Francisco would trade their heritage for an ounce of the Irish in me.

The sweater, like Bridget and me, had seen better days. It was something at least to see my suffering sister ensconced in an item of warm clothing our mother had poured the last of her love into. I wouldn't go so far as to say it was as if she was there in the room, the three of us returned to her tired, old kitchen that dark and rainy February evening, though it was some small comfort to think of her. You still wouldn't catch me dead in that baggy old rag despite my own reduced circumstances. To think that the last time I'd shopped for winter clothes I was armed with a slew of fat credit cards tucked into my wallet. There's little chance in the stars for a repeat round of that sort of spending, for the record, not since and not anytime soon. Anyway, I was in good company. I doubted Bridget had bought herself so much as a new pair of socks in years.

CHAPTER 4

JAZMIN

They call us the Dreamers, kids like me whose mom and dad snuck us over the border into the States with zero papers, raising us here in the only country we've ever really known. I never thought of myself as a dreamer 'til it came time to look into how to apply for junior college, put in for a driver's license and all.

I know as good as anyone what it is to live in the gray space between two cultures, two languages, two realities, two sets of laws. DACA is short for the official term of Deferred Action for Childhood Arrivals, a lifeline of an immigration policy that allows for some of us Dreamers brought here unlawfully as kids to be granted a renewable two-year period of deferred action from deportation and be allowed to apply for a work permit or student status.

And so when my BFF Mia emailed me asking: "Hey, you wanna earn a stash of cash, babe? Make bank. Change your luck?" I stupidly figured it was my best option to fast-forward my plans to put my paperwork in. Plus, she promised me we'd be home by Christmas with five "G" a piece stuffed into our pockets. After I got going with my DACA paperwork, I planned on treating the familia to a whole bunch of sweet things we'd never been able to afford with the easy money I would make from trimming weed.

It wasn't an instant "hell yes". Despite being all pissed and frustrated on account of my not being able to apply for or pay for school already, my first thought was: "Are you bat shit crazy, bitch?" And yet, I knew this chick — she was most likely grinning all goofy at me as she typed. This one has always been full of surprises. Still is. We don't have a whole deal to speak of, aside from each other, my folks and me but thank God, we do still have a real strong sense of family and who we are and what we mean to each other. I'm holding on to that. It's my touchstone with all the shit I've gotta wade through now to get myself where I need to be.

Mom and Dad, all they do is work, work, work. What choice do they have? They work their fingers to the bone and they wouldn't have it any other way insofar as figuring out how to put food on the table and a way to get the papers for all of us. It's been this way my whole life. All through high school, I never complained out loud when it was me who was left home come evening hours and weekends, looking after the little ones when I was barely more than a kid myself.

I graduated high school with a frickin' 4.0 GPA no less. My mom, she was more than happy for me to go on being her muchacha, the good girl that I was, low profile, picking up the house, helping her out with her early morning jobs before Dad took off for his own long day. And I did it for a few months even after I left school because it was what was expected of me and I love those little ones. I never bitched or moaned. I looked after my little brothers and sisters like I was a third parent.

My dad on the other hand, he knew I had other ideas. I had been upfront with him about my dream to get myself into nursing school some day. All he'd kept on saying was that he was sorry. It was what it was. There was no money for college and no college without paperwork. I learned to drive his truck the times he'd downed a whole bunch of Coronas after work, me being the oldest and my mom being way too scaredy-cat to take the wheel. I didn't dare try to get a license once I figured out how slim my chances were, though Dad had somehow managed to swing one back when they were issuing them to the undocumented with proof of identity and residence. I figured it was way too risky for me to apply for a license after the immigration scares started up.

Mia said I was breaking the mold in getting my life together. "Dare to dream, babe," she'd rallied and encouraged. Mia is always laughing with me, never at me, despite all the serious crap we've been dealt, which is one of the things I love most about that girl. And hey, you know what? She knows. She's learned the hard way how to free herself from fear and shame.

The little ones, I figured, they were old enough to make do without me for a short while. I justified what we did as good practice for Mia and me in finding us a sweet apartment of our own some day. Santa Rosa is 45 minutes inland, by car. I pictured a small, affordable place somewhere within walking distance of the junior college, you know the kind of thing — cool coffee shops, thrift stores, music venues, what the heck — a real life of our own for girls of our age. It was totally chill to take our time with all this school stuff, Mia kept on telling me. "The junior college has been there a long time, as far as I know, it sure ain't going anywhere til we get back, J."

I'd fixed my mind on the idea of filling out the paperwork that would enable me to stay on in the system. It was gonna be one heck of a struggle, but I'd heard there are safe haven schools where I'd be able to transfer, later, in my junior year. I wanted to do things the right way. I still plan on it, after all. But OMG, let's make this clear, there was no way in hell I would have agreed to what happened if I'd had one single fucking clue of what was in store.

All I know now for sure is that it's all out in the open, what happened to Mia and me. It feels like the whole darn county is aware of the position I am in with my lack of papers and all, my hoping and praying they're gonna see how much I have to offer if they let me stay. I'm hell-bent on fully cooperating with whoever and whatever it is I have to do for them to let me out of here, so that I'm free to make a life for myself in California. I'll figure out how to get on my feet if it kills me. I'm gonna make it into nursing school if it's the last thing I do, you'll see.

It's not that it's easy for me to maintain this kind of focus. My heart is in a million pieces 'til I get to see Mia again. After all the pain and the humiliation the pair of us have endured, shit, something fierce has taken hold inside of me. No man will ever have the strength to smash my spirit again, let me just say. "Swim to the light, babe," I urge myself, on loop. "Breathe it in, go on, look at all that fresh, clean air up there just hanging around waiting for the intake." I go about my days like this, as much as I have the strength for, following my compass, shining my light all the way through the trees for Mia to see. In some moments, when I am at more determined than ever, I feel like a greedy little kid who never knew nothing bad in the world. It's the only way I know how to cope, how to go on with it all.

CHAPTER 5

MAGGIE

Rain that started in on Halloween pounded the Northern California coastal communities through the holidays and well into January and February. I had bunkered down in my half empty apartment in gloomy San Francisco, glum and pitiful while I'd still thought I could wait that winter out. Since Andres had swiped way more than his share of its contents, the apartment echoed with the sole sound of silver bullets pelting the single pane windows. Day after day, night after night, I'd drowned my sorrows in his expensive wine and a series of overpriced comfort food deliveries, waiting for something, what, I have no clue in retrospect, to miraculously change inside of me. I had sat and watched the rain as it hit the glass sideways and poured down in sheets.

It was the city that had made me soft and ever more vulnerable. I wallowed in the misery of those last, self-indulgent months of my life within the nouveau wealth capital of America. I'd already walked away from my work and I'd barricaded myself in the apartment with a Joni Mitchell soundtrack on loop. I made perfectly sure it was loud enough to drown out the sound of police sirens and car alarms. I love my music and it was all I had left. For years I had taken pride in having unwittingly escaped the old man's humiliating bet on me being the family's best breeding stock. This false claim of his was frequently and crudely pointed out, much to my humiliation, in my teens — in the form of my pair of wide, so-called "child-bearing hips". The fact I had not fallen pregnant after Andres and I had come around to thinking we should give it a shot was a topic I revisited countless times in my head that sad, solo, holiday season. I felt like the lone loser.

The night of the day I'd given notice on my lease, I double-bolted the door, stripped off my clothes and took a long, hot shower. Since I had newly declared my Joni Mitchell moping period over, it was time to revisit my substantially perkier New Wave, '80s playlist — first up, Boy George ramped to full blast as the warm suds of the last of my overpriced salon shampoo and conditioner splurge, washed down my back. I stepped out from under the cheap little showerhead Andres had switched out for the luxury version he'd mean spiritedly unscrewed and taken with him as he'd systematically dismantled my life. Who does this to someone? You've heard about people who take the light bulbs with them when they move. Well, that's my ex. I took a good long look at myself in the full-length mirror fixed on the back of my bedroom door. There was a fresh new batch of cellulite at the top of my inner thighs I hadn't noticed before and my backside appeared to have built up an extra layer of padding since the last time I'd looked. I sucked in my stomach and took stock of my general overall condition. I made a sort of peace with myself, that night and after carefully ensconcing my naked, overripe 46-year-old body in a fluffy robe for safekeeping, I cranked the music down a tad to the dulcet tones of Duran Duran, kicking back on a pile of pillows on my bed to polish off the last bottle of Cab that I'd started in on earlier that evening.

The next morning, hungover, I set about bagging up the bulk of the clothes that had served me as a sort of incentive-inducing mid-management motivational suit of armor. I had made the decision while feeling no pain the night before to shed my false and ill-fitting skin, donate it, the whole lot of it — countless thousands of dollars worth of skirts, pants, jackets, dresses, shirts, shoes, belts and bags. Granted, most of it I'd bought on sale. I've never been a complete idiot. I searched online for a program I remembered promoting in one of the internal memos I was in charge of sending out to several thousand fellow employees. It's a program that provides outfits to underprivileged women being groomed for the workplace. Within hours, they'd efficiently sent two members of their all women collection team over in a van. Two girls in their late teens hauled the substantial stash of designer duds away before I could so much as change my mind.

"Sign here," said the one with the most visible ink art. She held the paperwork in her decorated fingers, the back of her hands, her wrists and what I could see of her arms a self-inked journal of what was likely an emotional trip through turbulent teens.

"Are you worried I'll call in later and ask for my designer belt collection back?" I joked.

She laughed. "Something like that, ma'am," she replied, looking over my shoulder at the half-empty apartment. "You'd be surprised. Sometimes people have second thoughts."

At least I'd taken sensible precaution to check the inside pockets of my Fendi purses and my newly discarded jackets and pants. I'd salvaged several fives and tens and a handful of crumpled twenty-dollar bills along with a surprising amount of loose change from the many days, months, years of those foolish, carefree latte runs. Given that there'd been a free-for-all espresso bar at work and a rotating menu of no cost lunch offerings from the hippest Bay Area restaurants retained to keep the worker bees happy, I'd managed to spend a shitload of money on nothing.

"Not many family jewels to be found in this lot," I quipped. "Never had too many of those I'm sorry to say." Despite my tendency to overspend in the luxury clothing, food and wine department, other than my wedding band, engagement ring and my prized pair of diamond studs, the only other bauble or bangle I owned was a Rolex watch Andres had gifted me. The watch was his material idea of compensation after he'd talked me into sinking our combined fortune into the stupendously fucked-up startup failure.

Pairing down to my post-city regime, two pairs of J Brand jeans, T-shirts, a couple of soft, simple, Michael Stars cashmere sweaters and my favorite pair of ankle boots felt surprisingly good, liberating in fact.

Quitting work had been a whole lot easier than I had imagined when it came down to it. I guess I had been addicted to the rush of my own self-importance even though I'd worked for the same global brand tech company for way too long to remain relevant. It didn't take me long to learn that nobody is indispensable, no matter how pumped up the hype and the role-playing. News flash: As far as I know, the world is still turning without me playing my trivial bit part. The firm we worked for, Andres and me, morphed through a number of major overhauls as tech advancements progressed. I'd hung in, rising to the top of the internal communications team as the employee number grew from 500 into the many thousands. After the company went public, we'd been giddy with the greedy notion of making even more bank. And, after we found ourselves forced back into our longtime work roles, I'd found myself reduced to dodging Adderall-popping millennials like bumper cars — both in the treacherous minefields of the tech world as well as in the marital bed.

Andres had a thing for the doting younger-by-the-year women with techno stars in their eyes and stamina to match. His ego was all the more inflated by his work in the minefield that is AI. All I have to say on the subject at this point is that it's going to come back to bite him. If you ask me, the entire shit show of what's in the works with artificial intelligence is a waiting game; some would go so far as to say it is the most dangerous degree of society upheaval in-waiting in human history. If Andres thinks he's somehow exempt from being replaced by a more efficient robotic workforce, well, his bloated manly ego is only fooling itself.

I'd worked hard to stay in the game to make the world a better place, to keep myself in shape for it, it wasn't just the frequent shopping expeditions that perked me up, I'd desperately gasped my way through endless sweaty spin classes in my lululemon technical athletic gear in the company gym, paid top dollar for hair care, splurged on regular spa mani-pedis, Botox every three months — all the trappings of the forty-something female desperately trying to stop the clock from ticking too fast. You name it, I'd been up for trying it. And then it all became crystal clear what a colossal waste of time and money and effort it was.

Regardless of the degree of superficial preening I'd committed and subjected myself to, a revolving door of dot-com babes proved willing to overlook Andres' wedding ring for a quick fuck after work, a leg up the career rung while I was stupidly busting my sorry, ever-spreading ass on the spin bike.

I plopped myself down on a rickety stool, relieved to be back at our rust bucket ranch if only to be free of all that. I crossed my legs at the ankles and slid my beloved $398 Frye Sabrina Chelsea boots (in antique polished cognac leather) off from the heel, dropping them, one by one, under the narrow counter where, after Mom died, Bridget and I would huddle over endless cereal suppers. I remember well the taste of the tears that mixed into the milky pink excess at the bottom of the drab, brown-colored bowls that have been in constant use since our grandmother's reign over the kitchen. How we had laughed and cried and fought, Bridget and me. We'd done what we thought we needed to do in figuring out our scary, uncertain futures even if it had meant parting, doing our own thing. Now it was time to draw the line in some sort of a sisterly truce. We both knew we had to make things right.

It was me who made the first move: "I'm sorry that I wasn't here for you, Bridget. Truly, I am." Without a word, she was thrusting a heavy-duty black rain poncho into my hands. Despite my detachment, I knew what this was for without her having to ask, the old routine that had long since befallen her, checking up on flood levels in the old stock pond. I slid my swollen feet back into my boots. It worked both ways after all, she had never been one to ask for help.

Bridget was nineteen and I was fifteen when Mom died. It was the same sort of cancer, it turned out, that our mother unknowingly passed down to her oldest daughter. Neither of us had any idea how to deal with our dad. We'd been left with a washed up, drunken dairyman with no clue how to survive since his long-suffering wife was no longer taking care of his every need.

We braced ourselves against the driving wind and rain, flashlights in hand as we walked side by side in the dark expanse, frail beams leading us along the muddy track to the same stock pond our grandparents had dug. The pond was filled close to capacity from what I was able to decipher in the low visibility of the downpour. "What's up, heels sinking into the mud, Maggie?" Bridget asked, sarcasm lacing her voice as she pointed the beam at my feet. My beautiful, American-made boots with their one-inch heel were clearly not the best choice. "It's time you catch a clue. Someone has to keep a close eye on the pond in this weather," she added. "And that someone is me, whether I feel like it or not."

Dad had done a number on Mom as well as Bridget and me. His moods, his negative comments, his morbid, utter lack of motivation at the end. Parental encouragement had been nonexistent. Mom had been a saint to put up with him. Or plain weak, one of the two, though it has taken me a long time to be able to say something as uncharitable as this about my own mother. Once our role model for learning to accept less than we deserved had left this world, things had gone from sad to dire.

I looked around me in the cold, wet, inhospitable darkness and shuddered. By the time I graduated high school, I was totally over my fractured family and this failing ranch. I couldn't have cared less if I never saw it again. It proved another world from the privileged homes of pampered college friends I sought out during those first few years away from the godforsaken place I left behind. My criteria for studies had been simple — I'd gone to the best school that accepted me with some degree of financial assistance and it had to be reachable by bus. Four hundred and fifty miles to the south, give or take a few, Los Angeles was my first taste of escape, a perfectly wild, crazy, material tonic to wipe out my unsophisticated past.

After graduation, armed with a shiny new marketing and communications degree, I found work in the features department of a glossy magazine — where, despite my humble north coast heritage and limited exposure to the finer things in life, I surprised myself at how adept I was as an interloper in selling the sunny SoCal lifestyle. Southern California was ideal for the new, glossier me, about as far removed from the sinkhole of home as I could have wished for. Life there was surprisingly good, exciting for an ambitious and single country girl in the big city. And when, after a few years, I'd had my fill of Los Angeles, I crept back up the coast to join the ranks of the early tech titans in free-thinking San Francisco. I'm ashamed to say I waited to tell Bridget I was back in Northern California 'til our dad, for all his weakness, sold his entire herd of Jerseys, paid off his debts and, in no time at all, proved to us he was capable of succeeding in something. He drank himself to death.

It was Bridget who'd stepped up as ranch matriarch, without the slightest fuss. "I've done my best for the place," she said as we stood side by side, gripping the dripping hoods of our sodden ponchos under the shelter of the barn. An eerie, raspy call of a barn owl stilled our conversation. I caught my breath as his white face, chest and underbelly took flight from over our heads on a buoyant pair of widespread wings across the open fields. Bridget checked the door was secure for another rainy night, pointing out the owl's nest in the exterior rafters, ten feet above my head. I shared how I had read an article on how the owl is the symbol of the moon's cycle of renewal, of magic, of ancient knowledge, mystery.

"I'm sure I don't know anything about that. What choice did I ever have?" Bridget asked.

"You could have walked away, after Dad died, like I did," I answered, my voice being carried away on the wind. "I mean, who would have stopped you, Bridget?"

I wondered, as we headed back to the house, arm awkwardly in arm as we braced against the rain, what difference would it have made in our lives, if she'd sold the ranch — mine, Bridget's, Mia's? And where was Mia? What was she up to? We hadn't got to that. Bridget was busy thinking her own thoughts as we made our way back to the dimly lit house. "The doctors say it will take five years after radiation for me to be cancer free," she said, positioning her back to me as she pushed open the front door with one shoulder. I looked around for something to wipe the mud from my boots, resorting to a sheet from a stack of damp newspapers.

"How do you cope with the uncertainty?" I asked. She turned to face me in the light of the open doorway. Why hadn't I packed a pair of rain boots? Even a pair of hiking boots would have come in handy. Shows where my mind was. I ought to have known better having been raised out here.

"I've made a fresh start, Maggie," Bridget said, heading into the warmth and light of the kitchen. "I've launched my own business."

Fat snakes of rain slithered down the windowpanes, distorting any sense of scale of the shrouded expanse of land that rolled down into the savage reach of the Pacific swell. I fixed my gaze on the dark, bleak, void.

Forget the wine, I would've poured myself a stiff drink or two or three if there'd been any drop of hard alcohol to be had.

"What?" I asked? "How've you had the wherewithal to even think of working in your condition?"

"I guess you'd call it a cottage industry," Bridget had my attention, now. She motioned to a stack of measuring cups and wooden spoons.

I stepped closer to better take in the contents of the countertop, remembering the hippie herbs and potions that were Bridget's bag back when we were in our teens. She'd spent hours experimenting with and concocting her colorful natural remedies and beauty products, driven in large part by our geographic isolation and coupled with a lack of money in the home health care department, or any department for that matter. Besides, we have all the natural ingredients at hand in our abundant shoreline ecosystem and we know where to look. Granny had passed her peoples' pioneer cures down to Mom and, in turn to Bridget more than me, when she showed considerable interest in it, early on. We'd never seen such a thing as a store-bought cough syrup or an anti-itch cream as kids, we drank baking soda in water for indigestion, rubbed salt water on mosquito bites, dabbed cider vinegar and honey cures, cobwebs on scratches.

"You're cooking with cannabis?"

"Damned well, if I say so myself, " she said, jutting her chin out. "If you must know, I started out baking to bolster my condition," Bridget explained. "After I'd been forced to succumb to the chemo, I switched from smoking weed to edibles." She looked me in the eyes. "Micro-dosing is where it's at," she informed me with a markedly new air of confidence. "Instead of one big hit, a steady, longer lasting release."

Bridget patiently explained how she'd progressed into baking for herself and, later, baking for a cancer collective. She had grown too weak to continue her shifts at the roadhouse, but making edibles in her own kitchen was something she enjoyed and was able to manage. "I've expanded my range, now that I have fine-tuned dosage and flavor," she continued — "brownies, cookies, almond bars, canna butter, alternative sweeteners."

This was news. "You're making a living this way, Bridget?"

"Attempting to," she exclaimed. "I have my paperwork sorted out. Bobby's pulling extra shifts at the bar, I'm making ends meet with my edibles. We don't need much. I'm all about locally grown, clean product and reputation. If you like, you can sample some for yourself at supper this evening."

Muted headlights from Bobby's beat-up Subaru wagon shone a double spotlight through the kitchen window over the otherwise quiet domestic scene of my sister's revelations. Once indoors, the big guy threw his XXL, damp and dripping standard Carhartt jacket over the back of the nearest chair. Rainwater trapped in its creases rolled down the wax coating, forming a fairly substantial puddle on the linoleum.

"One of these days we're covering that cursed porch," Bridget snapped, as the two of us watched the pool of water expand under the chair where the super-size jacket drip-dried. "After everything else on the goddamn fixit list."

"Huh, Maggie, what are you doing here?" A less than enthusiastic welcome home from my brother-in-law, common-law, whatever.

"Bobby," I jumped off my stool in an effort to greet him. "Hey, it's good to see you, bro."

There was no move to embrace, to take a hand, nothing close to even the smallest of polite gestures of welcome on his part. I knew how the land lay and there'd be no sympathy for my shallow sorrows. Bridget shot her guy a stern look. Bobby was rough around the edges, certainly not my idea of a knight in shining armor, but he'd weathered pretty well, considering. He'd grown on the hefty side, his face well-formed, not quite handsome, yet still, he was somewhat doe-eyed, dark-lashed and undeniably masculine. Bridget's choice was a swarthy, tobacco scented, no frills, hard-core, traditional Italian/American. I was at least grateful that he had stuck by her in her hour of need.

"Sheesh, it's crazy out there. More than a handful of trees down tonight," he said.

Giant eucalyptus, "Beautiful Nuisance", as we call them 'round here — non-native and everywhere you look, thanks to an unfortunate move in mass planting in the late 1880s. By the time they'd proved themselves totally useless as lumber during the boom or bust years, eucalyptus had grown to dominate the landscape in their enormity.

Locals keep them around, largely for their beauty, for sentimental reasons and the shelter and shade they afford, but mostly due to the cost of felling. When a eucalyptus decides it's time to fall, holy cow, it's a calamity.

"Best not turn around tonight." Bobby eyed my bag by the door. He put his arm to his mouth. I looked away as he wheezed and hacked into the coarse fabric of his plaid shirtsleeves.

"Depends," I said. That same look again, the pair of them shooting spiky, wordless messages to one another, too complex for me to fully decipher. I hoped he wasn't smoking tobacco around my sister.

"If it's OK with you guys, I'll sleep on the couch," I ventured.

"No need." Bridget looked away. "Take your old room, Maggie."

"What about Mia? When will she be home?"

"Sit down, Maggie — Mia's not here. She's been away for a while now." Bobby cautioned.

"What do you mean? Away. Where?"

Bridget's eyed welled up. She cleared her throat.

"Look Maggie, we don't know for sure," she stammered. "We haven't seen sight nor sound of her since late summer," she confessed.

"It's February, Bridget. You have to be kidding. What the hell?"

"Mia pretty much freaked out after my diagnosis," Bridget continued. "Left me a note sayin' she was out of here, that she'd found work, both she and her friend, Jazmin from school, not to worry myself on her behalf. Took off without as much as a goodbye in person, never told me where, how long, who else they were with — nothin'."

I clutched the sides of the stool for balance as I processed Bridget's casual bombshell. This was my sister's teenage daughter, my niece and, aside from Bridget, my only other living family member we were talking about. I hadn't been the best of aunts, it's true, or even a halfway good one up to this point, but it shocked me how hard the news of Mia's disappearance rattled me.

"Why the heck am I hearing about this five months after the fact, Bridget? I can't believe you didn't tell me when we talked after your surgery."

"That's the point, Maggie. It was me who called to check on you, not the other way around. Oh no, you were way too busy dealin' with your own dysfunctional life to bother yourself with Mia or me. You never even asked about your niece. What else did you have to do over Christmas and New Years? You've never even spent a single holiday here with Mia and me, not in all these years."

"Are you saying because I had a life and a job that happened not to revolve around this far-flung ranch, I don't count in this family?"

Bridget pointedly stacked and restacked a set of glass measuring cups. "Last thing I want in my condition is to be a burden, Maggie. Not then, not now, not to Mia, not to you, or Bobby. I let her go, like I let you go — so she wouldn't feel the pain."

Fucking hell. Was my sister made stupid by her sickness, selfish or simply unobservant? "Bridget, does Mia have money? She and this Jazmin girl, do they have friends? Someone must know where they are. For god's sake, woman, have you traced her phone, checked her social media?"

Bobby cleared his throat before speaking up. To everyone's great misfortune, he'd taken Mia's phone off his plan the minute she finished high school. Bad move, as it turned out, but who am I to point fingers? "She barely graduated — such an attitude. Lazed around all summer, never even started lookin' for a job."

"We both felt she should be standin' on her own two feet by now, Maggie. I kinda feel like it's my fault for not pushin' her to try a little harder, I let her flop around here like she had no choice, which is the same way I felt at her age, if I'm honest, I guess. I truly never thought she had it in her to take off," Bridget said. "She was a big ol' fuckin' mess last summer. We all were."

"You sure you didn't see this coming? Teenagers hate to be without a phone. Even I know that."

Bridget attempted to control her reaction to my obvious fury. She took a breath and launched into how long she'd been distracted, missing cues, working all those evening shifts the last few years, long before she'd fallen sick.

"She dropped Facebook in junior high after she was bullied by some older girls who had it in for her. I don't do social media, you know that, still, I got her off it at the end of eighth grade. I never knew what else she might have been on after we got her a phone, I never saw her on it all that much so I had no cause for concern. After I found out about the cancer, I lost it for a few weeks, smoked myself into a stupor. I cannot blame my daughter for takin' off."

"Ok, you really aren't helping her in any way."

"Don't you start to piss and moan, now Maggie," Bobby warned. "It's a real bad time for us. If you want to come here and be of some use, for once in your life, then that's a different matter."

CHAPTER 6

BRIDGET

My flawlessly dressed, jumped-up and dearly estranged little sis was attemptin' to reengage. I get it, I mean, we never picked each other out as sisters, but that don't mean we can't at least put in some effort to make good on our differences after all that's gone down. We are trying. I'll give us that. History repeats itself, ain't that what they say? Maggie was the first in the family to break away when there weren't such a thing as a cell phone, email or a goddamn frickin' text known to mankind and now here she was again, after, what, oh, only three decades give or take? Yes, sir, she was makin' her grand reappearance, right back at the place she started out from.

Maggie ditched home for the student life, a world I have no business with. I never knew for sure where Mia was headed, though I'd had my suspicions. What I did know was it weren't no college education she was after given her poor performance in high school.

Despite my warnin' myself not to cave in to my sister as she was clearly tryin' her darn best to crawl back in under my skin, I'd be lyin' if I said it wasn't good to see her. When it comes down to it, to blood family, me, Maggie and Mia, for all our sins, we are all there is. And, for all my failings, family is unconditional when all is said and done.

As for Bobby and me, too bad we never did tie the knot. It's my big regret. We'd just sorta drifted along, makin' do.

My fancypants sister started lettin' her shield slide down durin' that first supper, at least layin' off the accusations, some. Still, she kept on pressin' me on Mia's motives in takin' off.

"Have you filed a missin' person's report?" she asked, like she was takin' up a goddamn investigation at the kitchen table.

I tensed and snapped, no. "Mia's workin', okay? She wrote as much in her note. She'll be back when she's good 'n' ready, when the money runs out."

"Mia's eighteen, Bridget," Maggie shot back, all puffed-up and pink-cheeked in that porcelain doll face of hers, all of a sudden, meanwhile, puffin' out her already more than ample chest and wrappin' her arms in front of her in a confrontational fashion. "Even you have to know she's hardly streetwise."

Bobby shot up from his seat in my defense, God bless him. "For fuck's sake, Maggie, what do you know about it? Now's not the time to come here freakin' your sister out like this. She's givin' the girl space to grow up is all."

I reached out and touched my sister's arm. She's big-boned, our Maggie, broad shouldered, nothin' like me, inside or out. "You've looked after yourself well enough in all these years, haven't you?" I asked her, motionin' for Bobby to sit himself back down. "Mia's a smart one, despite her school failin's, she'll manage well enough."

Maggie raised her eyes in a way that made me wonder if she'd not done nearly as good a job of lookin' after herself as I had figured all these years. She lowered those green eyes of hers to the table so I'd not be able to read more into what was sittin', stewin' behind 'em. I waited 'til she raised 'em upward again, flashin' interest and lightin' up at the sight of a big ol' bowl of oven-warmed comfort food, my leftover canna mac 'n' cheese if you please, its crispy breadcrumb toppin' and a rich, creamy sauce bubblin' away like nobody's business with a pinch of paprika atop. She always did like her food and it showed. A few tablespoons of my cannabutter melts good and proper in a cheese sauce. I had taken pains to bake Bobby's portion of cheesy pasta aside, unadulterated on account of him being sober so long and, I thank the Lord, though I've no religion to speak of after we both let any last spark of the Catholic left in us lapse, he'd stuck to it.

We sat awhile, avoidin' the Mia subject while we awaited the trace amount of edible to kick in. Maggie was up front about not bein' sure of her personal tolerance. "Only one way to find out," she said, frankness personified, without the snarky edge I was expectin'.

I've learned through trial and error the ins and outs of the levels of psychoactive and medicinal compounds in the strains I've grown the best, out back. "There's nothin' much in what you're gettin' here to do you any damage," I did my best to assure.

It is the healin' properties I am after, not only the high, though for sure, I'm not adverse to a manageable amount of that, neither, considerin' all of it I've been through. "You surely know that cannabis is being used for treatin' all sorts of ailments from seizures to autoimmune diseases to migraines, nowadays," I said. "It helps folk sleep, eases the menstrual pains . . . this little ol' Wild West frontier business of mine is set on goin' mainstream."

"So that's it, I'm your guinea pig tonight?" Maggie asked, "a willin' subject of Bridget's quasi-legal kitchen experiments." She said she'd read plenty on the medicinal properties and breakthroughs bein' made but never had taken to it herself.

We've been fightin' for more than two decades for cannabis legislation reform in these parts. About damn time local elections in the last few years are finally turnin' the laws around in favor of legalizin' medical marijuana and, its limited recreational growth and use. "It's legit," I replied.

"Don't count your chickens," Bobby piped in. "The Feds still don't care much for these newfangled local laws, Bridget and you'd best keep that in mind."

Our folks had subscribed to a conservative school of thought. And they were proud of it. Bobby's family, as with most old-time ranchers out here were all pretty much of the same mindset — limited government, low taxes. It was Maggie who never cared none for the politics of the place, windin' us up with her loosey-goosey liberal ways. Now it was my turn to be shakin' things up. She weren't expectin' this none.

"I never would have dared done it back when Mia was a kid," I had to admit. "Times are a changin'. If I have myself all the right paperwork in order, implementin' appropriate security 'n all, why not grow the good stuff out here where it's well away from anyone else's business?"

Bobby nodded: "All I see is the rich growin' richer, the regular folk in these parts gettin' ripped off. If we do this right, Bridget's business I mean, we have a chance to make a go of it, fix things up out here."

While Bobby was taking care of the dishes, Maggie asked me what I was thinkin' the impact of this so-called "Green Rush" means for our farm culture out west, the natural environment 'n' all. "It's all well and good, Bridget," she pressed on. "But from what I hear, there are as many people against this widespread legalization as are for it. Specially when it's right next door."

"None of this happened overnight," I shared what I know of the big legalization debate as far as I understand in our home county, at least. "It's been a gradual movement, real slow. The advocators, the growers, the lawmakers whose job it is to legitimize, to govern and protect our region, truth is, none of 'em really knows how in God's green earth it's all goin' to pan out."

What I keep my focus on is that the laws are openin' all manner of new windows and doors for medical research and treatments. In my mind, women such as myself, those of us without too many options, if we're smart, we're gonna get to the top of what was for the longest time, pretty much a man's world.

"In the meantime, I'm takin' advantage of everythin' I'm learnin' along the way, thank you very much," I declared. "For me, Maggie, it's personal. It's not only about my goddamn health for me, it is my livelihood." My so-called progressive sister looked at me real confused. I figured she never expected to hear this. It's called initiative, the pioneer spirit. I guess she never knew I still had it in me, lame ol' Bridget, kickin' around the roadhouse waitin' tables the rest of her life. Hey, if I don't launch myself into the future, who else is gonna do it for me?

"Well, thanks anyway for the meal as well as the hefty dose of food for thought, I'm heading upstairs to unpack," she flounced off in her usual fashion. Maggie was unfoldin' the clothin' she'd packed as her escape gear as I climbed the stairs to check in on her. I figured I had best keep an eye on her, take responsibility in monitorin' her tolerance level.

I perched on the edge of the double bed we'd shared as kids watchin' her real close as she went through the motions of puttin' her stuff away. It was the exact same bed, same saggy ol' mattress that Mia slept on since she was a toddler. That oughta been my first clue, her climbin' up out of her cot the second she could stand on them chubby little legs of hers. Both Maggie and Mia were the restless type. When my sister acted on her bigger, la-di-da ideas, it'd come as no big surprise. I truly never did see it comin' with Mia.

"I've rented a budget storage unit in the city," Maggie explained, her way of lettin' me know she was here for a while. "I've packed up the rest of my stuff, the few items Andres left behind."

I listened as she told me how relieved she had been that her neighbors, two young programmer dudes who work for one of the big search engines, had come to her rescue in haulin' her couch, a mattress and a big, ol' bed frame down three sets of stairs and into the U-Haul van she'd filled with the dregs of her marriage. "I didn't have to ask, but, thankfully, they took it on themselves and helped me unload it all over at the storage place," she said.

If you ask me, Andres is and always was a douchebag. I'd sized him up early on, the few times I'd been graced with his company. I never liked him — he was way too wrapped up in himself, his ego, his image, his so-called brains and starched button-downs. Upscale Silicon Valley our Maggie had first described him to me. Ha! I never forgot it. She, on the other hand is a royal pain in the ass but somewhere inside of that manicured exterior you'll find a good enough heart. I'm her sister. I know these things.

Maggie had chilled out a degree, given what she'd been through, despite the lingerin' airs and graces. "Give the girl a throne," our dad used to say. Goddamn it, I had been so jealous of her good looks, her easy way of puttin' herself first in line. Even now, her long, dark wavy hair lets loose with barely a touch of silver. Those lively green eyes of hers bore bright in the low lit room as they locked with mine, a contrast of tired, ol' watery blue.

She wanted, then, to know what it was the surgeon had done to me, what it looked like in the flesh. Her eyes widened all the more when I held up my sweater for the show and tell she sought.

"Oh, sweet Jesus," she gasped, her hand to her mouth. "Bridget, damn, I had no idea."

My sister was seein' her first tit-less woman's torso, up close and personal, if you please. The core of my body was still freshly scarred, somewhat raw to be brutal honest about it and there was a strange, lingerin' aroma clingin' to the stitchin', two diagonal red slashes all that remained of the soft little buns where my breasts used to be.

"Christ. What happened to your nipples?" she asked, aghast. "Did they forget to sew them back on?"

"Not without any reconstructive surgery," I explained. "Stop your fussin', Maggie, I'm over it," I said. "Anyway, it was me who said no to a new pair."

When I'm well, I'm plannin' on a big, ol' chest tattoo. I'm picturin' a beautiful owl, based on the one in our barn, its wings spread real wide to cover whatever remains of the scarrin'.

I reached down, my T-shirt and sweater still halfway up around my armpits and plugged in a string of fairy lights Mia had tacked to the wall in a half-hearted attempt at a grotto surroundin' her headboard. The room twinkled, softly.

Maggie's eyes welled. I watched, taken aback, as she wiped the first of her small, fat tears with the back of her hand.

"Bridget," Maggie whispered, tenderly for once. For the first time in forever, my sister voluntarily reached out her hand to me. "You're going to beat this, honey," she said, tracin' the line of scars across my chest with the tip of her finger. "We'll beat this. Together."

I have grown weirdly accustomed to the strange sensation that is, in truth, no sensation at all when it comes to bein' suddenly and totally flat chested. Maggie dropped her hand and laced her fingers in mine.

Dingy granny curtains hung lifelessly across the bedroom window, the same cheap ol' lacey drapes from J.C. Penney our mother had hung up to keep the midday sun from strippin' the varnish on her ancient wooden furniture. I wondered why it was I had not taken any notion to better care for the place? A wash would have done these dull and dreary drapes some degree of good, though in truth, I figured they'd only disintegrate due to the compoundin' years of dust and harsh sun.

The old man hauled in the same ol' rug of worn green shag the week the drapes and wallpaper went up, a million years back, now.

"You know, they don't tell you any of this before they chop 'em off," I said, motionin' to my chest. "There's no feelin' there, now, none."

It's real strange, walkin' into things and not havin' even the smallest of what I'd call a boob buffer. I lie on my stomach at night and wonder at the flatness of it all.

It tends towards chilly upstairs so close to the rafters in the wet winter months. I shook out a musty smellin' patchwork quilt I'd stashed in an old blanket box at the foot of the bed, checkin' for mice. I spread it as a second layer over the dusky pink chenille coverlet that Mia picked out in junior high from a pile of first-rate used beddin' in our favorite thrift store in Point Reyes. "Good as new," I'd reassured her.

"One by one, over the years, I let go of everyone," Maggie spurted. "My friends — all of them, they left the city and its corporate life for the suburbs, one-by-one, two-by-two, starting businesses, families of their own." She was showin' signs of attemptin' to ready herself for bed, though she kept on stoppin' mid-sentence. I watched as she prized off her weddin' band, her flash diamond engagement ring and her watch. She wandered about the bedroom lookin' for somethin' to put 'em in, settlin' on a small satin pouch she found in amongst Mia's stuff, tuckin' her treasures in beneath the neatly folded clothes she'd carefully placed in a dresser drawer. Maggie brushed her glossy hair with one of Mia's hairbrushes and set about cleanin' her face with cotton wool and cleansin' lotion from a half-used drugstore bottle my daughter left behind. I followed her closely as my sister made her way downstairs.

"What do you need, Maggie" I asked. "How's about a nice glass of water?"

"Bridget. I've been a fool," she confessed, as we stood face to face in the dim light of the kitchen. I poured her a glass of ice-cold water from a pitcher in the fridge. I figured Maggie was pretty much bombed by this point. What I had wagered would have been a more gentle effect of our supper was kickin' in with way more impact than I had cause to anticipate, though the timin' was about right, an hour or so after we'd left the table.

Like I said, tolerance levels differ person-to-person, sometimes it's real dramatic and may feel dangerous to the partaker, though, as a rule it generally is not. I've seen cannabis take hold in all manner of ways. With Maggie, she started to giggle, spillin' water as she wandered on into the sittin' room.

I looked into her eyes as they filled with more of the same fat, watery tears she'd spilled on the bedcovers earlier. This time, though, she was laughin'. She clutched her curvy hips and for a good ten minutes or more, I listened as she hollered and went to, makin' silly talk about nothin' in particular.

Maggie's inhibitions took a nosedive. It was like she had launched herself off a hilltop on one of those paraglidin' contraptions or somethin'. So much so, she declared it was fuckin' good to be home, flyin' free and she never would have believed it.

"I feel like I'm floatin' on a cloud, Bridg'," she said, as she puttered around the room in slow, deliberate circles, fairly beamin' her face off at Bobby and me. Though it was kinda funny, watchin' my uptight sister relax into an altered state, I was all the while makin' sure that she was okay. Nothin' bad was gonna come of it, after all, I was the one who'd made the goddamn mac 'n' cheese, I knew just how much cannabutter I'd put in an' I saw how much of it she'd gobbled. What we was findin' out for the first time was how my sister reacts to edibles and how long she'd be high.

After about a quarter of an hour of her wanderin' around in this fashion with her arms out in front of her, bride of Frankenstein style, she walked across the room, stood with her back to us a minute or two more before she faceplanted her body the length of the couch. I stood by patiently as my holier-than-thou little sister hummed herself into a deep and contented lookin' sleep.

Bobby was all for leavin' her there, out cold. "Serve her right, silly bitch," he said. "She'll find her way to bed soon enough."

Instead, I pulled out a fuzzy ol' black and orange Giants blanket from a stash of beddin' I had tossed behind the couch at some desperate point durin' that eternal wet winter. I tucked the fuzzy coverlet under my sister's bare feet and arms and gently slid a pillow under her head, turnin' her face to the side so as she was able to breathe right.

As I lay in bed that night I thought it through. I'd never considered my self-centered sister the type to keep things bottled in. I was as guilty as she. Granted, Maggie had made the first move in showin' up. I'd give her that. She had climbed her way out of her crumblin' ivory castle, exposed herself to my resentment, to Bobby's impatience and ridicule. It was some sort of start toward me forgivin' her for bein' such a no-show.

Surely what Maggie was in need of was to feel wanted, useful. I guess she'd gotten used to bein' at the top of her game; brainwashed into common corporate goals and all the bullshit she swears she is done with. As for me, insomnia creepin' in as it does most nights, my mind was fair to racin'. What I did not need was for my sister to see me as the tragic figure she kinda wanted me to be. It dawned on me, the one who needed Maggie most was not in any shape or form myself, it was my baby girl, my Mia. They had no beef with each other and I figured that would prove a whole lot less complicated than the mother-daughter deal whether I liked it or not.

I'd made it this far with my struggles. If what Maggie had said was even halfway true, it was all my doin', whatever the mess Mia was in. I was the one who let her go without so much as a word. I'd failed her, like my sister had failed me. Hell. We'd all let each other down in our own fucked-up McCleery way.

I'd blinded myself and now I was startin' to see the light. I tossed and turned and settled into a restin' position on my front, one arm bent under the pillow for extra support. Shit had to change.

Next mornin', I woke her with gentle nudge and a mug of hot tea. A flurry of fallen leaves from the storm the night before was whippin' against the grimy window behind the couch. As I had tossed and turned in bed in the early hours, unable to sleep, I'd gotten to thinkin' back to when we were kids. We'd gotten by with barely as much as a toy or trinket, Maggie and me, we knew nothin' different. It was the way it was out here, same for all us kids in isolated outposts up along the coast. What we'd had was the freedom of imagination, roamin' around the countryside, free as birds without any supervision. And in the darker months, the idiot box as the old man called it, was our golden portal to an alternate reality.

"Remember when we sat here and watched TV like it was goin' out of fashion?" I asked Maggie, as she propped herself up against a couple of cushions, huddled up in her blanket like a kid again, crossin' her legs up under the covers, sippin' at her tea. Pretty much all we knew of the world outside of dairy ranchin' we'd gleaned from our favorite television shows — endless episodes of Happy Days, The Waltons, droolin' over David Cassidy in The Partridge Family.

"Cagney and Lacey, remember them? Ha! The Bionic Woman?" Maggie recalled. "It's a little sad how the best nostalgia for you and me comes in a box-shaped package, Bridg'."

When my own daughter hit her teenage years, I was barely around in the evenin's to see what it was that she was gleanin' from the box. At the same time, Mia had taken to hangin' out with the wrong crowd, the travelin' types, lean, hungry, feral-lookin' kids from who knows where, those that stopped off and camped along the coast in bigger numbers come July and August.

I warned her hangin' out at the beach after dark was gonna lead to trouble. All sorts pass through our remote community. I was convinced I'd made damn sure the kid was wary of strangers, to steer well clear of the extra dubious characters out there. In truth, I had no idea the extent of what she'd gotten herself into.

I set about organizin' the kitchen for the mornin's Bake-Off. If Maggie was gonna insist on forcin' any more sisterly bondin', I figured I'd show her how it is I go about makin' up a batch of my cannabutter, base substance of the bulk of my edible concoctions. I tend on makin' a supply once every week to last me a full seven days of cookin'. I heated up the stove to 240 °F in readiness to activate my weed stash for maximum potency and placed the plant material on a bakin' sheet to heat through in the oven 'til it was nice and dry and suitably crumbly. After, I placed a pot of water on the stovetop to boil, addin' in sticks of organic butter. I don't ever skimp on quality. I set to sprinklin' in the newly activated weed from the oven and left my concoction to simmer on the back burner for a couple of hours.

"The secret to cookin' with cannabis, is fat," I explained. "Look, see," I said, motionin' with a wooden spoon. "When the top of the concoction turns from watery to thick and glossy, it's ready for strainin' through a double layer of cheesecloth." I demonstrated tyin' string around the glass storage bowls I keep 'specially for this purpose.

"And that's all there is to it?" Maggie asked.

"No, not exactly," I replied. "You have to let it cool for an hour, before you place it in the refrigerator. At this stage, we wait for the butter to rise to the top of the liquid to solidify before we get to runnin' a knife across the top to scrape off the actual cannabutter. All the good stuff's in there," I explained, maintainin' my patience as best I was able, not bein' accustomed to an audience, especially one that consists of my sister.

"How do you keep your baked goods from tastin' too much of weed?" Maggie asked, her interest piqued.

"Now that's a challenge even for the most experienced of cooks," I answered, scrapin' the last of a batch of cannabutter from the previous week's stock. "It may not have felt like it, the way you were last night, Maggie, but truth is, I use smaller doses than most other edible makers in the market."

Most people overeat with edibles at first, though Maggie had consumed only what I'd served her. "To be honest, I never expected it to hit you as hard as it did," I confessed.

"Now you tell me! I feel fine," she replied, her face breakin' into a smile. "Did I make a fool of myself?"

"It knocked you out, for sure," I admitted. "You'll figure out your tolerance level soon enough; never pegged you as a lightweight."

"At least when it comes to weed," Maggie laughed. "Give me a bottle of wine, no problem."

The kitchen is generally chilly first thing, though the heat of the stove soon warms it through. I slid Maggie's old battery operated boom box, the size of a frickin' carry-on out from under the countertop. Both radio and double cassette heads were in good workin' order, despite its age and the hours I've spent tunin' in for the mornin' news and the playlists that keep me company in my kitchen. I tuned into KZST for a steady stream of songs to take the edge off the friction that remained between us. Heck, tension was hangin' in the air like a plume of smoke from a pile of burned toast. "Every Breath You Take," the Police, Simon & Garfunkel's "Cecilia", Bon Jovi's "You Give Love a Bad Name." One after another . . . it was the best way to clear the air between us.

Maggie pawed through a stack of old tapes I pushed over for her to have a look through. They were stacked in an old Tupperware box: Michael Jackson, Billy Joel, that time frame. The kitchen windows were all steamed up and we found ourselves engulfed in a comfortin' cloud of flour, the crackin' of eggshells and the soft and unmistakable scent of vanilla essence, a pleasin' concoction of which was makin' it hard for me to go on bein' too grumpy with her. Maggie cranked open a window, stickin' her head out into the mornin' air and inhalin' the damp breeze like she'd been deprived of vital oxygen all these years. I guess she'd all but forgotten what good, honest, clean air tastes like livin' in the City so long.

I took in the tape cassettes afresh. Back in the '80s I'd signed up for a mail order music club that ripped me and millions more kids off good and proper, reelin' us in with the too good to be true offer of eleven albums on vinyl or cassettes for a single penny. Once this deal of the century panned, suckered teenagers the length and breadth of the country found themselves on the hook for a small mountain of records and tapes of music they'd never even heard of. Like most of 'em, I was way too naive to mail back the tapes I had zero interest in, along with the necessary return form.

My folks went totally nuts when the bills started comin' in the mail at the end of each month. We can laugh about it now, but it was way out of hand at the time, a notorious, negative billin' option scam entrappin' ignorant youngsters such as myself who never had the wherewithal to read the fine print. Eventually, the Feds stepped in and made it harder for companies to rip off kids this way. When I think of it though, there's a whole trainload of new ways to be ripped off today.

"How did you get out of that whole mess with the mail order music scam, Bridget?" Maggie asked, readin' my mind.

"Mom wrote them a threatenin' letter to stop sendin' me any more seein' as I was under age." How could I forget? In short, I'd racked up a big ol' cassette tape collection comprisin' of all manner of random shit and I was still hundreds of dollars in debt by the time it was over.

"I owed that racket money for years," I recalled. "It was the internet that finally put the mail order clubs out of business." It was a relief for sure when I heard that the company I still owed money to finally tanked a few years back.

"Wow, to think, I was in junior high when you started that lark," Maggie remarked. "I still remember you playing me Starship for the first time — 'We Built This City', remember? Dire Straights — 'Money for Nothing' . . . oh God, yes, Madonna — 'Crazy For You' . . . " She flipped open the plastic cases of a dozen or more tapes, porin' over their faded inserts, eventually settlin' on Meat Loaf's "Bat Out of Hell".

I set about tyin' small, brown cardboard luggage tags with dosage content and other vital info carefully handwritten, onto each package with lengths of twine. In my book, "Paradise by the Dashboard Light" demands bein' played on full blast. Bobby used to like helpin' me with the labels, the two of us sittin' at the kitchen table at it, a couple nights each week. I was still awaitin' the sticky labels I's arranged for havin' printed up.

"Part of my small profit," I felt the sudden need to better inform my sister, "I've been donatin' to a local nonprofit. It's one that puts money into the hands of women like me who struggle to pay their cancer treatment bills."

Maggie swallowed, as well she frickin' should. She knew full well I had lived paycheck to paycheck my whole damn life while she'd been livin' it up like money was goin' out of fashion.

"Any profit that remains, I put back into my business," I was proud to say. I felt a rare flush in my cheeks at the same time a blessed break in the endless goddamn rain carried the welcome sound of birdsong through the open window.

"I don't think I can take much more of this weather, Bridget," Maggie said. "It gives me the blues on blues."

"Hey, no more complainin'," I shot back. "We were in a real bad shape for the serious lack of water before this wet winter brought us some relief." The rains had come in answer to a million or more prayers sent on up to heaven or who knows where from all over the state of California. A multi-year drought was finally over, at least for the time bein'.

I was still feelin' stabs of fresh annoyance in her presence, I couldn't help myself, yet, it slowly dawned on me, standin' there at the same countertop where Mom used to feed us her St. Paddy's Day corned beef and cabbage, at least we still had in common our connection to the land, to good, honest food, the basics of survivin' this crazy thing called life.

We were, we are, the McCleerys, together again, good and bad and all that comes between. I boiled some water for tea, scooped a teaspoon or two of a favorite aromatic herbal blend into an infuser and hooked it inside the squat little Brown Betty teapot that belonged to our grandmother. How many pots of tea have brewed in this old pot is anyone's guess. I poured in boilin' water and waited a couple minutes to remove the infuser, stirrin' a teaspoon of cannabutter into the steamin' hot tea.

Its potent aroma calmed my nerves, bringin' back memories of the backyard herbal concoctions Maggie and me had so much fun mixin' up back when we were kids.

"Tea?" I asked, tryin' to be nice, still. "Did you sleep well, all things considered?"

"Like a baby, in truth," Maggie replied. "Best sleep I've had in months". She asked about my clients.

"The folk I work with are what those in the business describe as the 'cannasseurs' —savvy enough consumers to know what works for them and what doesn't."

"And what if someone makes a mistake? Or you do?" Maggie asked.

"Fortunately, it's not that easy to ingest a lethal dose of cannabis," I explained.

"Well, that's a relief," Maggie laughed.

"Body size and weight are not always an indication of a person's tolerance level," I explained. "The most important thing to be aware of is that it may take as many as several hours to kick in. I make sure to tell a new client to take small doses to start out with and wait it out before ingestin' any more. That's where most newbies go wrong, scarfin' it all down and freakin' out when it hits."

"Jeez, Bridget," Maggie said, her tummy growlin' and rumblin' at the mention of food.

"There's sourdough if you're hungry, Bobby brings the good, day-old bread back from the roadhouse most nights."

Maggie sliced and toasted herself two thick wedges and slathered them with a thick layer each of fresh, creamy ricotta cheese from the fridge, another of Bobby's salvaged delights. I watched her slice a banana onto the ricotta-covered toast and sprinkle it with walnuts and a drizzle of honey on top. "Want some?" she asked.

Despite my feelin' I oughta go on givin' her a hard time, I surprised myself by smilin', as I shook my head. My little sister, lickin' her fingers like she was six or seven again.

"Go," I said, after she'd licked them all clean. "Why doncha get yourself down to the beach before it starts in rainin' heavy? Bobby'll be back soon, he's gonna drive me to drop off my delivery."

"What do you think of this old relic?" Maggie asked, slippin' her arms into the soft, butter leather sleeves of her favorite high school jacket she'd found upstairs. "It's almost back in style — and hey, by some miracle, it still fits."

I was wiped out and yet at the same time, I felt like I was slowly wakin' up to reality for the first time in months. My mind was racin' round and around in circles. Where the hell was Mia? Why was Maggie here with me in the kitchen and not my daughter? Everythin' was out of whack. Mia shoulda been hangin' out here with her aunt and me, shootin' the breeze, gettin' to know her, havin' my back. Whatever was goin' on with that girl last summer it had been way too much for me to handle in my state. Maybe you think I must be one hell of a lousy mother, but in my mind, I did it for love, my lettin' her go.

CHAPTER 7

MAGGIE

The way I remember it, Bridget, to her defense, had pre-warned me and therefore, I was a fully consenting guinea pig when it came to my consuming her homemade mac and cheese.

If I was to bum off my sister awhile, I figured I may as well throw caution to the wind and I tucked in, despite my lack of experience with edibles. Ordinarily, I would have been way too uptight and skeptical to partake, but since I was already feeling like I'd veered way off the conveyer belt of normalcy, I figured, why not? I am not about to slide gracefully and unapologetically into my late forties by sitting back and merely thinking about life, what I should be doing and how others may view me. I'm all about grabbing it now, truly living it. What is there to lose other than a little too much control?

We'd sat down to eat, the three of us, that first night, attempting to ignore the steady dripping of water from the leaking ceiling into an assortment of buckets and bowls that Bridget had positioned for maximum catchment.

"We barely ever ate like this, all together, before I got sick, except for the occasional Monday or Tuesday and holidays, of course," Bridget confessed, shuffling macaroni around her plate in a disinterested fashion with her fork.

"What did Mia do for dinner?" I asked. "The evenings you both worked?" I shoveled in my full share while my sister hardly ate. No wonder she was brittle.

"We pretty much left her to her own devices during those last years of high school", Bridget admitted. "I made sure to keep food in for her — a bunch of leftovers from the roadhouse mostly."

"Mia was old enough to figure it out," Bobby said. "Kid was more than capable of cookin' up some pancakes, sausage and eggs, pasta, the basic stuff. Teenagers nowadays are too lazy and spoiled. It was good for her."

"Mia never did have much of an appetite for homework, Maggie, not like you," Bridget said. "I made sure to be on her case when her report cards came in, but, truth is, she'd lost interest in her schoolin' somewhere along the line."

"So what, you were way too stretched with your own workload to keep an eye out for your daughter?" I shot back.

"Look, don't turn this on us," Bobby was quick to jump in. "It's too bad — the kid's super smart when she tries." He shuffled across the kitchen in a pair of plastic sports slides and socks, expertly balancing a pile of dirty dishes. "And when all's said and done," he added, "it's up to her, ain't it? It's her future. She has a goddamn roof over her head, here, whenever she needs it, food, heat, hot water."

I knew too well Mia's intrinsic need to bolt. Having her basic needs covered wouldn't nearly cut it in the rebellious stage she was in. Teenagers are simply not designed to settle. Mia was most likely terrified of being trapped here, as her mother had been, forever stuck in the same godforsaken place, retracing the same footsteps for the rest of her life. Instead, as I had, she'd upped and left, though not, regrettably, with the same ways and means I'd finagled, my getting myself into a decent university with a scholarship at the tail end of the state.

The McCleery clan is part and parcel of this property having settled on its bare land during the Gold Rush. In fact, a tinted, tintype portrait of Mary and Patrick McCleery no less sits above the dresser in the dining room to this day. I took my first good, long look at this tough old pair in years as I headed upstairs to ready myself for bed. There they were, decked out in their Victorian best, the first of the McCleerys; Patrick, in his thirties, captured for time immemorial with a firm hold on the reigns of his sturdy horse and cart. His wife was equally stiff backed, stoic and determined looking. She was seated straight-faced beside him, tough, Irish settler stock — proud new Americans.

Mary and Patrick were the brave generation that journeyed an entire continent only to take on a second, even more perilous cross-country expedition to California by wagon trail across the plains.

Little more than the natural beauty of the rolling hills, the wind, fog and the steely blue Pacific was in wait to greet them when they'd finally made it to the edge of the western world. Many early pioneers perished along the way. Getting here was one thing, making a go of it, another. And though the climate is inhospitable to all but the toughest, I'll wager they welcomed more sunshine in this western coastal land than they were accustomed to in the weeping, wet Ireland they'd left behind.

Never since the mulish McCleery bloodline dug its roots deep down into Northern Californian soil has one of us set foot in the old country. It's kind of pathetic on our part not to travel when I think of the trouble they went to, this pioneer pair, just to get here in the first place. I've been thinking that I may apply for my Irish citizenship through descent and travel the Emerald Isle and into Europe on it some day, find myself some perspective. I'll even bring Bridget and Mia along if they're up for it.

Mary and Patrick set up a rudimentary camp. They built their homestead with their bare hands from Pacific redwood bartered from the Russian River sawmills. Commercial logging was just getting started. A rudimentary three up, three down would have fit their basic needs with its open front porch serving as a shelter in the rainy season and a shade barrier in the sparse, sunnier months.

There was no bathroom in the early days, as the old man was fond of telling us when we were kids, a tin tub and an outdoor latrine served the needs of the family until my grandparents put a bathroom in some time in the early 1950s.

Since milk and dairy products were in massive demand in the storefronts and markets of early San Francisco, the Point Reyes Peninsula and coastline proved itself to be cow heaven, birthplace of the California dairy industry. Dairy ranching is one of the toughest forms of farming if you ask me or anyone who was born and raised into it, yet there must have been plenty of money to be made during the initial frenzy of the Gold Rush. Hundreds of thousands flooded

Northern California in search of an easy fortune. They were, as you'd imagine, desperate for good food and fresh dairy products that didn't stink from being transported cross-country. Mining camps of the Sierra Mountains swelled with fortune seekers as newcomers jumped ship in the ports of the Barbary Coast and made their way to the foothills.

I stepped up to closer scrutinize the faded photograph. Mary was a serious woman to say the least, intense and brooding. I closed my eyes and pictured her in an early version of Bridget's kitchen, seated at a lamp lit table with paper and pencil as she figured out the numbers for the milk and handchurned butter Patrick readied for regular shipment to the city.

By now, Bridget and Bobby were facing a vastly different set of demands for agricultural product. I wondered what Mary would have made of our times. Maybe she too would've gotten on with it without judgment of the latest cash crop, just as Bridget was evidently trying to do.

Wander through the Catholic or Protestant cemeteries in our small farming and fishing community and you will see surprisingly ornate plots peppered with headstones of pioneer families. We played amongst these same headstones as kids, Bridget and me, spooking ourselves in games of chase among the familiar last names, known to us from the stories we'd heard from the old-timers.

Six generations of Irish, Swiss, Portuguese, Italian — keeping each other good company, first on neighboring dairy and potato ranches and later, one by one, tucked in, deep beneath the rich, sandy soil that sits atop the region's Jurassic age volcanic bedrock.

Not all that much has changed in the landscape since the McCleerys first set foot here, aside from the sad reality of most of the dairy herds having vanished from the hills and horizon.

Bridget, as with other struggling souls left in charge of otherwise abandoned family ranchland, had little wherewithal for even the smallest of income generation after the milking cows were gone. At least not until the cannabis laws came in to stir things up into what is basically an ongoing storm of controversy.

Sharp wisps of salty, frigid air slipped through the cracks in the wooden window frames, chilling me sufficiently to remind me of the winters of my youth. We'd roamed this ranch at all hours and in every type of weather as little girls, Bridget and me, gathering and collecting animal bones, sticks, stones as we scoured for feathers and other treasures. We'd chased lizards, thrown rocks, searched high and low for flint arrowheads, abundant remnants of the lost people — the Coast Miwok our grandparents told us of. The fact the first people lived off only what they were able to use and replenish has become all the more poignant to me in my currently frugal situation.

Back when my grandparents were youngsters themselves, the last of the first people were still a big part of the fabric of the place, in specific pockets of the community — oyster fishing, boat building. I can picture my Grandmother on the porch, seated on the swing that, like her, has long since vanished into the past. I watch closely as she points west with her bony, arthritic finger. "The Pacific you see here before you is an ocean like no other, mark my words now girl," she'd say, a faraway look in her steely blue eyes. How she'd regaled us with stories of these waters being filled to the brim with whales and dolphins when she herself was a girl, numbers and oceanic activity we sadly can't imagine today.

Big Bobby De Santis, rough around the edges, larger-than-life with a deep bass baritone and shoulders to match, moved in on my sister when her daughter Mia, was five. Bridget was a single mom from the start. I'd never said a word about selling the place, though it was ours to share, on paper, for what it's worth. I had not had the heart to raise the question after Mia was born and I'm glad of it. Anyway, somehow, some way, we're still here, holding on tight to this wild patch of earth that is ours.

Tomás, the guy who fathered Mia, had raveled north from some unknown small town in central Mexico. That's about the extent of what we know of him. According to Bridget, he was a looker, fit, funny, charismatic, hardworking. I never set eyes on him. He was, she'd told me, an industrious, seasonal worker possessed with a charming mop of thick, glossy black hair, big brown, bedroom eyes, a limited grasp of the English language and a natural ease with women, not least my sister. What the elusive Tomás did not have going for him was any scrap of documentation. He'd driven back over the border to visit his family two weeks prior to Bridget finding out she was in the family way. She was 32 at the time, single after a stream of loser boyfriends and pleased as punch at the prospect of a baby despite having zero support system. As for Tomás, he was never seen again. Bridget feared he had fallen prey to the cartels that notoriously ransacked moneyed Mexican laborers for their fat wads of American dollars tucked under the floorboards of coveted Toyota workhorse trucks. If you ask me, I was never so sure. The virile Tomás might just have easily stayed put where he'd come from with a pretty young wife and gaggle of little ones who'd also been patiently awaiting his seasonal return.

Each spring, those first few years, whenever the migrant laborers showed up looking for work, Bridget had clung to the false hope that the new season would bring Tomás back north, kind of like a human form of the monarch butterfly in reverse flight I used to think, when she talked of him.

Bobby, on the other hand, he wasn't going anywhere too far from home. He'd had his fill of life's brief adventures in the outside world. He came back to where he started, only slightly worse for wear, rattling out Rat Pack hits for the locals while pouring shots behind his brother and sister-in-law's bar, an old speakeasy known as The Daniel Boone, the isolated roadhouse where Bridget would soon be waiting tables.

Bobby was made from hardscrabble farming stock. Not Irish — like us. Northern Italian, through and through, Genoa, fishing people, old guard, hence the propensity for the old-school Italian American playlist that rolled off his tongue like nobody's business. Bobby was well familiar with the pros and cons of an isolated coastal life. All of us, me, Bridget and Bobby, we were raised to be tough, to get on with it, to deal with the depressing bouts of fog and bone-chilling wind. I may have lost my edge in this more remote stretch of the craggy west, but I figured I'd soon get it back if I stuck around what was left of my family for any length of time.

We all knew Bobby had a thing for Bridget back in high school. He'd tried all the usual tricks to turn her head. She had never given him so much as the time of day. Like me, Bobby ditched his family's failed ranch. The difference was the time it took us to crawl back. After giving up on Bridget the first time around, the impatient hothead had gone and married another local girl, too soon out of high school for it to stand a reasonable chance.

Mia was in kindergarten when Bobby and my sister finally hooked up. Bridget called me out of the blue one night, asking if I remembered that Bobby De Santis guy. He was back on the scene, officially divorced and on the wagon, she'd said. He'd had his fill of a dozen years or so of marital unrest, fueled, on both sides, by drugs and booze and bar fights. By that time, my sister, who'd struggled through the early years of raising Mia on her own, was way more inclined to take notice of Bobby's newly sober and never more adoring gaze.

"He sings to me, Maggie. We slow dance like a couple of kids." I clearly recall how she was tickled to admit it, her voice, light and hopeful, for the first time in years. "Just the two of us, here in the kitchen after he's closed up for the night."

Mia's juvenile posters were plastered over the same flowery wallpaper I'd studied each and every interminable night of grade school as I'd fantasized about the glamorous world of celebrities from the television shows to relieve the boredom of my own reality. A poster of Miley Cyrus depicted her captured in a wide expanse of butterfly wings, bedazzled in body sparkles and silver eye shadow. In stark contrast, a sepia photo in a medium-size wooden frame balanced on the top shelf of a half empty bookcase, caught my eye.

"Ever heard of a duster, Bridg'?" I asked, walking over to take a closer look. Bridget had followed me upstairs. I'd squeezed myself into an old, brown leather jacket, a relic from my high school years I'd been more than taken aback to find was still there, exactly where I'd left it in the bedroom closet. It had been one of my more successful thrift store finds, its short, leather fringe dating it's design to classic '70s. I remembered well how its zip-out liner had come in handy during the chillier winter months. It just about fit me still, snug, but wearable. Aside from a couple of scrunched up Bubble Yum gum wrappers circa 1988, I was disappointed not to find a love note or at least a phone number scribbled hastily in class in the pockets.

It was like I'd simply shut the door to my old bedroom and walked away. I guess that's what had happened and Mia's subsequent impression on it, aside from the obnoxious posters was a minor imprint. The small, wooden frame held an awkward portrait: Bridget; me; Mom and Dad, all decked out in one of those touristy Wild West photo booths, a goofy "Wanted Dead or Alive" poster shot, captured during one of our rare overnight trips into Old Sacramento. "I don't remember any other fun outings as a family," I said, as Bridget looked over my shoulder. On that occasion, we'd visited the rail museum after it was completed, if I recall, an added outing after spending the night in a cheap motel close to the California State Fair.

"We'd gone up for Grange Day, remember? Most of our neighbors were there, along with their wives and kids," Bridget replied, a cloudy look in her eyes as she brushed her thumb over the dusty glass.

It was Mom who had sprung for the souvenir, a spontaneous, tacky photo taken on the boardwalk outside of the rail museum despite the old man's pissing and moaning, on the count of it being a foolish waste of his hard-earned money. There I was, a kooky teenager dressed up as a rifle-toting frontier woman. Inside, I was already bursting with big ideas, secret plans. Back then, the months and years had moved at a snail's pace. That evening, ironically, all I wanted was to slow it all the hell down.

I sank into the lumpy mattress beneath the pink chenille coverlet. Bridget sat beside me. I realized I had absolutely no idea what a double mastectomy looked like in the flesh and so I had taken the opportunity to let her know I truly did care about how she was doing in that department, specifically the recovery part. "The scarring," I asked?

What came next was not what I had expected. Bra-less, because, let's face it, she has no need of one now, Bridget pulled her sweater and T-shirt up under her armpits so that I could see for myself. Though to me, it was something like the misplaced seam of a crudely stitched rag doll, my sister was evidently in no way ashamed of how her body looked. I could see she was proud of it in a way, like a warrior. This made it seem less barbaric, somehow.

"The world's not gonna end because of my surgery," she'd declared. "I'm still the same old Bridget."

Supper's special ingredient was beginning to kick in by then. From what I remember, this was good timing in that it was helping take the edge off the heavy-duty heart-to-heart and show-and-tell we were having, at least for me. I recall desperately needed a drink of water. I couldn't shake the image of the four of us in the photo, posed in our stiff western outfits, forced smiles plastered to our faces, gripping a fleet of fake wooden guns. An ill-timed urge to giggle came over me as I'd headed down the stairs, clutching the handrail to steady myself. I felt my eyes welling, not sure at first if I was about to laugh out loud or burst into a flood of tears. Initial stifled giggles turned into a bout of full on, side-clutching hilarity, while my mind and body traveled through time and space, completely weightless, unburdened, free. I was aware of Bridget and Bobby watching me with some degree of concern but there was no stopping myself.

"I'm floating," I announced. "I'm light, so very light . . . " Until I wasn't — and the last thing I remember was crashing face down on the couch. At least one of them was kind enough to cover me with a warm blanket. Bridget, I'm sure.

At some point during supper, I'd apparently agreed to assist in the preparation of Bridget's edibles. I'd had little else to do, besides, I guess I was curious to see what she was up to, to be of some small help in the measuring, mixing and making up of a batch of my newly enterprising sister's chewy, chocolate, nut and pot granola bars, as well as her signature peanut butter 'medible' cookies and whatever the heck it was she'd described as her 'special' almond bars.

CHAPTER 8

BRIDGET

Bobby drove me into town, our weekly routine. Since I'd started treatment I'd felt weak and scatterbrained, nowhere near fit to take the wheel on the bumpy, waterlogged backcountry roads. In truth, his bar work had barely paid the bills. We both were hopin' I'd figure out a way to make a little money out of this new enterprise of mine.

"You ready, babe?" he asked. I sure as hell was not feelin' like much of anyone's babe but it was his way, bless his heart, to keep on with his kind words. Bobby never once flinched, the way I had at first when I'd stood myself in front of the bathroom mirror some time after my surgery. No offense, but I couldn't help but feel like I'd been butchered like a farm animal, basically, no matter how skilled the surgeon — a walkin', talkin', Raggedy Ann bag of sewn-up skin and bones. And yet, darn it if Bobby didn't look at me in the same dumb, lovesick way he always had. I'd gotten real lucky with my guy and I knew it. If he felt bad for me, he dug real deep. He took pains not to show it.

Bobby stepped up and hauled the basket off the countertop like it was light as a feather. I followed as he turned the door handle and nudged the door ajar with his big, ol' broad shoulder, motionin' his head for me to walk through before him, chivalry bein' one of his strong points. Whatever you might say about Bobby and his country ways, he was ever the gentleman when it came to me.

As I have said, women like me were few and far between in the legitimate side of the cannabis business until recently, though times they are a changin'. I could never have gotten this far without Bobby's help haulin' my product to market. Enterprisin' gals such as myself are really steppin' it up with the launch of all manner of new cannabis-related businesses, not just here in my home state of California, but clear across the country. In time, you'll see, what we're doin' is creatin' a ton of decent payin' jobs for hundreds of thousands more ordinary women just like me.

It's a frickin' wonder, breakin' through the barriers of what was for the longest time one of the biggest of the white male dominated arenas. Keeps me motivated in the darker moments if you really wanna know. I've taken the sorts of risks I'd never have dared to go anyplace near before the cancer, before Mia took off. If pockets of the general public are still shit-scared of legalizin' the pot market, hell, they should know, it's the deeper pockets of the black market they should be afraid of. Anyhow, the way I look at it, from a purely personal point of view, now that the door is open, what's the worst that can happen to me?

Let's face it. I have little left to lose. After I'd joined the collective, it was the other women who gave me the strength to see myself as part of the change. And, after all, it is women, not men, for the most part who are seekin' out alternative medicines and not just for themselves, but for their partners, their parents and other family members. The best part of bein' in an alliance, for me at least, is learnin' how to best ease a person's pain by bouncin' ideas off and brainstormin' with the other women in the business I've gotten to know.

I'm payin' it back now, see, sharin' my own newfound know-how with those who need it most. If I play my cards right, I'm bankin' on my carefully made concoctions bein' my future, bridgin' the gap that has grown between me and my sister and most importantly, my kid. I need to show her I can run a business, legit like, support myself, an' her if she'll allow me to help her in some motherly way.

We pulled up outside of the collective and Bobby switched off the ignition. I watched him as he lumbered around to retrieve my basket of goodies from the back seat and haul it up the stairs to the dispensary door. "Take your time, Bridg," he said, touchin' my arm as he headed back to the car. I saw him crank back the passenger seat, tip his head back and close his eyes. Bobby had no interest in comin' in and makin' small talk, it was vendor day and that means a whole boatload of motivated women and banter to match. This was his habit on delivery days, in all honesty he was happy to make the most of a rare half hour of shuteye while I took care of business.

The first giveaway that A Bloom of One's Own is a dispensary and not a goddamn florist shop is a set of sturdy metal bars fitted on the windows of the women's collective, a converted Victorian bungalow. The dispensary is the childhood home of Helena, one of the co-owners. When she inherited the property after her mother passed, Helena and her business partner, Nancy, a real smart retired nurse made a plan and started off by paintin' the old place all bright and invitin' with a wrap-around mural in the form of a field of wild flowers. Aside from the metal bars, though they've been painted white to soften the look, the buildin' has a welcoming vibe, inside and out that makes me smile each time I walk up those stairs.

A canary-yellow painted porch swing hangs to the side at the top of a short, wide staircase that leads to the front door. Clusters of painted terracotta pots spill out onto the porch filled with all manner of strangely shaped succulent plantin's that dig this misty climate.

I used my bony ol' hip to push open the door to the right side of the swing and walked on into what was the property's original hallway, a small size waitin' room with a glass paneled, bulletproof security window inset into the wall. I buzzed the lovely Luna — dispensary receptionist and our collective's go-to girl for vendor cheerleadin' and customer concerns. To say that Luna is a tried and tested true friend is an understatement. She's the most compassionate person I know without ever once feelin' the need to be goin' over the top and gettin' too gushy. That would never work for me.

It was Luna and Bobby who'd taken it in turns drivin' me to chemo, hangin' with me, real patient the both of 'em, hour after hour while I sat there with poison being pumped into my body. I've asked a whole lot of her and trust me when I say that she's been there through the worst of it with me.

Luna's knockout smile spread across her face showcasin' a dazzlin' set of large, perfectly even, pearly white teeth. "Hi there Bridget. Good to see you. How you doin' today, sugar?" she asked, her genuine warmth of spirit shinin' through. "Come on in, you know why? Today is an exceptional day for doin' business," she laughed, in a spontaneous burst, as is her way. This girl is always laughin', always positive, no matter what amount of shit is thrown her way. She deals with some challengin' individuals at times. I've never seen her handle the real difficult and demandin' ones with any less grace than she greets those who make our dispensary work so rewardin'.

She is younger than me by more years than I care to count. I have never asked Luna what her exact age is. She's a hard one to gauge, natural, through and through — soft and round, barefaced and beautiful with tan, freckled skin and thick lashed, deep brown eyes the color of the earth after the rains. Luna wears her felt-like dreadlocks in a long braid and I followed in the wake of its chunky swing as she walked me through the inner door. We bear-hugged. "What's new, Bridg'?"

"Well . . . my sister showed up, big surprise — helped me out in the kitchen today, would you believe?"

"Better late than never." I'd never heard Luna say so much as one bad word about anyone, except for her ex who deserved it and worse, havin' been one mean motherfucker from what she'd told me. Maggie's Andres was an angel in comparison.

"Well, good for her and good for you," she said, taking a hold of the heavy basket. "That's quite a load you've put together the two of you, Bridget. There's gonna be plenty happy customers today."

We went through the routine formalities required by the dispensary, the usual checkin' of my medical marijuana card and ID and various other necessary papers. Luna knew I was up to date with my permits and all. Still, she followed the usual protocol and I was happy to go through the motions. I was doin' things the right way for once in my life what with the paperwork. Security cameras followed our every 〜there was no cuttin' of corners even if I wanted to.

〜 the go-to girl for settin' me and all the other local 〜lors on the right path to enter the industry 〜-to-day details of the dispensary's business 〜 women entrepreneurs, organizin' weekly 〜kin' events with other vendors, that sort of

It's not that guys aren't welcome to the dispensary to purchase whatever it may be they need in the medical weed department — they just can't sell it. That's the whole point of this women-owned collective, see and it's not hard to figure this out the second you walk through the door. The way I look at it, this is my new and improved method of waitin' on tables all those years, my life work is takin' care of folk one way or another. Not that I did much of a good job with Mia these past few years.

Helena and Nancy set out from the start to make the dispensary an intentional healin' space, nothin' like the dingy, stereotypical stoner central of the old-school dispensaries that are as grim on the outside as they're unappealin' on the inside.

The main room is softly lit with crystal chandeliers in an open, airy space converted from the old home's front and back parlor. Lucky that Helena's husband, Pete is a contractor. He did all the renovation work himself. Pete salvaged the original hardwood floors and refinished them like new.

Luna likes to joke that she's the "lonely only sister" in our out-landish community. To say she's in the minority is an understatement. I'd never thought about it bein' mostly all white and Latino in these parts, 'til I met Luna. She was the one who opened my eyes, when she said to me, "look around Bridget."

I've never known anythin' other than this with my bein' born and raised here where the McCleerys and their tough-ass neighbors, the all-white Europeans were the only non-natives who'd braved the brutal combo of this geographic isolation and damn blisterin' hard work. They were on their own in their determination to make a go of it — come hell or high water, hard as it was — as it still is.

Only the devil knows how crazy determined folk must be to make it here, no matter where it is they're from or the color of their skin. This ain't about to change anytime soon, not one iota.

The first settlers, they figured out soon enough the raisin' of cattle. They planted their potatoes and tended the land through those wicked first winters, all the while shelterin' their brood in little more than the wooden shacks they cobbled together with a bunch bartered lumber. Wet winters and heavy fog would've disconnec wagon trails for months on end. Day-to-day life was a matter of survival of the fittest, plain and simple, those who were out-and-out the most resourceful. Still is. I've watched as countless folk have come and gone over the years, romanced by the lure and the wild beauty of the coast. Dismal reality never fails to hit home soon enough, generally straight after even the shortest of rainy seasons. Mostly, nowadays, it's the hardworkin' souls from south of the border that prove tough enough to take it on and stick it out.

Life out west is no sorta game for the feeble. In my book it's mind and body and spirit workin' together, a goddamn trifecta — all or nothin'. Bein' stubborn helps. And I keep on askin' myself are we gonna be tough enough to keep on weatherin' it, me and mine? It'd break my heart to throw in the towel at this point. We McCleerys, we're hellbent, we're gonna prevail, somehow, I hope to God. As for Luna, well, she's for sure gone and proved herself willin' to infiltrate our tough coastal clans. As she says, she is her own kind of crazy. And Luna had better reason than most to go against the tide in settlin' here.

Helena and Nancy were busy hangin' several large canvas paintin's on the wall behind a series of glass counters that looked to have been jewelry cases in another life. "Hello Bridget," — Aiko, a small, slim and smiley Japanese-American artist-chick in her sixties stepped over and took my hand. Aiko supplies the dispensary with a rotatin' display of original art made by local folk. "What do you think?" she asked, as she motioned to a groupin' of wild lookin', multi-colored abstracts painted by the regular students in her popular puff-n-paint community class.

"Neat," I said, though I had no idea what to make of any of 'em except to say they were cheerful enough. "You sure have unleashed the creative genius." Aiko and us go back years. She taught Mia art a few years back in elementary school when she was a volunteer art docent on account of her grandbaby bein' in the same class. She wrote me once, urgin' me to nurture Mia's creative side. I had no time for artsy-fartsy when I was workin' all the hours to make ends meet. I shoulda paid more attention, listened more.

I took a good long look around this energetic scene. It was a 'specially busy day in the dispensary. Aside from me there were several other women vendors in the buildin', enthusiastic and hopeful all of 'em, patiently waitin' to talk with Nancy or Helena to showcase their products. In addition to the usual granola-eatin', peace lovin' west county core members of the biz, legalization and our collective's stellar community outreach is bringing a whole new wave of seniors, veterans and disabled patients through the doors. Everyday folk. Heck, practically everyone's comin' out as a cannabis fan now it's been given a thumbs up on both the state and local level. The Feds can go fuck themselves.

"I guess the handheld joint is a thing of the past?" an older, wrinkle-faced hippie chick with hair to her hips asked in a crackly voice. She was seated in a wheelchair, smilin' and shakin' hands with Helena, whom she, like most of us, was previously acquainted with from Helena's former guise as a bank teller.

"We're pushing way past smoke, Lou-Lou, as you know," Helena replied. "What'll it be today? Are you ready for a fresh supply of your tincture? Do take a look at our new lozenges and teas before you head home."

Nancy advocates to seniors 'specially. "A lot of them have held on to their misconceptions for far too long," she'd informed durin' one of her weekly rally calls for all of us to work on better educatin' people. "There's something for every ailment," she said. And she's right, there's a balm for every issue. Transdermal patches, for instance, beat the pants off inflammation and they reckon that if you smoke a little pot a day, it fends off the brain from agin' too fast.

These women have an almost encyclopedic knowledge on the subject of top-drawer medical cannabis products, tonics for the future, I say.

Helena nodded her head as the wheelchair woman described at length how she was doin' with her aches and pains since havin' been prescribed a tincture—goin' into graphic detail about droppin' it under her tongue and all. "I'm glad to hear it's fast and effective, Lou," Helena replied, "on account of the tincture absorbing directly into your sublingual artery in a matter of minutes."

The enlightened Lou-Lou remarked on the added wonder of her prescription bein' somethin' she was okay takin' when away from home, given the "odorless, discreet, undetectable high."

An equally spirited group of women were patiently waitin' for me to set out my range of freshly baked goods. I have my regulars and boy, am I thankful these girls are always primed to shop.

It's perfectly clean and spotless inside of the dispensary. Though I, for one, dig the dense, musky smell of marijuana, they've somehow managed to keep it from bein' too much in your face when you walk in. That afternoon, chatter was gettin' louder by the minute. Dispensary assistants busied themselves selectin' various strains and takin' pains to identify them for customers perusin' the long, glass display cases stocked with glass petri dishes filled with various buds. Jars of Indica lined up on the left, Sativa on the right, hybrids in the middle, all organized and efficient.

After makin' my sales, I looked over the day's range of orange tinged, yellow and purple-hued buds with mysterious and equally colorful names dreamed up by the creative cannabis breeders themselves. Each strain in the dispensary is outlined with an information card indicatin' its main psychoactive ingredient, its specific primary intoxicant, THC percentage, as well as the content of its naturally occurrin' non-intoxicatin' medical benefit compound, CBD and its effects. One of the most in demand varietals in our dispensary if you care to know, is the strangely named Sour Diesel, a pungent and grassy strain of the Sativa plant. It's mostly grown outdoors and sought after for its reputation as havin' a pleasin', energizin', yet dreamily cerebral effect. In my experience, Sour Diesel grows real tall and lanky and stretches out while flowerin', makin' it way too hard for me to grow.

I was hopin' to get my hands on another strain I'd been wantin' to try, this one more enticin'ly named Little Lamb's Bread and said to emit a comfortin' sage and pine needle aroma with properties that help keep depression at bay. I figured if any two people were in need of some sort of soul soother, it was my sister and me.

I glanced up and made unintended eye contact with a tall, willowy woman whose extra long, slim limbs were layered in muted, earth colored, tie-dye. A row of hammered silver hoop earrings dangled from ears that appeared too small for her head. A mini version of the same hoop earring pierced her left nostril. She wore her gunmetal gray hair cropped close to her head and I wondered if she used an electric hair trimmer on herself like the one Bobby had me buzz the unruly hairs that grew in swirls on the back of his neck.

"Hi," she said, thrustin' a firm, yet sinewy hand with short, neat nails into my reluctant grasp. She read the name badge I wear when I'm at the dispensary. "I'm Serena, Serena Joy, medical cannabis massage therapist. Nice to meet you, Bridget. Care for a demo — how about a quick foot massage?"

I found I had little chance to resist Serena Joy as she swiftly levered me into a seated position on her portable massage chair, peelin' my boots and socks clear off my feet before I could summon the words to say no. I looked down at my bare, white feet as they were being submerged into a round copper bowl filled with a bunch of fresh herbs that were floatin' around in the comforting warm water. I flinched. I am naturally suspicious of bein' touched by a stranger, no matter the pamperin' environment. I'm not accustomed to such self-indulgent activities.

Dang, if I'd even so much as entertained the decadence of a spa day, I have never once had that much spare cash floatin' around. Mia and me, we'd taken a double mani-pedi date into town for her birthday several times after she hit her teens, but that's about the extent of a health and beauty cosmetic regimen in my books. I cut my own hair, when I still had hair that is and Mia's and Bobby's too. Since Serena Joy, assumin' that's her given name and not one she's made up for business purposes, was offerin' me a massage for free and as there appeared to be no arguin' with the woman, I decided to give in, lean back and close my eyes. I surprised myself with how easy it was to submit to the scent of the warm eucalyptus oil she'd made such a fuss of droppin' into the water.

"Don't worry, you're not going to get stoned from one of my topical treatments," Serena reassured. I paid attention to her tellin' me how she makes her own massage lotion with arnica, juniper and peppermint, coconut oil, beeswax and Aloe Vera, lacin' her lotions with relaxin' selections of the Indica cannabis strain. "And wouldn't you know," Serena added, "it's your lucky day, my dear." She described how she'd prepared her lotion with a small batch of organic Blackberry Kush that very same mornin'. "What we have here is a fantastic, fresh, anti-inflammatory blend that works as an antioxidant, without ever penetrating the bloodstream."

I felt the strange sensation of my muscles workin' double-time in an attempt to relax despite the physical intrusion of Serena's probin' deep into the soles of my feet with her powerful fingers and thumbs.

Maggie's showin' up had me riled to the extent that the foot massage, though undeniably good, was still no way close to makin' much of an inroad into my muddled mind. Aside from the Mia situation, my sister and the mess she'd gotten into with quittin' her marriage, her job, her home and all, well, my own worries and mainly of Mia were way more than Serena's strong hands could erase.

My mind raced around and around in ever-widenin' circles, unleashed and free for a few minutes to roam and explore in every goddamn direction possible. Maggie had fallen for Andres hard. It was a blessin' in a way that the old man was gone by the time they'd wed. I hate to admit this, but he would have been nothin' but nasty about it. By then, I'd been the only one left of what Maggie considered our old-guard, patriarchal family to show my face at the weddin', if you'd call it that, a fast and furious ceremony by any standards, at City Hall, in San Francisco. It wasn't like the old man had been aware of the fact he was prejudiced, the ignoramus that he was. In his whole life he had never known anythin' other than the faces of the same ol' traditional white European stock we'd been stuck with, for better or worse. He passed on before Mia came into the world, my own multicultural contribution to our community, born out of wedlock to add to his turnin' a couple more times in his grave. Maybe a good thing Maggie and Andres never had kids, given their split, though I always did think to myself they would have made real pretty babies the pair of 'em, her light skin, his dark, the both of 'em blessed with the sort of looks that make folk stop in their tracks.

I twisted my head to glance over at Luna as Serena continued to apply pressure on the knots in my feet. Luna, who was head-to-head with a vendor over a bunch of paperwork, washed up out here with a couple of kids in tow. Thank the Lord she'd had the gumption to run to the remote safety of the coast. First time I met her at the collective, Luna spilled whole darn life story, poured it out — all that happened to her before she and her little ones made their escape with no more 'an a small backpack apiece. They'd headed as far west as they could run without falling into the ocean.

"No way he would have thought to look for us out here," she'd said of her ex, who is now in jail: "a no-good, mean ass, sociopathic drug dealer, I'm sorry to say." Luna had lived with the asshole, unwed, in Sacramento for the good part of a decade.

"When I finally had enough, I packed a change of clothes for the kiddos and me, held their hands and walked on over to the nearest freeway ramp," Luna told me. Makes me real sad to think of it, the three of 'em stood there with their thumbs out for a good, solid two hours. Poor baby, she was scared to death the bastard would come lookin' for them before they'd found a ride.

Serena persisted in her mission to explore the tenderest spots on the soles of my bony feet. She slapped on extra cream, rubbin' in a circular motion, diggin' in and addin' pressure on a bunch of trigger points 'til she felt me finally give in to the cause, relaxin' my feet a little at the ankles.

Chance had taken a hold of Luna and her little ones' fate when a woman driver pulled over in her mini van on her way back west from a high school soccer game in the Central Valley. There had been plenty room in the van for three more, alongside two sweaty teenage boys with mouths full of expensive metal braces, a big ol' bag of soccer balls in back. Luna was aware that the woman knew full well this was not your run-of-the-mill road trip. And yet she told a series of white lies so as not to overly freak out her ride. Luna had asked to be dropped off in downtown Petaluma. She shared how they dined, hungrily, the three of 'em on the few dollars left in her wallet on a supper of cheap Mexican tacos, the tastiest they ever ate, flavored with freedom and purchased from a food truck in the parking lot of a floorin' store.

Shortly before nightfall, a friendly-faced ol' rancher from the Point Reyes Peninsula pulled over and offered Luna and her little ones a ride. Good thing, for if not for him, she'd have been left with no choice but to hold onto their small hands and walk them out along the unlit rural road from Petaluma all the way to the ocean.

"We could not have landed better luck that night," she'd said. Turned out the rancher had a workers' cottage sittin' vacant on his property. His wife was sick and the family was in dire need of help. It was as darn remote a place as any out here and findin' good folk to work is always challenge. Not long after Luna and her kids were settled, the rancher's daughter talked her dyin' mother into a regular hit of medical marijuana to help her sleep at night. A connection was made with the collective and Luna found herself extra hours in a decent payin' day job, runnin' the dispensary books and reception while her kids were settled in school.

With all this talk of drugs, I will put it on the record that I am for sure, no angel of purity, myself. There'd been no lack of access to all sorts of shit durin' my teens and twenties. We never had much else to do in the way of entertainment out West.

The muscle relaxant in Lydia's lotion kicked in. It's not euphoria I'm lookin' for these days, it's the calmin', relaxin' stuff that hits the spot. I'm even thinkin' of tryin' my hand at makin' a few different types of balms myself. Expand my line. Why not? From what I've figured, balms are not all that likely to be any more troublesome for me to make than a batch of my cannabutter. I made a note to self to pick up some essential oils, wintergreen and clove — beeswax and cheesecloth.

My restless mind is forever chargin' away with itself. While Serena was rattlin' on about the psychoactive effects of transdermal patches and how they deliver cannabinoids into the bloodstream and all, my brain was still flippin' around, blurrin' in and out of focus and windin' itself in reverse back to a time when Maggie and me were teens. We'd taken care of our early mornin' ranch chores before school, as did all the neighbor kids. Nothin' original in that. Partyin' in town at the bowlin' alley or the pool hall was reserved for the most special occasions. Mostly, on account of someone had to drive. We were stuck out in the boonies, drinkin' and smokin' all of the pot we could get our grubby hands on, out back, behind whosever barn it was we happened to be hangin' at. It was how we rolled in the small, tight-knit crowd I ran with and most of us were happy enough to go along with it.

It was not so much of a crowd, as a hangout group, built out of necessity with no choice of any alternative company. Crack cocaine swept our rural scene in the late '80s, cheap compared to most of the other drugs, plentiful and, dang addictive. I thank the stars I was never hooked. We lost more than a handful of our high school friends to crack and heroin, Maggie and me. Bobby too. Molly and crystal meth followed suit in the '90s. I hate to say it out loud, but I dabbled more in my fair share of all of the above. Lucky for me in the long haul, I had way too much to deal with in the general pullin' up of my bootstraps to let the partyin' take over my life.

Most of us who made it through the '80s and '90s are confirmed stoners by now, takin' to the beer of an evenin' an' all, wine for some, with plentiful whiskey and vodka flowin' come nightfall. It's how it is — been that way with one substance or another since the first of the old Irish came west cookin' up gallon after gallon of moonshine, their crude pot stills filled to the brim with the same rough-ass potato potcheen as they'd sucked from the teat back in the old country.

I've shared most of my crazier stories with my buddy Luna. I hate for her to feel bad about her own history, you know? Hell, who am I to judge at the choices she made? She got out, that's what counts. She put her kids first.

I ran my eyes over a stack of pre-rolled joints in the glass case displayed beneath a colorful array of cannabis-infused chocolate, candy, breath sprays and spritzers. It's all about the customer and the individual need. I stand by this even if the Feds will insist on stickin' their heads in the sand on the legalization issue. An additional, narrow, glass front cabinet is home to a specially curated collection of pipes, bowls and bongs.

Another cabinet displayed a range of fancy packaged teas, new to the dispensary that same week — real nice lookin' packages with appealin' logos toutin' a range of blends designed to ease a variety of pains and cramps, elevate mood, boost libido, aid sleep. You name it.

On impulse, given my enhanced mood of rare, semi-relaxation, I settled on a half-pound of organic weed bacon and a thick slice of locally smoked cannabis-infused salmon to take back to the ranch — way more money than I had reckoned on spendin', but what the hell, I seldom splurge and I was cravin' some extra protein.

"Someone is looking for you, Bridget," Helena came over to inform me. I've known Helena since she was a kid. In fact, I babysat her and her little brother back in my teens. We made good money that way when we were in school, me, Maggie, even Mia, for a short while, though, my daughter, being an only child, demonstrated little patience for it.

Helena wore the same sort of business-style fitted wool dress she favored when she worked in the bank. She motioned to the reception area with a perfectly manicured hand.

Nancy waved goodbye to me from across the room as I made to leave. Luna looked up from her paperwork and blew me a kiss. It was Nancy who brought Helena into the business after she'd accidentally fallen into it herself while caring for HIV/AIDs patients back in the major epidemic in the Bay Area in the eighties. Later, she'd figured the need for access to a dispensary while carin' for her dyin' husband. As a retired nurse, she sure is enthusiastic about extendin' the same canna care she'd learned to ease the sufferin' of her husband. Nancy drew Helena in after she had problems bankin' cash from the cannabis deals she passed on to other seniors she knew would benefit most from its medical use.

"I never was able to make my way up the ladder at the bank," Helena confided in me after I'd worked myself into the collective. By co-launchin' the dispensary, she works around her twin boys' busy school and baseball schedules. It's she who calls the shots and sets the bar. I admire that. "Nancy and me, we're making our own rules, within reason," she explained. What they've done, these two women, is to build a framework for others, women like me, to figure out a future with a business of our own. Lifesavers are what they are, in more ways than one.

Bobby was outside in the car, snoozin' like a big ol' contented baby. I was on my way out, basket in hand, when a small, round, Latina woman jumped up from a chair in reception, blockin' my exit.

"Señora. Mia's mama?" Jesus — she pounced. I took a step back, my heart stoppin' for a second. "Um . . . yes, that's me. What is it you want?"

"I find you, thanks to God. Mi hija, my daughter . . . " she stumbled on her words in her broken English. "Jazmin, mi bebé. She with your Mia."

The woman's face looked vaguely familiar — crap, maybe I'd sat beside her at any one of the numerous high school fiestas over the years? I was embarrassed not to remember havin' met her. She was way younger than me, not a lot older than I was, it flashed through my mind, when Mia was born.

Why hadn't I taken more interest in Mia's friends?

It took a minute more for to me register why she was there before I spat out a garbled: "Oh my God, do you have news? Are they safe, the girls? Where are they?"

A hundred and one questions shot through my head. I needed to know, right then and there, that Mia was safe. Months of denial burst the floodgates as my worst fears raged, unbidden but unstoppable.

"They gone north, senora, to Humboldt. Mi esposo, he no find. They there though, we know this."

"Come with me," I took her arm, gently but firmly, despite my suddenly wobbly knees and I walked her down the stairway and over to where Bobby was parked. I rapped on the window, wakin' him from his state of ignorant bliss.

He rubbed his eyes and, after figurin' out it was me who was makin' the commotion, he opened the door to a barrage of new information. "Whoa, slow down, Bridget . . . she . . . this woman, Jazmin's mom, she knows this how?"

Bobby had picked up his better than basic Spanish from years in the roadhouse kitchen and bar where most all of the staff hail from somewhere south of the border.

Maria Fernanda took a breathe and slowed her words as she did her best to explain how some young dude who had declared himself her daughter's boyfriend had showed up at her family's door, tellin' them how he was rightly concerned for the girls' welfare and why. Accordin' to his account, Jazmin and Mia were last seen or heard of after takin' off on foot durin' a nighttime raid on a cannabis farm in Garberville, shortly after the start of the harvest season.

"Miguel told Diego and me, Jazmin's Papi, he in charge of the crew."

Bobby gleaned from Maria Fernanda's garbled words how it was that this Miguel kid had met Jazmin and Mia down at the beach the previous summer. Just a few weeks later, it transpired he'd hooked up with the girls, by arrangement, in Garberville, transportin' them to a property in the redwoods in the back of a truck. Miguel told Jazmin's parents the girls had worked with him and his crewmates for barely two weeks, sleepin' in a trailer and trimmin' on a small mom and pop growin' operation semi-legit enough for the girls to have the sense to stick with — until it went belly-up.

We learned, much to our alarm, how it was that in the dead of the night, a mere couple weeks into Mia and Jazmin acclimatizin' to the hectic harvest trim culture, the farmers and their unsuspectin' crew were rudely awoken by the sound of helicopters hoverin' overhead. They'd fled, by foot, all of 'em, in all directions. Accordin' to Miguel, he and the girls were separated soon after makin' their way out of the forest and onto a paved road. The scared and anxious kid told Maria Fernanda how he'd assumed the girls had waited for daylight, hitchhiked into town and headed home.

"He no forget her, my Jazmin." Maria Fernanda cried, tears runnin' down her plump, round cheeks. "Miguel, he come looking for her. We tell him no, we not see her. She no home."

He'd made it clear to Jazmin's mom with no bullshitting about, the longer the girls were gone the more serious danger he feared they were in.

"Diego and me, we have no papers," Maria Fernanda cried, wavin' her small hands around her head, pullin' blue-black strands from her pretty, long, braided hair. The family was undocumented and way too afraid of the consequences to consider goin' to the authorities.

Shit. The timin' sucked and it still sucks for so many to be forced into the silence of fear. Immigration and Customs Enforcement (ICE) sweeps and fearmongerin' amongst the undocumented in our region is the real life fuckin' bogeyman. Mia is half Mexican — as American as myself and yet, for the first time in her life, I feared for the color of my baby's skin. On the orders of the government, ICE runs this reign of terror, puttin' the fear of God into good people when it's only the bad guys they should be goin' after. The undocumented folk in our Latino community are scared to death of being forced out of their long-time homes and deported, their American-born kids sent into goddamn camps. It don't bear thinkin' of to live in this level of fear, little kids afraid to go to school should their parents be taken away while they're in class. A person does not have to be a card-carryin' liberal to know in their heart that this is nothin' short of inhumane.

"Diego", Maria Fernanda's husband, Bobby further explained, had desperately driven up to Garberville and back on two occasions during the previous few weeks. "Damn, they're freakin' out, Bridg'. We've got nothin' to go on other than Miguel's word as to when and where the girls went missin'."

For the first time since Mia ran off, I gave myself permission to dig down deep inside the most painful inner part of me. I was startin' to recognize how it was I'd silenced this pain in order to deal with my own selfish struggles. I was gonna have to muster up the courage and energy to get up off my ass and quit my denial, or else I was gonna regret it for the rest of my life. Christ, Mia and Jazmin had gotten themselves in deep trouble, I knew it, we all knew it.

CHAPTER 9

BOBBY

Inside the Daniel Boone, the lights were fit to blazin'. Angelina flapped around the kitchen in a panic. She's all of five-foot-two and a whirlwind to behold, my family is real lucky to have her, she sure does keep a lookout for us all.

"Your brother's stuck in Petaluma with a truck bed full of meat and veggies, Bobby — road's flooded," Angie informed.

"What was it he was plannin' on fixin' for today?" I asked.

"We're fish heavy," she replied. "You're gonna have to come up with your best cioppino, bro, that's all there is to it."

One thing I do have is this classic San Francisco fish stew down to an art, cioppino being a staple of the De Santis family Sunday suppers since way back in the day. City folk might well assume we sit around twiddlin' our thumbs through the long days and nights of the rainy season, restin' the worn heels of our western boots on the edge of the bar. Not so. Roads in and out of here flood over so as to cut off all access in and out of the more remote, small seaside villages, hence the roadhouse servin' as nothin' less than a community lifeline come this time of year.

Unless it's one of them 4-wheel monster trucks you happen to be drivin', an outsider such as yourself would be wise to steer clear of any unwarranted expedition through three feet or more of standin' water — mud and asphalt damage at every turn. Hell knows, the creeks do rise. Best take my word for it. You won't be hearin' no more on that subject from me.

All manner of folk tended to hang at my bar on a dark, wet, winter's day and night, rallyin' the spirit with some reassurin' banter, a bite of somethin' warm and tasty and a libation or two or four. Company keeps the blues at bay. We been doin' it this way, holdin' up with nothin' but local folk durin' the rainy season since the first of the old families settled these parts. Even durin' the so-called Prohibition years, the booze was flowin'. Oh yes, sir, despite the fact the Feds were out here in force, armed as they were with their substantial arsenal of pistols and long rifles, bulldogs and handcuffs. Tried their darndest to catch the bootleggers in the act, though the law was generally always outsmarted for the most part. I could tell you some stories. Hijackin' and murders that took place in the 1920s and '30s, hair-raisin' tales told a thousand times over under this roof. Same goddamn floorboards under foot hid stash holes filled with more bootlegged Canadian whiskey than the local cheap home brew. As soon as the agents left the premises, it was up with the floorboards and what'll you have?

I grabbed me a super size stockpot for the doin's, lightin' the gas to a steady flame. A generous glug of olive oil hissed in the pan 'til good and hot to sizzlin' for heatin' through a mess of finely diced onions, the more onion, take it from me, the sweeter the sauce, along with a good handful of garlic, chopped, fresh fennel and parsley. Next up, a mess of stewed tomatoes from the pile of big ol' tins stacked up out back, extra paste, clam juice and a half fist full of crushed red pepper, some chopped, sweet basil, thyme, oregano and four or five of the same bay leaves I picked and dried myself from the granddaddy bay tree out back. I set the pot to a steady boil, lowered the flame to simmerin', every once in a while steppin' back into the kitchen to stir the pot between my tendin' to the regular mops hard at it paintin' their tonsils with cold beer and Jack Daniels.

I scrubbed my hands for next part — the stealth extraction of soft, pink, fleshy meat, fresh from the shell of that morning's haul — Dungeness crab trapped by an old buddy of mine from high school, hard at it fishin' out in the cold and abundant waters of Bodega Bay. Mindin' its tenderness, I slowly submerged the crab meat into the stew, real gentle like, addin' in what we locals call saltwater vegetables 'round here — scallops, clams, sea bass, salmon and my favorite, real succulent fresh halibut chunks.

A quarter-hour more on simmer and my prize cioppino was ready for a taste test, only after the classic De Santis finishing touch, mind — a hefty addition of fresh calamari rings and prawns. I dug in for a spoonful. Never tasted a finer mess of my own fish stew, that mornin' if I do say so myself.

Angie popped a few corks on our house red while I set to slicin' the sourdough, fixin' a creamy Caesar salad dressin', goin' heavy on the anchovies and croutons as I generally do. You bet the punters appreciate it — our house special bein' as familiar in these parts as a blanket of fog on the water on account of it being the Italian immigrants, the fishermen from Genoa, my people, the ones who invented this gem of a San Francisco stew, utilizin' all what they had access to durin' the crazy days of the Gold Rush, a haul of canned tomatoes, the last scraps of bread, home made red wine and whatever their catch of the day. The trawlers, they threw their load into one big ol' communal pot. Variations depend on whatever catch a family is most accustomed to.

The years had been a creepin' up on me for sure. Cookin' was one thing, but I'd gotten slow as molasses in the clean up, even slower than usual due to the uncontrollable coughin' bouts that came on real violent at times through the damp winter months.

Back in Nonna Lucia's day, the killer cioppino that good ol' girl served up was the very best known on this stretch of the coast. Damn. She made magic out of whatever it was the ol' man and his ol' man before him brought home, different haul each time. My Nonno, he ran a rough darn skiff out of Tomales Bay, long line fishin' for food and for pleasure the hours he was able to steal away from the ranch.

Listen to me. I'm a-dawdlin' on the past again. Always was sentimental. It was gettin' on time to move on to the next round of my daily duties and get it done before the evenin' storm rolled in. I'd grown accustomed to drivin' Bridget around with her deliveries durin' my afternoon break — ridin' for the brand I liked to call it, to coin a good ol' western phrase. There was not an iota I would not do for that girl and that's the truth. She'd had a hold of the muddy end of the stick, Bridget, what with the goddamn cancer and Mia takin' off the way she did. Bridget's business, the bakin', it was the one thing that was keepin' her together. As for me, best part of my day was a chance to catch myself some sly forty winks while I waited on her outside of the dispensary. No double espresso for the road ever stopped me from takin' a nap.

If there was any way I coulda switched places with Bridget for the worst of it, I woulda done it, honest to God, believe me. It fairly broke my heart to see her suffer. What you gonna do? What I never saw comin' was the other girl's ma showin' up at the dispensary lookin' for Bridget that same day, settin' the wheels in motion for what was comin' for us next.

It was later on that same afternoon, after I had dropped Bridget back at the ranch, when I returned to the roadhouse for my early evenin' shift when fate played its first hand. I was stood there behind that old mahogany bar with its silver dollars inlaid into its counter top, after I had finished off the last of the smokes I'd rolled the night before. Jesus, my fingers forever reeked of tobacco and garlic.

"More of that famous fish stew going begging, Bobby my man?"

My buddy, Marcus settled himself down on a barstool directly across from me. I had not set eyes on him for a couple of weeks.

"Stew, for you, you hairy-faced rabble rouser, hell no, you're clean out of luck," I replied, flicking his arm with a wet bar towel, inadvertently setting myself off on another round of hacking up phlegm into my shirtsleeve.

A broad smile spread across his open face, laugh lines showin' deeper by the year since he'd survived past his twenties. Dark was closin' in and shadows were castin' over the bar. We was in the company of some three dozen, dusty ol' taxidermy heads, hunted down and shot by the original owner of the roadhouse, one Henry "Shorty" O'Shea and his wild bunch of cattlemen cohorts. The place was otherwise, more 'n half empty.

"It sure is shaping into one hell of a gully washer out there," Marcus remarked, tuckin' one of Angelina's heavily starched red and white, checkered napkins down the front of a frayed flannel work shirt.

"You cleared those damn eucalyptus off your property, yet, Bobby boy?"

"If I don't die first waitin' for you to fell a few of 'em for me," I shot back. Marcus and me, we go back a whole long ways. We first crossed paths the time I fell off the wagon good and proper. That boy and me, we had each other's backs from the start, milkin' cows and plantin' lettuce durin' a stint in a subsidized rehab program at the Catholic Charities farm that bit the dust durin' the recession.

It was Angie and my brother Franco who'd finagled gettin' me into the goddamn place, weanin' me off the wild mare's milk a second time. Bridget was havin' none of it, not another drunk to deal with all alone out there at the ranch, no sir. Made me an ultimatum, she did and I thanked her for it, later. Her old man was one too many when it came to the bottle. My jig was up. In my own defense, I was not so much a mean drunk, nor a fully lame one at that. Though I continued to go about my daily business, it was more about me bein' a danger to myself and every other poor soul out on the road. It had come down to my woman, my driver's license and, in turn, my livelihood, or the booze. After I got out, firmly back on the wagon and all, Bridget and me, we started workin' the same shifts pretty much so's she could keep eye on me.

Marcus tucked into a big ol' bowl of stew, barely lookin' up at the sight of his own image in the bullet-riddled mirror behind the bar. The dude's real good-looking with those fine chiseled features the women fall for. Twelve years my junior with a long life ahead, though we were of a similar mindset, Marcus and me, right from the start. Kindred spirits I'd call it. No need for an overload of folk in our lives. It had taken me several weeks to figure out the feller's disability after makin' his acquaintance in the rehab.

One evenin', after doin' the dishes and other assorted kitchen duties, he caught his pant leg up in takin' out the trash, exposin' the artificial leg he'd mastered as darn good as real. Titanium alloy knee joint an' all. Holy cow, he coulda fooled me, havin' outworked my sorry ass in most every task, his bein' ex-Army and there was no hidin' his youth and strength — it was all there in his posture, his stance and intensity; that pure, physical drive he still has about him.

Marcus was one of the lucky ones given what he'd been through. He'd been real fortunate to make it into recovery for his goddamn addiction to the prescription painkillers. It may not sound like a whole barrel load of laughs, gettin' clean an' all, but I'm tellin' you, it woulda been Marcus pushin' up daisies if not for the stroke of luck of him bein' pulled out of a brief, but fuckin' nasty bout with heroin.

I liked the guy from the get-go. Marcus and me, we made a competition out of it all, more from a mutual desire to clean up and get the hell outta there than to show one another up. I'd made my mind up to whoop his ass at somethin'. Truth is, only thing I did better than Marcus was cook. Prosthetic and all, the dude never failed on makin' dust of me with any singular physical challenge. I kinda took on the role of older brother, uncle more like, I guess, given our age difference . . . I was glad of it. We were a great deal better off for the camaraderie, the both of us and we knew it. We'd kept tabs on each other ever since. As for Bridget and myself, well, we were the closest the fella had to family.

"Reckon on this bitch of a rainy season endin' any time soon?" I asked him, while I was sortin' empties from under the bar.

"Matter of fact," Marcus replied, "I'm off work for a week of furlough due to the conditions being so bad."

I popped a bottle of daytime ale, a popular choice amongst the ranchers, be it breakfast or lunch. I slid it over to him. "Go on then. Just the one," he said, takin' a hold of the bottle "Gets the job done". Marcus being what we in the liquor business call a mealer, a partial abstainer, a person who drinks booze only when there's food afore him.

Unlike me, my buddy has no problem with the occasional alcoholic beverage, it's all of the other shit he's darn well gotta steer the hell away from, or else. As for me, my days of getting roostered whatever the hour, they were long gone by this stage of the game. After rehab, Marcus started workin' for the park service as a groundskeeper come carpenter, repairin' all manner of structures out at Point Reyes. It was me who helped him get the job and he soon made himself a decent shake down in one of them park owned cabins in the middle of nowhere, not one darn neighbor to bother him other than a whole bunch of deer and a small team of rotatin' rangers and park interns.

"Week off, eh? You'll be hittin' town when the road is clear?"

"Yeah — road trip, Vegas? Wanna tag along? Come on now Bobby," Marcus did enjoy a wisecrack, though I knew full well the dude was never happier than when he was outdoors, the wilder the better — for the most part, optin' for his own company over others.

"In that case, if you're intent on stickin' around, come out and keep us company later this evenin', brother, even up the numbers seein' as me and Bridget have a house guest." I explained how it was I'd be clockin' off early since I'd volunteered myself on supper duty back home. "On account of Bridget's sister showin' up."

"The hoity-toity little sister nobody speaks of?" Marcus asked. "Man, when's the last time she was home?"

"Don't ask," I replied. "Not long enough. And she's not so little in any way, shape or form. Do not leave me outnumbered by those formidable McCleery women, Marcus, come on now, you're the man, I'm countin' on you to bail me out."

He tried his darn best to weasel out of it, as I knew full well he would. I was not takin' no for an answer despite the fact I'd yet to tell him of Mia's takin' off. It was awkward, for sure, but it was women's business, or so I'd thought. Men like me, we don't care to talk of things we have no understandin' of if you had not noticed.

I watched as he polished off the cioppino, moppin' up the last drop of sauce with a heel chunk of sourdough slathered in butter, fairly wipin' the bowl clean. "Always the best part," he said. "OK, I'll come on over later as a special favor to you, Bobby, work up a fresh appetite, balance the numbers with you and your womenfolk some."

Hell knows it was high time that Maggie showed up, given how her sister had been through the ringer that past year. Selfish bitch never so much as sent over Bridget a bunch of flowers. Meanwhile, what Bridget and Mia had been successful in developin' was the classic mother-daughter deal — they were worse than a pair of cats in a room full of rockers at times, the two of 'em together. And as for the sisters, they had a hell of a deal of ground to cover.

"Be seeing you later, then," Marcus said, pullin' a handful of dollars from his pocket and droppin' them in a heap on the bar.

Hindsight being what it is, for what it's worth, I shoulda laid down the law with Mia years back and we woulda been tellin' a different story now. You bet Mia had her mom and me wrapped 'round her little pinkie finger when it came to the subject of basic discipline. Takin' on the role of her daddy was not in my wheelhouse. Where the hell was the rule book for what went down? Still, I'd gone in eyes open and I wish to God I had been way more involved in the kid's life.

It had taken Bridget's pa passin' and a no-show, deadbeat baby daddy — the old man cold as a wagon tire, before she had given me the time of day. And I had considered myself the luckiest son-of-a-bitch in the state of California the night our stars aligned. It was enough.

What I never bargained for was Mia's hurricane teenage years hittin' shore so fast and furious. Talk about ignorant, goddamn clueless on my part. Still, I harbored no resentment, considerin'. Hadn't we been some form of family, done what we could do for one another given the circumstances? It was never my place to step on her mother's toes.

After Mia took off, I'll admit, it was more than relief I felt, sorta like lettin' loose a wild colt to the mercy of the open plains. There was no lookin' back for any of us after the filly had bust herself out of the trainin' ring, kickin' and snarlin' hither and yon.

It was around Christmas time I began to worry in all earnest. In small ways I was startin' to miss the old Mia, the curious, lively kid she was before the darn hormones set in. It was Bridget who had point-blank, flat out refused to talk about her. Every time I broached the subject, the woman froze. I figured when she was ready, I'd hear about it. After that, I'd kept my concerns to myself.

CHAPTER 10

MAGGIE

My grandparents had the master bedroom, my parents the smaller of the two upstairs rooms and it had been only after Bridget was born, that the old timers moved downstairs into a makeshift bedroom in the dining room. I picture them so clearly, before they passed away, back when I was six and Bridget was ten.

The perimeter fencing around the ranch appeared in dire need of help. I figured it was the illusive Tomás who had been the last to work on the fencing and that was 18 years ago. Yellowing-once-white paint peeled and curled off the exterior siding as I ran my fingers over rough lengths of old-growth redwood paneling.

Neighboring dairy ranches, abandoned by the last of their people, have surrendered their decrepit outbuildings to the rats and skunks, raccoons, opossum and any other opportunistic omnivores who've taken fancy to this rudimentary shelter. That we are still here says something about the McCleerys, generations of whom lived their whole lives in this same ramshackle place, an unapologetic relic that clings on to existence, a curiosity of another era, a haunted remnant of our family's past. It was the basic economics of dairy farming that brought on the rot, before our father's drinking, putting an end to the good old days. Though I don't for the life of me know why anyone would romanticize the ranching life.

I was never cut out for the grueling demands of a managing a dairy herd so, in a way, I am relieved the cows are gone. Still, Bridget's and my folk surely felt gratitude and pride in toiling the land that belonged to we McCleerys and nobody else, for the longest time, for better or worse. And isn't that what it's about? I fear for the last of the small, family-owned dairy ranches, a near impossible way of life in this harsh modern world. Money matters slipped downhill dramatically for the ranchers back in the '60s and Bridget was born into that. Pile on over half a century of further decline and the years have only wrought further wreckage on the yawning wooden ranch structures built in the path of the ceaseless wind and the fog. Dairy ranchers were forced to sell out as fast as they could, squeezed out by a plunge in milk prices that dipped senselessly below the cost of production.

No one other than Bobby and Bridget had come or gone from here in months, I wagered, as I dodged deep puddles engulfing the flooring of a long-abandoned chicken coop with its caved in roof. I kicked around a crushed and rusted, barely discernable Dr Pepper can, a favorite of mine back in the day, long before I'd learned of the perils of soda induced diabetes and tooth decay and all of the other no-nos the soft drink industry insidiously hooks its addicted consumers into pouring down their throats. We'd taken it in turns as kids to feed the hens and gather eggs, Bridget and me, soda cans in our hands. Mom's raised veggie beds were knee high by now with wild grasses, except for those closest to the barn, the ones that Bridget had cultivated for her cannabis crop. Year after year, she'd taken such pride in her garden, routinely planting the basics for our Mediterranean California coastal climate: basil, lemon verbena, sage, Italian parsley, thyme, oregano, garlic, tomatoes, onions and potatoes. On closer inspection, I could see that a few relics of leggy rosemary and mint plantings had managed to survive, doubtlessly thriving on the wintery wet conditions, left alone to roam at root. Mom had stored her excess garden bounty in the same small dark cellar beneath the house that Bridget claimed was now proving the best spot for drying weed. I tried to picture our mother helping her firstborn in the hanging of her green skunky-smelling boughs on the laundry lines that Bridget had strung the length of the cellar. I wondered what she would have made of this New Age farming era had she survived to see it and what it would have taken for her to embrace Bridget's enterprising ideas.

I was reminded of those summers long ago when the bounty of fresh tomatoes had been almost impossible to keep pace with. We'd crushed them in a team effort, at a makeshift production line set up on a trestle table under a plastic shade canopy out back. It was our neighbor rancher, Maria Baldassano who'd taught my Irish American grandmother the Italian method of tucking sprigs of fresh basil into gleaming rows of freshly sterilized glass jars. All the families around here stored this same, delicious crimson pasta sauce for the leaner winter months when a tray of lasagna was a Sunday staple, highlight of the week.

While other people's parents jumped on the bandwagon of TV dinners and convenience foods that flooded the market in the '60s and '70s, we McCleerys had little option both geographically and financially but to look to the earth for sustenance. Mom managed her meager budget with meals made almost entirely from our own backyard. I pinched a sprig of mint and pressed it to my palm, closing my fingers around the pungent leaves to hold to my nose. Smelling it in its freshest form, the strong, sharp distinctive aroma of mint transports me back to happier times, kicking around in the spring sunshine after school, my long hair swinging loose around my shoulders, my feet swimming around in my sister's too big, hand-me-down, western boots, the two of us picking herbs and making daisy chains out in the long green grasses of the dairy pasture.

I leaned against the rusty hinges of the door to the milking barn. It opened with a low groan and I tumbled in. Someone had clearly spent time cleaning it out; except for a few ranch tools, a mower, two or three rakes and a slew of thick, green tinted ropes that hung from the walls, it was empty. The milking equipment and clutter of the old dairy days, three single unit Henman Milkers, the old man's serious pride and joy, along with his DeLaval vacuum suction pump and all the pipelines were gone.

You don't have to believe in ghosts to be haunted. Though in the off chance the old man's spirit was lingering around, I wanted him to know that I was not in the least bit fazed to find myself back in his domain. "It's OK, Dad," I called out into the shadows: "It's me, Maggie. And believe me, I'm not here to give you a hard time."

The cracked concrete floor was coated in only a thin layer of dirt, an indication it had been scrubbed clean after its contents were removed. I climbed the narrow, wooden staircase into the raised, glass-fronted cubicle Dad had rigged up as his office for overseeing the milking bays in what had been the best of the old days before he was left to manage it all on his own. He'd had his own father by his side, 'til he'd passed, plus a few ranch hands on and off, not to mention Bridget and me when we came of age, helping out with some of the milking duties. His rusty iron desk and a squeaky old swivel chair was all that was left in place of the old man's long abandoned workspace. Somewhere in the midst of the overriding smell of damp, I detected a lingering scent of the Brylcreem he'd used to hold his hair in place, old-fashioned stuff squeezed from a black tube with its unmistakably musty, floral, soapy mix. Three hundred and sixty-five days a year you would have found him right here, when he wasn't outdoors feeding calves or tending the land. I half expected to see him at his desk, in his trademark denim coveralls, one of his motley collection of free hats from the feed store perched on his head, the type with plastic mesh at the back for ventilation. The old man was never without one, worn high on his greaser head, except for in bed, I assume or certainly at the dinner table and then, only on our mother's insistence. He treasured these tall, stiff, foam caps he carefully assembled on a long, narrow rack by the front door. Each was emblazoned by the name and logo of some protein feed supplement or other. I never knew him to throw one away, no matter how grimy.

Dad took out loans to keep his dairy operation afloat. He was so stretched so thin he mortgaged the ranch his family owned outright prior to his making his final, desperate move of selling the herd. Feed and fuel prices soared yet milk prices stayed the same. In order to produce more milk, the herd required far more food than grazing would provide. Dad had trouble paying off his loan. Half of the ranch families we went to school with lost their shirts this way along with their land. The math was simply not there. The Holsteins were a burden and he had to let them go. Hell, he let it all go — anything of value, the old wagon plus the harness and collars from his parents' generation's old workhorses, even the family's once-prized 1929 Chevy truck. In turn, he took his solace in the bottle.

I'd spent years not thinking of all that we'd lost, refusing to feel my father's pain. It had been bad enough being raised around his disappointment with the world and with himself. I didn't need any reminders of how fucking unfair life is. And I had no clue how much Mia was aware of the level of disappointment and loss she was born into. If my old man was hiding there still in those dark shadows of the past, it was on account of his shame. The old folks, the first of the McCleerys, they'd milked their small grazing herd by hand, squirting milk into a pail, taking pride in separating the cream from the milk.

Since my grandparents' day, the Holsteins they'd favored for their plentiful milk production have morphed into beasts of human engineering, genetically modified for a substantially higher volume of milk than the humble dairy cattle that grazed my family's ranch when I was a child.

My footsteps echoed as I made my way over to my dad's old built-in desk. I felt so alone I may have welcomed his ghostly apparition should it have appeared. I twisted and turned in my father's chair and placed my hands palms down on the cold surface of the desk, recalling the wire-haired skin of the old man's calloused and leathery hands.

A penetrating chill rose up from the frigid floor. I swear I could smell the cleaning fluid that was used to wipe off the milking teats, a distinctive solution containing iodine as a disinfectant. Tears welled and free-fell down my cheeks in a cascade of sudden, unexpected overwhelm, a compound of sorrows. Why was this still a thing? This place? Who the heck declared the McCleerys must press on here come hell or high water? Bridget and me, if we'd sold the whole deal, lock, stock and barrel, the minute Dad died, what would have become of us?

There was no way the old man would have been the one to let it go, if he'd lived. He would have considered it a double failure, losing the herd and later, the ranch itself.

CHAPTER 11

MIA

Thinking about it, I developed what I can only describe as a kind of allergy to my mom and Bobby when I was about 13. That's when every little thing they did around me began to irritate the hell out of me. I don't know why, but it did. I felt this overwhelming urge to be different from them. I hated the faded old, ill-fitting clothes they slopped about in, the dumb stuff they talked about, their annoying music, Mom's ugly sneakers, the way she drove, Bobby's endless and predictable doggie bags of leftover food for supper from the roadhouse, you name it, it was on my list.

My mom ignored my behavior for the most part. Bobby told me every now and again to shut it, but only if I was pushing it too far with my disrespect. I guess it wasn't Bobby's job to keep me in line, though I'm telling you, if it was my kid or someone else's dishing me such a crock of shit, I would figure out a better way to deal with this kind of sassy and mean-spirited behavior, at least acknowledge them.

I'm not saying that some of my feelings wasn't justified, though when it came to my mom sitting me down to tell me she had been diagnosed with breast cancer, that last summer evening, I was old enough to have known better, to have put my annoyance with her aside, to have comforted her, hugged her even. I had nothing else to do and I never reached out so much as a second.

CHAPTER 12

MAGGIE

I'd left a message for Andres first thing that morning. It pained me beyond words to have to make communication with him, but for once, I put the urgent needs of my blood family before my own feelings. The only one who had a strong shot at getting through a locked computer was my conniving soon-to-be ex, an individual who prides himself on his ability to hack his way into just about anything password controlled. He is paid to do it, after all, the tech world being a bottomless pit of information mining, legal and illegal.

Since I had made Andres aware of my whereabouts, I was quick to make myself scarce from the ranch. Last thing I wanted was for him to show up ahead of our assigned meeting point, full of bravado at my lingering dependence on him in front of my sister. I knew this would be something he'd enjoy, if I let him in, sticking the knife in a little deeper, twisting 'til I squirmed.

I made my way down to the beach behind the wheel of the old man's rusty Toyota truck — stick shift — the one workhorse he'd failed to drive entirely into the ground. Bridget had managed at least to keep it gassed up, if only a quarter tank, keys she'd said were in the glove compartment.

You'll find a near identical, trusted, rust-encrusted pick-up truck out back of just about every barn in the county. Worth their weight in gold, though I doubted Bridget had bothered to keep the insurance and registration up.

Rain clouds produced spittle not nearly heavy enough to deter me from taking a restorative walk along the shore in order to bolster myself for my meeting with Andres. Cold, slate blue waves rolled in from the depths of the wild Pacific, a bitter reminder not to be fooled by its beauty, not even for a second. Archaeologists claim 100 unexplored shipwrecks sit below these frigid waters rolling in from the Sonoma Coast to Mendocino County's shoreline in the north. It's a deceptively treacherous stretch of coastline.

A middle aged blonde woman with a medium-sized, jaunty black dog strode by. The dog was of mixed breed, its red collar embroidered with a heart shaped pattern. I watched as its human unleashed her pet, the eager dog leaping through the grassy dunes in that cheering display that is gleeful canine delight. We only had the one dog growing up. Bram. He was a mix, though we never could say what his particular combo may have been. He had a distinctive shaggy, gray and white coat and he'd been impressively devoted to our dad, despite the old man's miserable demeanor. Bram was just as good with cattle. How we'd adored that oddball, scruffy character. And he, in turn, loved nothing more than running down to the beach with Bridget and me, chasing birds up and down the shallow surf where he dashed, back and forth, full tilt, all day long if we'd let him.

Bram is buried on the ranch in full view of the ocean. For the first time in many years I sensed him beside me, his soft, fluffy coat rubbing against my legs as I made my way down to the frothy water's edge. Though it had been a long time since I'd spared a thought for him, I felt a pang of longing for his unconditional companionship. More than I miss the old man, that's for sure.

I walked barefoot a while beneath the looming storm clouds beside the ocean's prickling swell, slipping my hands into my pockets, my gloves and woolen beanie heavy from the salt spray. I could feel the chill from my feet up as I climbed on into the dunes, dodging a run off of a narrow rivulet from the previous night's storm. Dune grass whipped against my exposed skin as I turned back toward the shore at the point of a spindly dirt road, narrow and barely two track that follows an early stagecoach trail that transported beachgoers from a long gone, narrow gauge train station in the nearby small town of Tomales.

It's a short, downhill walk from tiny Dillon Village to the sand. I looked up at the clustering of weathered cottages that cling to the hillside above, cute little wooden cabins that sit here, huddled together, side by side, as they have since Victorian times, first serving as summer homes for the growing population of the Gold Rush riverfront city of Petaluma, then a 20-mile horse and wagon trail ride away from the beach.

The village is named after its founder, pioneer potato farmer, George Dillon, who, along with my great-great-grandparents' generation, traveled a continent to cross the plains in order to settle this land.

I stomped my feet in a feeble attempt to increase the circulation.

Lawson's Landing sits at the far end of Dillon Beach — a fisherman's trailer park positioned at the mouth of a skinny little inlet of water known as Tomales Bay. It is there that a modest wooden pier stretches out from the trailer park into the pristine waters of the bay, a waterway known for its kayaking and oysters. It may appear fairly tame and certainly scenic to the newcomer, but believe me, the scenic natural beauty of its surface hides a dangerous undercurrent that is deadly if miscalculated.

I watched a lone kite surfer dip in and out of the pounding waves in his shiny black wetsuit, harnessing the wind in order to propel himself against the frigid water. I might have mistaken him for a seal if not for the strange and multi colored wind sail, a crazy combination of windsurfing, paragliding and skateboarding.

Winds from the Pacific whip up without warning and as I've already said, it's a cruel trick of Mother Nature to lull the uninitiated into any kind of false sense of security on these dangerous waters. The shallow area that sits at the mouth of the bay causes the ocean swell to build, as it was doing that day, creating a breaker line of two or three big waves at a time.

My Grandfather on my mom's side made sure to drum his warning words into us as kids as to the dangers of these waters. He knew this to be absolute, having been raised in a rudimentary shack on the banks of the bay in the small fishing community of Marshall. How I had reveled in his stories of the bootleg years up and down this same stretch of water.

One of the scant few subjects my own dad cared to discuss at any length was that of the region's rich Prohibition lore, the romance of the old days and the lure. There was and still is an element of the outlaw factor in our heritage, I'm sure of it. His dad claimed it had been near on impossible for the law to contain the smuggling of booze on shore during those heavily romanticized bootleg years. This being so far west, it proved an ideal place for hiding contraband loot. Everyone was in on it, according to the old man. And a maze of unlit back roads proved impassable for the Feds.

Nocturnal high tides in the bay are especially risky to outsiders. I watched as the kite surfer flew dangerously close to the narrow waterway, the key spot, apparently for those daring nighttime drops of coveted Canadian whiskey and rum. It took a skilled navigator, my Grandfather claimed, to risk running the notorious third wave of a moonlit high tide. That's how they did it. That's how they brought the contraband bounty into the 50 foot mouth of the bay. You had to know the risks and work the perilous currents in order to survive. Silently, I wished the solo, wet-suited sportsman safe anchorage as he continued to battle the waves.

Down at the pier, I came across a tin can abandoned on a ledge. Instinctively, I dropped it into the water below, dangling it on its string. It was the height of Dungeness crab season and the ocean appeared at once calm, ominously so, despite the storm brewing.

Drop a single line or a can into the water without a license from the Department of Fish and Game and you're liable to run into trouble. I'd learned this from one of my numerous teenage misadventures. Still, the bait shop at the landing was closed. I doubted anyone was out there checking on folk, what with it being a deserted weekday in the dead of winter with yet more rain coming in. To catch a crab, even the most basic of a fisherman or woman must have access to bait. Whoever walked away from the can must've placed it there that morning, for inside was a single, raw chicken wing — common bait of the casual crabber. Crabs being carnivorous creatures, they feed on small clams, oysters, fish, shrimp and worms.

Minutes after I lowered the can into the water, I felt the old tug and thrill.

I hauled it up, peeking inside to inspect its contents. Sure enough, I'd caught myself a crab, its pincers at the ready. This one was way too small to take home to Bridget for supper. We'd learned from our dad how to identify which crabs were okay to eat and which to throw back into the ocean. Undersized, the young crab was reddish/brown with a slight purple tint, five intact pairs of legs and ten small teeth. I inspected its hard shell that, given the right conditions, would molt away in order for the crab to grow. I carefully lowered the can down to release the fortunate fella back onto the eelgrass bed below.

On each of the countless occasions I've ordered crab from the menu of some fancy restaurant in the City, it paled in comparison to the pink flesh and flavor of the ridiculously fresh crabmeat I'd taken for granted growing up. The melt-in-the-mouth flavor of delicious, same day ocean caught crab was a given during the holiday seasons of my youth. I never once tasted any as sweet, fine and tender as the salty, pink-fleshed crabs fresh caught in these home waters.

I tore myself away from my nostalgic crabbing expedition or I would've been soaked to the skin within the half hour. My feet were freezing, pins and needles making it painful to walk as I headed back toward the truck, but still, I held on to my coveted boots.

As I hurried back, I reminisced how Bridget and I had learned to best to prepare a fresh-caught crab from Granddad's fishing boat. It was the one time of year the old man had taken over the kitchen. Dad showed us how to cook a crab and to stop us squirming, though we had to brace ourselves in order to plunge the poor creature head first into the boiling water to simmer a quarter of an hour. What a mess we'd made, I recall, while Mom kept herself out of the kitchen 'til Dad and Bridget and me had the whole scene cleaned up.

To ready a cooked crab for eating, we cringed for first few times when we were taught to rip off the triangular belly flap before we pried off its back shell and drained the internal liquid, removing the reddish membranes that covered its core. A good rinse under cold water readied the poor crab for the further necessary evil of twisting off its legs and claws. It's hard to shake the image of the old man stepping back in at the end of this intense activity to give the shell a good, hard crack with his wooden mallet, before cutting its core into quarters for the family to devour. It's brutal, yes, the more I think of it, but we sure did learn the importance of understanding where our food came from and appreciate its primal dignity as we dug in with our fingers, savoring at the last juicy pieces of flesh with the aid of a little crab fork.

I drove back over the rise toward Tomales, my appetite piqued as the truck climbed and dropped in turn on the narrow road that cuts through verdant green hills studded with giant rock formations that make for panoramic viewpoints on a clear day. I checked my watch as I pulled into a deserted main street for one last stroll down memory lane. I was hoping to score a cup of soup of the day from a hole-in-the-wall bakery that closes shop at random hours according to when the last of the daily specials have completely sold out.

Single gauge tracks and trains have long since gone from here, another of the vanished lifelines in the region's dairy farming and logging history. I parked the truck on the side of the half empty road and walked along Main Street where there's little left to indicate the once bustling era of a depot town aside for a small strip of stern commercial buildings built in the Victorian style.

A little ways down the street, I looked up at yellow lights that illuminated the stained glass windows of the pretty, white Catholic church where Bridget and I'd been baptized and where we both received our first holy communion like the good little Irish girls we were. Needless to say, neither of us made it through to confirmation. Mom had given up on any sense of piety, holiness and sanctity I guess by the time she fell sick. I wondered if Mia had been put through any Catholic rights of passage? At least I'd not been invited to attend.

If, in some altered reality, the railroad had remained a feature of the landscape, this sleepy little place might well have grown into a much larger town. It would have meant a whole different story for those of us who grew up around here had the trains continued to run and larger industrial towns and even small coastal cities emerged. I dare say most of the folk who live out here prefer it the way it is. Those who pass through experience and surely appreciate a one-of-a-kind glimpse of the way life used to be. To spend any amount of time here is to turn your back on the conveniences of much of the modern world. All well and good for a long weekend but living here permanently takes a significantly more robust resolve, trust me.

When the trains stopped running, most of the smaller waterside villages were frozen in time, if they survived at all. Tiny fishing communities consisting of no more than a handful of shacks on the banks of Tomales Bay have disappeared into the mists of time. Aside from that, the region has been preserved pretty much as it was when George Dillon and his potato farmer pals rode their horse and buggies down this same main street.

The sky had turned a darker shade of gray with an ominous tint of blue in thick streaks. I walked on, peering over several fences of the childhood homes of old school friends. An old man with a long beard gawped back from an unlit downstairs window of a house built closer to the street. I jumped back, not expecting to see or be seen, an opportunistic voyeur of the past.

It felt like I was strolling through a silent movie set of bygone days — although one without the players. When I reached the bakery, the last serving of a seasonal soup of the day was mine for the taking and just in the nick of time, served up piping hot in a heatproof paper cup. I savored, standing, each warming spoonful of the rich, thick and creamy crab and Bodega red potato chowder with its familiar flavoring of nutmeg, fresh parsley, thyme and Old Bay seasoning, the same that Mom used to sprinkle into the satisfying fish soups she'd concocted from whatever seafood came her way.

~

It was raining on and off, harder by then. I slid onto the vinyl seat inside the musty truck; it was held together with a thick crisscross of disintegrating masking tape. I had a good rummage around in the glove compartment, inquisitive as to what I might find. Besides a few packets of rolling papers and a stale pack of American Spirit, there was nothing more interesting than a yellowing pile of expired documents and ancient receipts, a cache of unopened ketchup pouches, two hair bands and a small, handwritten sheet of mostly 707 and 415 area code phone numbers, the majority of which I guessed I'd need a hotline to heaven or hell in hopes of reaching a living person on the other end. The floor of the truck was carpeted with a dozen old Lays potato chip packets and a stash of brittle, yellowed newspapers, most of which were antiquated copies of The Santa Rosa Press Democrat from the '80s.

Rain was dripping through a rusted portion of the roof onto the left side of my head and shoulder. Sensibly, I'd wrapped Mia's laptop in a couple of large plastic garbage bags for protection from the elements. I double-checked the package was still where I'd tucked it under the driver's seat.

Hanging a right turn to the south, I levered the truck into gear, hit the gas and took off in the general direction of the bayside oyster farm where I'd arranged to meet my soon-to-be ex. I could see that Andres had tried calling me while I was at the beach, as I suspected he might, but my phone had dropped his calls. "Double-checking that you do have the computer with you," he'd texted, as if I'd forgotten the entire point of it, or maybe he thought I was tricking him into meeting me with the laptop as an excuse. My plan was to connect in a neutral zone that just so happened to be the oyster farm that supplied his favorite bar in the City.

Newly single, unemployed and technically homeless, it would have been wise for me to save the last few dollars in my pocket for a more practical temptation than splurging on oysters. To hell with that, I decided, if I had to see Andres, even for the briefest of meetings, I'd damn well make the best of it, bag myself a haul of oysters as compensation. The urge to indulge in the fruits of the bay was stronger than ever that day — one way of dealing with the futility of my situation, I guess. Plus, I figured once my face-to-face with Andres was over, my peace offering to Bridget would be the double whammy of access to Mia's email along with a big bag of briny bivalves.

These remote oyster farms are a hell of a trek for city folk, even during the best of conditions. I joined a slow stream of traffic snaking its way into a narrow sliver of a gravel parking lot where a hooded, hairy-faced dude in a heavy set of waterproof jacket and pants signaled for me to pull over by a big, nautical-themed, blue and white, hand-painted valet parking sign.

"OK, you've got to be kidding me. I grew up out here," I said, reluctantly rolling down my window in fear of it sticking open in place. "Since when the valet parking?"

"No choice, I'm afraid, ma'am," he replied. "Not a lot of real estate for parking out here on the water's edge you see."

Ma'am, please, I flinched at the formality, though technically, I was more or less old enough to be his mom.

The briny delights of the oyster farm have achieved a cult-like status amongst the food aficionados of the Bay Area. The downside being that it faces a popularity problem when it comes to accommodating an increasing swell of crowds that choose to step away from the marble counters in the Ferry Building en masse for a wild drive west to taste at the source. Traffic routinely jams this narrow highway on weekends. And in the summer months an even more insane scene ensues in search of the seductive qualities of the half shell.

But this was February and many of the roads out West were under water. I experienced a perverse stab of pleasure at the thought of Andres running into trouble, ill-equipped in such conditions in the Mini all this way out West. And all he was going to get from me would be a thank you and whatever sense of smug satisfaction on my being reliant on him for something so important. The commonly held myth of the aphrodisiacal qualities of the oyster briefly crossed my mind and I shuddered at the thought of my soon-to-be ex trying on any of his old games, holding me in his debt with inappropriate references to the oyster's exotic nature — glistening, slippery, alive, just like him.

A group of noisy young people gathered around a blazing fire pit by the shore, all manicured facial hair, piercings and hoodies, tech startup T-shirts and designer sneakers, guys a lot younger than Andres, laughing and toasting as their glossy, long-haired girlfriends bopped around in their skinny jeans and woolen ponchos, bright, happy faces beaming under wide-brimmed, felted hats in earthy shades of olive green and brown. I know the type. The heavier rain from earlier was holding off and yet I was impressed that a few of them had managed to establish a decent fire in such pervasive damp.

I watched them a little longer as they chuckled and flirted, clinking small, round stemless globes of chilled white wine, layers of crushed shells crackling under expensive winter footwear. A pinprick of jealousy hit me in the center of my chest as the young and the beautiful reveled in each other's company. When, precisely, had I stopped being one of this tribe, I wondered?

The waterside ghetto was abuzz with well organized, rainproofed hipsters in their beanies and branded puffer jackets snapping selfies in their small groups. The wood fires crackled in pits beside a fleet of wooden picnic tables, laden with photo worthy picnics, overlooking the brackish bay.

My phone vibrated in my pocket. A text from Andres: "I'm here, where are you?"

I'd fed him the short story in my initial text message, reluctant as I'd been to speak to him directly, especially in the flesh.

"Maggie, babe, how you doing?" Oh no, he hadn't lost his touch, laying on the velvet voice with its killer delivery, the slightest hint of breathiness. His warm breath on the back of my neck told me he'd had no trouble honing in on me. Talk about radar instinct. I braced myself for my own reaction, how easy it would have been for him to render me wobbly at the knees once more. Stepping back, instinctively in a standard self-protective move, I felt an instant relief in not falling prey to his charms, not even the slightest tingle.

I turned. "Hello Andres . . ." He sensed my hesitation as I stood my ground — a conscious separate entity, barefaced as he'd rarely ever seen me during the daytime hours, my hair scraped into a ponytail, wet from the rain. "We're not here to talk about me. It's Mia I'm worried about, as we've established. I'm really grateful that you're not above cracking her computer passcode." Best get straight to the point, I told myself. No more broaching the subject of our uncoupling. It was over. I kept it civil, averting my eyes from his as best as I was able. He was about to do me a big favor, he owed me that much, we both knew it.

"So where is Mia's laptop?" he asked, his eyes brushing over the damp fringing on the front of my funky jacket, "You do have it with you?"

"Why do you keep on asking me that? Of course I have it with me, it's in the truck," I snapped. We walked side by side, my leading the way to the junky vehicle the parking attendant had wedged into an almost impossibly tight space. I wrangled the keys and unlocked the door, wiping the leak-splattered seats with a greasy looking old towel I'd rescued from the clutter of the back seat.

"Are you serious, Maggie?" a look of distaste on his face as Andres assessed the general state of the vehicle's interior, of me. He was a little too close for comfort, so near, in fact, that for a second time, I recoiled at the sensation of the heat of his breath on the side of my exposed neck. I handed over the laptop and swiftly dug my hands into my pockets, taking extra care to avoid any unnecessary skin contact. He kicked aside an ancient bottle of Mexican Coke on the passenger seat floor, asking: "Jesus, how long has this been here?" After shifting around uncomfortably in his seat a few seconds longer, he released the computer from its layers of plastic, opened it and positioned it on the knees of a pair of expensive looking thick, heather colored corduroy pants. New life clearly meant new luxury clothing for one of us at least.

Andres removed a USB stick from a small cloth pouch he'd taken from his coat pocket and inserted it into the side of the laptop.

"I'm using a data security program to unlock Mia's computer without a password," he said. This time it was he who was avoiding looking directly at me. "Don't ask."

We sat in silence for several long minutes while the computer took its time to wake up. Andres tapped away at the keyboard. "And hey presto, we're in." He said he had every confidence it would be of help in our figuring out where my niece had gone. Ever the optimist, though he'd never shown such interest in my family when we were together.

"Bridget has a lot on her plate, we both do," I said. Let's not pretend he cared about Mia, my sister, or me for that matter other than as someone who had been in love with me, once. "We'll be alright. This at least will give us some idea of what Mia was up to before she took off. Thank you for this, Andres, I mean it."

The man I no longer loved sighed, softening his voice as he reached for my hand, an old trick I'd fallen for a million times in the past. No more of the old-times' sake stuff, dear God. I'd been there, done that plenty. Not happening. I pulled away.

"And you? The apartment, I hear you've let it go, reduced yourself to what, driving this old wreck around, Maggie, what's next? You've lowered your standards a tad, haven't you?" he asked, gracing me with one of his patronizing half smiles, as if my reduced circumstances had nothing to do with his taking off. "Does this mean you're back at the ranch for good?"

"I'm undecided but I'm fine. Don't you worry about me, in fact, I really do have to go — thanks again for your time," I said, reaching across him to release the passenger door. I caught an exotic whiff of the cologne he'd favored for as long as I'd been in his life, sweet, sandalwood, essentially masculine, classic Andres. I did my best to block a flood of sensual memories. "Bridget and me, we appreciate you going out of your way to help. You take care now . . . "

"Come on, Maggie, let's have a nice, chilled glass of white, share some oysters for old times sake at least," he suggested, "seeing as I've driven all the way out here." He extended a tailored arm toward my shoulder, his chiseled, clean-shaven features closing in and, before I could stop him, landing a warm and lingering kiss on the cool skin of my cheek. Andres always knew exactly which buttons to press and when.

I cut him off, sharply, though, to be honest, my mind did wander a brief moment at his offer of a glass of wine. Hell, if you spring for the whole fucking bottle, I thought, then maybe. I caught myself shivering, in equal part due to the damp leather jacket and my unbridled fear of caving in. I shook my head fervently and watched him as he extricated himself from the truck and walked away, shoulders back, head held high. He turned to look back only the once, those big, brown, beautiful eyebrows raised and a shrugging of his shoulders to remind me the whole thing between over us was my loss. As if he'd played no role in our demise. Take it or leave it Maggie. I continued to keep an eye on him as he took shelter beneath a stupid, giant designer golfing umbrella out there on the water's edge, looking as he always did, like a million dollars, even in the rain. He was not oblivious, of that I'm sure, fully aware of my watching him as he, in turn, took in the actions of an oyster shepherd in waterproof wading gear hanging large sacks of freshly harvested oysters onto racks for hand sorting on an open-air conveyor belt.

His silhouette shifted behind a filter tank of bay water bubbling with newly bagged oysters undergoing the natural cooling process used to slow down their metabolism in readiness for transportation to Bay Area restaurants. The line at the oyster take-home window had shortened with the onslaught of now heavier rain. I watched 'til I was sure Andres was out of sight before I stepped out of the truck. I waited my turn in line, intent on placing an order for a dozen oysters to go, mentally patting myself on the back for mustering the courage to deal with my soon-to-be ex in such a clipped and businesslike fashion. Any sense of achievement did not last long, however, before the all-too familiar, ice-cold onset of anxiety crept in and a swift and strangulating hold swept over me. This awful condition had been the bane of my existence since Andres left — unpredictable, overwhelming feelings of sudden and irrational fear, a suffocating sensation of helplessness. I'd experienced my first, a preview of what would fast become a series of frequent panic attacks a few weeks prior to Andres' threatened departure.

My heart pounded. I could barely catch my breath. The last thing I needed was for Andres to stroll back over and find me like this. I felt instantly weak and vulnerable, aware of the extra weight I was carrying as I stood against the wall of the oyster shack, closing my eyes in an effort to find calm. I told myself to conjure the Maggie of my post-supper state of the previous evening, the strange sense of inner power that I'd felt, a fleeting feeling of ease, of wellbeing and self-contentment. After about five minutes of forcing myself into channeling whatever amount of positivity and strength I was able to muster, I somehow managed to pull myself together and, in the after effects of having gotten myself into such a state, I purchased a bag of oysters and drove myself straight back to the ranch.

CHAPTER 13

MARCUS

As I climbed the dilapidated porch steps to Bobby and Bridget's place, I took in a couple deep breaths — a coping mechanism I'd learned from rehab that most times helps in calming my stubborn social phobia issue sufficiently enough for me to walk on in.

No matter how many times I go through this, it's never easy to shake the crippling fear of making a complete dick of myself. That particular evening I was even more revved up than usual and ready to roll with my standard round of self-punishment at the mere thought of having to make small talk with a stranger, even if it was my buddy's sister-in-law. I was dry mouthed, experiencing the shakes and all. My heart raced and my palms began to sweat. I knew full well this was idiotic considering my feelings for these guys, Bobby and Bridget and them being my only real friends, the two of them. It's not as if these troublesome anxieties of mine are based on any one real thing. I mean, who the hell gives a shit, aside from me, should some dumbass statement spurt out of my mouth? I reminded myself for the millionth time to shut the interior monologue the fuck up. Being around a woman I had never met before was no big deal, but still, the mind of the introvert will press on with its dirty work of self-assassination.

I figured I was going to have to work double time for Bridget's sister to be convinced of me as any kind of normal, happy-go-lucky dude grateful for some company and a decent meal. Don't get me wrong, it was no way on account of her being a woman of a certain age that had me all riled up. I'm not one to discriminate. I have trouble connecting with folk in general. I've grown accustomed to my own company, my own space, peace and solitude you see. Idle conversation, table talk, typically filled me with dread.

A bead of perspiration rolled down my spine. I felt it trickle beneath the heavy twill of my button down shirt, the most presentable item I managed to dig out of my laundry pile on the short notice of Bobby's sudden supper mandate.

The decrepit porch sagged underfoot. This sorry ol' place is in serious need of shoring up. I vowed, come spring, after the rains stopped, I'd be a good friend, help take stock of the place, formulate a list as to what all would be required to help make a start.

Bobby, who'd spotted the lights of my truck, flung the door open to greet me as I reached the top of the porch steps, his big ol' frame filling the narrow entryway, all but blocking out the light from the hallway.

"Yo, it's the castaway," he boomed, slapping me on the shoulder, beaming. "Storm chase you in?"

The front door slammed shut behind me on a gust of wind strong enough to swoop a smaller guy, fling him over the cliff and clear into the Pacific, beyond. "No sign of her lettin' up, man," I replied. "No mercy tonight."

"Wood burner's earnin' its keep, come on in and warm your bones, bud," Bobby said.

I had not set eyes on Bridget since she'd lost all of her hair. Hell, I was in an awkward position, not knowing if I should say something or go about our greetings as if she wasn't altered any. Something or other had to be said in order to get it out of the way, I knew that much. I swept my own discomfort aside for once and went for the safe bet: "Nice head scarf, Bridg', how're you holding up?"

It's a crime, Bridget being so sick. She nodded with a thin-lipped, wry-faced smile that led me to believe that if she was keeping her shit together on the outside she was raging hell on the inside.

"It sure does appear I'm makin' some small progress, Marcus, thank you for askin'," she said, looking away to end that particular line of conversation, a relief for both of us. She'd taken my jacket in one hand and my hand in the other — thin, small and real bony, yet surprisingly strong. I looked down at it, white as white could be, pale blue superficial veins close to the skin's surface raised up on the back like a bunch of creeping earthworms.

"Prepare yourself for meetin' Maggie, my sister, shinin' jewel of the McCleery crown," she said, "she'll be back any minute now, Marcus, at least she ought to be, the queen bee's been gone for hours."

"No messing around out there at this time with another of these goddamn storm systems coming in," I said. "I hope for her sake she's close by." It was no night to be rambling around waterlogged, unlit roads, reacquainting, reminiscing, whatever it was she'd been up to. Tall domes of leaden, stone gray clouds were smothering any chance of moonlight breaking through.

There would be no stars to look up at in the sky that night. Indoors, the air was thick with smoke, the kitchen filled with a briny steam.

Bridget handed me a big, ol' mug of sweet, hot, honeyed tea. It warmed my hands and eased the tightness in my chest. The heat of the wood burner flushed my face as we stood there, waiting for her sister to make her appearance. In the narrow slips of silence between the necessary small talk I forced out of my mouth, I heard what sounded like ball bearings plink into plastic bowls in the kitchen, the shrill, metallic rattle in stark contrast to a soft, groaning croak and hiss of burning wood, an orchestra of fire and water. Bridget seemed distracted, disconnected, as Bobby applied himself to coaxing my ongoing pitiful attempt at chitchat, piping up with something, anything to plug the uncomfortable silences. My awkward ways never bothered him none.

For years I'd trusted no one but Bobby. And Bridget, God bless her, she never presses me too hard, as is her way. It's time that has won us over with each other, her and me. That's how it is for shy folk. Good people like the McCleerys are well worth the effort, worth their weight in silver and gold.

Let me make this clear, I have never been a man to will the fragile pieces of my heart on another, not since all my troubles started as a kid. If you'd told me that evening I would find myself so instantly undone, that a few split seconds was about to change the mindset of my life, I'd have laughed in your face, suggesting that you to take the giant bug out of your ass, for you'd picked the wrong guy to play such foolish games with.

Oh yes, I'd be the first to admit I was an authentic, card-holding skeptic of the strange and mysterious, invisible force of womanly bewitchment. A dude such as me had no previous reference or concept whatsoever of a stealth invasion in the feminine form. I guess the best way for me to describe it is a magnetic attraction that strikes when you're least expecting it, the crazy shit that goes down when two people are drawn together by their opposite pole.

In the briefest of moments it took for her to walk into that house, her eyes were almost instantly locked onto mine. I felt myself flush and reddened, undoubtedly to a sudden, deep shade of darkest maroon. I've gotta say we both sensed it, a door to somewhere strange and new and foreign, one that neither of us had thought to pass through, least of all that night. It flung itself open in a hot flash. Looking back, any fool could've heard my heavy heart pounding ten to the dozen, visibly raising the breast pocket of my shirt. I stuttered a short greeting, my mouth and throat as dry as the barn floor out back as I stumbled toward her, offering Maggie my hand in a bungled attempt to disguise this rash onset of irrational and totally out of character behavior.

It was a clumsy introduction at best and she threw me further off balance by taking a tactile hold of my hand a few seconds longer than was warranted. This mesmerizing stranger of sorts, Bridget's sister, had zero problems in maintaining direct eye contact. Her piercing green eyes docked into mine like a bullet on target. I blinked fast as she held her gaze. A surge of something implicit and unfamiliar continued to pass between us and it hovered a minute more in the heavy charge of air. Bridget's little sister, of all people in the whole dang world, was reading me for the fool I was, frozen on the spot, dazed, confused, blindsided, an open book, chapter and verse. It was as If I was written solely for her.

Up close, I took in the smell of her. It was of the Pacific, a mixture of sea breeze, salt water and that strong, earthy scent of damp sand. She let go of my hand in order to reach up to the back of her head and loosen her hair band, shaking rainwater from a tumble of dark waves, an alluring first move, one that made me think of the ocean at night, its unleashing of scent-bearing chemicals secreted deep within her core. Call it chemistry, pheromones, whatever mysterious matter it is that fuels most all-animal behavior. Truth is, I'm as dumbfounded now as I was then, in having fallen hook, line and sinker within seconds of her call.

"I hope you like oysters, Marcus," she said, awakening me from a swift and intoxicating self-analysis. It was like I was on something, high on her.

She handed over her icy loot. "You shuck?" She asked me with a sly, half smile.

"Beg your pardon," I stammered, stumbling forward. My face flushed anew. What was I, a sophomore schoolboy crushing on a senior girl, one who was way out of my league?

The wind howled and chased in through the window frames and under the doors. It swept in on the gusts that whipped across the old pastureland in the front and back pounding so heavily on the thin, single pane glass, I feared at once the windows might shatter.

I laughed, in spite of myself, standing there, hypnotized, clinging on for dear life to the bag of ice and oysters Maggie thrust upon me. I'm no stranger to the shucking of a half dozen oysters, still, semi-paralyzed as I was, I passed the bag over to Bobby, whom I duly followed, with a sense of relief, like an obedient puppy, into the kitchen. He rattled around in the kitchen drawers, unearthing a couple hook-tipped, dull-pointed, thick-bladed oyster knives. "Swiss," he said as he set about our appointed task at the kitchen sink. "Indestructible. Belonged to my folks."

Bobby filled a bowl in the sink from a bag of ice Maggie hauled in from where she'd left it on the porch and he set about arranging the oysters evenly on top. I watched him as he took two clean kitchen towels and folded them into thirds to both brace the shells and protect our hands from any accidental slippage.

The art of oyster shucking is a learned one that takes skill and patience and practice to perfect. Bobby shared how he'd learned at any early age how to inspect each of the oysters for any that were already open, reminding me that a healthy, living oyster is clamped shut at the outset. If an oyster's open even slightly and will not close when tapped, it's a done deal, dead. I watched as he took a good sniff of each of the shells, one at a time.

"If you come across a fishy one, avoid it like the plague," he urged. "You know what they say," he let out one of his deep chesty smoker's chortles: "eat a bad oyster, you'll soon suffer a reversal of fortune."

As the big guy vigorously scrubbed away at the outer shells, removing mud, sand and dirt, I stole myself a stealthy glance at Maggie. Not surprisingly, given my performance earlier, she caught me in the act. I averted my eyes and looked back down at my task at hand.

Bridget asked her sister to go light candles in the dining room. "It's been a whole year," she remarked, her arms full with a pile of old mail she'd cleared from the dining table and carried into the kitchen, "It was you who was here last for supper, Marcus and that's been a good twelve months since. First time this old table has seen any action in a long while."

The belly side being the bottom and the flat side the top, I picked out one oyster at a time, holding each shell firmly between one of the folded towels. Working my knife into the hinge, I wiggled and finessed the hook-tipped blade 'til I was able to exert sufficient pressure 'gainst the top and bottom, twisting and prying, rotating it so as to feel the familiar "pop", the sweet spot, the moment the oyster yields. I pulled off the top shells, severing the muscle that held each shell together before I made a close inspection of the half dozen my unsteady hands had managed to shuck.

Top shells went into the garbage as I slid the knife beneath the clear, shiny, lively looking oysters inside the bottom shells, so as to swiftly release them to eat. Bobby and I placed the half shells onto a platter Maggie had prepared with coarse salt to stabilize the mildly metallic, mineral scented bivalves. My hand trembled as I passed the platter over the countertop. Seeing as I was feeling extra scrutinized, pressured to say the least, I focused on the shining, silvery, almost iridescent color of the sweet oyster meat. Its mild, salty aroma was seductive.

Bobby hauled a steaming pot of pasta from the stovetop to the sink. He poured spaghetti al dente into a large, metal colander as Maggie stood directly across from me cutting lemons for the oyster platter. Bridget was busy stirring tomato sauce with a wooden spoon, seemingly oblivious to any agitated tension on my part. The cacophony of leaks I'd been aware of earlier was steadily filling the bowls and buckets that were dotted around the kitchen.

The three of them worked well in the kitchen together. They sure made a good impression of a tight-knit family, if I hadn't known better, that is. According to Bobby, Bridget and Maggie were not nearly close. Not for a long time.

Maggie walked directly over to stand before me. She was radiant, her hair still damp and fragrant and her cheeks all rosy and glowing from the chill night air. I watched as she took an oyster on its half shell and holding it close to my mouth, her fingertips brushed my lips. "I always eat the first one naked," she said, flashing a three by nine smile wide enough to knock a dude for six.

My wide eyes spoke for themselves. "Don't worry, Marcus," she laughed, applying the slightest touch of her palm to the back of my bare arm. I'd rolled up my shirtsleeves for the shucking. "Keep your clothes on. Forget the lemon. Bring the oyster to your nose, smell its essence, then, shoot it in its juice . . . like so, now, chew it, slowly, and swallow."

She was clearly getting a kick out of making fun of me. What the hell does a guy like me from the Central Valley know of oyster etiquette? I'm no food snob, though I eat all the oysters I get my hands on, outdoors, in their natural habitat. "Squirt a little lemon on the next one," she said, her hand on my arm a second time. "Eat an oyster eyes first and taste the bay, isn't that what they say?"

"My sister's such a geek, a total food elitist," Bridget said. "Don't mind her, Marcus. Way too many fancy oyster bar bills in this girl's history."

"She's right though, Bridget," Bobby came to Maggie's rescue. "In my humble opinion, oysters are best enjoyed fat, plump and unadulterated."

I took myself a second shell, squeezed a drop of lemon on it, slurping its delicious contents down in a manner I hoped was halfway acceptable given my sophisticated newfound companion. "Each to his own," I said. In other words, I meant take me as I am, or not.

Maggie made no qualms in fixing her eyes on my mouth as I chewed on the slippery oyster deliberately and slowly, as directed and duly swallowed. Her face lit up with something like approval of my having fully savored the experience just as she'd instructed.

"Heavenly. Yes?"

I smiled back and nodded, taking extra care than usual in the wiping of my lips and beard with the cloth napkin she'd handed me. It might as well have been the first time I'd ever tasted an oyster given the explosion of tastes in my mouth. Man, the range of pain and pleasure flooding through my veins was confusing.

Maggie took care of the bulk of our conversation while Bobby and Bridget were fixing to serve supper, rattling on about a chef in the city making waves in the restaurant scene by cooking with seawater. "Who knew, it's all the rage in some parts of the world?" she asked. "Bread bakers are swearing by seawater, apparently."

Neither me nor Bobby or Bridget passed comment on the sort of crazy who pays for the luxury of filtered, sanitized seawater. I know from my own experience, boating with my Grandpa as a boy, any fool is free to take as much seawater as he or she should reasonably need. Dang well bring it to a boil and pass it through a coffee filter. Job done, though I never said as much.

It wasn't until halfway through supper that Bridget chose to spill the beans on her disturbing meeting that afternoon outside of the dispensary. Mia's being gone sure was news to me, the last to hear about it. Bobby shuffled his eating irons uncomfortably.

Tension is generally the first trigger for me to make a swift exit. I was out of my depth in the middle of a complicated family matter of which I had no part, nor wanted one. A familiar urge to make a hasty retreat, to recharge, alone and in private called. My palms began to sweat again, my heart was fit to racing. I stared out of the window into the depths of the sheeting dark. Lightening flashed across the night sky.

"She's in Humboldt, we know that, for sure," Bridget announced.

Maggie leapt from her chair, sending it crashing to the floor. Heavy wood caught my leg at the point where the prosthetic joins. I flinched and instinctively I leaned down to tug at and pull my pant leg back into place. Maggie took it all in, though she was polite enough to give no pause to stare.

"Jesus, Bridget, this is unbelievable," she turned her attention to snap at her sister. "I'm sorry but I just cannot get into your head. Mia may be anywhere in the whole damn Emerald Triangle by now, it's not just Humboldt you know, Mendocino and Trinity counties make up a massive trifecta of potential trouble," she said. "Lord, what I need right now is a drink . . . what the hell do you think happens to young girls their age in the middle of fucking nowhere?"

Bobby was the next to blow a fuse. He picked up his salad plate and smacked it on the side of the table in an uncharacteristic show of force, cracking it in two and shooting salad leaves across the surface. I sat upright, on red alert for I'd never seen him react this way. "Enough," he yelled. "Quit your conniption fit, Maggie. You come here, raisin' sand, with no right to point a finger at your sister or any one of us."

"Calm down, both of you," Bridget stood and raised her voice to be heard above Bobby's. "Mia is my daughter, Maggie, and despite the fact you seem to think I've given up on her, failed her, I will decide what the next move will be. You all know how hard this is. The timin'. It sucks."

I froze to my chair in fear of further aggravating the situation by offending my friends in slinking off. As I've said, I am a solo operator, more than used to saying hell no to any form of social responsibility, but this time I found myself offering no excuse and I stuck it out at the table. I did the right thing and kept my mouth shut.

"I'm sorry that you're on edge, that you're bein' forced to give the booze a rest, Maggie," Bridget said, "You know we don't keep alcohol in the house. I dare say, you'll survive by doin' without it for another night. After that, you are free to go do whatever the hell it is that gives you the courage to be so righteous."

Maggie kept her mouth zipped a minute or two more as she mulled things over in her head. "It's time we take a look through your daughter's email," she said, calmly, when she deemed it sufficiently safe to speak. "Together. See if we can't find some leads at least in what she was thinking when she took off. Andres proved himself good for something. He unlocked her password this afternoon."

"What? You met with him out here?" Bridget asked her sister. "Where?

"Briefly," Maggie replied. "He drove out. And the bastard better not be thinking I owe him one."

Maggie retrieved a laptop from the messenger bag I vaguely recalled she'd worn slung over her shoulder when she'd made her electric entrance, earlier. She uncovered it from its wrapping of plastic bags, using its weight to push a stack of plates to one side before she flipped it open.

"We already know that the girls were last seen in a forested area in Humboldt," Bridget said. She took her time in composing herself, steadying her voice in order to recount what she had learned that afternoon from Jazmin's distraught mother.

"All I am able to pray for, since it seems I am officially the winner of the worst mother of the year award, is that the girls are together and they're unharmed," she said.

Maggie fiddled with the laptop. "I don't get it, why has neither of them made contact with anyone?" she asked. "A text at the very least."

At that late hour it was looking increasingly unlikely the storm was in any mood to temper its hissy fit that night. "I'd best be leaving, afford you all some privacy," I announced, before the weather took a turn for the worse. It struck me they were all three of them way out of their league in knowing what in the hell to do with the scant information they did have.

Three sets of rattled eyes bored to mine. They shook their heads in unison at my suggestion of taking off. The situation was deeply troubling. And so like it or not, there was no way I was getting out of it, either.

"The Emerald Triangle has a shady and dangerous side, as we all know," I said, breaking my silence. Commonplace shootings, robbery, bodies buried in the forest, kidnappings, I hated to say it, but the distressing nature of news from the northernmost neck of the woods was becoming all too frequent. I never intended to alarm anyone without due cause, no more than necessary but I felt it my duty to share what I knew. "Even the most seasoned of weed trimmers know to best steer clear of the more remote areas," I said. "Let's hope the girls have that good sense about them."

"Marcus is right," Bobby said. "It's the lure of the big bucks that draws the innocents into the seasonal gig. What I don't get is why in God's name they've chosen to stay up there? They should have headed on home by now."

The idea of two girls of eighteen wandering around in the forest, months after harvest and presumably without any basic gear or training for survival was what concerned me most.

"Do you think I'm stupid?" Bridget burst out. "I know full well what it's all about, the whole trimmigrant deal, the good grows and the bad. I'd be a hypocrite if I said I wasn't aware of what goes on, what they might have gotten into."

"So you just let her go headfirst into it, knowing all of this?" Maggie asked, scrolling through the icons on the computer screen in search of her niece's email. "OK, I get that you're a stoner yourself, Bridget, too lazy or weak to get a grip on your one and only child. What I want to know is why did the other girl's parents wait so long?"

Bridget's eyes flashed once more with fury. "I'll thank you not to cast any further judgment, miss perfect on your high horse. Who the fuck are you to barge in here and point fingers? If you must know, Jazmin's family is undocumented. They've been way too afraid to deal with the authorities to make a complaint," she explained, angrily. "They've tried their best to find the girls and they're rightly terrified of bein' deported if they make themselves known to the police."

This shut us all up. ICE has been a genuine threat in the region, terrorizing people over the previous few months, arresting many. I saw it myself as they handcuffed a terrified and distraught woman, a single mother of three young kids as she worked the checkout where I buy my bread and milk. The only thing they say she was guilty of, aside from having no papers, was a black mark against her for an outstanding warrant for some minor traffic incident years back. It makes no sense. They say that some good soul at her place of worship stepped up to take those kiddies in, the three of them born and raised in the same small ranching community where it all went down.

The way I look at it is I never joined the army in order to defend some and not all. This new regime makes me sick to my stomach. I've put away my medal, the Purple Heart no less, the one thing I've managed to keep ahold of from my army days. I've stuck it where I don't have to look at it 'til things in this country are running the right way again. One thing that I'll never forget, many of the best soldiers I served with, stand-up Latino guys and gals, they signed up for these documents — they put their lives on the line for the love of this country, no different from the rest of us.

Maggie finally pulled up Mia's email account. She clicked it open. "Looks like her last entry was in early September," she said, scrolling through her niece's communications from the previous summer.

The two sisters sat side by side, softly illuminated under a low beam cast from a heavy overhead light fixture. Maggie painstakingly backtracked through messages sent and received the previous summer between Mia and her friend.

"Garberville. That's where we need to start," Bridget said, slamming her fist on the table, her mind working to absorb the basic motivations of her teenage daughter's unfortunate decision-making. "Shit, I had no idea how much she hated it out here, how mad she was at me."

"It's the usual teenage angst to a certain extent, Bridget," Maggie reassured, making nice after her earlier outburst. "Rebelling — it happens to the best of us, though more often than not, it backfires, hopefully, in Mia's case, not horribly."

"None of these emails give us much to go on, other than the knowledge they were primarily money motivated," Bridget said. "We have to get up there, you guys."

"There's no wasting any more time," Maggie agreed. "We're talking first thing in the morning, Bridget. Get your shit together, sis, even if this is all the info we have to go on, it's a starting point, we're headed north. Who's in?"

~

"It's called the Redwood Curtain for good reason," I confided in Maggie, after Bridget and Bobby took off upstairs to bed.

"Once you travel beyond the divide, it's a different world — one that spans thousands of miles of twisting, turning, winding dirt roads that lead deep into the wilderness," I said, calm and clear, upfront though I didn't want to freak her out entirely. Last thing I was trying to do was deflate her go-get-'em enthusiasm for finding the teens.

"We're talking hundreds of thousands of acres of dense forest canopy, Maggie. An unimaginable number of nooks and crannies for hiding out in a vast goddamn realm that for the most part, is completely impenetrable to outsiders."

She perched herself on the high-back wooden chair she'd flipped to face me as I sank back on the couch and crossed her arms. "My take on their emails," she said, "is that it's the sort of friendship that fosters taking risks they might otherwise never have dared to take alone . . ." The chair back served as a buffer between us, our physical proximity. I was acutely aware that it was now just the two of us.

"Sounds to me they've made the only move they figured was open to them," I ventured. "Whatever it is that is keeping them from coming home, it has to be something to do with their not knowing what they were getting themselves into and where they are."

It had been decided I was to spend the night on the couch. The woodburning stove crackled from the last of the firewood Bobby threw into the burner prior to turning in for the night.

Maggie stood, stretched, stepped forward and reached behind the couch for a stack of blankets and a pillow. She smiled as she informed me that it was she who had warmed my makeshift bed for me the night before. "Never quite made it upstairs," she said, yawning. "Long story." She wrapped a blanket around her shoulders and sat herself beside me, close enough for me to feel the spark of static from the sides of our thighs as they barely touched. Outside, the rain fell and distant thunder rumbled and clapped above the midnight tide. The last of the glowing embers jumped and furled. I focused my gaze on the dwindling fire.

I found talking with Maggie a whole deal different from the usual small talk I so detest. To my relief, our conversation flowed, comfortably, surprisingly naturally. She reached out a hand and I braced myself as she rested it lightly on my disfigured limb, the exact place she had seen it join with the prosthetic under the dining table. I took it on to be up front with her right from the get-go that night as I revealed the source of what she'd seen. "Well, you know what? I respect your honesty, your humility," she replied as I fought the urge to take her face in my hands, to kiss her on the lips. Instead, I employed my better judgment and I let it pass, figuring, this, whatever it was, if it was going anywhere at all, would have to come from her. Her face was flushed by the firelight. I felt the blood flow under my skin as I garbled, distractedly at how I was okay with what others may consider a disability. "It's not that I am . . . that I am overly courageous," I said. "I'm getting on with my life is all, making the best of a bad deal."

What I never said was that once she doused the lights and left me for the night, I was liable to feel my whole darn leg like it was still there. Sometimes it happens this way, though it pains me, the mind playing its cruel and humiliating tricks. And it hurts like hell. There are other night terrors I have learned to deal with. Not every night, now, but more times a week than I care to count.

Despite the howling outside and the practical matter of the short, lumpy couch, I fell into a few hours of oddly untroubled sleep. By morning I had mulled it over, my position. It was clear to me before I so much as put my one foot on the ground. I was off work a few days anyways due to the storms and the flooded roads. I'd pretty much figured during supper on my heading north with Bobby, Bridget and her sister. Hell, no, this was not me going along for the ride, I would be the ride — my truck and me. I would be the one to take the driver's seat in this emergency expedition into the wild.

If anyone owed this family, it was me.

"That's a big deal for us to ask of you, Marcus," Bridget said over a mug of fresh brewed coffee. The way they'd had my back over the past few years, Bobby and Bridget, they've been as close a thing to my own people as I've had in this world.

"I'll not see the three of you off as innocents," I said.

Bridget raised her mug and declared a toast to me, a sucker for punishment, she said and one with a taste for rough terrain. "Yes, ma'am, that sounds about right," I said.

"Will you walk with me out to the barn, Marcus?" Maggie asked. "I'm hoping to hunt down the emergency supplies Bridget says she stuck out there in storage, years ago." I noticed Bridget shoot Bobby a look.

Our plan, outlined by Bobby himself, was to head north by way of the Sonoma coastline and up into Mendocino and the more remote neighboring region known as the Lost Coast. He thought maybe the girls would have innocently taken that longer, more winding route north, neither of them having been up into the Emerald Triangle before.

It had pissed down earlier that morning, though patches of blue attempted a weak push through the dark layers of clouds. Storm conditions had calmed temporarily, as far as the wind, but the rain was turning itself on and off like a faulty bathroom faucet, showering the green and sodden earth in random intervals. There was no end to it. Conditions were dire for embarking on any such shoreline expedition. I knew this to be the case and yet I ignored my instincts in order to appease Bridget's desperation and please her sister. It took over any voice of reason in my head. The one that told me we should wait it out.

The dairy barn was in good shape compared to the house. I already knew this, as it was me who had helped Bobby and Bridget in clearing out the last of her old man's milking machinery three summers prior.

Maggie opened and shut a half dozen doors into cold, drafty storage recesses, rustling up sleeping bags, camping gear, a water canteen, a couple big flashlights, candles, a rope and a big ol' metal spade that Bridget had referred to as the shit-shoveler. "No food, or the rats would have had a field day," Maggie said. "We'll take what we can from the kitchen."

It is not have been out of the realm of possibility to find ourselves cut off from the world for days, weeks, a month even, in these remote parts, should the 'Big One' rumble and hit this part of the Bay Area. My tank is always at least half full of gas and that day was no exception. I'd filled up on my way to the ranch. We'd need it if we stuck to the coast road, for there'd be no more refueling for many miles.

I scanned the general condition of the sturdy old barn from my former trade perspective as an army construction carpenter. My job had been to assist with the building of temporary and permanent structures on tours in Afghanistan and Iraq. I know my way around lumber, plywood, plasterboard, concrete, masonry and bricks. I'm adept at hunting and cooking in the outdoors. Ask me to build you a structure and I will happily set about concocting a suitable shelter from almost any available material.

Before the inconvenient incident of having half my leg blown off, I worked with dozens of outfits ordered to build and repair bridges, buildings, foundations, dams and bunkers.

The barn was rendered a hollow, empty space back when we'd stripped it of the last vestiges of its former use. It had struck me as a gloomy, solemn place back then. Standing in the barn that morning with Maggie by my side, its still solid structure began to show surprising signs of new life. It was like it was pleased she was there. I looked around and pictured the barn repurposed, doors flung open wide to let the sunshine in.

"Your barn here has real solid bones, you know," I said.

"The old-timers, they built it to last," Maggie replied. "It's in serious need of some fresh air if you ask me — time to flush out the ghosts," she said. "If I'm honest with you, Marcus, this whole sorry place is trapped in the past."

"We all have history," I said. "Trick is not to let it take you down."

Maggie looked up into the cobwebbed cubicle office, the corner of the barn where her old man had ruled the roost.

"He's here," she said. "I can almost see him sitting at his desk, usual scowl on his face, wiry gray hairs poking out of his Wrangler shirt, a goddamn toothpick stuck between those tobacco-yellow teeth of his."

I could see no such sorry vision in the silvery, thin light, though if I had caught the old feller glancing over at us, I believe it would have been on account of his awaiting this particular daughter's return. If old man McCleery is still here, he darn sure willed Maggie home to fix his failings. Maybe, after all and despite her best intentions, she'd heard his call.

"Do you know?" I asked, as I stepped closer and took a hold of her hand in mine: "In some African societies it's said they divide humans into three categories. Those who are still alive, others who have recently departed — they're known as the living dead. And then there are those who live on in the minds of the living. When the last living person to remember the deceased passes over, he or she who has been the longest gone is finally able to move on."

Maggie laughed. "Not sure where you are going with this."

"If your old man lives on in your mind and Bridget's mind, then you have nothing to fear is all. Way I see it, he's likely gonna hang out here 'til nobody remembers him."

She reached through the air with a wide sweep of her free hand. "Well then, to my old man and all the other ghosts in the barn, I see you, I remember you," she said. "Have at it."

She pulled me gently towards her, so close I could see for the first time the crinkle of a set of fine lines that framed her beautiful eyes, their color intensified by the beam of daylight through redwood, reflecting a different shade of green from that which I had noticed in our brief walk outdoors.

A thin streak of wintry sunlight shifted through the narrow cracks in the soft boards of the barn's siding, gentle rays further highlighting her features and the luster of her loosened hair.

The moment was broken by the whistling sound of a barn owl, calling out from the cross beams in the space between the barn roof and the briefest of a first embrace.

"I dare say your sister will take off without us if we dally here much longer," I said. "Catch your breath, Maggie, it's time to make our move."

CHAPTER 14

MIA AND JAZMIN'S EMAIL THREAD

Jazmin Marques
To: Mia McCleery
RE: Hey Girl!

On August 15, 2018, at 11:00 AM, Jazmin Marques
jaziswag.m@gmail.com wrote:

> *I've been up since five, out the door by five thirty. These early mornings are killing me, M. I want you to know, between us, me and my mom, we cleaned three stinky fish restaurants top to toe by the time you rolled your lazy ass out of bed, ha ha!*
>
> *BTW, not a peep from you these past few days, so what's up?*

On August 15, 2018, at 11:15 AM, Mia McCleery
macbrae98@gmail.com wrote:

> Let me see. Oh, nothing much. Except for the fact that my mom might die on me (insert operatic sigh).

On August 15, 2018, at 11:17 AM, Jazmin Marques
jaziswag.m@gmail.com wrote:

> *WTF? You kidding me, right?*
>
> *What's going on?*

On August 15, 2018, at 11:19 AM, Mia McCleery
macbrae98@gmail.com wrote:

Breast cancer. And if that's not bad enough, she's totally nuts, claims she's taking care of it with her lotions and potions and the weed she's been growing out back. Pretty much stoned the whole time. Fuck this.

On August 15, 2018, at 11:21 AM, Jazmin Marques
jaziswag.m@gmail.com wrote:

You gotta trust her, let her do her thing.

Give her a minute, M. Takes time to process this sorta heavy shit.

On August 15, 2018, at 11:23 AM, Mia McCleery
macbrae98@gmail.com wrote:

It's fucked up is what it is (insert wads of soggy tissue up sleeve).

I just wanna be someone else for a while, quit the hick life. What about you? Who do you wanna be, my sister from another mother?

On August 15, 2018, at 11:25 AM, Jazmin Marques
jaziswag.m@gmail.com wrote:

Girlfriend, you know who I'm gonna be. Just watch. You see if I don't get myself into the J.C. and pre-nursing classes next year, somehow, someway. One thing for sure, I'm not planning on cleaning scuzzy floors for the rest of my life.

On August 15, 2018, at 11:30 AM, Mia McCleery
macbrae98@gmail.com wrote

Oh yeah? Right on. And what's your momma gonna say about that, you in school? Who's gonna look after the little ones when she's on her hands and knees scrubbing floors while you sit yourself in an air conditioned class all day? (Insert gasp).

On August 15, 2018, at 11:33 AM, Jazmin Marques
jaziswag.m@gmail.com wrote:

> *Don't you talk bad about my mom for working her butt off, M. It's not like she doesn't want the best for me and the other kids. She's afraid if I start the application process it could trigger the deportation process. My dad, he gets it, though. I know he does, he knows of undocumented students who've gotten themselves into junior college with the Dreamer papers, scholarships and all. Anyway, it's my plan and I'm sticking to it. I'm gonna get my pre-requisites done, work a transfer into a nursing program at one of the state schools in no time. Illegal is a state of mind, believe me.*

On August 15, 2018, at 11:37 AM, Mia McCleery
macbrae98@gmail.com wrote:

> More power to you, J. You made the grades girl, not me. All I know is it's time to get outta this shithole with action plan A — make us some cash.

On August 15, 2018, at 11:39 AM, Jazmin Marques
jaziswag.m@gmail.com wrote:

> *If we do this together, M, it's the J.C. next semester for both of us, agreed?*
>
> *Just cuz you didn't do it all in high school doesn't mean you can't ever get your shit together. You could take your pick of vocational courses at the J.C. There's a whole bunch of trades to pick from, maybe even train as a dental hygienist, a radiology technician or a pharmacy tech, that way you'll earn yourself a job that pays enough to get you the hell outa Hicksville with me.*

On August 15, 2018, at 11:45 AM, Mia McCleery
macbrae98@gmail.com wrote:

> Maybe, baby. Right now what I need is a class in how to stop myself from blowing my brains out. I am so bored (fake holding gun to forehead).

Meet me down at the beach tonight at seven. I cannot stand being forced to listen to Van Morrison half the day and night. I'm done watching my mom lie around in a cloud of smoke. Total denial is what it is. She's gonna kick the bucket if she doesn't get real.

~

Mia McCleery
To: Jazmin Marques
Re: Bored Brainless Continued . . .

On August 17, 2018, at 12:08 AM, Mia McCleery
macbrae98@gmail.com wrote:

You still awake, J? Might as well be dead as not have a goddamn phone. I need to text and Insta and Snapchat like I need a life.

Hate being forced to communicate this way, what is this, the frickin' dark ages? Email for God sakes. Listen, I have an idea. Wanna make bank & get out of here? And I mean sooner not later. You in? (Insert truth detector eye scan).

M

On August 17, 2018, at 12:15 AM, Jazmin Marques
jaziswag.m@gmail.com wrote:

I'm awake. Can't sleep.

What's your plan, Veronica Mars? What we gonna do? Set up a detective agency?

On August 17, 2018, at 12:17 AM, Mia McCleery
macbrae98@gmail.com wrote:

Ha! If only.

Seriously, J, the dude from Santa Rosa, weed trimmer, big mouth bragger 'round the bonfire at the beach that night, fastest trimmer in the west. You still crushin' on him?

On August 17, 2018, at 12:18 AM, Jazmin Marques
jaziswag.m@gmail.com wrote:

> *Yep. We've been messaging on FB, on and off! Miguel — man of emojis. Dude persists.*

On August 17, 2018, at 12:20 AM, Mia McCleery
macbrae98@gmail.com wrote:

> Hey girl. WTF —you still do Facebook? Tell him we'd be up for it, the weed trimming. You and me, as long as he's vouching for us.

On August 17, 2016, at 12:22 AM, Jazmin Marques
jaziswag.m@gmail.com wrote:

> *WTF back, Mia? My parents would kill me.*

On August 17, 2018, at 12:24 AM, Mia McCleery
macbrae98@gmail.com wrote:

> Fast cash, Jazzy, think about it. I've been doing some serious home-work, here, digging around online. Two hundo a pound. Easy. Trim, make bank, get out of there. Five weeks, five thousand a piece.
>
> Why the fuck not? And we're not telling anyone what we're up to, so keep your pretty mouth shut and no posting. What they don't know won't hurt. (Insert evil grin).

On August 17, 2018, at 12:28 AM, Jazmin Marques
jaziswag.m@gmail.com wrote:

> *M, you're bad. There's sketchy shit up there, Phish fans with acoustic guitars, sex starved rednecks and all . . . And for your information, I don't post shit, I'm only on FB on the pc for Messenger seeing as I broke my phone by accident.*

On August 17, 2018, at 12:32 AM, Mia McCleery
macbrae98@gmail.com wrote:

> Duh. Miguel and his friends, they're cool, right? You said as much yourself. They'll look out for us. Who cares about the rednecks and crust-punks, the tent dwellers, they're everywhere these days. Anyway, I hear there's plenty of semi-legit seasonal work to be had, money for nothing. Come on. Say yes.
>
> Think about it. Ten thousand bucks between us gets us a sweet down payment, first, last and security on a place of our own. A chill little apartment is sitting there waiting for you and me to move in over in Santa Rosa, walking distance to the J.C. I can see it now, pots of cool plants on the deck. We'll have plenty of money left for our enrollment fees, brand new iPhones a piece — spring semester. It's ours, babe.

On August 17, 2018, at 12:36AM, Jazmin Marques
jaziswag.m@gmail.com wrote:

> *U crazy! BCNU.*
>
> *xoxoxoxo*

On August 17, 2018, at 12:40 AM, Mia McCleery
macbrae98@gmail.com wrote:

> Fuck Yes! Though I'd prefer to be known as badass than bat shit crazy.

On August 18, 2018, at 10:38 PM, Jazmin Marques
jaziswag.m@gmail.com wrote:

> *You got me. Shit.*
>
> *BTW, I messaged Miguel after work.*
>
> *Been thinking on it all day.*
>
> *We're on.*
>
> *Miguel's down to meet up with us in Garberville early Sept. He's headed up there now to get things going, says he'll set us up on his*

crew, camping and all. Real nice people, same family he trimmed for last year.

On August 18, 2018, at 10:45 PM, Mia McCleery *macbrae98@gmail.com* wrote:

Hell yes! Can't believe you're this ballsy, J.

On August 18, 2018, at 10:48 PM, Jazmin Marques *jaziswag.m@gmail.com* wrote:

You're fucking insane, M.

How am I doing this to my parents? They're gonna freak.

On August 18, 2018, at 10:50 PM, Mia McCleery *macbrae98@gmail.com* wrote:

Babe, we're all afraid of something. How the hell else are we gonna get outa here anytime in the next ten years if we don't take a chance?

All we have to do is show back up at Christmas, act all sheepish, say sorry for the worry we caused. Better off begging for forgiveness than asking permission.

Think of it, a backpack each, crammed full of cash by the time we get home. You can even buy the little ninós some presents.

On August 18, 2018, at 10:54 PM, Jazmin Marques *jaziswag.m@gmail.com* wrote:

This is one big, fat massive deal for me, M.

So much worse for me than it is for you. Do you get that?

My dad. He's old school. He'll be mad as hell. It's a pretty crappy stint to pull.

On August 18, 2018, at 10:56 PM, Mia McCleery *macbrae98@gmail.com* wrote:

K. Stay. Clean floors. Have fun with that. I'm going. Besides, Miguel might like me better ;) ;) ;)

On August 18, 2018, at 10:58 PM, Jazmin Marques *jaziswag.m@gmail.com* wrote:

> *I said I'd go, didn't I?*

~

Mia McCleery
To: Jazmin Marques
RE: Operation Weed

On August 19, 2018, at 11:08 AM Mia McCleery *macbrae98@gmail.com* wrote:

> Meet me at the beach. Tonight at seven.

On August 19, 2018, at 12:00 PM, Jazmin Marques *jaziswag.m@gmail.com* wrote:

> *K. Tell no one.*

On August 19, 2018, at 12:05 PM Mia McCleery *macbrae98@gmail.com* wrote:

> K. Who would I tell?

~

Mia McCleery
To: Jazmin Marques
RE: Get Me Out of Here

On August 20, 2018, at 10:00 AM Mia McCleery *macbrae98@gmail.com* wrote:

> Girlfriend, I am done with this place, these people. If I hear one more Janis Joplin track on that shit record player, I'm gonna slit my throat. Unfuckingbearable.

On August 20, 2018, at 12:05 PM, Jazmin Marques *jaziswag.m@gmail.com* wrote:

> *Chill. We'll be outa here soon. You gotta give your mom a break, M. She's sick.*

On August 20, 2018, at 12:15 PM Mia McCleery
macbrae98@gmail.com wrote:

> You try being around her dark cloud of misery. Fuck, now it's
> Leonard Cohen on loop. Depressing is what it is. Trapped in the
> past. Totally sucks.
>
> All of it, J, it's driving me insane. No work, no wheels, no money,
> no food in the house except for the sorry leftovers Bobby brings
> back from the roadhouse.

On August 20, 2018, at 12:20 PM, Jazmin Marques
jaziswag.m@gmail.com wrote:

> *Hey babe, you'll see, you're gonna have it all once we get up to
> Garberville. I heard a lot of semi-pro skaters and surfers trim to pay
> the bills. I know that's your type — Miguel says that after dark is
> party time.*

On August 20, 2018, at 12:25 PM Mia McCleery
macbrae98@gmail.com wrote:

> Girl, I cannot wait.
>
> xoxoxoxo

Jazmin Marques
To: Mia McCleery
Re: Countdown

On August 21, 2018, at 11:00 AM, Jazmin Marques
jaziswag.m@gmail.com wrote:

> *Shit. I'm a nervous wreck. I hope it's not a total asshole move. I feel
> real bad for the lil niños. They're gonna miss me so.*
>
> *BTW, you packing some party wear?*

On August 21, 2018, at 11:30 AM Mia McCleery
macbrae98@gmail.com wrote:

> What are you, nuts? Do not screw this up, girl. NO party wear. Cut-off shorts so your cute little butt cheeks stick out the bottom and a bikini top is all you're gonna need. That's about as hot as it gets in the backwoods, babe. And hey, watch one more round of Frozen with the ninõs for the seven billionth time, they'll get over it.
>
> Meet me at the beach tonight. Seven.

On August 24, 2018, at 11:00 AM, Jazmin Marques
jaziswag.m@gmail.com wrote:

> *Babe. We're outta here. Eight days to adventure time.*
>
> *Can't stop thinking of Miguel, now I know I'm gonna see him soon. Help? How dumb am I? Romance in the redwoods, ha ha!*
>
> *Best get you hooked up with your own hillbilly-surfer hottie!*
>
> *Meet at the beach again tonight. Usual time. Tell me everything is under control. (Insert scoff).*

On August 24, 2018, at 11:53 AM Mia McCleery
macbrae98@gmail.com wrote:

> K. No more emails. Just in case. Last of the logistics to go over tonight — sunscreen, don't forget tampons, toothpaste, basics a chick can't live without in the woods. Condoms?!?!
>
> J, you're the bomb. I love you babe. CUL8R.
>
> xoxoxo

CHAPTER 15

BRIDGET

B obby paced the kitchen after callin' Jazmin's boyfriend Miguel on the number her mother had handed over on a small piece of paper carefully folded into a tidy square. In his defense, it appeared the kid had never stopped tryin' to make contact with Jazmin after the raid on the pot farm, in September.

Miguel explained to Bobby how he and his friends had hidden out in the woods for almost an entire week, livin' off the little food and water they'd managed to grab ahold of after the choppers had scared the shit out of 'em. He and his buddies had found more work that took 'em through the season.

"He figured the girls had most likely freaked and made their way home," Bobby said.

Miguel and Jazmin were together, Miguel told Bobby, as in a pair and in their minds, at least as seriously as any kids their age consider themselves a couple. At any rate, the lovesick Miguel maintained his concern and his feelin's for Jazmin and he'd every intention of reconnectin' after he made it back to Santa Rosa with his season's earnin's. "He knew somethin' was wrong when his emails went unanswered durin' the holidays and after," Bobby said. "Poor kid has little more to go on than we do."

If all this was not nearly enough to set my rusty alarm bells ringin', my sister had decided to make this her moment to hit on Marcus, the first unfortunate guy to cross her newly single path.

That's Maggie for ya. What she wants she gets. I don't know why I never saw this one comin' when Bobby told me he'd invited Marcus over. It may sound harsh for me to say it, but knowin' how she reels 'em in with her flirtatious ways, any decent lookin', unsuspectin' dude stuck out here in the boonies would be easy prey for the likes of my sister. The look on his face when she'd walked through the door said it all.

"Don't mess with him, Maggie," I warned her, as we packed up the truck. "I swear to God, he's one of the good guys." For her part, she totally denied startin' anythin' at all.

"For God's sake, Bridget," she'd said. "Ease up. Romance is the last thing I'm looking for."

Whatever. So now we were four. Group therapy on the road — could things get anymore fuckin' complicated? Me and Bobby, my sis' and Bobby's love struck best buddy sounded like a recipe for trouble to me.

I looked over at the guys as they were lockin' up, the two of 'em haulin' an ancient, grimy ol' Coleman cooler between 'em, the pair havin' bonded as brothers of sorts since rehab. Marcus bein' the younger of the two, poor baby, was real messed up back then. His was a common tale. He'd come back to the States from a tour of Afghanistan with post-traumatic stress disorder for good measure as well as a disability discharge in his back pocket.

His grandfather that raised him, passed, while Marcus had been servin' overseas. The kid had no place to live, no backup money, nothin'. Marcus had not a single soul to look out for him other than the folk at the veteran's hospital. It was durin' that time that he'd come accustomed to gettin' loaded in order to handle the physical and mental pain he was dealin' with. Marcus might have had a fancy new leg, but a part of him, his soul, that is, he surely left there in the mountains of Afghanistan, blown to smithereens, a classic narc addict in the makin' Bobby said.

He wound up in Sonoma County coming from a VA rehabilitation facility across the bay in Martinez, searchin' for someplace well hidden to hole up off the grid. He chose to hide out in a redwood grove on the Russian River after he set up camp and by the grace of God he had managed to keep from dyin' out there durin' those first few summer months.

Folk in this region's non-profit outreach groups scour the land from time to time lookin' out for ex-military men and the occasional former armed forces woman like Marcus. Plenty of 'em go underground in whatever their freaked out post-combat condition.

They sure don't print those pictures in the military recruitment brochures, do they? Hell no. A kindly group of volunteer counselors pulled Marcus out of the forest. Lucky for him, these people know what to look for, the right way to approach an ex-soldier. As fate had it, he was placed in the exact same drug and alcohol rehab center where Bobby was and just in time. Marcus had resorted to the street heroin that's way more accessible amongst the homeless. Many like him switch to heroin when the prescription drugs are done and illegal opiate supplies dry up — sad truth is the heroin costs less and is way more deadly.

Bobby took Marcus under his wing. He'd seen how opiate addiction opened the door to friends who were snortin' or injectin' heroin and, over the years and as I've said, we'd both lost count of folk we'd hung out with who eventually died from overdosin'. Thing is, Bobby never judged. He knew the lay of the land and how best to help his young buddy take steps to deal with his demons.

Settin' Marcus up with the park job after rehab was hands down one of the best thing Bobby ever did. Unlike most guys his age, the kid was happy with an isolated, outdoor existence, far from the rat race and temptations of civilian life, I guess. Marcus was well in his comfort zone out there in the wild. We felt protective of him, Bobby and me, both, what with no family to look out for his welfare and Marcus bein' high risk for relapse, due to the PTSD. He'd come a long way in the years since, contented out there all on his own, an occasional woman to warm his body with, I heard, though no one he'd brought to the house.

If the dude was about to drop a lifetime's reserve, why did it have to be my sister? I could not fathom it, despite her more obvious charms. Maggie later insisted it was Marcus who made the first move. Right, like she never gave him the come-on, shakin' her hair loose down over her shoulders like she did, battin' those dark eyelashes over her flashin' green come-hither eyes.

Anyways, since he has agreed to hitch a ride on our worry wagon, he sure has taken on a whole fresh set of troubles for himself, though none of them his makin'. He keeps on sayin' he shoulda known better but it was not his sole decision to make and I only had so much energy that day to deal with the choices we did make.

I took the opportunity to survey my baby sister from my position on the back seat of Marcus' truck. It must have been a good two decades or more since we'd driven in the same vehicle, she and me. Though my memory flashes in and out from the aftereffects of my treatment, I remember tellin' myself to quit frettin' on what the hell Maggie's plans were for the long haul and let her get on with it. The only thing I had the bandwidth for was figurin' out the trackin' down of my daughter.

And besides, it was Marcus who knew his way around the forest. He was the one to take the lead. I watched as he shifted into gear without ever grindin' the clutch. Marcus' truck bein' manual transmission like the old man's, prompted me to make a mental note to re-register the ol' rust bucket if Maggie was plannin' on sticking around awhile. Forget all her talk of the self-drivin' vehicles startin' to take over in San Francisco. Every fool oughta know how to drive stick shift. I'd been about to get Mia behind that ol' wheel when I fell sick.

"I've been thinkin'," I announced after I came up with the one plan I shoulda absolutely enforced. "We oughta switch things up regardin' our route, before we're too far in," I said. I was all for drivin' directly east into Petaluma, catchin' highway 101 and headin' north on the freeway, avoidin' any potential trouble along the coast. "It's too darn unpredictable in this weather," I warned.

It was Bobby who was the more stubborn-headed, damn well insistin' we stick to our original plan to forge on up the rugged pathway of Highway 1, the Pacific Coast road.

"It's gonna be dicey whichever way we head," he said. "If we take the 101 back, Bridg' we'll have covered all routes out on the off chance someone along the way may have news on their whereabouts."

Bobby and me, when had we ever sat in the back seat together, holdin' hands like a couple of smitten teenagers? I snuggled into his warm, tobacco-scented, fleece-clad and oh so familiar bulk.

With Marcus in the driver's seat, Maggie rode shotgun. She wore a real dopey look on her face as she twisted around, dealin' me a grin like she was the teenage girl who'd landed a date with the hottest dude in high school. She was so darn obviously stoked, it was hard for me to stifle a smile.

Instead, I relaxed my body into Bobby's arms as best I was able, dog-tired from all the preparations and the last minute shuttin' up of the ranch. I caught sight of myself in the rearview mirror. The strain of the past six months had caught itself up, etched into a deep crevice of fresh lines across my forehead and smaller, spindly ones around my eyes. My cheeks were sunken and my skin lacked the color that Bobby used to say gave me the sorta "country girl complexion" he had a weakness for. I discreetly pinched at the skin above my cheekbones but it made little difference.

"Rest up a little, Bridget," Maggie said, turnin' to me a second time. "We're in this together now," she said, softenin' her tone, reachin' out and squeezin' my hand in hers. She, for one, appeared the picture of health despite her worries and woes. Flushed, with the first throws of infatuation, I guess.

We drove past a cluster of giant volcanic rocks, those familiar, monolithic boulders that mark so much of the land out here. These hulkin' lumps, nature's monuments to the past, are scattered in random spots across western Sonoma and Marin counties. Tidal patterns and waves shaped these strange, stone sentinels back in a time when sea levels were said to be so high they sat below sea level.

"What was it the old folk used to tell us about these rocks, Maggie?" I asked. "Somethin' about the wooly mammoths, long extinct, rubbin' the rock surface smooth with centuries of groomin'?"

"Ha," Maggie answered. "I do remember. Scientists dubbed this stretch of the coastline the Sonoma Serengeti, if I remember right, seeing as it once rivaled the African plains for wildlife?"

Bobby hacked his nasty, chesty cough into the fold of his shirt-sleeve. I was well aware he was havin' issues from the heavy tobacco smokin' he did when he was not around me and yet I kept my concerns to myself. One of us sick was enough. He piped in with his take on what he termed as his local knowledge of natural phenomena:

"And to think, it was commonplace for packs of saber-toothed tigers to hide out behind these stones," he said. "Wild."

"What was it made all of that wonderful ancient wildlife vanish?" I asked.

"Climate, I guess," Bobby piped in.

Maggie and Mia — hadn't they upped and gone and vanished on me, the minute they'd each turned eighteen? Maybe it was the climate that drove them away, also, the prospect of more miserable winter months. I rubbed the steamy glass with the back of my hand and watched the waves crash onto shore. The Pacific Ocean is as perilous as it is breathtakin'. You'd better believe it.

Those unfamiliar with the sleeper waves, the riptides and the sheer, relentless power of those deep, dark, swirlin' currents beneath, have so little idea how truly dangerous it is to dawdle on the rocks, which reminded me, we were coming up to the same craggy point where Mia and me once witnessed a dramatic helicopter rescue back when she was in junior high.

We'd taken a spontaneous mother-daughter afternoon road trip up the coast, one of those rare, balmy evenin's in summer when I was not needed at the roadhouse. It was a rare event for me to pack a picnic for the two of us and we'd set up on the rocky bluff at the top of Bodega Head in time to watch the sunset from our foldout chairs. While we were happily munchin' on our supper of egg salad sandwiches with a pickle apiece, a teenage boy wearin' nothin' but a baseball cap and swim shorts hauled himself over the top of the cliff edge some 20 feet ahead.

We could see straight off that the scrawny kid, not a lot older than Mia, was close to hyperventilatin', havin' clearly been in one heck of a precarious position on the other side of the cliff. Thank the Lord the cliff was not more sheer, or there was no way he would have made it to the top. Still, there was little substantial ledge to grab a hold of. It struck me that nobody in half a right mind would make an attempt at such a climb. Unless it was his only option.

He gestured wildly when he set eyes on us, unable to spit his words out, sheer panic written all over his face. I had no instinct to be a hero or nothin', though I carefully approached the cliff edge to take a look for myself as to what was goin' on down there in the surgin' ocean.

Sure enough, two more boys about the same age and size were clingin' to the cliff, one of them about 15 feet down, the other, closer to 50. I clapped a hand to my mouth. Below them, the frigid Pacific surf crashed against a series of smaller rocks.

"Call nine one one," the kid who'd made it to the top screamed and hollered as he caught his breath. "We need help, oh God, they might not make it up."

I pulled my phone from my backpack and dialed with shaky fingers, a mixture of massive relief and surprise runnin' through my veins the second the call went through. The sheriff's department's helicopter, Henry 1 hovered overhead in what felt like time suspended. The Coast Guard, state park rangers, Bodega Bay Fire Department, the whole nine yards of emergency services appeared in what felt like seconds to assist the helicopter crew.

Dozens of volunteers pulled into the cliff edge parkin' lot in a dusty caravan of cars, trucks and motorcycles. The first boy, who we had hastily cocooned in our picnic blanket to calm him from his uncontrollable shiverin' rallied and called down to his friends as they clung on for dear life: "Don't move. Hold on. Hold on," he cried.

I was almost sure one or both of the boys was gonna make a wrong move. As it turned out, I read in the paper later, the three young bucks were celebratin' the boy with the baseball cap's passin' his driver's test when they made a series of foolish choices, not least takin' a hike down a steep cliffside trail to the beach below to smoke a joint and nap. By the time they'd been rudely awoken by the risin' tide, there was no trail no more. They were stranded. Between them, they'd figured their only chance was to climb. It was the driver who made it to the top, though who knows how the hell he did it. "I had to save us, somehow," the kid was quoted in the article.

The crew of Henry 1 had made a swift assessment of the situation by flyin' in a deputy officer on one of those long-line rescue apparatus. We'd watched, openmouthed, silent, as darkness fell, us and the whole big crowd that had assembled, as the deputy secured the teen who was closer to the top of the cliff in a rescue device, haulin' him to where we were gathered within safe distance of the edge.

This second one buckled at the knees and wept. Mia stepped forward to comfort him just as, unbeknownst to us, the remainin' boy on the crumblin' cliff changed position, causin' rocks to slide beneath his feet. To everyone's immense relief, we learned how the superhero deputy made it back down within a minute of that poor kid losin' his footin' entirely. The crowd let out a huge roar of cheers and applause as the third boy was dropped to the safety of his bawlin' friends.

Fresh tears welled in my eyes as we drove by the site of where it had happened. Mia had promised me, as I was drivin' home later that night, each of us still shakin' that I need not ever worry on her account — she'd never do a thing as stupid as that. And to think I had believed her. Anyways, I'd say I am a fatalist by now. When it's your time, it's your time. We all do the dumbest things. There's no real sense in it.

~

It was Bobby who brought up the subject of other real and present dangers that lurk along the coast. He always was obsessed with earthquakes, primarily the San Andreas Fault that runs directly beneath us out west. The guy had a morbid fascination with the rumbles of our region's epic and infamous earthquake culture. He was ready, almost willin' for the big one that we all know is on its way and soon.

I sat back and humored him as he rattled on in his usual fashion, though I'd heard it all too many times before to count. "You know," he said, this time: "Back in the great quake of 1906, the earth shook so violently it pushed the land mass north some fifteen feet." We all four gawped at the road ahead, half expectin' it to crack apart and shoot us off the slick, wet cliff.

Maggie, Marcus and me were his captive audience: "Imagine it like this," he said. "If you were to place two slices of pizza on a countertop and slide them by each other at the part where they touch at the two straight sides," he was reachin' forward to demonstrate or mimic the movement with his hands, "chunks of toppin' would soon start breakin' off one slice and topplin' on to the other. The same thing happens with earth and trees and structures atop the San Andreas as the slidin' boundary between the Pacific Plate and the North American Plate shift."

This was not what I needed to hear right then. It's not that I don't think it's gonna happen. I had other, more pressin' concerns and the brain can only take so much. "What we have here, folks, is a fault that has the capacity to slice the great state of California in two," he declared: "all the way from the border of Mexico to Cape Mendocino in the north."

Marcus egged him on in this banter on tectonic plates. "It's true, brother," he said. "These plates you're talking of, they yield the very real potential for massive damage. People don't like to acknowledge it." This was another of the things the two friends had in common, their tendency toward earthquake preparedness. Today, tomorrow, ten years from now, Bobby's box of emergency supplies won't make much of a difference however much he liked to think it would.

"Take the '06 earthquake trail in Olema," Marcus went on, despite my attempts to shush the pair of 'em. "You won't find a better spot to see the effect of just how far the earth moved. Most of the wake is covered in brush by now, though I know where to look if you really want to see it."

"Thanks for the scary-ass geology lesson, guys," I butted in, raisin' my voice so they knew I meant it. "I am feelin' like I know all I need to on the subject for now," I said. "We've lived our whole lives tryin' not to freak out about the next one, Maggie and me. We are not in need of any more constant reminders at this particular moment in time."

"Babe, you're livin' in a bubble of denial when it comes to quakes," Bobby shot back. "The San Andreas is not the least of it. Do you have any idea how many other plates there are to threaten us out here?"

I fixed my gaze on the ominous, blue-violet sky. Bobby was dogmatic at times.

"OK, really, enough," I snapped, turning my head to look out of the window, willin' him to hush. "Fuck." Marcus fiddled with the airflow to let in some air.

We were about to pass by the crab shack, the one that Bobby and me liked to drive out to every once in a while on the occasions when we were off work together, before I was sick. I figured Bobby would be easily sidetracked by the prospect of fresh seafood. It was me who suggested we stop off for a bite.

The cheerful little crab shack was packed with noisy commercial fishing crews comin' in out of the rain for mornin' coffee and donuts, chili and chowder, hot dogs and crab sandwiches.

We feasted, the four of us, in the cozy confine of the truck, over-lookin' scenic Bodega Head, half keepin' watch for the spurt of the Western Pacific Gray Whales that journey to and from the warmer calfin' lagoons of the Mexican waters from December through March. I bit into a fresh crab sandwich, its toasted, buttery juices running down my fingers onto a stack of paper towels I'd knowingly stacked on my lap. I believe it was the first time in months I'd felt my facial muscles relax.

Food had never tasted so good, truly, a sense of something like hope rose through me from the stomach up. I was gonna make it, Mia was gonna make it. It was OK to enjoy the sandwich, I told myself. It would all be OK.

Back on the road, it was Marcus who broached the subject of his work along the National seashore and how unlawful cannabis grows are tendin' to encroach more and more on the parkland. "I'm forever on the look-out for roads and vegetation that's been clear cut for access to these illegal grows," he said, explaining how a big part of his job to preserve the coastal wilderness is protecting it from increasing numbers of rogue grow cannabis operations.

"Wherever I am, in any open space, I can't help but keep my eyes peeled for telltale signs," he explained, as he filled us in on how illegal grow sites are more often than not blatantly poisonous — pesticides and herbicides wipin' out the habitat, leachin' into groundwater, pollutin' waterways, poisonin' insects, birds and animals. I'd never heard him talk so much.

Marcus fears that most at risk are the endangered woodland creatures. "Human waste, abandoned garbage, fertilizers and other hazardous materials take vast amounts of time and money to contain and clear up and more often than not they're left to rot," he said. "These are toxic disaster zones for wildlife."

"Makes me mad as hell to hear it . . . " Bobby muttered. If there was one thing he'd retained from his family's ranchin' background, it was his deep respect for nature.

"Those at the start of it all, back in San Francisco in the Summer of Love, they were communal-minded folk and most of the growers still are," Marcus added. "They were folk like me, wanting nothing from no one, not least the government. They set about leaving the City and making themselves invisible," he said. "Survival depended on living in as sustainable a way as possible. The first growers produced most of their own food, they hunted, fished and figured out how to bring in pot-growing supplies without raising suspicions in town."

It was these first, underground, back-to-the-landers who settled the forested regions of northernmost California, raisin' their kids and now, later, their grandkids.

Not much different from my own folk, I reasoned. Once they'd put down their roots, they were fully entrenched on their land. These northern neighbors, homesteaders of the '60s and '70s soon figured which specific crops and farmin' methods made the most money. Sadly, loggin', millin', dairy farmin' . . . all but a few of these regional strongholds since reduced to relics of our proud agricultural heritage.

Marcus kept on, still, talkin' of how outta hand it's all become, how he's found water lines buried underground when stumblin' on illegal cannabis grows planted in partial shade and hidden under Manzanita bushes on some of the hardiest hillsides of the national seashore.

Maggie opened the window a sliver for a lungful of damp air. She'd tied her dark curls up into a ponytail. There is barely a silver thread runnin' through her head of hair, lucky bitch. Marcus was steady and focused in his drivin', handlin' the slick curves of the road with ease.

"Let's get real. Who, here, was a stoner in high school, other than my sister?" Maggie asked.

It was Marcus who answered her first. "Not me, on account of my being a jock. We snuck beers in after games with no choice but to steer clear of weed." He'd been relatively clean of substances in the army, until the incident, he added. "If I'd failed a drug test, I would have been at risk of a pay cut at the least, a cut in rank, slammed in military prison, kicked out."

Bobby freely admitted he'd been introduced to weed by the age of fourteen. He'd had his fill of it as well as downin' a potent concoction of spirits — whiskey, vodka even the cookin' sherry from his mother's pantry, whatever it was he'd laid his hands on.

I'm dead sure I would have known if Mia was smokin' while she was at home. She hadn't gotten into it in high school as far as I could tell. She took after Maggie in that way. Maybe it was the reverse psychology of havin' a stoner for a mom.

Me, on the other hand, I'd smoked like a chimney since I was in junior high. On and off in that I managed to quit for the time I was pregnant and almost a year of breastfeedin'. I've finally been able to wean my way off smokin' since makin' and experimentin' with my edibles, figurin' out lower dosage and frequency of dependency so as to get better and go about my business. As with any addiction, caffeine, tobacco, alcohol, gamblin', even sex, I guess, withdrawal is just as much a big deal for longtime weed smokers like me. Dependent dosin' was maskin' what was really wrong and after Mia took off, I started to wake up to what I was doin' to myself and my family, or not doin'. It's taken me to this point in my life, 50 years old, for fuck's sake to face the fact I'm a weed addict, however I choose to justify it. And it was the same weed that lured my baby away from me. It was past time to get it all out in the open, to start takin' more control of my life and, unbeknownst to me, I was headed into the eye of the storm with little clue as to the consequences.

Chapter 16

Jazmin

So, if you really wanna know, this is how it went down.

Mia and I look kinda similar. Her skin and her hair are as dark as mine on account of her dad being Mexican, who, by the way, she has never even met. She has eyes the color of toasted nuts, amber sorta, while mine are more of a deep chocolate brown. That's pretty much where the similarity stops. I've had plenty of fun teasing her for being one wild chica due to the Irish/Mexican hot-blooded combo that runs through her veins. Mia's mom's folks go back generations on that ol' ranch of theirs and whatever she has to deal with in the future, she knows, in the back of her mind, she has that to run back to. Me, I'm way more reserved in comparison to Mia on account of my family being uprooted from the country of my birth. I never did care for drawing too much attention to myself, except, I guess, when it came to Miguel. Aside from Mia, man, he really got me there while it lasted.

"Stay in the shadows," that's what my mom has told me since I was a little girl. Keep out of trouble — so much for that.

"Fuck the shadows and fuck the expectations," Mia said. Her mom, my folks, none of 'em knew a thing about making the sort of serious money we had in mind.

"Let's get outta here, see a bit of action, make some dough," Mia urged.

I was not so sure. She pushed me and I'm not laying any blame, I was happy to let her. Mia warned me over and over if I stayed home, I'd be knocked-up in no time, a trail of sticky-fingered little ones holding me back, dragging me down, stopping me from getting into nursing school.

Hell no, I'd said. I'll go.

My family, they're the brave ones. I mean, would you have the guts to cross a border with your kids for a better life the same way they did? Would you hold on tight to their little hands, all the while afraid of 'em being ripped apart from you, forced as they are being today into some unknown child custody facility, those hideous camps in empty Walmart buildings in some unknown hellhole of America? I was just a small child at the time, yet I remember our crossing as if it was yesterday. Who could forget such a thing? We all know by now that horrible stuff happens all the time to families like mine, those who are so desperate for a chance to live a good life they'll go so far as to sign up for some shit-show smuggling operation through the rugged border terrain.

We were the lucky ones. I've had plenty of time this past winter to think about the sacrifices my parents made for me to be here. All I've dreamed of these past months is walking back into our tiny apartment or waiting at the gates of the elementary school for my brothers and sisters to get out of class and gather them into my arms, spill my warm tears of regret into their soft hair. I would have given anything to turn back the clock and go back to working those goddamn early mornings with my mom. If my foolish actions bring an end to all their hopes and dreams I will never forgive myself. That's why I have to fight it out. Be smart.

Those first, happy-go-lucky summer months after graduation, they were the last of our childhood, Mia and me. Before the shameful, screwed-up introduction to adulthood we'd naively gone looking for. There is no going back. I'm sorry to say it all happened for real and it went from being a stupid idea to truth when I grabbed my backpack from under the bed in the dead of night.

"Pack your cut-offs and a bikini top." Mia had been clear in her instructions. "We won't be needing a whole bunch of clothes where we're going."

I'd never owned a bikini. Not in my house, no way, no how. My dad, he'd have been madder than hell at me showing myself off in a skimpy two-piece like the one Mia bought on sale from Target.

She gave me an old one she'd worn in the summer of junior high, poking fun in that it was: "Small enough for your little boobies."

Mia's a whole lot bigger than me in that department, she's taller and sturdier in general, which proved a good thing in a way given what she in particular has been put through. To think how she'd claimed her stack would prove our security in getting us hired. How we'd laughed, so fucking clueless, I tell you. I, for one, had planned on keeping my chest semi-covered, at least until I met up with Miguel.

"There's extra pay for trimming topless," Mia had only half joked. "Don't worry, J, we'll keep 'em undercover," she promised.

Mia packed a few pieces of basic makeup in the front zipper pocket of her backpack. I did the same, even though our drugstore mascara and lipstick stash was not on her official list. We planned on looking good for the hiring. "In case there are busloads of bitches jostling for the best pay and conditions. Scissor drifters," she'd heard. "Trim bitches" — paid by the pound of pot, trimming up to sixteen hours a day.

We'd stolen off while it was still dark, two hours before my folks woke up. I'm sorry to say there was barely a thought between us for the chaos we were about to cause. We managed to hitch a ride up the coast to Jenner at daybreak with few questions asked by two chicks not much older than us who were driving to work at one of the lonely old inns on the side of the ocean.

I was stoked at the thought of making big money for the first time in my life. And there was the extra bonus of having Miguel to myself with no parents and no curfew to keep us apart. We'd done the deed already, Miguel and me, two times, me lying on his jacket in the dunes on the beach and him fumbling about in the dark.

One of the girls who'd given us that first ride reckoned the quickest way up north to the big weed farms was to get off the coastal road and cut across to the main highway. We'd walked a fair ways beside the Russian River before scoring a second ride to Santa Rosa. It was an old couple that picked us up in their beat-up station wagon that was so full of junk we barely fit. We took in the early fall scenery as we wove through redwood groves and alongside fields of grapevines, heavy with low-hanging fruit.

We soon changed our minds on hitchhiking all the way up to Humboldt, foolishly blowing most of our cash on a forty dollar apiece Greyhound ride all the way to the small town of Garberville, which, we discovered that evening, straddles the south fork of the Eel River.

I've never in my life seen a place as strange as this. Guys, girls, most of them a few years older than us, were hanging out in big, rowdy groups, some of them stringing up a mess of jewelry for sale along the main street, others juggling or playing guitars as they sat around in circles of dusty backpacks with scary-looking dogs. The stink of weed was everywhere.

"This is what they call a one-horse town," Mia said. Population just shy of around a thousand according to the first city limit sign we saw, though that number looked to have swollen by who knows how many with so many hopeful trimmers in town.

We'd landed in a crazy cowboy movie gone wrong. I'd best describe it as a mix of a western set meets hobo-punk/zombie apocalypse.

The crowd made a racket, a competing mix of live and recorded beats loud enough to wake the dead. How many ukuleles and banjos and covers of Somewhere Over The Rainbow can you fit into one city block?

Mia and me, we stuck out like two sore thumbs, though neither of us said so, but I knew she was thinking the same thing as me by the little she was saying and the look on her face.

The music and sounds of all these mismatched free spirits and stoners carried on the wind that rushed through the mass of redwood trees. It's easy to act like you're too big for your boots 'til you're forced to fend for yourself. For the first time since we'd made our plan, the hair rose on my forearms. I felt small and vulnerable.

"Who the heck's gonna hire all these wild looking dudes? What if Miguel never shows?" I started to panic. I couldn't figure how in hell we'd ever manage to get ourselves noticed in such a mob scene. I suggested we head into the restroom in one of the coffee shops on the main street to make ourselves up, maybe if we were more appealing looking, older, we'd have a better chance of fitting in.

"No backpacks," barked a ropy-looking woman with a bony face and a long, thin, ponytail that hung, limply, like a rat's tail from under her purple faded baseball cap. The coffee shop was half empty and despite the late hour and its sketch proprietor, an aroma of powdered donuts and fresh coffee was hard to resist. We were hungry and tired and left with little choice but to make an about turn and walk back outside into the mob. We didn't have a chance to pee, let alone fill our faces before applying the battle paint.

Handmade signs filled the bustling street scene. A crowd of loudmouths jostled for position on the sidewalk in front, spilling us into the street. Mia announced if Miguel was a no-show the next day, we'd have to work on finding ourselves an attention-seeking gimmick to set us apart.

"I'm not sure about this anymore, Mia," I admitted, tears welling. "Let's just forget it happened, head back on board the next bus south."

She looked at me like I was a dumb-ass: "Do you have a stash tucked away somewhere, babe, 'cuz I sure don't?"

We'd splashed the last of our cash on sandwiches for the bus and a couple of cheapo sleeping bags in the hardware store when we'd arrived. All we had was a few dollars left between us. We'd been foolish to think it would all be so easy and now we were stuck. I missed the little ones, already, their small hands reaching out for me to comfort them at bedtime, pleading with me to tell them one more story.

"Buck up, Jaz. If Miguel is a no-show, there's always the bikini top move," Mia said, eyeing me for my reaction.

It didn't sit right with me, chicks of all shapes and sizes, their suntanned bodies barely covered, bouncing around in the street in broad daylight for anyone to see. I felt sick. As much as it was making me uncomfortable, Mia didn't appear to be as bothered as me.

"Chill out," she urged. "And don't you dare cry." She could see I was getting myself into more of a state by the advancing hour. "We'll stick to the mom and pop farms, it's fine, J, I promise, don't get cold feet."

She made me pledge, palm to palm that we'd stick together, whatever. She said I'd be sick of the sight of her by the time we were done making the big bucks.

At dusk we scoped out a spot down by the river, setting ourselves up with a makeshift camp on the rocky shore. All I could think of was home and my cozy bed where, if I'd had any sense, I should have been cuddled up with the little ones.

Giant redwoods lined the distant horizon. I felt even smaller than I had earlier and lost and far from home.

After dark, the bugs had bit at us so bad we covered our heads with our towels. People were partying while a few around us looked at least to be attempting to sleep.

"We'd best be on a farm and undercover by this time tomorrow," I told Mia, "or I'm outta here, even if I have to walk back home."

I thought about the clerk in the hardware store and how he'd asked us if we wanted to buy a raffle ticket for a rifle draw. He must have been my grandfather's age. And he had to know what we were doing here. We'd wandered wide-eyed through aisles stacked with two-way radio sets, propane stoves, canteens, knives, guns, camouflage, all sorts of shit, every type of military gear imaginable.

"You never mentioned us being headed for the jungle," I whispered to Mia in the store. It had never occurred to me to pack a weapon of some sort and anyway where would I have got ahold of one? After dark, I'd found myself wishing I'd slipped a pocketknife into my backpack for self-defense without the store clerk catching me pilfering the stock.

Some time during the night I woke to the sound of footsteps crunching on the rocks at the foot of my sleeping bag. There was just enough moonlight for me to make out the silhouette of a dude with long, matted hair as he set his blanket and a ratty old sleeping bag way too close to mine. Seeing as we were not alone on the riverbank, I hoped to God there was safety in numbers.

Still, I wasn't sure what to do, make a fuss and piss him off by asking him to move over or simply try to fake sleep? I decided if he dared come even a step closer I would bash him in the head with the nearest rock. I slid myself down deeper into my sleeping bag and turned slowly, uncomfortably onto my side, placing my back to him so that he could not see my face. The slow murmur of the running river and the wind in the trees failed to drown out the noise of partiers downstream. I barely slept a wink.

People were in the river in their underwear soon after daylight, a few of them naked, others semi-clothed. I'd never seen anything like it, guys and girls dipping their dreads in the cool, murky, river water, washing the dust away from another night on the rocky riverbank.

Mia said we'd best take a dip ourselves as soon as the morning fog rolled off. "Wait until it warms up a bit," she said. "And don't worry, we'll keep our clothes on."

I watched a heavyset woman wearing nothing but an oversized white Grateful Dead shirt and dingy white panties wash her face at the river's edge. Here was another crucial thing I hadn't thought about. I can barely swim. I'd been in the Russian River only once or twice in the summer months, just often enough to learn basic dog paddle and that was it.

My mom, she stayed home on all those Labor Day holidays when my dad would take us kids to the river. I remembered with a pang how she welcomed us back at sundown with Champurrado — a warm, thick and delicious drink she made with corn masa, milk and hot chocolate. How tired and sun-kissed and happy we'd been from our splashing about in the water. It made my heart ache to think of it, that morning. What I wouldn't have given for a warm shower and a mug of hot chocolate.

"Today's the day," Mia declared. "Miguel or no Miguel, we're going to get ourselves hired." She broke a granola bar she'd dug from her backpack in two halves and we scarfed our meager breakfast. "We can't last long like this," she said. My tummy grumbled in agreement.

We washed beneath the green, swaying grasses of the river, in our shorts and T-shirts, underwear and all. I stayed close to the edge so as not to slip into the stronger current of the deeper water. The river was cool and refreshing under the warm sun.

"Let's look for a bush to change into our bikini tops and shorts," Mia instructed, as we balanced barefoot on the slippery rocks of the riverbank. We watched out for each other's privacy as we put on dry clothes in turn.

After we'd freshened up and dressed, or half-dressed, more like, we readied for another attempt in tackling this strange and mysterious place, not the Northern California either of us were familiar with. We walked into town and searched out a shaded spot in the company of a couple dozen or more hopeful kids closer to our age.

Hours passed. It was a hot and airless day. No sign of Miguel.

A girl in a sundress with a shaved head and a full sleeve tattoo of multicolored butterflies announced she was headed to a soup kitchen a couple blocks away. "First timers?" she asked. I nodded, nervously, expecting her to laugh, but she only smiled.

"If you're hungry, you'd best make it zippy," she said. "Food runs out fast." We tagged along with her and a couple of Canadian chicks, blonde and athletic looking in comparison to the butterflied skinhead who was busy inviting us to meditate and do yoga on the riverbank later. Mia looked up at me and rolled her eyes. I barely stifled my giggles.

One of the Canadian girls directed her attention at Mia and me. "Free food is free food, honey," she said. "A rare gift in the U.S. being given something for nothing." Mia and me wolfed down the chicken salad sandwiches we gladly accepted from the outstretched hand of a kindly old guy serving from the shadowy inside of the soup kitchen window. We stuffed our faces in minutes, half way down the block.

Shortly after noon as we anxiously awaited Miguel's showing up, we practically willed it so. We had arranged to meet outside of the hardware store the previous afternoon and he'd said if there was a problem with his schedule, we were to wait there again the following day. I hoped to God he wouldn't let us down that second afternoon, me, especially.

I can't tell you how relieved I was when I spotted him springing out of a truck parked a little ways down the block. He stood there in the shade of a tree on the sidewalk, stick thin in his big old cowboy hat and boots, scoping out the scene like he owned the place.

"Jesus, are you kidding? This place, Miguel, oh my God, it's so freaky," I said, throwing my arms around him. Hot tears welled in my eyes. I linked my arm through his. I could've jumped for joy I was so happy. Miguel's lean, tan face broke into a broad smile. "Let's go, Bonita," he said, grabbing my backpack.

There was no dust on us, Mia and me, as we hopped up into the back of the truck that was being driven by and belonging to a chick named Ruby, a coworker of Miguel's who he introduced to us as having been at the farm with him the previous year.

"Bruce and Bonnie and their daughter, Fern, the folk who own the farm, you'll see, they're real good people," Miguel said. "They've been growing the good stuff, plenty of it, mostly indoors in greenhouses, for years. There's nothing to worry about. It's real safe."

She was totally rad looking, Ruby — real small, with spiky, violet hair shaved off at the sides. From my seat in the back, I was able to checkout the gages in her ears, her lip and nose piercings visible from the rearview mirror and the tattoos that were etched on the backs of her hands as she turned the wheel. A small half moon and star was inked on the back of her neck. This short boss chick in her big ol' truck was something else and for the first time since we'd made it to Garberville, I was excited to be invited to be a part of their scene.

Ruby was raised on the East Coast, Boston area, she said. She was real open with us, though we'd never even asked as much as she hauled ass around the corner onto the main street and out through town, rattling on, all cheerful, telling us how it was she'd made her way out West to study art in Santa Cruz two years prior. It was there that she'd discovered the weed-trimming gig soon after she arrived.

"First year I trimmed in the Santa Cruz Mountains," she said. "Last year, I met Fern through mutual friends and me and a bunch of girlfriends came up to trim at her folk's place for a working vacation. As soon as school is set to start at the end of September we take off back to Santa Cruz."

Mia said, smiling like she got it: "We're planning on heading back to school ourselves."

"Gro-hoes is the game in the meantime," Ruby said. "Beats stripping in order to pay for school."

It was Ruby who outlined the lay of the land as she drove a good half hour on a super intense series of twisty turns through heavy forestland. "Bruce and Bonnie hire the guys to harvest and haul. It's us girls who trim," she said. "A sexist industry and culture some might say, for sure. But I prefer to think of it as making serious inroads as women getting into the business, building our nest eggs, biding our time."

Miguel turned his fine head and grinned at me, the sunkissed skin around his eyes crinkling at the corners. It was a massive relief to be with him at last. And he seemed just as pleased to have made it happen, more or less as planned. "Bonnie and Bruce have been at it so long they grow their crop in record time," he said. "It's a lot of work."

"Growing indoors speeds up the process," Ruby explained. "Right now, as we speak, the guys are harvesting the early crop, hanging the branches up to dry. We'll be trimming shortly," she said. "Good timing, girls, we'll be needing your help."

We listened, though we knew so little of it, as Ruby and Miguel discussed the value of being ahead of the market when it came to moving product south.

"It's critical to beat the rush," Ruby turned to explain. "Otherwise, the bosses will go out of business. It's a big worry for these mom and pop grows," she said. "So much competition and if we're late, then, basically, we all get paid a whole lot less per pound."

It was hot and humid. Ruby rolled down all four of the truck's windows in an attempt to keep us all as well as the supplies she'd picked up in town, as cool as possible. "Forget about air conditioning," she said. My skin was sticky, the truck cabin as muggy as the inside of an oven. The still air from outside barely cut through a potent aroma of body odor, liquor, sunscreen and whatever assortment of perishable foods Ruby and Miguel had stashed in the back.

Ruby pulled up in front of a high fence with a heavy set of double gates positioned a long ways up a steep green, rocky mountain-logging road several miles off the paved road. Miguel jumped out to unlock the gates by tapping a code into a black metal box. I felt a mixture of something like fear and relief run through my veins.

Bruce and Bonnie's place appeared pretty basic at first sight, a small ranch house with a bunch of sturdy looking cherry trees set around, the type that would burst into fluffy pink blossoms come April or May.

A group of tarp-covered camper vans, six or seven tents, four-wheelers and water tanks were scattered around the far side of the house, backing onto a barnlike structure. A young, dark-skinned guy was hanging laundry on a line tied between two trees.

"This is home sweet home for the next couple of months, ladies," Ruby announced. "We have a whole bunch of tents and air mattresses, not all of them occupied, take your pick, you'll find it comfortable enough. Mia watched the laundry guy at work. "Look at that, Jazmin," she remarked: "the men do their own laundry here." She laughed. Ruby turned: "Something you'll learn here pretty quick," she said. "If you don't pitch in, you're out."

They took off out of the truck ahead, leaving me with Miguel.

Barking dogs and a flock of chickens roamed free. "Where do we wash?" I asked, thinking back to the cool brown waters of the river earlier that morning.

"There's a single shower stall and toilet off the drying barn," Miguel answered. "We take it in turns, it works out."

I overheard Ruby talking to Mia up ahead.

"Real nice bunch of guys, Miguel and his buddies," Ruby said. "Otherwise, let me tell you, sweetie, if they were dicks, they'd have been outta here by now."

We met Bruce and Bonnie that afternoon. First thing they asked us was if we were eighteen.

"We want you to feel welcome," Bonnie said. "Our place is as good as it gets." Bruce told us that we would be working long, hard hours but we would be treated fairly, fed well and made to feel comfortable, safe. I noticed that Bruce took no pains to disguise the pistol he carried in his belt.

"They are doing as best they can," Ruby explained. "They're cool and they give us trimmers a fair deal." We learned that Fern, their daughter, was running the family's sideline business, a hemp boutique in a neighboring town. "There's little point in the family obtaining any medical grow permits," Ruby explained. "If shit goes down with the Feds, it'll make no difference if they're legalized or not."

Miguel had sectioned off a pullout bed big enough for Mia and me by hanging up a sheet in the same rusting RV he slept in. He had staked out his own tiny bedroom with sheets on the windows. Two more guys shared a small bedroom in the front.

I spent most nights in Miguel's bed soon after we'd settled in, the sound of others snoring a steady reminder to keep our make-outs on the down low. Though it was the first time I had spent the whole night long with a boy, to be real, Miguel was not the first guy I'd slept with in that sense. There'd been some minor action in high school. I'd kept it fully undercover from my folks. My dad would have blown a fucking fuse. This was different. I'd run away from home in part for this. And boy, at least he was worth it — while it lasted.

Part of me couldn't believe he'd waited for me. Miguel is as good to look at on the outside as he is every bit as kind and gentle on the inside. I was shocked some other chick hadn't cornered him by the time I dragged my ass up there.

It was more like we were away at camp. We were housed and fed, mostly the simple, tasty Mexican food I'm used to, tortillas, a whole load of rice and beans with fresh salads, fruit and eggs from the farm. Yes, the days were long and the work monotonous, fifteen to sixteen hours once we started trimming, but the company and the music kept us going and we were happy.

We laughed and talked and drank beer by the campfire 'til the early morning hours. I kid you not, though I do not partake, the joints they passed around were the size of beer bottles. For once in my life I felt myself growing more confident, freer by the day.

"We don't allow any funny business with our girls," Bonnie had told us, after we'd arrived. "We never hire trimmers from the street and no outside boyfriends. Anyone bothers you, uninvited, you come straight to Bruce or me."

A lot of us were hooking up. Hey, what else was there to do up there but have some fun when the long day's work was done?

Mia held off on a couple of contenders of both sexes. "Not my type," was all she'd say.

She was a little pissed at me for making it more of a thing with Miguel than she'd bargained for.

At first, I was intimidated by the speed in which the others were trimming weed into neat little nuggets. The days were hot and it stunk to high heaven of pungent skunk in the trimming shed. The only sound above the chatter of the trimmers was the whir of large ventilation fans.

A thousand pounds or more of weed was strung up inside the shed, waiting to be trimmed. We never took a single break during trimming sessions except for if we needed to pee. It was Ruby who gave Mia and me our first lesson. She handed us our own tubs and sewing scissors, aprons and a pile of plastic gloves.

"Clean off the scissors after you trim each and every bud so as not to transfer any insects or mold," she instructed. "Look out for bugs — spiders, caterpillars, they'll eat through after if you don't spot them."

It was a seriously sticky business. The first day it was all in my hair, green flakes of itchy, dry weed down my bikini top, messy goop on my shorts. The smell intensified during the trimming process once we broke open the more pungent buds.

The best way to describe being in the barn was like being on another planet, someplace where time stood still and we were the only ones. We sat in a circle as we removed the protruding leaves, carefully and slowly trimming around one dried flower bud after another.

"Make it look like a tidy, little hedge," Ruby further instructed as she kept a close eye on our early efforts. "No leaving stems too long. It's very important that each one looks the same." We watched intently as she rotated a raw bud slowly between her fingers, demonstrating the perfect shear.

Gloves kept the brown, sticky resin off our hands and we soon got the hang of dropping each trimmed bud into a big plastic container before we started in on the next one.

It was muscle aching work as far as sitting down so long. My legs ached when I stood up. I coped better with the boredom of repetition than Mia did. She never had the training I'd had in getting my head around the business of all that routine mopping and scrubbing. That girl was ill-prepared for manual labor, doing the same thing over and over, hour after hour.

Miguel was my incentive at the end of those long first days. "Hang in there, Jaz," he'd encouraged, as we lay together looking up at the moon in the early hours. Miguel told us it was almost time to start shipping it out in order to get ahead of the game. There would be bonuses involved if we trimmers worked hard to beat the rush.

Mia and I had settled into the general routine with the goal of making even more money than we'd dared hope for.

Less than two weeks into our trimming initiation, though it felt like months, we awoke in the middle of the night to the sudden sound of whirling helicopters swooping overhead. An intense search beam probed the barnyard, at once flooding the RV with a white, blinding light.

"Shit! Fuck! Wake up, everyone up," Miguel yelled, shooting out of bed, spilling a half empty box of condom packets across the floor. He grabbed his jeans and boots in an instant. "Throw some clothes on." His face was lit up by the search beam that moved on, leaving me to fall over myself as I hurriedly readied as best as I could in the dark.

"Mia", I yelled — that girl could sleep through an earthquake. She murmured in her sleep as I rushed towards her, Miguel screaming in the background ordering the others to run and leave it all behind. I shook her awake and she sprung up, slipping her feet into her dirty old tennis shoes in her half-awake confusion. We stumbled out of the RV, holding hands. It was pitch-black outside. The others were tumbling out of vehicles and tents, rubbing their eyes and looking up into the night sky. Thumping blades chopped through the star-studded darkness.

"It's a fucking bust," one the guys yelled. "Run."

I lost sight of Miguel. Mia pulled me back in through the door of the RV. "Grab your stuff," she said. "Quick."

Picture a stampede of wildebeest in one of those Netflix documentaries with the old British guy doing the voiceover. It was like we were racing through the plains of Kenya, not Northern California, running together in a group formation in our panic as we left. We ran with some of the farmhands and Ruby to start off with, Ruby, Mia and me splintering away into the trees as soon as we were out of the gate.

One of the farmhands tripped on an exposed root, howling. Ruby slowed. "Shit, we might as well face it," she said. "We always knew this could happen." Mia shook her head no and motioned at me. "She doesn't have papers," she cried. I didn't realize 'til then how much I was shaking. I had broken out in a cold sweat. Ruby stood as tall as she was able, seeming at once fully in control of her surroundings even now. "You two run, we'll distract them," she said before turning to face the law.

A bunch of U.S. Marshalls were waiting at the entrance to the property in a handful of trucks and a U-Haul van.

We watched, wordlessly, from our hiding spot as officers searched the buildings. Others set up floodlights. An officer walked in our direction and we froze. We looked back over our shoulders one last time, taking off as fast as we could run. Two officers took down Ruby and several of the guys and were handcuffing them on the ground. I looked over at the house. Bruce and Bonnie stood, watching, helplessly from the kitchen window. I guessed there was no point in running when it was your place that was under attack.

The low hovering helicopter swung its search beam through the area, casting menacing shadows amongst the trees.

I spotted a narrow clearing in the brush by the outside of the gate, and, yanking Mia by the arm, we turned back on ourselves, squeezing into the shadows of the brushy hillside as we slipped down a densely wooded dip.

Mia scraped up her knee and she whimpered slightly. The bloody rash glistened in the glow of the search beams that continued passing over us.

"Shush," I whispered. "We'll wait it out here 'til the last of them have gone in," I said. "Once they're all on the property, we'll make another run for it."

We huddled together hardly daring to breathe for fear our hiding place would be discovered. It was chilly. Mia was shivering. Rummaging around in our backpacks we pulled on our hastily gathered sweatshirts, covering our heads with our hoods.

We crawled through the forest for as long as we could stand the rocks and scratches from tree branches, resting at daybreak, when we were sure we'd escaped capture.

There was no sight of any of the others. I was worried for Miguel but my feelings for him didn't stop Mia and me from acting on survival impulse and getting the hell outta there.

We made it back down to some sign of civilization in the form of a nameless, one block scrappy little town, later the following afternoon. We must have looked a mess, our hair all crazy and full of leaves and other random bits of tree bark and sticks. If Mia had not managed to grab our metal water canisters from the RV the night before, we'd have been in a lot worse shape. We'd filled them before going to bed, as was our routine, ready for a day of trimming come morning. Neither of us had a dime to our name. We had needed nothing at the farm while we'd awaited the payday that now would never come.

We'd worked our butts off for two weeks and we weren't about to head home empty-handed. "Shit. How much do you think we would have made if the Feds hadn't bust in?" Mia asked. "There's no use in even guessing," I said. "That money is gone."

"What an adventure, you have to admit," Mia grinned, brushing leaves from my hair.

"Are you fucking kidding? You nearly got my ass killed, or deported," I snapped.

We watched as the cars and trucks on the highway sped past, each of them with their separate lives, homes to go to, families waiting, sacks of food for their refrigerators.

"Still," Mia said. "We have time to get on another grow-op, like, immediately." It was her idea to hang out at the gas station on the edge of the town we'd stumbled into.

I was feeling increasingly anxious by then, famished, my hollow stomach rumbled and my hands shook. I scratched at my head and feared for Miguel. What would happen to him if he'd been arrested, along with Ruby and the others?

"We're headed for another night outdoors," I said, resigned to it. Now I wished we'd stuck with Miguel, whatever the consequences.

Mia hushed me. She held me by my hands as she looked me in the eyes. "Come on, J," she said. "You're tougher than this." Besides, she added, "Miguel will catch up with us eventually."

I readied for tears as a shiny, newer-looking, big-ass truck pulled up at one of the tanks. The truck's hood blazed blue red in the castoff light of the setting sun. A Latino dude my dad's age hopped out from the driver's seat.

He tipped his hat that was half the size of him in our direction. Dude looked like he was making the big bucks from the size of his vehicle.

We watched him pump gas and fill a second 50-gallon portable tank.

It was starting to get dark. The florescent lights above the pumps flickered on at once. All the while we kept our eyes on his every move.

Mia pushed me forward. "Speak to him in Spanish," she said. "Tell him we're fast trimmers and we're neat."

I asked him the time. "Señor, me podría dar su hora?" He looked me up and down, slowly enough to creep me out. I noticed that the buckle on his belt was a painted metal with thorny roses engulfed in flames.

Please, Jesus, no, I said to myself. If this guy turns out to be a creep we're in serious trouble. Mia continued on with her nudging. His eyes were tired and his deadpan face gave nothing away. Just like my uncle on poker night.

"We're looking for trimming work," I announced, in Spanish. "We're ready to start today — um, now, I guess."

It was almost dark out, except for a few pockets of yellow light quickly fading behind the redwoods on either side of the gas station.

He was a man of little words. Nodding and without so much as breaking a smile, he opened the passenger door by the driver's side and motioned for us to get in.

Without a word ourselves, we climbed up and into the truck, hauling in our backpacks and our rolled up sleeping bags.

A little ways out of town, Jefe Hombre, the boss man, as we would call him, pulled over into a dirt turnout at the side of the road. He kept his eyes on us in the rearview mirror breaking his silence by announcing there was no need for concern. Still, something in his voice made me uncomfortable, despite his urging us not to be afraid. He informed us all matter-of-fact that he was about to cover our eyes for the remains of the route. It was for our own safety, he said.

"It's OK," he repeated. "No hay de qué preocuparse," — there's nothing to worry about. And we sat there, a pair of dumb ass idiots, despite the distinct warning in the form of a sharp prickle in the hair on the back of my neck as he reached over and promptly blindfolded us with a pair of weed scented bandanas.

I'd heard the trimmers talk of it being a common thing for workers not to know where they are.

I figured we were headed along a vague northwesterly route away from town. I'm weird that way. My sense of direction is one of my few natural gifts, for all the good it's done me.

We kept quiet, Mia and me. The whole time we were in the truck the fucker never said another word. An hour passed, maybe more. Belted, blindfolded and bumping around in the back, I searched for Mia's hand, digging my nails into the skin on her palm as I held on tight.

He swapped through several Spanish music CDs as he drove. One was a ranchero CD my dad used to play when he picked me up from school. I missed him. He was a half forgotten memory already.

It was late when we reached what I figured was a winding dirt road. Night owls hooted and big birds screeched. My ears popped, an indication of a high climb, altitude-wise. I've been to Lake Tahoe with my family, once, it was the only other time I've felt my ears pop like this. I kept them peeled, though I never heard a single truck pass us in the time it took to get where we were going.

Another 15 minutes went by after we'd turned onto the bumpy road. The chills were creeping up on me; man it was cold. I could feel the goose bumps on the back of Mia's hand. The temperature had dropped big time since sundown.

It was what we'd planned on, I kept on reminding myself, so as not to frickin' hyperventilate. How bad could it be? It was all an adventure as Mia had reminded me, so quit the chickenshit worrying, I told myself. Still, looking back, my sixth sense had kicked in early and I knew from the start it was a bad move.

The truck came to a halt before a heavy, metal gate. We heard it scrape the ground as it opened on the rough terrain. Jefe Hombre drove us a further half-mile or more over the rocky surface and into the compound. He pulled the truck to a stop, switched off the engine, opened his door and climbed out. I waited, frozen in place as he walked around and released the handle of the rear passenger door and roughly untied our blindfolds, mine first, then Mia's. We looked out into the dark, like a pair of timid lambs to the slaughter, taking in our first glimpse of what would be our stark new reality.

"Get out," he said, gruffly, in Spanish. We climbed out, clinging on to our backpacks and sleeping bags in our last, false sense of fast-dwindling security. The sky was moonless and starless. I squinted through the inky black. Where the hell were we? And what had we done?

CHAPTER 17

MAGGIE

The heavens opened as cold rain turned into small, hard, ice-bead balls of hail, pelting the windshield and all but blocking our view of the road.

Marcus continued to adjust the airflow, slowing the damp breeze that flowed in through the air vents. He turned on the radio, tuning the dial to a news station with a sufficiently strong signal to reach this far out along the coast.

Maintaining a steady 50 miles per hour, his thick tires hissed on the wet asphalt. We snaked our way north. The road was our own.

A female newscaster with a husky voice employed her best "keep calm and carry on" tone, reinforcing our worst fears. "Severe storm weather conditions are set to persist through the coastal region this afternoon and into this evening," she warned.

She listed, in her perfectly polished on-air cadence, a series of notorious highways already closed or likely to be closed due to hazardous driving conditions, cautioning drivers that a one-way traffic control had gone into effect a few miles to the north of us. Mudslides on the road above the small seaside village of Jenner had made the highway an impassable mess.

We were a few minutes south of the slides at the precise point where the coast highway intersects with highway 116 to weave along the curve of the Russian River, inland towards the cities of Healdsburg, Windsor and Santa Rosa.

The newscaster wrapped up her traffic report with a series of flash flood warnings in Sonoma, Marin and Napa Counties, issuing further terse instructions. "Do not, under any circumstances attempt to drive through any rising water," she warned.

Bobby concurred, although still somewhat begrudgingly, that his preferred route was now completely out of the question. "If we push forward and the mudslides worsen, we're gonna find ourselves in trouble," he admitted.

Marcus suggested a second and a third option. We could head back south to wait out the storm or, if we were all in agreement, take the river route east.

"If we've timed it right," he said, "We oughta be able to make it through to the freeway before the river crests."

The size of the truck and its grip on the road was reassuring. It seemed to me that Marcus was an extension of the vehicle, in tune with its every vibration. He'd driven in war zones for heavens sake.

He signaled, though there was no other vehicle in sight, turning off the ocean road, heading inland at the mouth of the river where it meets the State Marine Conservation Area.

The breathtaking beauty of the watery vista was teeming with wildlife despite the dire weather. It had been years since I'd ventured this far north on this especially scenic stretch of coastline.

We passed a scattering of rudimentary shacks with tarps tied over ramshackle rooftops. The countryside was drenched to the core. This whole lonely ledge on the edge of the world was all ours for want of any other vehicle in sight. I suddenly wondered where do the woodland creatures take shelter when the earth is swollen to this extent? Come spring and summer, it's a different landscape entirely, a shaded wonderland of redwoods and warm, rippling water, a safe haven for foxes, jackrabbits, deer. The rainy season on the other hand, is dark and foreboding, frequently transforming this remote outreach into the inhospitable, sodden, danger zone it proved that day.

A shiver ran along my spine. I checked my streaky reflection in the rain soaked passenger mirror. Black Irish. The old man claimed the dark complexion he and I shared came from a Spanish shipwreck off the coast of Ireland. That's a load of bull, a popular tale, nothing but an Irish American myth.

I tilted my eyes to steal another look at Marcus. Truth be told, I'd found it hard to take my eyes off him the whole time we'd been on the road. Even without me looking directly at him, his physical presence next to me proved intense. I closed my eyes and breathed him in through my nose, a potent mix of Old Spice deodorant and soap, an old-fashioned manly drugstore scent that Andres would have snobbishly described as a trailer trash aroma or something similarly mean. And you know what, I love the way that Marcus smells. It reminds me of the squeaky-clean scent the ranch guys, young and old had about them on churchgoing Sundays back when I was coming of age. To me, it's the lure of an honest aroma, the washing off of the week's hard work in preparation for the next.

A tangle of his thick, sandy hair rested on the frayed edge of his shirt collar, a softly worn flannel, unbuttoned to the point of exposing just the slightest tuft of flaxen chest hair. Marcus' beard is the same golden hue as his thick head of hair with its flecks of a paler blonde color. His dark-rimmed, blue-gray eyes mirror the color of the line at the outer reach of the ocean.

I drank in every detail of him as he maintained his steady focus on the road. It felt almost preposterous, the chances of my rapid and completely unexpected feelings being real and reciprocated. Hadn't I given up on the idea of such a thing? I sat back and savored the moment anyway. Blissing out on my luck in landing there beside him did not last for long.

Storm conditions had worsened; the heavens jolted me out of my doe-eyed, dopey zone. I gripped the bar on the glove compartment, bracing on instinct for the aquaplane ahead.

Marcus swiftly maneuvered the wheel to the left. We were headed uphill on an elevated side road carved into the rocky hillside. He pulled the truck to a sharp stop beneath a canopy of overhanging trees.

"We won't not make it through," he warned. "Either we turn back now and hope for the best or we wait it out for the next few hours."

We sat in silence. Bridget was the first to speak. "I've put us in this position," she said. "Damn it, I waited too long. I should have gone to look for her when she first took off, back when it was warm and sunny and safe out on the roads."

I twisted around at the waist as Bobby took her hand, tipping it upside down and gently tracing her palm with his nicotine-stained forefinger. "I'll go take me a look," he said as he pushed open his door, dropping his cash-stuffed wallet onto the seat beside Bridget. He unfolded his big torso and lumbered out onto the surface of the streaming dirt road, pulling a pair of baggy, black, waterproof pants and a pair of rubber waders from a plastic tub in the covered shell of the truck bed.

"You all — stay put," he barked, that damn hacking cough starting up again as he stepped into the waders. Bobby turned back to throw his heavy, leather boots onto the floor of the truck, grabbing a flashlight from the rear pocket of the driver's seat as he closed the door. The sky had darkened from the heaviness of the cloud cover.

A cold blast off the Pacific sent a second heavy shiver up the back of my neck and down along the length of my spine.

As I remember it, there was no single glance back, not the briefest goodbye, just a man, who, for once in his life, had made up his mind to take charge.

Marcus made a move to go after Bobby. He opened his door and jumped out. "Don't either of you leave the truck. Not for a minute," he warned as he made his way around the front of the vehicle.

The storm was sweeping violent sheets of cold, dark water through the heavy redwood canopy and the forest, soaked to its core, emitted a stench of wild, green life layered with the rank odor of death. The open door strained on its hinges. I imagined we were seated in the path of an oncoming train as a deafening vibration shook the very metal of the truck.

Sounds of screeching forest life woke from its trembling shelter. The bank of the river breached.

"Bobby!" Bridget screamed, flinging open her door.

"Stay inside," Marcus yelled, as he clambered back inside and slammed the door shut behind him. "Holy shit! It's . . . nobody move."

I strained my eyes and caught my last sight of Bobby, his flashlight held above him, way down below. He reached up, lurching in an instinctual, desperate attempt to grab on to any sagging, sodden limb.

I saw it coming in that moment and there was no way to stop it from happening.

Something vile rose up in the back of my throat. Bridget slumped forward, her body pushing into the back of my seat — she blacked out.

Later, she asked me what I had seen. A powerful curtain of liquid mud — sludgy and ravenous — a flood of water swallowed the scene in a vicious onslaught of trees, tents, television sets, shopping carts, trucks, all sorts and sizes of floating debris from paint cans to the side view of an almost entirely submerged Airstream trailer, sweeping below us in an angry, dark brown current of hell.

Bobby was there and then he was not. Rapid and relentless, the furious floodwaters overpowered him at shoulder height, sweeping him under and over in their wake.

Flash floods occur when the ground is saturated from excessive rainfall and is unable to absorb a single drop more. It came on in reality way faster than I ever would have fathomed.

Bridget came to and went into an immediate state of shock. We all did, in our own way. I lost track of how much time passed before a first responder air rescue crew swooped down further along the side road we'd taken shelter on. An hour or more at least. There was no designated landing spot to speak of. I would not have believed they could have made it down into such a narrow space if I hadn't seen it with my own eyes. By that time I had climbed into the back of the truck to hold on to Bridget, the both of us shocked, horrified and disbelieving at the same time. She'd been silently rocking for what had seemed like forever.

Marcus' reaction to this sudden freak tragedy was to shut down, slowly, staring into the dark. He'd desperately tried to call 911 immediately after Bobby was swept under, but to no avail. And I'd made several frantic attempts on both my and Bridget's phones but reception was sketchy.

There's no way to undo a trauma such as this. I'm afraid we're going to be dealing with these grainy flashbacks, mired in the horror of the scene for the rest of our lives.

We sat there, the three of us, frozen with horror and fear, praying for the floodwaters to subside as heavy rain continued to pound the truck from the canopy above.

Eventually, after I'd persisted with our phones, one bar of cell reception on mine enabled me to make it through to 911. The dispatcher had calmed me down enough to take note of our location and the basic details of our situation and our panicked SOS as to Bobby's slim chances of still being alive. I was told to stay in the truck and wait our turn. Help was on the way, though there were several others being picked up in the region and we had no option but to be as patient as possible. Later, after we were briefly medically assessed, the rescue crew took us by helicopter to an emergency evacuation center, the county's largest, the monolithic 1950s Veterans Memorial Building in Santa Rosa. With no concern for traffic or road conditions, air transportation was scary but fast. All I remember is looking down at the ravaged scene as the helicopter whirled its direct route, the same as the bird flies — super fast and further vomit inducing. Army engineers had already been sent out to deal with the foot of sandy loam and detritus of all kinds that lay beneath the diminishing floodwaters where the water had crested on River Road.

We landed on a makeshift helipad. It wasn't clear at first, in all the confusion, how to differentiate well-meaning volunteers from incoming evacuees. Red Cross workers at least wore the red vests that set them apart. It was sheer and utter chaos all around initially as dozens of vehicles lined up in a slow crawl to file into the large parking lot. A bunch of kids, some confused, others jostling and pushing one another, excitedly, almost, the way only kids do, oblivious to what was going on, spilled out of a yellow school bus. I watched their unflustered teacher gather them into some semblance of a line and calmly take a roll call. She methodically counted them, her hand on each head, one by one, child by child.

I still couldn't tell who was in need of emergency shelter and who were the ones who had come out to help. A mad jumble of people jostled for position. Looking back, I can understand the Red Cross position of pissing off well-meaning folk by discouraging unauthorized help in and turning away random donations in fraught situations like this. Cavernous old buildings, funded by the government after World War II, are not exactly the safest spots for too many folk to shelter in place, given the age of the structures and the types of materials that were used to build them. I guess when it comes to putting a roof over the head of a mass amount of people in any emergency situation, there's not a whole load of options. I can't help but think if there'd been an earthquake in the aftermath of the flash flooding, Jesus knows what may have rained down from under that roof.

Take it from me, when you find yourself in a fight or flight situation, the mind starts to imagine all sorts of fresh horrors coming your way. Personally, I was praying for no more than we were already dealing with. Being on the receiving end of emergency services is a wild, out-of-body experience I'd never thought to experience. One minute I'd been awash in admiration for Marcus as he handled the rough terrain of the coastal road, the next we had watched his best friend disappear in a horrifying, nightmarish split-second, the same guy who'd given my sister reason to keep fighting. I was grappling hard with reality. I still could not believe what I'd seen, the sheer, deadly power of the river.

We somehow made it through the paperwork at the front of the line, as a fleet of efficient, pre-approved volunteers hauled heavy-duty foil food containers onto a makeshift production line of foldout tables at the entrance to the main hall.

A growing crowd milled around under the grim glare of commercial florescent light, old people, young people, the disabled, families, homeless tent dwellers, kids; nobody seemed to know what to do with themselves other than simply follow their basic human instinct and line up in an orderly fashion for food. I didn't yet have the stomach to even contemplate eating.

We were handed folded squares of bright red blankets wrapped in plastic. I took the blanket from Bridget's outstretched hands, shook it open and draped it around her shoulders.

"Listen to me, we've gotta to stay right here and wait for Bobby," she begged. "They'll find him, they must. I'm sure of it." She gripped me on the forearm with a force that left a series of small, round purple bruises on my skin.

Marcus pulled the two of us in toward him, protectively. He had barely spoken the past few hours. "We're not going anywhere tonight, Bridget. We're staying here, together, the three of us. I don't know where he is, but what I do know for sure is that Bobby was looking out for us. We'll do right by him, I promise."

I was shaking. I tried to hold my raw emotions in but I burst into tears. Though the initial hysteria I'd felt back in the truck had worn itself out, I was only just beginning to absorb what had happened. Bobby wasn't coming back. I knew it. Marcus knew it. What I didn't know was how we'd even begin to deal with having witnessed such a swift and brutal end.

If I felt this way, what private hell was Bridget going through? And how would we ever make it out of here with enough strength to go forward?

Evening turned to night. I kept on thinking if there was the slightest chance he had survived, then poor Bobby was out there on his own. If he hadn't drowned, he would surely have died of hypothermia by that late hour. The temperature outside had dropped below freezing.

Some faceless person herded us into a new line. Single file we trooped past made-up cots set up in neat rows of military precision.

A soft voiced, efficient, elderly man had been put in charge of moving us around. He suggested the three of us make our way into a second, smaller room that was less populated and not nearly as pungent with the odor of the unwashed. I focused on a bingo wheel stored on an open shelving unit as we entered. I wondered how many times in its three-quarter of a century existence, this room had been cleared for emergency use.

I figured it was a meeting room, used for small gatherings and budget weddings and such, with its high ceilings, long, narrow windows and institutional, waxed floors. Not a room in which I'd describe in any way as festive or even inviting in as far as spending the night, though, I told myself that being safe and dry, sheltered and somewhat secluded from the bigger crowd was the best we could ask for in such terrible circumstances.

Bridget was in no position to argue and Marcus was looking decidedly green around the gills. We stuck together, the three of us.

"You'll rest better in here," the people-mover man said. "First we need to transfer your details to a crisis counselor and a nurse, if you should continue to require these services."

Evidently, the room had been reserved for those of us who had been caught up in the core crisis of the flash flooding zone — several other small groups and individuals who had assumedly and inconceivably lost their loved ones and pets to the rising river waters. I'd caught sight of a slew of handwritten notices posted on the walls as we'd walked through the auditorium, the most striking of them had been scrawled in desperation in the hands of the young, adorned with hearts and question marks, colorful childlike stick figures and beloved dogs and cats.

The man with the clipboard tried his best to reassure in his genteel, southern accent. Who knows what horrors of Mother Nature's disaster path he'd seen in his line of work.

"We're doing everything we can to locate those caught up in the waters, ma'am," he explained. "Ya'll in the best place now for us to keep you sheltered and informed."

An equally sympathetic young woman wearing a "trained volunteer" vest with a heavily made-up face, set us up with cots, pillows, sheets, extra blankets and towels.

I couldn't take my eyes off her eyelash extensions and the thick line of turquoise, sparkly eyeshadow that emphasized a pair of otherwise well-intentioned pale blue eyes as she handed each of us a zippered plastic bag containing socks, a toothbrush and travel-size paste, a washcloth, bar of soap, stick of deodorant and a sleep mask.

"No way in hell I'm sleepin' tonight," Bridget declared. "For God sake, Bobby's out there, he's all alone. Do not let me close my eyes, Maggie." She clung to me, her fingers gripping my forearms in the same tender spot that she'd held onto earlier.

I ran through an abridged version of our story three or four times to various people with clipboards and walkie-talkies over the next hour or so. Some kind soul brought us trays of food that we never even touched.

Marcus took off, mumbling something about needing a basin. He wandered back with a metal crutch under one arm and the handle of a plastic bucket of water balanced over the other.

"There's a large pack of highly agitated dogs and cats in wire pens out in the parking lot," he said. "Poor creatures are all riled up, terrified."

I watched as he lost his cool openly, abruptly turning away a medic who was handing out sleeping pills like candy. "No drugs," Marcus snapped. It might have been easier to tell the medic he was in recovery. We'd talked about it only briefly the previous night. "What I really fucking need is a clean elastic bandage," he barked.

Seating himself on the edge of his cot, Marcus asked me if I would hold up a blanket for privacy. "Brace yourself, Maggie," he said, locking eyes. "If you've never seen a prosthetic removed, I'm telling you, it's not all that pretty, especially the first time."

I listened as he explained how if he were to leave the artificial leg and liner on too long without a cleaning, it would lead to blisters and sores.

My first test, I figured, as I readied myself for the intimacy of Marcus' most private world. I was learning fast.

I maintained a steady eye contact as he demonstrated graphically the mechanical extension of his body connecting to a socket that fits over his residual limb.

He was searching for any sign of reaction, I sensed. There was no point in any polite bullshit between us given the brutal pace and fast-forwarding of our getting to know one another. Marcus explained how each morning he fits a liner over his limb in order to make for comfort and cushioning and to provide a barrier between skin and socket. The design of his artificial leg is coated with a cosmetic cover to make it look more realistic, though I'd recognized it as a prosthetic from the start.

"It's to please myself," he said. "I've never felt the need to make any one else feel more comfortable."

He told me how after the accident, he had ranked high on the scale the military used in deciding the level of prosthetic mechanics he would best respond to.

"Seeing as I was a soldier, relatively young and an athlete," he explained, "I was considered way more likely to be successful with a high caliber artificial limb."

I watched intently, expressionless, as he methodically removed the fake leg and socket, carefully laying them down beside him on the cot.

"I was reliant on a wheelchair at first," he continued. "The crutches came into play as I waited for the surgery to heal and the swelling to go down. First year was a nightmare, worse than the blast itself. It took time to recondition my muscles, to relearn balance, to walk on different surfaces, climb stairs, drive."

Bridget looked on with a glazed expression as Marcus peeled the liner off his stump and dropped it into the bucket of water. Afterwards, he took a washcloth and soap from one of the plastic bags we'd been given and soaked it in the warm bubbles. Soaping and squeezing, he gently cleansed the reddened scar tissue at the amputation site. Only then did I let him see me look away.

"Don't be embarrassed on my account," he said. "It is what it is. Took me enough time to get over my own anger and disgust. It's alright, though you know. I'm one of the lucky ones."

He spoke of Bobby and how they'd depended on each other after the rehab.

"Will power is never enough," Marcus said. "It was a holy hell of a day-by-day deal for the both of us, Bobby and me. Addicts are never fully cured. You are aware of that, right? Any slight setback makes me yearn for it, even if only for a brief second, the relief I'd sought from the drugs," he said.

Marcus looked down at the ground. He choked back tears. "Son of a bitch, Bobby kept me going," he said. "Man."

I watched as he ran his fingers over his scar tissue, feeling for signs of swelling from the day's exertions. I resisted the urge to sit beside him, to hold him.

He dried his skin meticulously with a second, clean cloth before positioning the elastic bandage he'd requested over the top of his stump. "This should prevent any swelling overnight," he said.

Next he washed the socket with the same careful process, setting it out to dry alongside the liner and the prosthetic on a towel that he'd carefully unfolded and laid out beneath his cot.

I listened, as he opened up on the subject of his friendship. "Bobby helped me figure out it was grow up or give up," he said. "He had his shit together, more than most in recovery. I never once considered I would lose him first."

We looked back over at Bridget. She was in a trance-like state, lying on her side on the cot, facing away from the two of us by then. I crouched down to touch her cheek softly with the back of my hand, checking to see if she had fallen asleep despite her protest. She turned at my touch, awake, wide-eyed, staring, blindly, into the room.

"Rest, Bridget," I whispered in her ear. "Don't sleep, but it's OK if you close your eyes and doze a little."

Marcus was up from his cot and back on his crutch. "I'll be back," he said over his shoulder as he left, I assumed, for any update he could get out of the folk with the radios.

I felt an unfamiliar pang — his strong presence was much needed, it was comforting to the Bridget and me. As soon as he was out of my line of vision, I felt his absence, acutely. I wanted him back beside me. And, having shared with me so much of his emotional weakness, I figured he needed me as much as I needed him at that moment.

I moved my cot closer to my sister's, reaching out to be of some small comfort to her. "Remember when we shared a room when we were kids, sis?" I asked. "The stories you told me to help me sleep, Bridget. Remember the imaginary magic rabbit hole at the bottom of the bed? Down we'd go into fairyland, night after night. Everything was so happy-go-lucky and vibrant in our land of make-believe, wasn't it?"

Bridget turned to me amidst the sound of muted texts, a thousand pairs of feet shuffling around in the dark. "I remember," she said. "Those silly, childish stories were my way to escape it all. The sum total of my adventures, Maggie, while I still had some shred of an imagination." Tears. A sudden intake of breath and Bridget launched into a rocking motion, sobbing with a level of intensity unlike any I'd experienced in the lowest points of my life, not even when our parents died. I was powerless, sick to my stomach at the lack of privacy afforded us in this most primal of moments.

I felt a familiar flickering sensation rising in my chest, a tightening of the lungs, my heart pounded in a throat-closing readiness for another one of my ill-timed fucking panic attacks.

This was not the time for working on my self-regulating routine, that whole bloody business of breathing in, breathing out. Instead I tried to picture something pure and good and beautiful. I dug down deep inside my head and conjured an old image of Mia that I'd posted on my refrigerator. It was one of her first school photos and I'd taken it with me on every move. Bridget had sent it to me after she'd paid for one of those overpriced packets filled with an excessive number of prints. "Who else is going to want a picture of my kid?" she'd written on a sticky note on the back. My one and only niece, cute as a button, her long brown hair tied into two neat braids, thick blue ribbons the same color as her sweatshirt with its white pony motif on the front.

I concentrated on the mental image of young Mia in tandem with my breathing in and out, tuning in to the sound of a coffee machine in the main auditorium, drip drop, the mutterings of the half asleep, the thrum of the ventilation system.

Bridget rocked from side to side in the narrow confines of her cot, loosening and releasing her hand from my tight, clammy grip. We were not alone in our heightened state of anxiety. I managed to maintain a sufficient mode of defense so as not to come completely undone for my sister's sake and I somehow slept though fitfully and only after Bridget had cried herself to sleep from the sheer exhaustion of it all. I awoke to the sound of Marcus' return sometime during the night, opening my eyes and propping myself up on one elbow as he balanced a plate of foil-wrapped food in one hand, while navigating his way around his cot on his crutch.

We sat, side by side, the pair of us, at once made suddenly ravenous by the savory, spicy aroma of a small pile of steamed tamales. I peeled off layers of cornhusk and devoured the spicy red chili and pork filling that was wrapped in a soft and especially comforting masa dough, the same sweet, pungent scent and texture of the street food I had purchased from the baskets of Mexican grandmothers in San Francisco's Mission District on my way home from work in a different life.

"Can you believe they turned these delicious morsels away?" Marcus asked. The humble tamale maker who had walked to the shelter to share her homemade comfort food was deemed, along with so many other benevolent givers, as unauthorized in the supply of perishables. "It's crazy out there," he said. "Crowds of folk showing up with all kinds of stuff."

"What else is going on out there, Marcus?" I asked. "How did you manage to get a hold of these if they were rejected?"

"You need details? Why? Are you keeping tabs on me now?" he shot back, clearly on the defensive all of a sudden.

"No. Just wondering."

Marcus put his hands to his face and covered his eyes.

"If I tell you, do you promise not to judge?"

Test number two as Marcus described to me how he'd approached the night shift volunteers for any news on Bobby, while I was comforting my sister.

"There was a rush of activity around midnight," he said. "One of the EMT guys had gone outside to handle an emergency situation with an elderly man."

Marcus had found himself alone in a room with an open drawer and a ready supply of painkillers in plain sight.

"I had a bottle in my hand, Maggie. Fuck. I don't know how it happened, but it did. I slipped the pills into my pocket and took off outside. I stayed there, on a bench, in the shadows of the outer parking lot, holding on to it, shaking the bottle, rolling it around in the palm of my hand."

It would have been that easy. Only, something stopped him.

"It was Bobby, I felt like he was there looking over me," Marcus said. "It was then that I walked outside and into the path of the woman who'd been sent away with her basket of tamales. She was more than happy to hand them over to me."

I moved closer, wrapping my arms around his shoulders, brushing the skin above his beard line with my lips. "I'm here for you, Marcus," I said. "You can trust me."

I stirred after an hour or two more of fitful sleep as Marcus caressed my cheek with the back of his hand. I opened my eyes directly into his, noticing for the first time the tiny speckles of brown that floated in a deep-sea of blue.

"The search, Maggie, it's resumed," he whispered in my ear. "It's daybreak, though you'd never know it in here."

According to Marcus, both Bridget and me had slept way more than we'd thought we had. He'd stayed awake the whole night through.

"What did you do with the bottle of pills?" I had to ask.

"Slipped them back into the drawer where I'd found them," he said. "My single most disciplined move, Maggie, through this whole damned ordeal."

Bridget stirred and rolled to the side of her cot. She opened her eyes, swung her legs into a seated position and let out a deep, instantaneous moan. Her scarf had slipped from her head, exposing spiky tufts of short, white, newly sprouting hair. The sight of this took me aback and I gasped, promptly clapping a hand over my mouth.

My sister was both vulnerable and alert, all eyes and ears, like a fawn searching for its family. She reached for the bucket of water beneath Marcus' cot, retching whatever little contents remained in her near empty stomach.

I gagged, in sympathy. My instincts told me it was time to bolt, to get us out of there, find someplace else, anyplace in order to wait it out. I feared the onset of another panic attack as florescent lights flickered strobe-like and incessantly over a sea of huddled heads.

Marcus was back on two feet. He took Bridget's arm and led us through to the main room where the aroma of fried sausages, eggs, bacon and maple syrup failed to mask the sweet and cloying smell of fear and the unmistakable odor of so many unwashed bodies.

What we needed was fresh air. We made our way over to the main door, heading into a flurry of activity and buzzing walkie-talkies.

Two men interacted with one another over the radio chatter. We heard them talking about a body that had washed up on the roadside near Jenner that morning. "We'll get to you shortly," we were told.

I bustled us outside and found a space on a bench for Bridget and me to sit. Marcus took off and returned a couple minutes later with disposable cups of hot, sweet tea before he set to walking the perimeter of the building as we awaited news from the sheriff's department.

Around 8 a.m., the three of us were taken into a small windowless room at the front of the building and informed, in shockingly plain speak that the recovered body fit our description of Bobby.

We desperately wanted to believe it wasn't he who had washed up on a bank of weeds and rock where the river met the ocean. "Please, God, let it not be him," I begged. Whosever's body it was would need to be formally identified as all clothing had been ripped off by the strength of the current.

Bridget dropped her head between her knees and wailed like a wolf. I crouched down beside her and holding her tight, I placed my hand at the back of her head to steady her in her continual flailing. The sheriff's deputy asked Marcus if he was able and willing to identify Bobby's body. Marcus nodded, turned to Bridget and me and said: "You two best wait for me here."

"I should have stopped him," Bridget moaned, tearing at her clothing. She was inconsolable. Someone sent a counselor in. She was quite a bit younger than Bridget and me and despite her sympathetic manner and evident training, really, what could the poor woman possibly have done to make this any more bearable?

My mind raced. I couldn't comprehend the injustice of it. What kind of world is it when a good guy like Bobby gets dealt the death card? It's bad of me to admit it, I know, but my first thought was why the hell was Andres spared some similarly horrid end? He's still free to go on playing around for the rest of his miserable life, thinking only of himself, treating women as disposable commodities. Bobby, on the other hand, what had he ever done to deserve such a cruel and sudden fate? I pictured him lying there in the morgue, ice-cold and bloated from the bacterial activity in his corpse.

How my sister and I found the strength to sit there and wait on Marcus coming back, I'll never know. The pain of the high probability of a conformation of Bobby's violent death pinned us to our seats. Awful visions floated into mind. Hours of binge watching CSI have taught me that when a person drowns, their body floats due to the gases that build up inside. I remembered how I'd once watched a grim show about the dozens of people who drown in lake Tahoe each year. It's a weird thing to retain, but it's a known fact that of all those who drown, 90 percent of people do so in fresh water as opposed to salt. Lakes and rivers are evidently way more dangerous than bodies of salt water. It's something to do with the chemical constitution of fresh water being a lot more similar to blood than its salty counterpart.

When Bobby took his last breath, he inhaled a flood of murky river water into his already compromised lungs. "The flood water passed through into his bloodstream, bursting his blood cells," Marcus explained in overly technical detail during his shell-shocked delivery of the news we'd so desperately hoped not to hear.

It was fast. At least there was that. I still can't get it all out of my head. The coroner told Marcus that in Bobby's case, his organs would have failed in two to three minutes at most given that his lungs were already shot from the hand rolled smokes, those lethal "casket nails" as he'd jokingly called them.

Was it any consolation to learn that Bobby went without a fight? Hell no and I'd never say any of this to my sister, but if he'd been doubly unlucky and he'd drowned in salt water, it would have taken more like eight to ten minutes of his desperate thrashing about. So that's something, I guess, that he never made it out into the ocean. We found out from the pathologist who conducted his autopsy that they'd discovered bits of plant life, rocks and stones in his lungs.

Bobby's physical wounds, his cuts and bruises were caused by debris in the current, his body washed up on the rocky bank. Thank God he wasn't swept away at sea, along with the Airstream trailer that floated by, the cans of paint and television sets that rushed through and rolled out into the open waves. If that had been the case, there was every chance his body would have drifted miles through the open salt water before resurfacing on some far off beach to the north or south. Even in death, Bobby had chosen to stay in the familiar territory of his beloved home county.

His body was given back to Bridget for burial in his family's coastal cemetery plot. For that, at least, we were thankful.

CHAPTER 18

MARCUS

Maggie made the call to Luna, Bridget's friend from the dispensary. She came for Bridget less than an hour after I'd broken the news. It was Bobby's body I had identified.

Life is too easily stolen from the best of us. Jesus. I've been witness to this more times than any one man should be forced to recount. I don't expect I will ever in my whole life shake off the recurring visual of raw flesh and severed limbs; way too many army comrades blasted by machine gun on some godforsaken desert goat path. Since I'm no longer at war, except for the shit storm in my head, Bobby's swollen body was way tougher for me to deal with in a way. I freely admit I struggled to maintain composure seeing him like that, fresh from his watery grave. And yet I held myself together, though I almost lost it several times, standing there in that fucking ice-cold morgue staring at my barely recognizable best buddy.

I figured it was high time to off-load Bridget from the lethal expedition we were on. I was sick to my stomach to pull the plug on her last drop of hope that Bobby had somehow clung on to solid ground. I let her know it came over him real fast, the floodwater, taking him down at shoulder level with such violent force he'd been under in a mere couple seconds.

The coroner had been somewhat delicate in his manner despite having given me the graphic details pretty much straight up. The fella deduced I was able to handle it, I guessed. "It's the sudden intake of water flooding the sinuses that proves fatal, I'm sorry to say," he'd explained while my knees turned to jelly.

My one and only true friend, my brother for all intents and purposes, lay there in that cold morgue, waxy, frozen solid — distorted, his arms folded across his bloated stomach, his eyelids fat and closed tight like a marble figurine laid out on top of one of those ancient stone caskets I've seen in magazine pictures of cathedrals in far-off lands.

My last impression of Bobby was of his feet — blown up like surgical gloves, black and blue, like balloons. Ten sausage toes all messed up and bloody from being scraped along the rocky bank in the deadly current.

I knew then it was me and me alone who was gonna have to man up, step it up big time — for Bobby. I owed him. There is nothing I wouldn't do for the guy, for his family, for Bridget, Maggie, Mia. Bobby never asked for much. I knew if he coulda risen up and asked something of me from his bed of stone, my being there for his womenfolk was what it'd be. And I'll do it gladly, if they'll have me.

Bridget freaked when I broke the news, as I fully expected she would, throwing up and wailing in turns, her face devoid of its last trace of color. The woman was in need of rest and medical care.

"Find Mia, Marcus, bring her home," she begged, weeping and sobbing in intervals, grasping my hands in a viselike grip, her face a crumpled mess of tears.

When Luna arrived, she started in right away on calming Bridget with the promise she would deal with the sheriff and all the necessary paperwork back at the ranch. "Don't worry, I'll look after her, me and the kids will. You and Maggie do what you need to do to find Mia. I'll get Bridget in for her treatments and all," she assured us.

As the two of 'em were leaving, Bridget turned to me, said how she wanted me to know, of all people, how she would never forget him.

"The touch of his hand, his big, ol' bear hugs. All the stupid stuff he ever said."

I heard her. Bobby had kept us both on course with his chilled, steady way of being solidly in the moment in this fucking, messed up world.

River Road was still under several feet of water at the ocean end. The Army Corps of Engineers were waiting for it to drain in order to clear it of silt and detritus and open it back up to traffic. We'd be forced to wait it out another night before we'd be able to safely retrieve my stranded truck.

Maggie started searching on her phone for someplace to hole up, anywhere that wasn't that goddamn shelter.

There was no way in hell I was going into a second night without sleep, pacing the place, tempted, oh Lord, how I had been tempted to down that handful of pills. Wash it all away.

I figured out who I needed to talk to and told them we were headed someplace nearby for the night, that we could be reachable on Maggie's cell and if not, we'd call in.

The Russian River Resort Cabins and Cottages was the first affordable place that fit the bill, tucked away in the hills in an old redwood grove along an elevated and accessible dirt road at the dry end of the flood zone.

Maggie found a volunteer to give us a ride, a young dude, a student from the junior college nearby, one of those kids in possession of a sense of service and community. Lucky for us, he'd turned up willing to run unfortunate folk like us around the river region in between his classes.

What I needed most at that moment was to lose myself in the forest, calm my soul in the monolithic presence of the redwoods, those gentle giants that blow my mind with their three-dimensional labyrinth that lives and breaths above the forest floor. It's almost impossible for the naked eye to scan these distant treetops for their magical hanging gardens of ferns, thickets of huckleberry bushes and all the many other amazing species that grow and thrive in the upper layers of soil that support this wild and crazy host of plant and animal life.

We thanked the kid for the ride when we reached the cabins. I handed him a bunch of small change and a five-dollar note to cover his gas.

"Good evening to you," said an aging hippie chick who sat in the ramshackle office of the main building of an otherwise deserted resort.

Her round, moon-shaped face emerged from a shadowy recess behind the desk topped by a big ol' mess of faded red curls that sprung from her large head.

"My name is Tanya, and I am your host," she announced, pointing to a badge pinned onto the psychedelic, tent-like blue and green colored kaftan she was wearing with its bright peacock design. She was a good deal to take in, this Tanya, the sort of woman who is to some degree more than a few years past her prime yet unapologetically set on refusing to give it up. Her voice was gravelly and strong. It spoke to a past I'd bet good money on being as wild as her taste in clothing.

A collection of faded, black and white photos of various Russian River scenes hung askew on the redwood panels behind the desk where she was perched, reminding me of one of the heavily made-up fortune-tellers at the traveling circuses we went to as kids. "Like that one?" she asked, following my gaze. "Last day of the train at Duncan Mills, 1935," she said. Another captured a steamboat on the river, a bunch of poker-faced passengers in Victorian hats and decked out in their Sunday best waving at the photographer from the upper deck. "This one's a bird's-eye view over the river as it was in 1940," she added. "Not much has changed around here as you can see."

She leaned across the counter to take a closer, hawkish look at Maggie and me. Her deep-set, milk-gray eyes that looked like the color of film on cold coffee, were magnified by a pair of small, round eyeglasses that she'd perched on the tip of a bulbous nose. Tanya pocketed my cash quick enough, handing over a pen and instructing Maggie and me to write our names in a worn, leather ledger that sat open on the desktop between us.

"You two sweet lovebirds are my sole guests tonight," she said, punctuating her claim with an unsubtle wink. "You're fortunate that I decided to stay put given these dangerous weather conditions. I almost closed up for the week when the flood hit." She launched into a long speech on how she had turned to her cards for direction. "My old Tarot deck. Never fails me," she said, as she retrieved a well-worn deck from a drawer under the desktop.

"And wouldn't you know," she decreed, placing a set of cards face up and, with a smile, exposed an otherwise intact set of weed and tobacco-stained teeth: "Look at this for a three card spread, if you please? Six of Wands, the Star, Lovers, a welcome reprieve after a period of destruction and turmoil — please do consider this a place of peace and compassion for the night."

In our quest to find somewhere private to process our pain, it appeared we'd at least succeeded in making her day with our preordained arrival. "Put faith in the universe and you will share your success," she said. "Though be prepared to take the high road, the more challenging and difficult path."

I don't go in for these sorts of showman's props ordinarily, but hey, if there is such a thing as destiny and it offers some element of promise, who the hell am I to challenge such a thing?

Maggie changed the subject back to the flood, explaining in brief how it had been our very reason for needing the room. "We've been through the most horrendous twenty-four hours," she confessed while Tanya hung on her every word. It didn't so much as give me the creeps as make me wonder if the woman was trying to see inside our heads. "We'll be on our way in the morning," Maggie added.

"No keys," Tanya informed, raising her hands, palms out. "No need. Lock your door from the inside, kids. Keep your valuables on you. Breakfast is served in here or on the porch if it ain't too wet outdoors, any time between the hours of seven and nine."

Maggie politely enquired if there was any small chance of something to eat before nightfall. "We'd be grateful. We're not fussy," she said.

"Leave it with me, my dears," Tanya replied. "It just so happens I have the last of a recent batch of my famous piroshkis waiting for you in my refrigerator — homemade, Russian style, everyone's crazy about them. I've got some good rye bread and a bowl of slaw I can spare. I'd be happy to warm them up for a token fee, given that you are pretty much stuck out here. I'll wrap 'em in foil and drop them on your porch a little later on," she said as she walked to the open door and pointed uphill with a shiny, silver ring-filled finger, her thick wrist jingling with a mess of matching bangles and beads.

"Along the path, through the grove and up above the creek, you'll find it. Rosemary's Cabin's the one for you. Can't miss it. You'll find plenty of wood for the stove, fresh towels, bed's made-up." One cabin. The idea of a shared bed set off a surge of the same level of electrical charges I'd experienced when I first laid eyes on the woman beside me.

Low light faded fast as we made our way up a narrow path that wound its way between the towering trees. We might have been the last two people on earth that night, the only other sound aside from our footsteps the rustling of a thick layer of pine needles and composting grass beneath the wet and springy ground. My senses were working overtime as the shock of the past twenty-four hours began to wear off. The forest reeked of wild mushrooms, damp wood, millions of decomposing micro-life-forms waiting for spring to come back around, for sunlight, for new life to emerge.

In the defused twilight we came across the small redwood cabin we'd been assigned. It was easy to find, squeezed into place between two giant trees. I was conscious of my heartbeat ramping up a notch or two as we moved toward the lamplight glowing through a pair of lace curtains drawn inside a small, square window frame.

An owl hooted from above. I took a hold of the wrought iron doorknob and rattled the rough-hewn door that had expanded in the heavy winter rainfall and was stuck in its frame. I pushed it open with the weight of my shoulder, facing off with a small deer's head that was mounted directly opposite and above the bed. I held the door open for Maggie and followed her inside onto the creaky, wide plank floorboards. Centered against the far wall, an old-time iron bedframe and mattress was made up with crisp white sheets and topped with a tartan wool bedspread in a dark red and black design. A potbellied stove sat perpendicular to the foot of the bed, with a full basket of wood, newspapers and kindling set out beside it.

Imitation gas lanterns glowed a pinky-yellow on the dresser by the window, two smaller versions of which were positioned either side of the bed.

"A perfect hideaway," Maggie declared, surveying the territory. "A refuge for rest to banish our woes — at least for one night."

She sat down on the edge of the bed where she wasted no time in sliding her feet from her boots and socks. Barefoot, Maggie stepped across the room to investigate a musty smelling closet bathroom.

I followed behind. The narrow confines of the bathroom consisted of an old commode and washbasin and a white vinyl curtain pulled across the narrow shower stall. I opened the sash window a little higher to let in some cool, fresh, forest air.

I found it hard to take my eyes off her fine boned, graceful and thrillingly bare feet as she turned and traversed the bedroom, taking in its equally scant details. Maggie's toenails were painted the same dark red color as her fingernails. I'm unaccustomed to being with the kind of woman who wears nail polish. I followed, a second time and lowered myself onto the bed where I lay on one side, facing toward her with the support of a pile of pillows I repositioned for comfort. I closed my eyes as she lay down beside me, her cold feet just short of touching my own, her warm breath on the back of my neck in the chill of the room. I felt a shiver of exhilaration and opened my eyes.

"Holy shit . . . it's an icebox in here," I said, feeling the need to deflect the intensity of the moment. I rolled myself over and up into a sitting position. Maggie tipped her head to one side, dishing me a wide, quizzical half smile.

The two of us rolled out of bed and worked together to fix the stove to crackling and hissing 'til much-needed heat cast its welcome glow into the room. I knelt down on one knee to secure the iron handle on the stove's glass door. Maggie squatted down beside me, reaching up behind her head to set her ponytail loose. I gathered a bunch of her hair between my fingers as it brushed my face. It was tangled from the previous night's unrest and it smelled to me of seawater and rain, of sweet Douglas fir and freshly dug earth of the redwood forest. I felt a slow, tingling sensation run through my body as she brushed the back of her hand against the bristly surface of my beard. Placing my arm around her waist to stand we warmed our bodies held together as one by the heat of the stove and she led me to bed.

There we lay on our side by side, fully clothed, two sets of eyes fixed above us on the beams of the redwood ceiling as we watched the light flicker upwards from the fire, her hand in mine. The mattress sank and sagged and the bed frame rattled its approval as she stirred, rolling onto her side and pressing herself to me, her arm resting across my chest so that I could feel the beat of her heart, the deep, steady rhythm of her. She threaded her hand through my hair and rolled me over onto my side, face to face. She closed her eyes. I kissed her eyelids, softly, one at a time, a heady mix of adrenaline, fear and arousal pumping through my body.

She moved her hands along my spine and up to my head, her mouth at last on mine. Her kisses unleashed a lust I'd never experienced before. Slowly, purposefully, she pulled back to remove her outer clothes and crouch above me on my back in her bra and panties. I rolled the straps of her bra down her arms and raised her elbows lightly, her fire-warmed and heavy breasts spilling out of their lace-topped cups and over my face. She pulled off her underwear with one hand, unbuckling my belt and slipping her free hand down the front of my jeans.

A primitive scent from the forest floor filled the confines of the cabin. It wrapped itself around us, entwined us. Meanwhile, a million night creatures sang their nocturnal chorus. A basket of food had appeared with pretty damn perfect timing around the time that dusk had slipped into darkness, though we'd been too preoccupied to hear our host as she made good on her promised delivery. Maggie wrapped her naked body in the thick, tartan blanket from the bed to step out into the chill of the narrow porch. "We kept the light on," she said, blushing as she came back in with our humble feast of two large piroshkis —Tanya's Russian dumplings, oven warmed and wrapped in foil, tucked into the folds of a cotton towel to keep them warm.

I draped my body in the crumpled top sheet we'd worked off the bed and we devoured this second gift of sustenance in as many days. We ate hungrily from cloth napkins we spread on our laps under the moonlit starscape of a blessedly clear night that shone in on us through the small window.

Sitting beside her in this simple act of post-coital nourishment, I felt like something far more significant had taken place between the two of us than basic intercourse, copulation of convenience, stress-relieving carnal relations, whatever. Holy hell, how does a man such as me try to capture in words the kind of mind-blowing biological union that left me thanking God, the universe, my lucky stars for the start of the most unexpectedly beautiful night of my life. It was out of this world — well, for me, at least. We sealed this new deal we'd established between us with mugs of hot and spicy tea poured from a heavy thermos flask that was tucked into the basket alongside the piroshkies, a tub of slaw and two thick slices of rye bread and butter.

"I would kill for a glass of wine," Maggie confessed as she peeled herself away and wandered into the bathroom to wash her hands. "Though I guess I'll settle for the natural high I'm feeling right now," she said, grinning as she stepped in front of me by the bed and pulled my body toward her. I sat myself down to set about the business of removing my prosthetic and she opened her blanket teasingly. My eyes were glued to the spectacle of her as I continued to free myself from my artificial limb and, after blindly succeeding with the task at hand, I raised myself off the bed, balanced myself on the crutch from the shelter, made my way over to the bathroom, turned on the faucet and stepped into the steaming shower stall.

Let me tell you, a hot shower, no matter how basic, is a godsend for the one-legged even at the best of times. Forget about a bathtub, though I would find a way to manage several good soakings and sooner than I'd thought, with Maggie's help.

Not more than a minute later, she stepped behind me into the steam of the muggy stall and set about lathering my back with a dense and woodsy smelling, scratchy bar of soap she'd removed from its paper wrapping deposited on a narrow shower caddy that hung from the faucet. Soap bubbles filled the vaporous cubicle with the heady scent of rosemary and pine.

I felt the weight of her full breasts rest against my back. She reached up to lather my hair, moving her hands across the contours of my head, deftly caressing the scalp beneath my thick, wet, sudsy hair with the strong tips of her fingers.

I turned, slowly and deliberately so as not to slip, holding her firmly around her waist with one arm while steadying myself with the other. Reciprocating her kindness, I lathered her breasts with the small bar of aromatic soap, cupping them beneath their swell to rinse them from the suds. Afterwards, I lowered my head to her chest, tracing each wet, rosemary-scented nipple in turn with the tip of my warm tongue.

In a single smooth move, she dropped to her knees to gently soap and lather the scar tissue of my stump, rendering me breathless as she gradually worked her way up.

We wrapped our freshly showered, towel dried selves in the already rumpled sheets, bodies entwined once again on the bed, arms and legs, full and partial, her hips, soft and round pressed against my own. "It's like piecing together the complicated puzzle of a pair," Maggie said as she wrapped a leg across my stump and tucked her foot beneath the calf of my good leg. My body relaxed into the easy, calm repose of her.

Three or four hours after I had given in to a by then desperate need for sleep, I was rudely awoken by one of my bad dreams, brought on this time by the mad jumble of disturbing memories that had resurfaced in the evacuation center — the smell of antiseptic a major prompt, for starters. That night in the cabin, I experienced one of my frequent flashbacks to the makeshift military hospital in Iraq, the place where I'd awoken after the blast. In this dream, though, I was back on the operating table. Bizarrely, Bobby was the medic. He looked down at me as I was lying there and he frowned, the fucker, as if he never even knew me. I kept on trying to tell him: "Bobby boy, it's me, your old pal, Marcus," but I'd been muted by the anesthetic. He looked a little closer, scrutinized my face and smiled in some form of basic recognition as he reached out a hand to comfort me. I woke up, sweating like a pig.

These sweats, this bad taste in my mouth, they come back to haunt me on an almost nightly basis, an unwanted reminder of the sickly berry flavors of the sugarcoated, fast release opioid lollipops the military medics doled out to us blast victims to take away the pain.

I've heard it said how idiotic rich folk in Hollywood serve these same deadly, narcotic-laced lollipops to their party guests on silver platters no less. Make no mistake, the sole intended design of a fentanyl infused lollipop is for combatting breakthrough pain. If you ask me, whoever it was who came up with this whole sick, twisted idea of making a drug as addictive as crack into a lollipop, should be made accountable for the string of lethal deaths they've caused.

Let me make it clear. Opioids are heroin times 50 in pill form. Keep on taking them and they'll kill you sooner than later my friend.

Fuck, some 50,000 people no better than me have kicked the bucket from opioid addiction in this goddamn country in one single year. I lay there thinking my usual thoughts on how the government never stops making a whole load of noise about it, pointing fingers at the addicts and the whole codependent system and yet fuck all is ever done to put a stop to this madness.

Maybe that's what they want, to get rid of the deadwood. The big drug companies, they're laughing their way to the bank while opioid addicts are dropping like flies. I'd sweated so profusely, the sheet was soaked beneath me.

I propped myself up on my elbow seeing as I was awake anyway, taking the opportunity to study Maggie's facial features in the still darkened room. One day I hope to wake up to this woman without the fucked-up PTSD triggers grinding me down. Much as I was enjoying my private study of her fine bone structure, the arc of her eyebrows, the slightest part in her lips, I was mindful of freaking her out if she woke up and caught me staring at her.

She opened one eye before the other, an endearing move and there it was again, that irresistible half smile. I shifted my position as she rolled over and lowered her body onto mine. She looked me in the eyes.

"What is it?" she asked, a frown crinkling her forehead. "Is this all too much, considering?"

"It's Bobby," I said, my hands shaking. "But not because of what we're doing here. I was dreaming and Bobby, he was back."

"Well, you're wide awake now," she said as she took my still trembling hand in hers. "And I'm the only one here with you. And you know what they say, third time's the charm." She whispered a number of enticements into my ear. Her morning hair smelled of wood smoke and rosemary. Warm from sleep, naked the whole night long beneath the sheets, her contours were smooth and tender to my touch. She rolled onto her back so that I was the one on top this time. I hooked one knee and one half leg beneath hers as she made good on her promise to take my mind clear off the misery and sorrow of mourning my dead friend for at least as long as it lasted. My brain temporarily stopped playing tricks on my central nervous system. The phantom limb pain I've grown accustomed to waking up with failed to materialize. Anyone who has experienced the loss of a limb will tell you how bullshit strange and disconcerting it is to go on feeling the full effects of discomfort in a body part that is no longer there.

A little after daylight we pried ourselves apart, showered again, though separately this time and we dressed. I fixed my prosthetic for the day ahead, one eye on Maggie as she towel dried and brushed through the tangles of her long, wet hair. We gathered our scant belongings and walked back downhill to sit ourselves at a wooden bench table on the covered porch of the empty reception area.

"It is a damn ghost town," I remarked, looking around the deserted resort. Tanya showed up a few minutes later, breaking the silence, a glint in her eye. Clearly she'd perceived a sense of the fervor of the night before even if she hadn't seen it for herself, though I am sure she had. She tamed her crazy hair, it was secured it in a tighter coil that morning, a wild crown of copper held in place with a large, multicolored plastic clip shaped like a butterfly. She floated around like a giant forest fairy bearing gifts, setting down a heavy, wooden tray. My stomach rumbled at the welcome sight of two big mugs of strong coffee and bowls of steaming oatmeal, plus a set of small, stainless steel containers filled with chopped bananas, walnuts, raisins, syrup and brown sugar.

A dog, heavy with pups, sauntered over, extending her ample girth beneath the table at our feet.

"Don't mind this one," Tanya said, shifting her own substantial weight from one foot to the other. Her fleshy cheeks were flushed and rosy in the chill morning air. "This one's been hanging around here since before the river broke," she said. "Dogs, they sense it coming, danger. She'll find her way home when she's ready, I don't doubt."

Maggie reached under the table and took a hold of the scruff of the dog's neck. "No tag," she said. "She looks pretty young for her condition, though I'll wager this is not her first litter."

The dog was in need of a heavy-duty grooming, her short coat caked with mud. The mutt appeared calm and friendly, relieved to find some company.

"Most likely she belongs to one of the travelers, puppy draggers they call them, though it's not a real nice thing to say in my mind." Tanya thought the dog was maybe part pit.

"I've fed the poor baby scraps," she added, "what with her puppies coming."

I petted the dog behind the ears and took a closer look. She was medium sized, stocky, tan and white colored with one blue eye, one brown.

Maggie liked the mix. "Look at her, a real sweetie. She'll make a good momma."

Tanya stepped back indoors in answer to the shrill, invasive call of her landline. We were alone, again, except for the dog.

"You never wanted any?" It just came out. I'd put her on the spot in an uncomfortable way. It was too late to take it back.

"Puppies?" she asked.

I reddened. "No. I meant kids."

It was unlike me to burst out with something so way out of line. It was none of my business.

Maggie took a second. She looked at me straight on, unwavering, as is her way.

"Yes, as a matter of fact," she said. "We tried for years. Never happened and the sad thing is, neither of us ever really knew if it was me or him that was the problem."

Her soon-to-be ex was not the type of dude to take any sort of failure lightly — "It would have hurt his manly pride if I'd placed the blame on him," she said. And so they had swept the fertility issue under the carpet.

I had to admire her honesty, though it flashed through my mind in that instant that safe sex, protection, all the shit you're supposed to think of before you hit the sack, well, that was the last thing we had stopped to consider during our throes of passion the night before — and again, that same morning. I mentally calculated the number of times we had taken that risk.

If it wasn't Maggie's problem, was it too late for her, anyway? Me, I was clueless as to when a woman's clock stops ticking and all. The few other women I was with over the past few years had taken pains with their own precautions. They'd been upfront about it, beforehand. Shows how little I'd thought things through. We'd leaped on each other without a second thought.

Maggie read my mind.

"I'm forty-six, Marcus," she said, in answer to alarm bells that continued to ring in my mind. Was I that easy to read?

"Technically, if I'm not the one with the fertility problem, I guess there might still be a small window of time for me to conceive," she said, forthright if nothing else. Her monthlies, according to Maggie, were as regular as clockwork, more reason for concern considering that I barely knew the woman.

I figured, oh well, fuck that shit, what the hell. Would it be so bad? I'd gotten away without impregnating anyone this far into my life. What were the chances? If our stars were indeed in some strange alignment in these first few wild times we'd been together, then we'd been fully consenting adults, the pair of us and we'd have to deal with it, though I had no clue as to what we'd do about it. Only time would tell. "Really, don't worry yourself," she said, making light of the subject. "I promise not to come knocking on your door with paternity papers."

She gazed over the fogged-in grove, most likely, I figured, mulling the subject over a minute or two more in her own mind. She turned back towards me, leaned over and took my hand in hers.

"I'm sorry, Marcus," she said, "We haven't exactly thought this through, have we? I want you to know, I have zero expectations beyond the day ahead."

I took hold of her upturned hand in mine, tracing the veins of the skin on the inside of her wrist with my thumb: "Taking it day by day," I said. "Best way in my book."

Truth is, waking up with Maggie was about the greatest start to any day I could remember. I'd thought I'd sealed off the part of me that would have allowed something this good to take a place in my life. I'd been so sure I'd lost all ability to feel anything more than the smallest pinprick of joy.

The sky, or what we could see of it through the heavy canopy of trees, revealed itself a thin strip of clear blue ribbon threading through a blanket of mist. It looked like we were in for a respite from the rain at least for the next few hours.

That meant we were free to make our move. I placed a call to the sheriff's department from Tanya's phone in reception, cell coverage being off and on, still spotty.

It took a fair bit of anxiously biding our time as we waited for a call back. We made our way down a wide staircase of muddy railroad ties that led to a grassy hillside ridge above a fast running winter creek. I laid my jacket down on a bench seat carved into a fallen redwood and we sat.

"It was a spot like this where I hid out," I confessed. "I settled on a hideout as far away from the world as I could find." After I'd waged an inner war on myself with the drugs and all, the towering redwoods were the closet place to a safe haven I could find.

Maggie linked her arm through mine and gently pressed me for more. "Why here, Marcus? Why the Russian River? Like the girls, you might have easily gone further north, inland, even more remote."

"After the explosion and my discharge, there was nothing for me back home," I explained. "I was sick and tired of people, noise, disfigurement, conflict. It was like the whole wide world was rotten to the core."

I'd wanted nothing more to do with it all, was the truth. "I figured if I hitchhiked my way far enough west I would come to the place where the world falls off its edge, the perfect peace of a vast nothingness."

"I can understand that," Maggie said, reassuringly. "You're not a total loser," she laughed, sharing how she'd suffered her own freak-out with regard to the rat race and all. "I guess that's why you do the work you do, out in the park, in the forest, steering as clear of the hamster wheel as is geographically possible," she said.

I had begun to heal in the redwoods, though I never knew it at the time, so much of it had been drug fueled. "Getting clean and finding work is what saved my life," I said. "If it weren't for these redwoods, I would never have met the folks who put me into rehab, never have met Bobby."

I found myself telling her how my grandparents had raised my brother and me in the Central Valley after our mom took off. My dad, their son, well, he walked out of the picture soon after our mother left. The dude was as selfish, cold-hearted and irresponsible as she, for he remarried pretty much as soon as the divorce came through and moved to Boston with his second wife and three kids from her first marriage. We were five years old.

"You have a twin?"

Did have. "He died. When we were ten."

I hadn't spoken Nick's name in years. If I'd talked to Bobby about him in the early days, he knew not to bring him up unless I did first. All things considered, my brother's death was way too painful for me to talk about. I'd kept memories of Nick firmly bottled up inside, all those years in the army and since.

"Nicholas and our grandmother, they were killed, together, car crash — drunk driver took them both out. She was behind the wheel of the old man's truck. Nick was up front beside her."

They'd been out running errands on a Saturday afternoon in readiness for Thanksgiving. Some old-timer who should never have been driving, let alone propping up the bar in town, had one two many and lost control when a stag leaped out into the road ahead.

"It would have been me in that truck with the two of them, only I was in bed with strep throat. Nick had just come through it, he was the one who'd passed it on to me."

Maggie touched my cheek lightly with her palm. "A twin brother," she said. "I'm so sorry, Marcus, I can't even begin to imagine your loss."

I thought of my gramps. The old boy died of a broken heart while I was on tour in Iraq. Loneliness and loss will do that to you.

"My grandfather was the one who taught me how to work with wood," I continued. "He was a union carpenter by trade. Gramps lost the home they'd worked so hard for in Stockton when tough times hit the industry. It wasn't easy for him bringing in those extra dollars at his age, taking care of me and all."

They'd lived on the poverty line their whole lives, my folks. They were good people and happy enough, given the cards they'd been dealt. "After Nick and my grandmother passed, it was never the same."

"That's a lot of heartbreak, Marcus," Maggie said. "And you never married? Have you ever been in love? Come on, surely so."

"There's been a few girlfriends over the years, nothing serious — one back in high school and one or two I've gotten to know working out at the coast," I confessed.

She smiled, said she was thankful for small mercies: "You're no stranger to the female form, I'll give you that."

Sex had never been a problem. It was intimacy I'd shied away from until I met her.

"Take it from me, Maggie, you've switched the light back on somehow. I'm telling you, sitting here with you is an exception to my solitary rule."

"One of life's great mysteries, Marcus," she replied. "Matters of the heart. Foolish to question these unexpected feelings when they come along."

"Hey, too much attention on me, the emotionally disabled," I said, only half joking. I was done with all the personal questions for now, eager to change the subject.

Maggie was quick to ease the tension. She kissed me lightly, warming her hands between my lower thighs. She changed the subject, recounting the times she'd swam in the calmer waters of the Russian River in the summer months when she was a kid. "Even though it's dangerous water in parts, whatever the time of year, due to the heavy undercurrent," she said. "Summer swimming at the river was something we all did, a rite of passage, you know. It was way safer for us to swim in the stretch of the river over at Johnson's Beach, roped off from the swifter currents."

Her grandparents had passed on all they'd learned about the river as kids: "The early Russian settlers, the logging," she said. "Come to think of it, do you suppose that Tanya may be descended from Russian blood?" Maggie asked. "She kind of looks like a pink-cheeked, round Russian stacking doll, doesn't she, perched on her stool, her hair, those high cheekbones of hers, the food?"

"Maybe, that would be cool. Tanya's a Russian sounding name —
makes sense," I replied.

If Tanya had Russian ancestors in the river region that takes its
name, her people arrived after they ran into a boatload of trouble in
maintaining stocks of food and supplies for their Alaskan settlements,
back in the early 1800s. Roaming Russian fur hunters spent years
scouring the Pacific coast south of Alaska for the best place to build a
Northern California settlement, one rich with sea otters for pelts. It
was these determined newcomers who built a fort some forty miles
north of where Maggie and I sat talking history of all things. The
ocean acted as a moat for Fort Ross on one side, the rugged Pacific
mountains protecting it on the other.

"Fort Ross proved as good a spot as any for the Russians, way
before the first coastal road came in," I explained. "To reach the fort in
those days, the only way in and out that rough and rocky terrain was
by boat, by ship, by trail and later, by wagon."

I pointed out a large patch of poison oak attempting to hide itself
amidst a bank of Scotch broom. "The natives who worked the land
around Fort Ross as day laborers and domestics were known to have
eaten poison oak to grow their immunity. Can you imagine? Many of
the Russian sailors married native women, so my guess is they tried it
out too."

Maggie had bit my collarbone lightly, the previous night. I moved
my hand inside of my shirt. No break to the skin, no swelling.

Birdsong broke out from high above, the soft yapping of the
Marbled Murrelet, preparing for flight, a small seabird that feeds on
the ocean by day and wings his way back home into the redwood
canopy come nightfall.

"You know," I said, "not all of the Russians and the natives got
along so well together within the fort's compound. It was not the
hunky-dory cohabitation of cultures we're led to believe."

Though the Russians were reportedly better behaved than the
Spanish missionaries who came next. "When they finally did push on
up the coast, the Spanish alienated the Russians and all but wiped out
the natives," I said. "Those who were left were rounded up and used
and abused like slaves in the early Spanish missions. Most of them died."

And, after they'd come close to wiping out the whole damn sea otter population in the region's waters, the Russians in turn, moved inland in order to launch their pillaging campaign on the redwoods.

"I guess they jumped at it being super lucrative, all this lumber, free for the picking," Maggie said, looking up into the canopy of the groaning giant beanstalks that towered above us. "Would've made more sense to them than farming the fort's blustery bluff," she added.

I've crossed paths in my line of work with conservationists and scientists who are setting up electronic monitoring in the more remote parts of the redwood forests. "It breaks my heart to think of the flora and fauna destroyed by the mass felling of an ancient ecosystem such as this," I admitted. "It's a crime against nature, that's what it is — the lumber that was stripped out of these forests over the past century and a half."

The key to the survival of the redwoods, I've come to accept, is to understand them, their function in controlling the movement of water in the forest, the sustaining role of the fog and the redwood burls.

"It's crazy to say it out loud," I said, as we sat there, dwarfed by giant redwoods as high as our eyes could see. "But the truth of it is, Maggie, all that's left of it is a tiny slice, a puny four percent of Northern California's early redwood forests are still in existence."

"So hard for me to imagine how magnificent a forest it must have been," Maggie sighed. "There's no end to man's greed, I guess." And, then: "What did happen to the Russians?" she asked.

I explained how, after Mexico and its rebel forces fought and won independence from Spain, land grants were drawn up to target the Russians, prevent them from staking claim.

"It was the more prominent Mexican families in California who took over the vast tracts of land," I said, taking pride of the knowledge I've gained in my years of working in the park system. "It would take another twenty years, but by the early 1840s, the Russians were gone." Not long after that, the U.S. wrestled the state from the Mexicans and the Gold Rush began, single worst thing that could've happened to the redwood forests of Northern California if you want my humble opinion.

Maggie inspected her boots, fancy footwear ill designed if you ask me for as rough an outdoor terrain as this. She picked at the dried mud that caked her heels with a stick. "Well, they're all gone now, the Russians, with the exception of Tanya," she said. The dog from the porch had followed us down to the creek. She nestled in a damp bed of crushed sorrel and sword fern, curled like a sleeping fox at Maggie's feet.

"What's your name, little honey momma?" Maggie asked.

"Little Honey, sounds about right," I said. "Look at her."

"Well then, Little Honey Momma it is. You'd best come along with us."

The dog appeared to grasp the randomness of the invitation that had come her way. She uncurled her heavy girth, stood to her feet and shook out her damp coat as a thousand droplets of mud and water sprayed our pant legs. Little Honey Momma stuck to Maggie like molasses, closely shadowing her as we made our way uphill.

Maggie's cell pinged back into service just as we reached the top. It was the sheriff's department calling back, giving us the green light to head on back along a cleared portion of River Road in order for me to retrieve my truck.

Tanya was visibly relieved to hear the news that we were taking the dog with us, her big face softened into a smile. "Don't suppose anybody's gonna come looking for her in truth," she said, reaching down to pet Little Honey Momma on the back of her head. "Better you guys than the shelter."

She offered to drive us the handful of miles to the spot where we'd left the truck. "Except for the shitload of mud and crap left behind, it's hard to believe this whole darn road was underwater, less than forty-eight hours ago," she said, hauling the rig of a dusty old Volvo wagon into gear, Diamonds and Rust blasting from a crackly cassette player. "I've seen it go under this way during many a rainy season," she said. I recognized the Joan Baez song from Bridget's playing Joan Baez at her place.

"Did you know that she wrote this song about Dylan?" Tanya asked, humming along loudly and way out of key. "King and Queen of folk there for a while, the pair of 'em. You'd be hardpressed to sing me a better love ballad," she said. "A complete novel in one short song, that's what they say." She cut Joan off toward the end of her hit as she pulled to a stop at a general store in the riverfront town of Guerneville.

The faded resort town enjoys what locals call a revival during the summer months. If you drive through anytime in July and August, a rainbow of colored plastic tubes and water wings hangs from hooks outside of the general store. Modest first and second homes line the riverbank, raised on stilts if the owners are smart enough and have the cash on hand to protect their properties against the onslaught of almost yearly winter floods.

Come storm season, the storefront, its neighboring small cafes and bars and all of the year-round residents of the town and other Russian River communities hunker down and brace themselves for the rising river water and, worst-case scenario, a flash flood such as the deadly one that we had the bad fortune to have been caught up in.

Maggie picked out a leash, a good, strong brush and a bottle of medicated dog shampoo. I pushed the cart and she tossed in two metal dog bowls, a gallon of drinking water and a bag of dried dog food.

Tanya handed us a pile of worn bath towels she'd pulled out of the trunk of her mud-encrusted wagon as we said our goodbyes. It was the ill-fated spot where we'd abandoned the truck.

"Make her a comfy bed in the back," Tanya suggested. "And let's hope for your sakes she holds on to those pups 'til you get to where you're going." Maggie fairly beamed as she petted the dog behind her ears, a small gesture of compassion in an unstable world.

Lucky for me and Little Honey Momma Maggie has a thing for waifs and strays. Who was I to say no to taking the darn dog along for the ride?

CHAPTER 19

MAGGIE

L ittle Honey Momma, Little Honey for short, perched in the back
of the truck for no more than ten minutes before the little sneak
squeezed through and squirrelled her big barrel of a tummy between
the two of us.

I surfed through a bunch of fuzzy radio stations for several minutes,
settling instead on a Bob Marley album from a CD with a cracked
cover I mined from an alphabetized stack of assorted Rocksteady,
Reggae and Ska in the glove compartment.

"Cool, man," I said, teasingly. "I never pegged you for a Rasta
dude."

"Believe me, it was all country music growing up," Marcus replied,
play-slapping my thigh with the back of his hand. "Never did care for
it."

Marcus was an easy and natural convert of the Jamaican rhythm
guitar, his body in tune with the strong drum beat of the music, his left
hand pulsating on the steering wheel on drum beats two and four.
Andres had been into Reggae when I'd first gotten together with him.

"I met myself a bunch of dreadlocked Rasta dudes the summer I
was camped out in the woods," Marcus explained. "They were headed
to the Reggae on the River festival up in Humboldt." It had been his
first serious introduction to the sound of the Kingston slums.

He'd joined them, working a stint on the festival's security team, a
bunch of guys in charge of the various duties involved in handling a
large, unruly festival crowd. His military background was just what
they'd been looking for. "No papers or nothing," he said. "Took me
on my word."

I rolled down the window and breathed in the fresh, moist, inland air with its own distinctive aroma of bay laurel and wet rain on oaks. Microclimates in coastal Northern California change dramatically according to the specific geographic terrain: quality of sunlight; fog; wind; rain; heat and cold.

I hadn't given a lot of thought to the soundtrack of my life. I'd had little choice but to conform to my older sister's musical tastes as a teen. Bridget pretty much dominated the theme tunes of my high school years. Her yard sales and thrift store buys in hippie West Marin built her a pretty impressive throwback collection any American rock music lover would be proud of — The Grateful Dead, Jimi Hendrix, Frank Zappa, Jefferson Airplane, you name it. As for me, I was happy to segue into the world of clubs and college parties in the pre-grunge era of the Los Angeles music scene. Michael and Janet Jackson, Madonna, Whitney Houston, Phil Collins, George Michael — the 80s' for me proved a far cry from the dulcet tones of the rock and folk music Bridget had spoon-fed me on.

Losing myself in the music, my mind drifted back to the night before, our impulsive and awkwardly timed coming together. I reprimanded myself for about half a second, but I had to admit, it had felt so natural, it always has. I raised a hand to the flush of my cheek as I replayed the conjoining of our naked bodies with all our imperfections. Simple truth is I was comfortable around him, above him, beneath him, beside him. I couldn't bring myself to feel bad about it. No more regrets, I told myself.

Marcus squeezed my hand, pressing on as we put the crazy events of the past couple of days behind us for as long as the music lasted. The truck's wheels whirred past green hills studded with red barns, 500-year-old oak trees and, fairly soon, mile after mile of pear orchards lining the freeway along the edge of the small Mendocino County seat of Ukiah.

Snowy-white tree blossoms looked like they were on the brink of blooming into buds despite all of the constant rain.

Ukiah is home to the ancient basket makers of the Northern Pomo, the last semiurban center before the modern day traveler crosses into the realm of the Redwood Curtain.

"Most of these businesses around here deal entirely in cash these days," Marcus said, looking out at the fringe of a Victorian farming community-cum-cannabis industrial center. "Forget the credit-heavy culture of the rest of this country, it's a cash pot crop that keeps this community afloat," he said.

"Well, hey, hasn't this been hunter/farmer country, in one form or another from the start?" I asked. I learned about the Pomo Tribe, in school, how they built their homes like beehives with sunken floors and willow walls along trails to the coast. "We could learn a lot from the first people."

"There were treaties that were set in place intended to preserve this land for its rightful owners, only they were never upheld," Marcus replied. "The brutal truth of it is that Pomo villagers were rounded up and moved to camps in less fertile reservations. The Bloody Run they called it." He continued on with his knowledge of this grave injustice. "The river waters ran red with native blood. A crime against humanity, that's what is was."

Rugged, wooded canyons came into view as we cleared the flatter lands. Marcus took his hand from my thigh to change gears as we made our way uphill, winding northward toward the one-time major logging hub of Willits, population nowadays around 5,500 according to the freeway sign.

The occasional lumbering RV, a brave motorcyclist dressed for the elements and a steady flow of larger trucks and vehicles passed us on the southbound lane. The driver's faces were a blur depending on their speed and motion in their downhill descent from the higher elevation of Mendocino and Humboldt counties.

Tempting though it was to put foot to metal on this clear stretch of open road, the storms had wreaked havoc on road conditions and, after our nightmare start to the journey two days before, Marcus was justifiably wary.

"Keep an eye out for repairs to the asphalt from here on out, Maggie," he said. "Heavy rainfall leaves a quick fix in the asphalt a gooey mess. It's a danger to the tires."

It was a relief to me that he was as in tune with the road and the vehicle as he was with the music that lightened our mood. Bumpy, scarred and potholed portions of the road surface reverberated at random through the core of our bodies.

"To think," I said, my imagination slipping back into the un-populated past, nudged by the scenery, I suppose, "in the old days, the only way up here was by horse and carriage. Rainy season such as this would have made for a rough old ride."

I'd never before set foot in Willits prior to the fortuitous pit stop I made with Marcus. I'd describe it as a more of an on-the-way-to-somewhere town than a notable destination though the folk who live here appear to have a genuine fondness for its strong sense of community and its intrinsic, rural charm.

We drove through a welcome to Willits arch with its testimonial to the fact we had officially entered into the heart of Mendocino County — gateway to the redwoods.

Marcus pulled over into the busy parking lot of a small, independent market, promoting itself loudly and proudly as organic in large, cheerful hand carved letters on a freshly painted, wooden rainbow-shaped sign.

"This is most likely our last chance for any decent food for miles," he announced. In contrast to the gloomy outdoors, the store inside was bright and inviting under its LED lighting. It possessed the peculiar, comforting aroma of a green, organic grocery store, a small market, the sort my folks would have referred to before the foodie revolution took hold as one of those "new fangled health food stores."

Together, we browsed the aisles of freshly baked breads, inhaling the smell of the brown paper wrapped sourdough, olive, jalapeño and round wheat loaves, the yeasty, oat-scented lure of the bulk bins. We passed by the fragrant shelves of incense, peppermint-scented natural soaps and essential oils in the heath and beauty department. Marcus stopped and picked out a small bar of soap, misshaped, unwrapped and rosemary-scented. "I'm a convert," he joked, causing me to blush again at the thought of our previous night's compact and erotic lathering. I emptied the contents of our basket onto the conveyor belt, the bar of soap, two bottles of ginger and hibiscus tea mushroom, probiotic kombucha (Marcus' choice), a share-size, turkey and sprouts sub sandwich, one large bag of black pepper Kettle Chips and a small bunch of bananas. A woman in a voluminous multicolored patchwork-knitted poncho with a matching bobble hat looked like she'd been standing in line since the 70s. I played with the bar of soap, inhaling its scent while I mused on her outlandish outfit and waited our turn at the checkout.

Expeditions to the grocery store with Andres had been notoriously longwinded and nearly always painful. We had never been on the same page, even on the smallest of things.

Over the air The Mamas and The Papas belted out their billionth rendition of California Dreamin'. I smiled again, for here I was indeed, on such a winter's day, buying groceries for God's sake with a guy I barely knew, a guy I'd had sex with three times in less than 24 hours. Even though I've been inexplicably connected to Marcus since the get-go, I couldn't help but feel at that moment that he had sprung out of nowhere, as in a dream. A really great dream, could he be for real? I took a good, long look at his profile in line and figured on the spot to take my own advice, there was no sense in questioning such rare good fortune.

My eyes hovered over his shoulder, drawn to the deals at the entrance to the wine aisle, a large stack of cases filled with attractive and enticingly labeled Mendocino and Sonoma County wines on special that week. If I'd been in the store by myself, I would've made a beeline for a bargain case. Instead, I reminded myself that kombucha is fermented. It had taken me several attempts to come around to this fizzy, vinegary drink that's supposedly good for the guts. I've since found it a surprisingly semi-decent way to half-fool my cravings for wine with its tiny trace amount of alcohol. I forced my eyes away from the cases of wine and focused instead on the counter stand, grabbing the next thing I saw, a pocket-sized handbook with a charming, hand illustrated cover on the history of Willits and surrounding area.

Our fresh-faced, patchouli-scented cashier with long, tousled, undone hair looked to be Mia's age, or thereabouts. She flashed us an endearing, lopsided lower lip-pierced smile as I flipped through the handbook. "It's worth a read," she half yelled over the din of the relentless Mamas and Papas and the noisy banter between the neighboring cashiers and customers.

"Make the author's day and buy one, go on," she urged. "And better still, pick up one of his favorite black bean and veggie wraps while you're at it and he'll love you forever. He'll even sign his book for you."

"Walter," she said. "Dude is the man, our number one favorite winter regular, we all love him in here. He volunteers at the museum — in fact, he's taking care of the garden, today."

We found Walter, mid-60s, full-bearded, raffishly good-looking still, intent in his work in pruning one of a double row of tall, thorny rose bushes that lined the pathway to the museum. I doubted he was one to let something as unimportant as a rainy day dampen his enthusiasm for the outdoor life. I felt an instant urge to hang out and chill, to watch him at his slow, careful work selecting which branch and where to apply the rose clipper for maximum effect for next spring's bloom.

Walter's laid-back, easygoing vibe was evident in his winter dress sense of surf shorts, hoodie, woolen socks and Birkenstock sandals.

He took the veggie wrap from my hands with a crooked smile, a deep pair of crow's feet crinkling at the sides of his eyes.

"Why thank you. Good gal to send you over with a bite to eat just as I was starting to feel a tad peckish," he said. "Creature of habit, me — and that one, well she is nothing short of the best darn natural bookseller in town."

The museum, Walter went on to explain, was his refuge during the rainy months. "On account of my spending most of my daytime hours here from the start of the holiday season, all the way through early spring as a general rule," he said. "The rest of the year," Walter continued, "you'll find me back at my own place up in Garberville."

We sat on the stone steps of the museum beside Walter as he ate, explaining at length, between mouthfuls, how he'd taught environmental science in high school for nigh on 30 years. "Til tragedy struck a few years back," he said, all matter-of-fact, like he'd come to terms with it. "My sweet gal, my bride, my Connie, love of my life, best school librarian in the west." They'd worked together at the same school for years, he said. "She passed on less than a month after taking early retirement. Never saw it coming. Heart attack."

Walter's parents are still alive and as well as is expected for their age, puttering around Willits, their hometown, the pair of them, each well into their eighth decade. They live alone, without his help for the warmer months of the year, comfortably rattling around the same old house that Walter was born and raised in, a block away from the museum.

"It's ever since Connie passed I've been making my way down from the mountains for the winter months," Walter said, his face crumpled a little and I could see he was watery eyed under his tough veneer. "My number one priority nowadays is taking care of my folks through the rainy season, that and helping out here at the museum when they need it most. I put this little booklet on the town's history together last winter in memory of my gal."

The cloud of sadness I'd detected lifted and his upbeat demeanor returned as soon as he stepped back to inspect his morning's work.

"Local lore was our thing, you see, Connie and me," he said. "She loved the history as much as she loved me. Man, I miss that gal."

He shook his head and changed the subject, asking what it was that brought us through these parts in his words: "During this godforsaken time of year." I was drawn to confide in him and I blurted out the truth of the matter, my whole increasingly practiced mini-version of the messed up story of our reason for being on the road.

Our new friend barely flinched as he finished chewing on a mouthful of veggie wrap. He looked me in the eye. "Honey, there are all sorts of folk up there in the more hidden tracts of the redwoods. Best you two hurry along, find out where it is your gals are holing up."

Marcus shot me a look that Walter immediately intercepted. This talk was starting to unnerve me. I felt my lower lip tremble.

"Matter of fact," Walter jumped right in, "if you've room for the company and you don't mind it, I'll take advantage of the ride and head on up there with the two of you."

He said he was due a check-in on his place in Garberville. "My neighbor, Lori, she knows everyone. Lori's your best bet, connection-wise — she'll point you in the right direction, help get you started in the tracking down of your niece and her young buddy."

Walter said Lori was a member of a group looking out for vulnerable kids such as Mia and Jazmin. "They do their best in talking the younger ones into turning back home. Keep track as much as they're able of those that do insist on hanging on in hopes of finding work."

Fifteen minutes later, on the porch of his parents' weathered, ramshackle, two-story Victorian home, Walter said a quick goodbye to his frail looking folk. The sky, though dry for a spell, weighed heavy with low hanging clouds.

"I'll be back real soon," he told them. "You take good care of each other, now, you promise me? Stay out of trouble!" The frail old pair appeared to be okay with his departure as they waved goodbye from their walkers, side by side. A set of antiquated porch furniture poked out from a tarp cover, as old, spindly and fragile as its owners.

"Never do know if I'm saying goodbye for the last time, at their age," Walter confessed. "I'm no spring chicken myself," he said. "It's bittersweet when the ol' folks battle on this long."

Our spontaneous traveling companion tossed a well-worn canvas bag into the back of the truck and hopped on up to the back seat with the air of a spritely young guy. "Travel light," he said. "That's my motto."

A nonplussed Little Honey Momma was more inclined to lounge on the back seat now she had a friendly and willing traveling companion to curl and warm herself against and in as comfortable a position as she was able to muster, given her condition. I turned to see Walter place his hand in the small of her back as she snuggled into her pile of towels. She closed her eyes and slept, her breathing deep and contented.

I wished I were as easily settled as we drove over the tree-lined border of Mendocino and into Humboldt County with the storm swollen Eel River, 40 feet deep in parts, snaking beneath us.

~

"Who was it who named it the Eel River, anyway?" Marcus asked, as we three peered down at the rushing water. Walter grinned, boyishly. Of course he would know how it came by its name. He seemed to know everything, including the fact there never was any such thing as

217

an eel in these waters. It didn't take me long to figure Walter is a man who likes to hear the sound of his own voice, waxing lyrical with his encyclopedic knowledge of the region.

"This swirling waterway was only lightly used by the sparsest of tribes until the 1880s rolled around and shook things up," he pontificated, setting the scene for more.

I closed my eyes and listened to the cadence of his melodic diatribe. He described the first outside explorers in the area making their historic trade of a cast iron frying pan for a native fisherman's haul of bloodsucking, snakelike sea creatures fished from the remote waterway.

"On account that they were half starved," Walter explained, "the boneless bodies of the Pacific lamprey looked a good deal more like eels than anything else that came to mind and so they decided that is what they were eating."

According to Walter, our newfound personal guide to the natural world, the hideous looking sea lamprey, a strangely popular dish in the Netherlands and France is: "A highly unattractive, overrated delicacy, if you ask me." He made a face. "Tastes more like stewed beef than fish."

The Eel River ran with formidable force that February afternoon. Walter told us how the average flow of the waterway in a wet winter season is more than 100 times greater than in the warmer summer months. I shuddered at the thought of how Bobby had zero chance against the fast flowing water of the neighboring Russian River.

The pitch and rhythm of Walter's voice drew me further in. I was learning how to dip in and out of his elaborate storytelling technique, honing in on the main elements of his bountiful stash of potentially useful information.

I opened the window to a welcome breeze carrying the aroma of damp earth, wet rock, and thick, fibrous bark.

Walter prattled on. "You'd be hard pushed to believe, considering the inhospitable nature of the place at this time of year, yet come the month of August, a swell of youngsters such as your niece and her pal converge from all corners of the world. Thousands of them milling around, pitching a sea of tents along the Eel in hopes of being hired on as trimmers."

It was hard to picture the river not raging.

"Truth is, locals such as myself, no offense to your gals — we consider ourselves fully justified in growing increasingly peeved by these large throngs of ukulele-playing, alpaca poncho-wearing pricks who converge on what is basically an escalating human circus up here," Walter said.

"Tell us how you really feel, Walter! Sounds like a freak show for sure," I said, picturing Mia and Jazmin in the midst of such a crowd.

"Aside from the fact there are way too many folk thrashing the place, shitting on the riverbank, urinating in the water and wrecking the ecosystem with their birth control and opioid piss — they are draining our community nonprofits. Safety issues are out of control."

Marcus shook his head. I guess he's been on both sides of this fence with his troubled past. Walter continued: "Never more dangerous out here than it is today, life is cheap since the lunatics took over the asylum. Welcome to the Wild West of transnational criminal activity." He took a deep breath. "Narcotics, money laundering, weapons, trafficked humans, it's all here, right under our noses, hidden in plain sight under a canopy of guerilla grows."

"Jesus," I said, wondering for the umpteenth time what corner of hell my niece had gotten herself into.

Walter claimed it was the criminal cartel growers that caused the most mayhem, those from south and central America: "And, as we're hearing of more frequently, now, Eastern European gangs that range in size and level of sophistication."

He was tracing the line of the river in the steam of the passenger window as I'd turned to look at him. Walter rapidly digressed into topography and how the Eel carries the highest suspended sediment load of any U.S. river its size. I followed his gaze as he pointed out landslide after landslide along the narrowed, two lane highway.

"The water, see —awash with rocks and soil and trees."

For thousands of years, Walter explained, it was the Eel River that supported the region's ancient and abundant forests as well as one of the world's largest salmon/steelhead trout runs.

"After the white man arrived, logging, grazing, rail and road construction combined to make a drastic impact on the health of the wild watershed and its increasingly fragile ecology." He described a series of dams built in the river's headwaters in the early 1900s, designed to provide water for the newcomers, the settlers of Mendocino and Sonoma Counties.

"It was these dams and diversions that slowly started on a long course of killing the river. It was so much so that native salmon and steelhead neared extinction." Walter cleared his throat and outlined the environmental crisis in more detail: "Think of it like an overdraft. When use of groundwater grossly exceeds the natural recharge, a river dries up. It's simple math — understanding efficient use of water is critical; it's the only way for all of us, now and in the future. Drought or no drought."

Marcus had kept quiet to this point, driving steadily uphill. "It's all gone to shit," he said, breaking his silence and shaking his head a second time as he reached for my hand. I wasn't sure if he was specifically referring to the state of the waterway, the underbelly of criminal activity in the region, or what had happened to Bobby.

Walter reached forward and rested the palm of his large hand on Marcus' right shoulder.

"I hear you, man," he said and, after a brief pause, "In other news, looking at the bigger picture, all of this here rain we've had this winter, it's a blessing of sorts. The salmon and steelhead populations, wouldn't you know it, they are slowly making a comeback? There's been a huge push to create awareness of the issue over the past few years and it appears to be working."

His profile looked like he may have stepped straight out of a 49ers mining prospectus. A head of untamed, silvery, shoulder-length hair and beard flecked with a suitable sprinkling of gold framed his weathered face inset with a pair of piercing blue eyes the color of the sky in the Sierras on a clear spring morning. I asked him if any of the tribes who lived along this waterway were still in existence.

"The natives in these parts were deeply wronged, segregated into reservations a good deal farther away from the Eel," he replied.

I caught myself wondering if Walter's late wife had dozed off to his well-meant, long-winded stories, or had she hung on to his every word? I peered out into the damp, dark corridors of trees, at least some of which I'd wager a guess, date back 2,000 years or more. The tribes Walter talked of had been driven like cattle, in all weather, corralled like animals.

"What sickens me most is when I think of the old people, the very young and the sick, those who never made it to the reservations, the ones who perished along the way," he said. This wild and primal place bears its past with a stoic silence. Several large redwoods visible on my side of the highway bore charred bark, sign of a past forest fire.

"Over time," Walter added, "those who did survive made their peace with one another, as best as they were able, intermarrying, their descendants forming a new tribe and, over the years, a common lifestyle evolved."

He talked of a sacred ritual known as the Feather Dances of the former river tribes. "A hopeful teaming up with a bunch of friends of the river takes place most years," he claimed. "It's said that these dances, gatherings of folk from all walks of life, have been a big part in bringing back the fish."

I stuck my hand out of the window, palms up to feel the misty drizzle of the late afternoon. The rush of the river, its furious swell would be fit to burst by springtime, when snowpack melt into the highest levels of the waterway. If the redwoods are the heart and soul of the forest, the river is the blood, a roaring terror in the rainy season, a swift, strong, force of life in the warmer months. High above the waterway, the sky had turned a dusky tone of watery lilac.

We three looked down at the swell of the river as it hungrily consumed the native plant life along its lower bank, whole bodies of grass, tree branches and rocks sweeping beneath us in its wake.

The Eel River basin empties into the Pacific at the northern end of the San Andreas Fault, the precarious juncture of the three tectonic plates Bobby and Marcus had talked of two days earlier.

I scanned a large information board ahead on the side of the highway — redwood roots, according to the signage, reach down to twelve feet underground in a maze of substructure burrowing deep into the earth of this seismic epicenter. "Something else I may as well ask you Walter," I posed, "is, should we find ourselves in the forest when the big one hits, what the hell do we do? Where do we run? And how is it so many of these giants have withstood past centuries of quakes?" I could only assume that any tree around long enough to grow to almost four hundred feet tall must have its list of natural disasters pretty much dialed in.

"I mean if the ground swells violently in the redwood forest, is there a warning pulse?" I asked.

"They say that the wildlife acts real strange, but it's never been proven. It's like waiting for the shoe to drop knowing full well that we're sure to get one big, honking shaker sooner or later," Walter explained.

"As with any earthquake zone wherever you are in the world, best step away from tall objects, trees or no trees, seek open space, drop and take shelter. What I do know is that if the movement along the fault is vertical, it's possible the sea floor displacement could trigger a tsunami. In that case, best act fast and make a move to higher ground."

Marcus pressed on, uphill, as Walter deftly segued on to the next subject on our list of natural disasters — landslides. The guy just never stopped talking. "Scientists refer to the soil you see around here as blue goo," he continued. "On account of the soil being blue-gray in color with a tendency to slip."

We had passed a number of small slides of damp green hillside cordoned off with bright orange traffic cones. I shrunk back into my seat, chilled by the prospect of even a slight chance of a big slide suddenly dumping down on us, burying us alive — truck and all. Nothing now seemed too fantastical after what had happened to Bobby.

If any substantial portion of the hillside slipped, covering us in mud, there was no one to come to our rescue. We were, for sure, among the only fools on the road that late in the day as the storm clouds continued to build.

Marcus eased the truck into a parking space in a scenic roadside rest stop, a spectacular, ozone encapsulated location for a pee break, lush, green canyon on one side, river on the other and creepily remote. Had I been driving this route alone, there's no way I'd have chosen to make a solo pit stop in such a lonely place. At least the eerie atmosphere did not deter Little Honey Momma from going about her business.

The four of us clambered down a soggy, slippery riverbank to the rocky shore, Marcus proving adept at coping with all-weather terrain. Walter was equally comfortable out there in the wild.

Yellow banana slugs slid around in startling numbers, a convention of them, reveling in the wet conditions. The largest specimen I spotted was a crazy full ten inches long. I tried my best to step around so as not to squash these strange, shiny, insanely colored creatures of the woods.

Who knew, the banana slug is mostly made up of water? Walter did, naturally.

"These slugs are amazing," he marveled, "Did you know they power themselves entirely by their own slime gliding along the roughest terrain, the healthiest of them living for as long as seven years? And, what's more, have a guess at how they find each other." I rolled my eyes, shook my head.

"Do tell."

"Darn it if they don't leave behind a lubricant chemical track. Even better, banana slugs leave no permanent or even semi-permanent trace — they actually eat one another's slime."

Scientists, Walter explained, are studying the banana slug to see what the future of slime might hold for the environment, for human life.

"Tell us more about the settlers here — the Europeans," I asked, moving on from our natural science lesson to veer back into a seemingly limitless anthropological knowledge trove.

Walter was clearly in his element with Marcus and me at once his most responsive, or at the very least, captive students.

"Most of the settlers were Gold Rush prospectors that never did get lucky finding any gold," he said. We were leaning against a large, cold, smooth-sided boulder, the three of us side by side, Little Honey by our feet. "Settlements gradually built up along the coast, those with good access to the Pacific, boats coming up from San Francisco. It was the more adventurous folk who spread east into the Eel River Valley, pushing their boundaries deeper into native land."

Wispy strands of creeping fog rolled stealthily upriver. The temperature had dropped noticeably.

"Logging companies established themselves in the region at a rapid pace, as they also did along the Russian River, stripping the river basin of hundreds of millions of feet of redwood timber board in no time," Walter said.

The wood was floated down the river to an estuary.

"Given the many twists and turns in the Eel, larger logs were cut into more manageable, more easily floatable pieces of wood that they called cants," he explained. We craned our necks to look down river at the pearl gray, by then fluffier curls of incoming fog.

By the 1880s, I discovered, the Eel River and the Eureka Railroad that was later deemed as being way too dangerous to maintain, transported tons of lumber from the estuary to Humboldt Bay. From there hundreds of thousands of lengths of solid redwood were shipped to San Francisco to build its famous Victorian structures.

I've rented apartments in countless Victorian conversions in San Francisco over the years. I thought about the last place I'd shared with Andres, the one I'd walked away from, a large, light-filled, top floor apartment in an ornate Victorian structure most certainly constructed from redwood logs floated down this very waterway.

I'd never given it much thought, the monstrous volume of raw material acquired in the mad race for development in San Francisco and the many emerging towns and small cities that popped up throughout Northern California during the Gold Rush.

I strained my neck and looked upwards into the canopy as daylight dwindled and the treetops faded into a dirty pink sky. The liner of my old leather jacket was proving insufficient for the necessary insulation and I shivered.

"Oh, hello . . . we have company," Walter remarked.

Across the riverbank, we watched as a family of three deer, a mother and her fawns froze in place. We none of us moved a foot until the mother deer backed slowly into the shadows of the forest, followed by her young.

"These beautiful, sacred redwoods, home to these and many more magnificent creatures, represent a mere fragment of the global forest it once was. We're talking millions of years," Walter whispered, in the deer's wake. "Gets me every time."

"We were just talking about this," Marcus replied. "Maggie and me. The fact that the redwoods covered much of the world's hemisphere . . . Alaska, Siberia, Greenland."

"It makes me happy to think of the dinosaurs that rubbed elbows with these trees," Walter continued as we made our way back uphill to the truck. I grabbed on to strands of longer grasses for support. "Continents shifted, climates changed. The ancient redwood forest shrunk to what remains today."

Marcus caught my eye and made a face as Walter rambled on.

"It only added insult to injury," Marcus interjected, moving the topic along a pace: "the logging industry coming into its own was a terrible blow for the already endangered redwoods."

Marcus helped a struggling Little Honey Momma scramble up a steep section of the bank, pushing her gently from her backside.

"We ought to be more than aware of our follies, by now," Walter added as he opened the door for Little Honey, avoiding the bulge of her belly as he carefully hoisted her up. "It's our responsibility, all of us, to protect these coastal redwoods — Sequoia Sempervirens," he said, quoting the scientific name of the colossal beauties that watched down on us.

If there was any place to reach out and hug a tree, this was it, the Redwood Highway being so narrow in parts that I could have easily rolled down my window and touched my palm to the rough, red bark of any one of these gentle giants.

Borders are easily confused when crossing out of densely forested Humboldt and into Mendocino and Trinity counties within the Emerald Triangle. I think of the region now not as a triangle as such, more like the side profile of a woman looking over from the coast to the east. Waist up is what folk say they see of her silhouette — her backbone forming the spine of the more remote parts of the Lost Coast.

"How many people live up here?" I asked.

"Less than a quarter million in all three counties," Walter replied. "Not counting the extras who flood in for the trimming during harvest time."

Marcus talked of it being the perfect place to grow weed given the warm, fertile soil and a typical 14 to 18 hours of sunlight every 24-hour cycle. "Airflow and breeze being optimal," he said.

Walter agreed. "Average temperature sits between 70 and 80 degrees," he said. "Most of the folk who live here are largely minding their own business, spread out among tens of thousands of square miles of curvy, narrow, isolated dirt roads in dense forest land, though most, these days, are directly or indirectly involved in or impacted by the pot growing industry."

"Why'd you quit teaching?" I asked. My eyes were immediately drawn to what looked like the flash of lights a ways up ahead.

Walter shrugged his shoulders. "I gave it up, called it a day after Connie passed. Lost the heart for dealing with a classroom of hormonal teenagers." I turned to him as he moved closer to peer through the windshield and check out the disturbance, one hand on top of his duffle bag, the other rested in the small of Little Honey's back.

"Looks like trouble ahead," Marcus said, slowing to a crawl and pulling to a stop beside a cop car's flashing lights. An empty sheriff deputy's vehicle was stopped at an awkward angle clear across the center of the highway.

We were close enough to see in through the open driver's seat door, to hear the engine running. My hackles rose. Visibility was fading fast.

"Wait here," Walter instructed as he slid a pistol out of his pack and slipped it into his jacket.

"What the hell?" My eyes popped wide at the sight of the gun.

"Never travel without one these days," Walter replied. "Connie, bless her, she would not have heard of it, old hippie that she was, but she's gone and times have changed. No need for you two to be afraid, it's called moving with the times, merely a safety precaution."

"Sure appears as if you're well equipped to protect what's yours," Marcus said, reaching across to stop me as I motioned to open my door.

In one smooth move, he released the latch on the glove compartment, keeping his eyes trained on Walter in the rearview mirror.

My eyes widened a second time as Marcus felt around and retrieved a fixed blade survival knife from behind the stack of CDs, the sort my old man had favored for setting traps, cutting branches, carving wood, skinning rabbits.

"Hop into the back seat with the dog, Maggie," Marcus instructed, keeping his cool. He slipped the knife into his boot. "Lay low and lock the doors."

"Hell no, you're not leaving me here, I'm coming with you," I shot back, my animal instinct kicking in, a rush of adrenaline charging my veins.

"Best you listen to Marcus in this instance," Walter leaned forward and intervened. "Don't take this the wrong way, but this may not be the right time for you to prove your mettle. You've got bigger fish to fry."

The city girl in me believed there was safety in numbers if nothing else, though I took short stock of what he'd said and slunk, reluctantly onto the back seat alongside Little Honey Momma, locking the doors behind the guys as they stepped out to approach the flashing vehicle. I peeped out of the side window to watch as they walked slowly, side by side, Walter pointing his pistol into the open door, while Marcus kept an eye on the surrounds.

Later, Marcus explained, it was on account of the sheriff deputy's shotgun being missing, removed from its strap in the front of the vehicle and there being nothing and nobody in the back seat or the trunk, not a single soul or evidence of another vehicle in sight, that prompted them to investigate further.

"Law enforcement is forever on the lookout for cannabis traveling south, narcotics, weapons and drugs being ferried in the opposite direction, the Redwood Highway being a major portal of illegal trafficking, drugs and people, both," he'd said.

Minutes after I spotted the tops of their heads disappearing down the riverbank, I came close to having another of my fake heart attacks at the sudden sound of rapping on the passenger seat window above my head. I flipped around and found myself eyeball to eyeball through the glass with a zit-faced kid — a teenager, dancing around on his feet, frantic. He was maniacally motioning for me to open the door, to give him the keys.

In a flash, I pressed the alarm button on the electronic keys Marcus had placed in the palm of my hand. I kicked the passenger door open and hurled myself out into a somewhat unstable standing position. The second I found my balance, I took off, running, leaving Little Honey Momma in the truck, initial thoughts rushing through my mind that she would jump out after me.

I never paused to turn my head though I heard his body stumble into the side of the truck as he came running after me. It didn't take him long to pick up sufficient speed to take me down. My knees and the bottoms of my palms stung, the weight of his slight frame on my back, briefly, as he rolled me around, straddling my torso on his knees, prying my fist open, yelling in Spanish: "Dame las llaves" — "Give me your keys".

He was more afraid of me than I was of him of that I was sure. Still, he'd had the strength to take me down and keep me there and he grabbed what he was searching for, leaping up after he'd pulled my clenched fist apart, taking off running in a cartoon cloud of dust, back in the direction of the two empty vehicles.

It took me a minute to compose myself, to figure out if I'd done any more serious damage than the stinging cuts and bruises of my fall onto the loose rocks on the surface of the road. I placed my hands back on the ground and slowly rolled myself up into a standing position with a view of the road behind me. I felt dizzy but my adrenaline continued to pump. I strained my eyes to better see what I could already hear — he was clearly having trouble getting the truck into gear, revving the engine over and over. The kid was clumsily attempting to figure his way around a manual transmission.

Finally the truck lunged forward a ways as he tried to make a U-turn. I raced toward the vehicle and launched myself by some crazy-ass impulse on top of the hood, pressing my body onto the windshield. I held on to the wipers for dear life; that served as double duty in blocking his vision from the driver's seat.

"Don't ever ask me to pull a stunt like this again," I warned Marcus, later, "Where the hell I found the strength I have no idea, but I was not about to let the fucker get away with your truck and with Little Honey Momma in her condition all shook up on the back seat and all."

"No messing with your gut-reaction, Ms. McCleery, that's for sure," Marcus replied, wide-eyed, turning my hands in his to inspect the damage. It dawned on me he didn't even know my married name. I was done with it, anyway. It felt surprisingly good to reclaim my bloodline and my fighting spirit. I should never have given it up for Andres.

Anyway, once I'd latched myself onto the windshield like some kind of mad, giant leech, the kid pressed his foot to the gas and screeched around a sharp turn in the highway, lurching into second gear and screeching forward in the southbound direction. Somehow, in my head, I sensed he was going to have even more trouble getting into third and so I clung on, despite my almost pissing myself in fear that he'd run us into a tree, or the river.

I'd say we were a little less than a mile down the deserted highway before he'd ditched his dumb-ass carjacking idea. He slammed on the brakes, leapt out and scrambled up into the dense grove of trees on the hillside running parallel to the road.

As for me, well, I took my driver's test in the old man's truck that I'd learned to maneuver around the ranch from the time I could see above the steering wheel. Stick shift is second nature to me. No sooner than he'd taken off up into the trees, I'd slid myself off the hood and onto the ground, raced around the side of the truck and hopped in through the open driver's seat door. I turned around just long enough to check on a surprisingly nonplussed Little Honey Momma, flipped an impressive U-turn and floored it back to where I'd seen Marcus and Walter head down the riverbank by the side of the still flashing sheriff deputy's vehicle. The two of them were standing in the center of the highway, hands on hips, a third guy, short and round in a sheriff deputy's uniform —the three of them looking totally dazed and disoriented. I'd felt like I'd been unwillingly cast in a high-speed collision course car chase movie scene, my fight-or-flight reaction having kicked into overdrive along with a rush of my body's vital defense mechanisms.

The teenage failed carjacker fit the description of one of two kids the deputy dude had pulled over for weaving over the center divide. It was the same idiot boy who had knocked him out with a punch to the head and tied the officer to a tree down by the river's edge.

"Did you see the second one, female?" the sheriff deputy asked. "Whole thing happened so damn fast. I figure given his move to jack the truck, she'd ditched him when he was down by the river, took off with the goods most like ... a solo mule makes a boatload more money than two."

He turned on his dispatch radio and proceeded to issue a multi-county alert. "This is Deputy Alejandro Hernandez — two suspects are on the run following abduction of a law enforcement officer during an apprehension for suspected drug transportation ... "

Walter volunteered to accompany the deputy in tracking down the boy. "Kid can't have gotten far by foot."

Marcus sat me in the truck beside Little Honey Momma, shielding me from any further incident or episodes of sudden bravery, at least for the time being. "You'd make a mighty fine stunt woman, Maggie," he joked, smoothing my hair with his hand, smiling, a little shakily. He could see I was energized. "Take it easy, now," he urged, looking into my eyes to evaluate how wired I really was.

Not ten minutes passed before the deputy and Walter returned with the kid in cuffs in the back of the vehicle.

"Cornered the quivering wreck up a tree, a ways up from the fresh tire marks where he'd skidded to a stop," Walter said.

He was wasted, cold and wet and he was shaking uncontrollably, poor kid. I felt a stab of sympathy for him. What was he? Barely sixteen? Real skinny, long, lank hair scraped back in a ponytail, pockmarked skin on a thin, sad face. He looked terrified to me.

"Came down pretty damn sharpish at the sight of us, seeing as he dropped my pistol half way up," the deputy added. "Looks like a regular dopehead. I doubt the kid's a serious drug runner himself on account of his age and his not knowing a whole bunch about how to handle a vehicle."

CHAPTER 20

MARCUS

B efore the whole truck-jacking episode occurred, we'd stood beside the flashing vehicle just as the creeping onset of dusk shrouded the river, Walter and me both, scratching our heads as to why we should give a damn. We both knew we could have just as easily driven by, carried on along our way without so much as a second glance.

"It comes down to common decency, man," I'd said. "Law enforcement's out here on the road doing its job. Least we can do is go see where they're at, if there's a problem."

"They're forever on the lookout for cannabis traveling south," Walter replied. "Narcotics, weapons and drugs ferried north, humans and all."

The rest stop we'd pulled in at earlier had been plastered with posters of missing people, girls and young women mostly, those the law believes to have been abducted and trafficked up into the Emerald Triangle.

"The cops are best suited targeting the big, old illegal grows, not wasting time chasing small time dealers on the road," Walter said.

"Why'd you reckon he made this stop?" I asked.

"Most likely on suspicion of transportation of ecstasy, meth, cocaine, I'd wager, possible outstanding warrant or stolen vehicle, firearms even," Walter replied.

"A broken taillight, expired registration, about all it takes to get yourself pulled over," he said. "Pretext stops — open the door and hey presto . . . "

"OK, so where's the other vehicle in that case?" I asked.

"It's the big dealers they're after," Walter replied, shrugging his shoulders. "This guy could be in a whole bunch of trouble if he messed up on an arrest. Come on, we best take a look down by the water."

I voiced my confusion as to why, being that the Redwood Highway is under the jurisdiction of the California Highway Patrol, a sheriff's vehicle would be this far out.

"On occasion, sheriffs and city cops dispatch officers outside of their jurisdiction," Walter explained. "This one's a Eureka deputy judging from the plates. Long way from home base."

I'd spotted signs of a struggle in a bed of flattened foliage leading down to the riverbank. "Take a look at that," I said. Maggie and the mutt were still safely inside the truck at that point. "You head north Walter, and I'll head south by the water's edge."

Dense fog rolled in. It was difficult to make out any other sound above the roaring of the fast flowing river. It was Walter who detected a shuffling of rocks beyond the waist-high ferns and he heard a series of low, stifled, grunts. He called me over and we kept to the shadows by the grassy bank 'til we came upon the sheriff deputy, a short, stocky, Latino dude, gagged and tied by the hands and knees to the trunk of a tree.

He'd spotted us as we clambered down the riverbank, hence his efforts to kick at the rocks that were underfoot, disturbing the scene with his kicking up a storm, urgently moaning, despite his gag, desperate to catch our attention. We scoured the immediate area for any further sign of trouble, deducing it safe enough for me to release him with two swift strikes of my knife.

The dude's wrists were red raw from the rope. I reached around the back of his head and cut through the old T-shirt that served as a gag. He sputtered and spit and bent forward to catch his breath, stumbling back against the tree to regain his balance.

"Man, is it good to see you two," he said, relief spreading across his face.

"How long have you been tied up here, officer?" I asked.

"A while, I lost track, blacked out I guess . . . kids, male and female . . . young devils long gone by now."

It was then that we were stopped in our tracks by the truck alarm, followed shortly after by a loud screech of tires and Maggie's screaming bloody murder from above. We'd thrashed and scrambled through wild grasses and brush to bust our way back up the riverbank to find both she and the truck and the darn dog gone. Maggie astounded even herself by making it back with our wheels.

I awoke sometime before sunrise the next morning, confused. I could not for the life of me figure out where I was. It was the waning moonlight that woke me as it stole through the window in the so-called guest room that was more of a junk room to be honest.

Walter had been insistent on putting Maggie and me up at his place after all the excitement on the road the night before. His home is a compact, one-story deal with a knotty pine cathedral ceiling in the living room, big ol' single pane windows, skylights and solar tubes. A typical '60's-build, I would say, back when boomers like Walter were kids.

The room where we slept was piled to the rafters with boxes of seed packets, stacks of plastic plant pots and gardening books, a mess of unidentifiable objects Walter claimed might come in useful someday.

Our host had shuffled around the room on showing us in, shifting a bunch of boxes from the top of the bed to the floor.

"Let's hope Bobby's quake doesn't choose tonight to hit," I'd whispered to Maggie.

"What's that?" Walter asked, absentmindedly.

Maggie winked at me, stifling a giggle.

A round metal spaceship of a wood-burning stove kicked out a substantial heat and the house was toasty in no time. Little Honey had been as relieved as us to be out of the truck. She was a deal less flustered by the carjacking as we were, as far as we could tell.

"Maybe she's used to drama," Maggie said as Little Honey yawned, closed her eyes and stretched out her swollen form on a large, lumpy cushion Walter had set down for her by the fire. The soft light from the stove turned the color of her blonde fur a blazing gold.

Despite how wiped he must have been, the dude had taken it upon himself to rummage around the kitchen cupboards for the makings of a late-night feast.

We'd sat ourselves down, three road warriors on rickety chairs pulled up to the stove. Though the closed-up room had warmed substantially, our breath mingled with the steam cast from the full bowls we'd set on our laps, filled with pasta tossed in one of Walter's prize artichoke pesto sauces he'd made a show of pulling from the freezer.

"Impromptu suppers are my forte," he'd declared, his chest puffed with pride. "Welcome to Waltersville, Maggie and Marcus. I will be honored to show you around the famous Walter's Garden come daylight."

We had been witness to the contents of the chest freezer he kept in the garage, filled to the brim with an impressive stash of vacuum packed fruits and veggies and cuts from our host's past hunting expeditions — venison, elk, duck, wild boar, turkey.

Walter wandered off in search of a towel and an extra blanket for the bed. "I'll figure out the hot water in the morning," he said. "You'll find a redwood tub at your disposal on the deck — nothing says Humboldt better than an outdoor soak."

Maggie's hair spread out over the pillow beside me, it's blue-black hue tinted silver by the moon's luminescence. I tuned in to the mesmerizing rhythm of her breathing, placing my arm on the round curve of hip, taking care not to awaken her. My eyes rested on her mouth, her lips upturned in a pleasing dream, which brought a smile to my face. Gently, I slipped my free hand to rest in the soft, warm space between her mid thighs and she slept on, untroubled by her ordeal of the prior evening.

This totally random thing, whatever the heck it is that we have between us, it frequently induces a most strange yet pleasant physical sensation like a bunch of butterflies let loose in my stomach. And I was all for giving it the green light to pick up steam that early morning, to grant it permission to grow into something real and good and solid for once in my goddamned life.

My last relationship, if you'd call it that, lasted one entire month, though, in truth, we never spent so much as one whole night together. Her name was Rachel. She was smart and all — a professor if you please from Sonoma State, out at Point Reyes on a late spring assignment to study wildflowers.

Though Rachel was the book smart type, she was impressively robust, with real pretty cornflower blue eyes, I recall. I admired her mettle though in truth, she never so much as set my heart on a medium flame. I'd been assigned to her for the purely practical purpose of preventing any mishap, accident or run-in with the wildlife while she navigated the more remote trails and rugged cliff sides of the National Seashore.

She had never learned to drive. I thought this mighty odd for a field scientist. Other than that, Rachel was resourceful. I could relate to her being happy enough with her own company.

It's so damn easy to escape from the outside world in a 71,000-acre preserve, let me tell you. The two of us spent many long hours together during Rachel's four-week study assignment, traversing the more remote corners and hard to reach interior of the park. One evening, early on, after she'd invited herself over to my cabin for a supper of cold cuts, pickles and bread, she asked me straight out, after we ate, if I'd care to go join her in bed.

I'd never heard it put so matter-of-fact. For the remains of her stay, Rachel switched her daytime attentions from wildflowers to her intimate study of the male form, every darn evening after dark, like clockwork.

I willingly obliged, though I doubt either of us would look back at it as an overtly passionate pairing in any wild stretch of the imagination. We liked each other well enough, I figured. And I never felt like she expected me to fake that it was any more than that on my part.

Rachel was fit and toned from frequent hiking on the trails on Sonoma Mountain and I guess I'd have to say, looking back on it, we were matched in a scientific sense, meeting one another's short-term biological and physical needs. Though we made the best of our time together, neither of us tried to hide any lack of sorrow when it came time for her to leave.

Two introverts do not make for sparks to fly. With Maggie and me, I have to say, it is the polar opposite, a primal pairing. Where Rachel was all sharp, electric edges of a purely technical focus, Maggie is soft and warm and generous. I feel it in the way she smells, her voice, her touch, her eyes and her kisses telling me exactly what it is she wants from me.

It was after nine when a glowing, bare-skinned Maggie propped herself up on her elbow, watching me quizzically.

"You look surprised." I said. "What? Did you think I'd take off in the night? Leave you here with Walter to figure things out?"

"I wouldn't blame you, Marcus," Maggie replied, her lips nibbling at the outer edge of my ear as she snuggled in closer. "I can't help but wonder when you're gonna tell me that we're making a mistake, rushing into things like a couple of dumb teenagers."

I shook my head and took her face in my hands.

"Darlin', I may not be a man of many words, but don't you be thinking I'm not bold enough to take you on."

"In that case," she said, kicking off the sheet that was wrapped around her middle, "since you're sticking around, I think it's only right that you check me over for damage from yesterday's ordeal."

I took my assignment seriously, my senses fully alert as I set about inspecting her body in close detail for any signs of more serious battle distress than the road rash I'd tended to the night before.

All's I will say is that it was a good thing her adrenaline had kept her holding onto that damn windshield. We would have been looking at a serious case of broken bones or worse had she lost her grip.

The house was silent. There was no evidence of Walter in the kitchen or elsewhere and, for the first time since we'd been thrown together on this fucked-up, crazy road trip, the time was right to get to know each other a little better in daylight, her contours, the curve and scar tissue of my stump. We took it slowly, it was less ecstatic than the first time, but hey, it felt every bit as doggone good to mix it up by morning light.

I rolled myself off the mattress onto my crutch and made my way into the kitchen for coffee. A flash of Bobby's being swept away in the floodwater washed over me afresh. Grief came close to consuming me as I stood waiting for the coffee to brew. A fresh stab of guilt flowed through my core. What type of dude rolls around the sack with his dead best buddy's sister-in-law so soon after his sudden and tragic demise? Maybe it was Bobby after all who had configured this crazy thing with Maggie and me. I could not so much as take my eyes off her when I was with her, how was I to stop what he'd started by asking me over there in the first place?

Strange thing is I would have been the first in line to declare it all a load of crock before I met her. This freaky, unnerving, despairing of wanting and needing to be with her all of the time — all new and totally foreign to me. Bobby's death would have done me in had Maggie not been by my side. And then again, if Maggie had not been by my side, then maybe Bobby would not be dead. I poured strong, black coffee into a matching pair of Save the Redwoods mugs, quitting the brain conniption and giving in to plain gratitude for what my buddy had brought into my life.

After we drank our coffee tucked on between the sheets of the toasty bed, we decided to make our way outdoors into the fine morning drizzle. Maggie helped me navigate the slick deck with me balanced on one crutch, carefully stepping down into the soothing waters of Walter's secluded redwood tub.

"Just look at that view," a naked Maggie pointed to a primeval world of redwood trees, the mountainous forest beyond. A thick, purple heather-colored layer of clouds floated on the upper reaches of the forest. The redwoods were busy doing their daily job, moving moisture out of the clouds, funneling it down those mighty 35-story trunks and into the thirsty receptacles of their root systems.

"At a risk of sounding too much like Walter, this forest, I believe this ancient, complex ecosystem serves to reinforce how truly insignificant and tiny our lives are." I reached out to trace her bare collarbone with my thumb. "We're here for so short a time, Maggie. Bobby, Bridget, you, me. These trees, on the other hand, they remind us not to squander the time we've been given."

I closed my eyes and pondered the god-dang fragility of life, the lives of those we love. A pang of fear ran through me when I thought of Mia and Jazmin still out there in the redwoods somewhere, who the hell knew where.

"Shush, now," Maggie replied, taking my hand as we soaked and savored a few moments more of peace and quiet in the comfortable embrace of the warm water. "You're a deep one."

Walter returned just as we were drying off. Maggie wrapped the extra towel we had wrestled from a pile of laundry around her torso in a modest move to cover the important parts. Anyways, I reckoned our new pal and fellow fugitive chaser is cool with a spot of outdoor nudity, so it didn't bother me none to hop on back indoors buck naked. Hey, last thing these old hippies are is prudes.

A basket of aromatic oven-warm banana nut muffins sat on the kitchen counter, wrapped in a yellow napkin.

"You can thank Lori for the baked goods," Walter said, following the hunger in my eyes as they honed in on the muffins. "I stopped in to see her this morning while you two young'uns were catching up on your beauty sleep."

Lori keeps an eye on the place when Walter is away and, I suspect, more than an eye on Walter when he's back home. "She's a good ol' gal, waters the garden when its thirsty, though Lord knows, it's not been in the least part a necessity what with all this rain," he rambled on with his well-versed diversion tactics, having detected my picking up on the glint in his eye.

Walter's neighbor's baked goods sure hit the mark. A satisfied rumbling from my belly testified to her baking skills. Lori's muffins revealed themselves deliciously gooey on the inside on account of a generous handful of dark chocolate chips she'd thrown into the mix.

Our host placed a heavy, blue, cast iron teakettle to boil on the stovetop flame. Maggie's phone vibrated on the table. She started from her seat, checked the caller, placing it on speaker.

"Maggie, it's me, Bridget."

We all three jumped to attention. You coulda heard a pin drop on the kitchen floor.

The connection was spotty, yet through its thin signal we clearly heard what it was that Bridget had to say.

"Jazmin — Maggie, oh my God, I just found out that she's safe, at least. Turned herself in last night."

Sharing this was all Bridget was able to muster before she broke down, sobbing, catching her breath. "Don't get too ahead of yourself, it's not all good news, I barely know where to start . . . she says she has not so much as set eyes on Mia these past couple of months."

There followed the deep and mournful cry of a mother in pain. We stood in silence, mouths agape, wide-eyed, waiting for Bridget to regain her composure and tell us more of how it was that Jazmin was apart from Mia.

"Oh dear God, the girl is scared to death as to what may have happened to Mia," Bridget sputtered.

Maggie tried her best to calm her sister. "How, why, whoa, what do you mean, Bridget, when you say that Jazmin turned herself in?" she pressed. "Let's start there."

"She showed up at the police station in Ukiah last night. Turned herself in along with a truckload of weed."

It took a little more than a minute for the light bulb moment to hit. Maggie, me, Walter, the three of us in unison — judging by the look that passed between us, it did not take a genius to figure out the freak coincidence.

Jazmin had made a run for it while her counterpart was otherwise occupied dragging the unfortunate, unconscious sheriff deputy down the riverbank. We must have passed her, unbeknownst to any of us, heading in the opposite direction on our way up along the Redwood Highway.

Bridget, Luna and Jazmin's parents were about to head up to Ukiah to reunite with the girl. Jazmin was scheduled to meet with a public defense lawyer and a team of psychological and medical professionals.

Bridget managed to sufficiently gather her wits about her to further explain how investigators were now aware of Jazmin's precarious situation given that she is over 18 and is no longer a juvenile, with no papers to her name. What Jazmin was claiming, Bridget explained, was that she had turned herself in as an innocent victim who'd been caught up in a drug-running ring.

"They're tellin' us if what Jazmin claims is true, it's suspected human traffickin' we're lookin' at in so far as her defense," Bridget added. "All we can do is pray this prompts a high profile search for Mia, Maggie. I can't bear it. How the hell do I keep goin' if we don't find her soon? It's the not knowin' what has happened to her, Jesus Christ, it's too much to bear."

Maggie cleared her throat and spoke real calm, taking great pains to reassure her sister we were on it. We were in Humboldt, she explained, with people who were already helping ramp up our hunt for Mia. "Trust me, Bridget," she said as she hung up, "We won't stop until we find her."

"At the very least, Jazmin turning herself in puts Mia on the law enforcement radar," Walter said.

On cue, Deputy Hernandez showed up at Walter's front door within five minutes of Bridget's phone call. The dude was a deal more chipper than we'd found him after his personal ordeal the previous evening. A shower and a clean uniform helped. He wore fresh bandages wrapped neatly around his wrists, visible beneath his long sleeved shirt.

"Good morning to you all," he said, shaking hands in turn. "I'm here to let you know I have been apprised of some interesting news. The passenger of the stolen truck surrendered last night. She was taken into custody in Ukiah," he announced, immediately sensing from our reactions that his news did not come as the surprise he had expected. He explained how he was on his way down to Ukiah after talking first with us.

Maggie patiently shared what we'd learned from Bridget's call and how we'd connected the dots. "It's vital that you help us find Mia, officer," she pleaded. "As soon as humanly possible. We have every reason to believe she's still alive and that she's in serious danger."

Officer Hernandez nodded, gravely. He seemed a decent enough cop, though my confidence in the speed of his detective work reinforced the fact in my mind that it was up to Maggie and me to find Mia and fast.

"There's no time to be wasted, I agree," he said. "Troubling thing is it's not at all as textbook as it should be up here."

He told us how he had confiscated such a volume of illegal weed haul that month alone his wife was sick and tired of washing his uniform. "If she don't launder it separate from the family wash, the kids, they darn well go to school reeking of it."

Walter pledged to call on each and every one of his own personal connections in the tri-county region. "I made a start with my visit to Lori, this morning," he said. "She'll be over shortly."

Lori is a short, solid woman with a wild mane of frizzy blonde hair that hangs loose to her thick waist and shot through with fine silver strands that remind me of the thin, metallic tinsel threads we strung on the Christmas tree each December when we were kids. I liked her from the minute she walked through the door, smiley faced, lively, light brown eyes honing in on each of our faces with an air of what felt like genuine warmth and concern.

A spark of mutual acknowledgment passed between her and Walter, reinforcing my instincts that the two of them were more than neighbors.

I guess neither of them is of an age to bust up a good solid friendship with the sorts of dull, routine domestic arrangements that living together calls for. If Walter and Lori choose to keep to their own routines, their own business, in the knowledge and comfort of their caring for each other at their age being more of a benefit than a commitment — hell, there is nothing wrong with that. For a second or two, my thoughts wandered to Maggie and me. Would that be the type of arrangement we would maintain down the line? I hope not. My desire is to be with her, beside her, the full deal.

Walter had been gone a while that winter, still, he and Lori moved comfortably around one another, close to touching yet maintaining a slight distance, as if it was a dance of some sort that they had practice at. I hoped at least, given their obvious enjoyment and appreciation of each other, it was a more private reunion they'd savored while the batch of banana nut muffins baked.

He handed Lori a mug of sweet and spicy orange scented tea. "Your favorite, I brought it up from Willits," he said, smiling at her, as she pulled up a chair. We three listened to Walter share with us how, over the past few trimming seasons especially, he had learned how to spot an abandoned grow site in an instant. "I'm well aware of all the telltale signs — diversion of water, withering stalks, dead song birds caught up in drying wire."

Walter told how a buddy of his had recently come across a clearing in the forest while hiking in what he thought was a safe area: "He was not the first to stumble on a pile of burned trash, empty sacks of toxic pesticides, more than a dozen carcasses of endangered animals poisoned, no doubt, by lethal bait."

"So tragic. Whatever happened to weed being a sacrament of the earth?" Lori asked.

She and a group of townsfolk had organized themselves into a neighborhood watch of sorts.

"Locals on the Lookout, we keep an eye out for the community," she explained. "At the same time, we do what we can for the safety of the younger ones, the trimmigrants who spill out onto the sidewalks downtown at the start of each harvest season."

Lori said they didn't have to do this, she and her friends and neighbors, but their efforts benefitted everyone seeing as otherwise, the dumpster diving, stealing and depositing of filthy waste in the river water and under the bridges would be way worse than it already was.

"It's a disaster of sorts," she said, her facial expression set into one of frustrated resignation. "One way or another and though we all do rely on the economy of the cannabis industry up here in many ways, it's simply grown out of control. The days of petty crimes have passed. Missing people and murders are now commonplace."

Walter spoke of private militia outfits hired on as SWAT teams by the big property owners that are rightfully infuriated by the volume of illegal grows.

"Leech bosses of bastard guerilla operations are razor sharp, they're fluid and adaptive and that's the problem. They've permeated the more remote pockets of the state with an interconnected network of crime and they'll stop at nothing."

Lori positioned herself with her plump round back held straight, her shoulders rising and falling as she talked of the ironies within the traveling culture that passes through the region, in particular, the so-called Rainbow People, those who choose to celebrate unconditional love and freedom devoid of consumerism within the forests and the rivers of the world. "Their values sound refreshing, but they too have a dark side," she said.

"Utopia's not all its cracked up to be?" Maggie asked.

Lori smiled. "It's a nice idea to build a world free from accountability and government, but so many of those who come here, they take, take, take from our limited resources, most of which are provided by our own community members," she said. "Those who do pay into the nonprofit system and local services do so with tithes if not taxes."

She took notes on a pad of paper from all that Maggie was able to tell her about Mia's increasingly troubling situation. Maggie dropped a photo of her niece directly into Lori's phone for her to share.

"She's a good-looking girl, for sure. Mixed blood?" Lori asked. "You don't know how sorry I am to say this, given Mia's present position being unknown, but it's the white girls, the German and the French and Canadian students, they're the ones who get hired up here first and they're the girls who the authorities take the most notice of if anything goes wrong."

"So, are you suggesting Mia being half Mexican puts her lower on the list?" Maggie asked.

"I'm afraid so," Lori replied. "It's all so wrong, you don't have to tell me."

We listened intently as Lori explained how the big-boned, blonde haired, blue-eyed international travelers, girls and guys both, students, the ones who hold up their handwritten signs touting their ethnicity and work ethic are able to use the race card as a surefire method for being snapped up out of the crowd.

I looked over at Maggie. She was growing visibly more troubled and restless in her chair, scratching her head, fidgeting anxiously with her hair. Walter took notice, and, after catching my eye, he turned his attention back to Lori. I reached up to take Maggie's hand from her head and hold it in my own.

"The legitimate growers are not interested in any funny business," Lori said. "If they don't already have a regular setup with a reliable trimming team, they want to know that they're taking on the type of trimmer who'll get the job done with minimal fuss, those who will be on their way once harvest is done."

"Lori's main concern is for the unknown numbers of exploited young souls such as Jazmin and Mia, those who find themselves enslaved on guerilla grows — men, women, duped into all manner of subservience, from manning the crop in the middle of nowhere for months on end to being chicaned and drugged and blindfolded and forced into domestic and sexual slavery," Walter interjected. "I'm sorry to be so brutal about it, but it's time to face facts."

I looked across at Maggie. Her face fell. Tears welled in her eyes. "We're going to find her," I promised, squeezing her hand. We'd been given no information as yet from Bridget as to who it was who had held the girls against their will over the winter months, but whoever it was, facts were veering toward Walter's depiction of the sorts of dire circumstances the girls had managed to get themselves caught up in.

Lori flipped open her laptop she'd carried in. Logging into Walter's sketchy Wi-Fi, she pulled up a photo folder of the faces of hundreds of youngsters snapped on camera during the pre-harvest and early harvest season.

"We do our best to urge these kids to move on," she said. "We let them know in no uncertain terms there's little chance of finding work. If they persist, or we see them again, we snap a photo and download it onto our files."

Maggie stood behind her as Lori scrolled through dozens of young faces, most of them hopeful, others more desperate looking, others more vacant, many displaying multiple piercings and facial tattoos.

"Stop!" Maggie yelled. "That's her, that's Mia."

Lori flipped her laptop around for Walter and me to see. Mia and her friend Jazmin were sat side by side looking directly up at the camera. There they were, captured in the moment, head to head, smiling for a photo with the innocence of youth.

The two girls were seated on a sidewalk, captured in their bikini tops, two girls in a sea of young faces. Mia held a sign above their heads — "Fast, Fun Non-Smokers" it said.

Each had worn her long hair tied back, their hopeful, open faces directed at the camera. Maggie zoomed in. Strands of wooden beads were wrapped around their wrists interspersed with three or four inches of brightly colored, woven bracelets. The sun shone down on the start of what they'd imagined as their first big adventure. I knew that feeling. The one I'd had when I was first deployed.

I detected a note of self-absorption in Mia's young face, a face I'd never taken much notice of, but one I had known from when she was a kid. She'd been in it for herself, I sensed, no clue of the trouble she'd dragged her pal into. Never underestimate a teenager.

Lori said she'd print out the image of the girls and walk it up to what the locals dubbed "Hippie Hill", a tent city just outside of town. "We'll ask around," she said. "Won't hurt to start there."

She went home to pick up the Taser she told us that she takes out with her more frequently these days. "Way too many vagrants hanging about for my liking," she said.

"It's not the students, or the worldly wanderers who are causing the trouble," Walter added. "They move on. It's the ones who stay, assuming they have stumbled on the land of buds and honey in answer to their prayers."

Walter described how he had been threatened and physically assaulted on more than one occasion over the previous year or two. "We've been forced to resort to arming ourselves one way or another," he said. "Hence the pistol."

Lori stood and tucked a thick strand of hair behind her pixie ear that was hung with a long, dangling turquoise-beaded earring. Walter told us she teaches English at the same high school that he and Connie retired from. "I came to it late after a difficult divorce," she said. "Found my calling."

The teacher in her placed her hands on her ample hips. "It's our job, those who love this place, to become a sort of citizen police," she said, glancing out of the window into the winter garden of collards, kale and Swiss chard she'd kept an eye on for Walter while he was away.

"Way too many people continue to pretend these terrible things are not happening," Lori said. "If and when the black market does settle down, maybe after time, the dangers will stop. Until then, we've had little choice but to take the law into our own hands."

CHAPTER 21

JAZMÍN

Two hella scary dudes with assault rifles strung across their chests stood guard in the middle of a rectangular group of shitty looking aluminum trailers and a two-story concrete building at the rear. It appeared to me at first sight, a stark, military-style setup.

Light shone through narrow slits of windows in the main building, otherwise it was pitch-dark outside. What I was able to figure out right away was that this menacing-looking compound Mia and me had wound up at was set in a densely forested mountaintop a hundred times more secluded than Bruce and Bonnie's place.

I reached out in the dark and squeezed hold of Mia's hand. She held on tight. My knees buckled and I would have fallen to the ground on the spot if it weren't for Mia's grip.

"In here," Jefe Hombre hustled us in through the metal doorway of the main building. I figured maybe it was some sort of abandoned station back from the days of the logging boom Miguel had talked about.

The mean-faced, gun-toting dudes carried in a bunch of cases of Corona, bottled water, boxes of groceries from the back of the truck, enough to supply a small army.

Inside, the stark ground floor was basically one big room, dimly lit with old fluorescent tubes, plastic foldout tables and chairs, a couple of ratty couches and a makeshift camp kitchen at the far end.

Two younger looking Latina girls in the kitchen area barely dared look up from their work to see who'd arrived. One of them was stirring a big, ol' heavy pot of some sort of stew, while the other was heating a pile of tortillas. It was almost like they were expecting us. No big deal

246

to them. Anyway, the food smelled good, despite everything and my stomach growled. We hadn't eaten in 24 hours by that point.

Jefe Hombre barked orders at the two girls. "Stop what you're doing. Take them upstairs," he said, pushing us toward them. "Carry their sleeping bags. Make up their bunks."

One, whose name was Camila motioned for us to follow her as she led us up a narrow stairway to the second floor. "You?" she asked, in Spanish. "What is your name?" — like we are going to be around long enough to be pals, I thought. Still, she looked kind, relieved for the female company, I assumed. We would soon found out why.

Valeria was the other one tiptoeing around in their dirty white athletic socks, no shoes. They led the way up into a windowless, loft-style room barely big enough for two sets of narrow steel bunks.

"Ours," Camila pointed to the bunk beds on the left. "Yours," she said, in Spanish. Long, thin, sagging mattresses were stained with God knows what.

It wasn't really a room, more an alcove with an old curtain drawn limply on a rail to separate the space from the drafty staircase and hallway.

Camila handed me a pile of shabby threadbare sheets. No pillow. She opened the door to a small bathroom. I stepped back. It reeked of men, of sweat and pee and of strong, nasty cologne.

Jefe Hombre stood at the bottom of the staircase. A sharp knife-edge of fear pierced the back of my neck. "Don't be getting too comfortable up there," he snapped, in Spanish, for he spoke no English. "There's work to be done down here."

The door opened downstairs, a noisy group of Latino men aged from late teens to early forties, I guessed, filtered in and gathered in the downstairs eating area.

I was shaking as I made my way downstairs behind my equally freaked out buddy. All eyes were on Mia and me. Mia, Miguel and Bonnie had promised to keep me safe. Well, so much for that.

Tears welled up and threatened to spill as I thought of my parents and the little ones, worried sick about me, I just knew it, like the cold sense of impending doom that had come over me. It was the shame of it that would be the worst, knowing that we'd done this to ourselves,

Mia and me. It was her idea but I'd agreed to it. We had no one but ourselves to blame.

After the men had eaten their fill of the tortillas and stew, we were given permission to eat whatever little was left of it. Camila and Valeria served the four of us in silence, scraping the pan for the last of scraps of the meat. Mia and me, we were so frightened and at the same time so hungry we could barely swallow. Jefe Hombre had rifled through our packs and frisked our pockets, whisking away our high school student ID's, our shoes. The only thing he'd left us with was our sleeping bags.

Right away he ordered two of his men to lead us outside by the shoulders, barefoot and single file. Mia whimpered as he forced us to sit. It was Jefe Hombre himself who tied our wrists to the arms of two rusty metal chairs set around a smoldering firepit.

It was the other fucker who gathered my hair in his fist, holding it above my head. I never saw it coming. I had no idea. The bastard sealed my immediate fate with the shock of burning flesh, a searing and excruciating pain, the sizzle of a smoldering iron beneath the thin surface of skin on the back of my neck. I screamed bloody fucking murder for all the good it did me, kicking my bare feet in the dirt. What were we? No better than the helpless cattle in the fields back home. Mia looked on, shaking, horrified. I heard her sob and plead as I threw up.

Mia's pleas for mercy made no difference. She knew she was next as she darted her dark, wide eyes back and forth between that group of monsters and me, transfixed, petrified, begging to be spared. She fixed her eyes on my trembling lower lip. I bit the inside of my cheeks to stop my screaming, for her sake.

They'd branded us with the sign of a cross, Mia and me before she too hurled the sparse contents of her stomach big time on the ground at her feet.

Camila and Valeria were given orders to untie our hands and take us back into the building. Once inside, in turn, they raised their long, thick braids from their shoulders in a show of silent unity. We each shared the same tortured brand. Camila was twitchy, super nervous. She kept on catching her breath like she was reliving her own pain as she gently soaked my scorched skin with a cold, wet towel. Valeria applied a soothing aloe vera gel she told us she had made herself, along with what I think must have been an antibiotic cream of some kind. The two girls taped strips of loose gauze around my and Mia's necks.

It was during that horror-filled first night of humiliation and pain that yet more of our miserable, immediate destiny was laid out for us to digest. Mia's main job from thereon out was to please Jefe Hombre. As for me, I was promptly handed over to his main man, Jose Luis, the devil himself, the fucker responsible for the branding.

Don't for a minute think that we were not disgusted, sickened, repelled to the pits of our stomachs. We were all of that and more. But we're no fools, Mia and me, we knew better than to resist to the point of greater punishment, total humiliation, death even, at least not until we knew we had a plan.

"We'll make it out of here if it kills us," she kept on telling me. "They don't know who they're dealing with," Mia whispered, rocking side to side, our arms around each other, much later, though still in the midst of the shock and the hurt and the total fear and degradation of the events of that first sickening night. We lay on our stomachs on top of our sleeping bags on our narrow bunks, our necks aflame with pain, our insides churning, the sound of those torturous maniacs snoring in the narrow rooms close by. A remember how a lone coyote howled in the distance.

"OK, this is what we do," Mia whispered into my ear the next morning, her fists clenched, tears rolling down her cheeks. "We're gonna force ourselves to play at being robots in our minds. Think of your body as not belonging to your brain, J. It's the only way we'll get ourselves through this." Mia was a virgin when she came to this place. Vomit rose in the back of my throat and I cringed at the thought of what had already happened, what was happening to her, to me what was to go on happening, over and over. Life as we'd known it was done.

To think, Mia had been waiting for the one. The skin-crawling abuse of our bodies was to be a nightly torment. At first, Mia tried to act brave, for my sake, mostly, but all the while I knew how much she was hating on herself for what she felt she had pushed us into. "These fuckers don't own us, not now, not ever," she'd repeat this, her mantra when we found a minute or two to talk without being overheard. Asleep or awake, we learned fast how to guard our own shadows.

Only after our daily duties of scrubbing floors, scouring the scum out of the big-shit bathroom and all the other lesser hideous morning hour duties, were we sent out to sit our butts on sticky swivel chairs along a line of foldout tables in the trimming tent. It was a whole different setup from the scene at Bonnie and Bruce's, where the trimmers had been all women. Here, aside from us four girls, it was all men, Guatemalans and Mexican dudes who were sent back to their rusted, cramped and leaking trailers at night and only allowed into the main building during mealtimes.

We worked by kerosene lamplight well into the evening hours. The other two girls joined us in the trimming tent later on, after the day's cooking was done, the four of us padding around like the inmates we were in our disgusting athletic socks. Our captors figured we wouldn't get far if we were either brave or stupid enough to run. We didn't have a pair of shoes between us.

"Don't get caught up in feeling too hella sorry for anyone aside from you and me," Mia warned, late one evening on account of my being visibly agitated watching Valeria being pushed around by Jose Luis. There was no such thing as a washing machine on that godforsaken mountaintop. The kid shivered with cold in the night air as she wrestled a bunch of threadbare sheets she'd hand washed and hung on a long laundry line that was strung under the eaves at the back of the house. "Get a move on, bitch," he'd said, pushing her around, like she was no better than a donkey. "Get back inside, make up the beds." She had rubbed her knuckles raw, scrubbing at sheets and clothing with nothing but a cheap bar of soap.

I prayed to God we'd get out alive, somehow, anyhow, despite being threatened each and every day that should we even try to attempt to make a run for it, the motherfuckers would not hesitate to shoot.

Mia was up and down in her handling of our total living nightmare. We were basically sex slaves. "Never in my worst dreams," she cried, over and over. It was like we'd become caged animals waiting for a chance to attack. All the while we tried our best to stick to the only plan we could think might work and pretend to become a little more docile by the day.

She'd worried the skin around her eyes into such a mess with the hideous stress of it all. I begged her to stop making things worse for herself.

"We have to do what we have to do to get out, Mia," I reassured her. "Keep our feelings under wraps. We're tough, we're survivors — you said so yourself, remember?"

It was the sex, being forced to fuck that was the worst of it. If you really want to know how we dealt with it, like Mia said, we reduced ourselves to becoming robot girls. Unfeeling half the time, numb, and yet other times, every tiny hair would stand on end. It wasn't real, it wasn't us, despite what they did to us we tried so damn hard to make ourselves believe that none of it mattered, that it was not the real us it was happening to at all.

"Come on, Mia, I've learned to do what you said we must," I reminded her, when I could see that she was starting to lose it. "Keep on moving your mind to a different space." I worked so hard it almost killed me to pretend to be one of the stony-faced figures I'd seen up close one time in the wax museum at Fisherman's Wharf. Once I was an effigy of Taylor Swift putting up with faceless strangers poring over her, day in, day out, the next I'd make out in my mind I was Jennifer Lawrence in the Hunger Games, ready to spear our captives with my fucking bow and arrow.

We were all slaves of some kind or another in that place, yet we were still alive and breathing in our hideous mountaintop existence. We had to stay alert to get out.

Most of the trimmers were as helpless one way or another, if not more so in the end. We found out how these men had been given zero choice but to suck it up, take the heat, grow the weed all summer, see the harvest through to the end. Most of them had been brought there by force. The cartel kidnapped them from small villages in Central and South America. If one of them so much as dared to refuse the work or tried to run away, his wife and kids, his entire family would be taken out. Just like that.

One of the guys told me this, one of the younger Guatemalans who dared whisper some of what happened to him in the long hours we together spent in the trimming room.

The girls had it worse in that it was their own people who sold them to Jefe Hombre, for Christ sakes.

Camila and Valeria said nothing much about themselves to Mia and me those first few weeks. Over time, they had slowly started to place their trust in us, confide. "We grew up together on the same street in Guadalajara," Valeria explained. They'd turned seventeen the previous summer, shit, they were kids, a whole year younger than Mia and me.

They were timid and kept a constant eye out during their work in the kitchen after the breakfast hour, terrified someone might hear them talking to Mia and me over the hum of the gas-powered generator. The divulged all this horrific stuff while the four of us were gathered around the sink, washing sweaty work clothes. Camila talked of the vile and horrendous things she'd seen firsthand, hangings, executions, kidnapping — fucking hell, she'd witnessed a beheading, can you believe? It was all they had known since they were small, the world of bad men.

It was after two dueling drug lords were crossed, we learned, the two of them were offered up to Jefe Hombre as payment to settle the feud.

Mia and me coming into the house was in reality, a pair of fresh bodies that provided the younger girls a reprieve from their dreaded bedtime duties.

"Camila needs to heal," Valeria whispered, taking my hand. "She lost a lot of blood," she said, pointing to the other girl's stomach. "I was afraid." She made us tea with small bunches of pungent dried herbs, tied and dipped into mugs of boiling water, wild stuff, nettles, twigs and leaves of clover they'd gather in their brief time outdoors.

Valeria began brewing more intense, woody concoctions into hot tea for Mia and me. "For slow down fertility," she said, patting our bellies.

It came down to sex for survival within the prison walls of a ten-foot metal and electric fence. I'd never wish such a thing on my worst enemy. I began to see that it was me who was keeping it together for the both of us. Mia had slipped into a trancelike state. She told me: "I feel like I'm watching myself in a horror film on TV." It was like none of it was real it was so bad.

She'd always been the one to take the lead, ever since we'd buddied up in tenth grade. No one was more surprised than me in that I was the one who was keeping Mia going much of the time, not the other way around. We whispered to one another in the dead of night, back in the sanctity of our bunks, after we'd done our best to scrub up, clean ourselves from yet another of those sick service sessions. We'd climb into one bunk, night after night, and huddle together to quietly brainstorm and plot our way out.

Somehow I even managed to make her laugh at times at the horror of it. Crying had grown old. Part of my dippy old self hung in there if only for her. I love that girl's laugh. It comes from somewhere deep inside. It's distinctive. I'd pick out Mia's big ol' belly laugh anywhere, low and rumbling and sometimes she lets out a loud snort. I can't wait to hear her laugh again. "We're out of here, Mia, real soon," I promised her. "Fuckers won't see us for dust."

Weeks passed. It was November, we guessed. We'd gotten to be good and fast at the trimming and the rest of it, human mechanization working at its best. The more efficient we were the faster it was over.

Jefe Hombre declared himself a softie slapping a couple packs of sanitary pads on the countertop after he'd made one of his three-hour round trip supply runs into town. We were faking how long we were on our periods, well, I was, Mia was working her own denial by then.

One time he came back with a stick of lavender scented deodorant and a bottle of cheap shampoo, two packs of new socks, women's size for once. "Go make yourself pretty," he said to Mia, handing over his gifts like he was the prince of charm.

Fights broke out in the trimming tent. A couple of the Mexican dudes mysteriously disappeared. We kept our heads down as tensions rose from being cooped up and overworked so long. Three more men failed to show for supper one night. The four of us girls began to exchange frequent knowing glances.

Pile after pile of resin-coated buds from the six-foot plants that had grown in the dappled sunlight of summer, crossed our laps for weeks on end. I'd learned to trim without looking, it was monotonous, staring out of the window yearning for the freedom of the sky. I spent most of my time willing the Feds to fly by, praying for the sound of helicopter blades. They never came.

We resorted to tying plastic bags over our socks when the rains came in. Camila and Valeria taught us how to pack the trimmed bud into turkey bags the men concealed under false flatbeds in a small fleet of freshly washed and polished trucks.

We were forced to sit at our trays all day every day and most of the night towards the end of trimming season. My butt cheeks were numb for weeks.

After the last of the crop was trimmed, the tequila came out. Demands on Mia and me picked up at a new, even more abusive pace.

One night, Jefe Hombre made a drunken tequila-trade with Jose Luis, switching Mia for me. This happened just the once. The boss man, he flew into a jealous fit over something that was said about Mia. Jose Luis backed off with a black eye.

By then, Mia wasn't doing so well. I'd been keeping tabs on our monthlies. I told her outright I'd kept a count of the sanitary pads in the bathroom. She point-blank refused to talk about it, first time she'd ever been unwilling to talk shit with me on any subject. Neither of us was ready to spit it out — the truth, I guess, to say the words.

"Chances are it's the shock of it all," is what I said "Slows down the regularity in between periods."

We were given a beating apiece after getting ourselves caught talking to the Guatemalan guy in the trimming tent one evening. Not he or any one of them had dared to make a move on Mia or me, not the whole time they'd been without their wives and girlfriends. We never knew if they were all more than halfway decent dudes in the moral sense or scared shitless of what would happen to them if they even thought of messing with us.

At night, they scuttled off to their shacks like the cockroaches they'd been reduced to. I worried what was gonna happen to those we'd gotten to be something like sociable inmates with given that their disappearance rate was getting more frequent. So far, I figured, Mia and me had made it through the worst of it. We were living and breathing. We still had a chance.

It was around Thanksgiving, we'd calculated. Mia grew wistful with the change of season, reminiscing about the leftover feast that Bobby would bring back to the ranch after working the holiday shift. "Big ol' plate of turkey, gravy, mashed sweet potato, cornbread, all the fixings," she said, her eyes glazing over. "My favorite. A whole pumpkin pie if there was an extra."

There was no feasting for us that Thanksgiving. No celebration, no such thing as TV, or radio, zero contact with the outside world.

We'd hatched our plan for implementation after the bulk of the weed was packed and gone from the compound.

Mia would go first. I'd follow. "Girl power, baby," I said. We watched and waited with the patience of saints for the moment the tequila resurfaced.

"It's a ballsy move," she agreed, "Us waiting for the moment when they're good and drunk." We poured them one shot after another, fooled around, waited until they passed out, one by one as we'd seen them do plenty of times before. Once we were totally sure they'd crashed out, Mia made a run for it, hacking through the fence with a pair of wire cutters someone had negligently left behind after securing the false flatbeds.

One of the goons must have detected a shift in our mood, earlier. Normally they turned in at that time of night. Mia wasn't even close to squeezing through the small, ragged hole she'd made when they were on to her like a pack of wolves on a chicken. It was the final unraveling of our having stupidly thought we could outsmart our captives.

One of them smashed Mia in the back of the head with a pistol. I was convinced she was dead when I was pushed out to watch, my hands behind my back as they hauled her away from the fence. I pissed myself with fear, more for Mia than for me.

A stumbling Jose Luis dragged my ass outside while they tied Mia like a sack of rice to a rail in the shed. They continued to make me watch and then they forced us apart. For two days they left her there.

On the second day they brought me out again to make me look on as they shaved her head and hosed her down.

I begged them to stop, I pleaded, promised I would do anything they asked of me. I was left alone for the first time in weeks, huddled on my bunk, crying, shaking constantly, and for the first time, I doubted either of us would ever make it out alive.

Camila crept up the stairs to feed me little bits of food, the same scraps it turned out she was coaxing Mia to eat. Valeria was too terrified to do anything other than shake with fright and look at me like she had seen a ghost. She begged me not to run. "Too, too dangerous," she said. "Next time, they kill us all."

CHAPTER 22

MAGGIE

Though Walter's kitchen is every bit as dated as our kitchen back at the ranch, the old-school copper tones were easier on the eye, homely, even, in a retro sort of way. As far as I could tell, Walter's house is thankfully watertight not to mention blessedly warm thanks to the heat that pumps out of one of those big, round stoves that look like a spaceship. Marcus helped him fill it with wood when he'd opened up the house.

After the ordeal of the evening before, my heroics with the car-jacking and all, the last thing I'd expected was to hear from Bridget so soon.

"Don't pin too much hope on the law," Lori warned. "They're as much in the dark as we are when it comes to locating the cartel's guerilla grows."

Walter concurred. "The more remote the site where Mia's at, the more likely it is heavily protected with booby traps and armed guards packing AK-47s."

"Aside from their heinous crimes against humanity, these bastards hack down hundreds of trees, though not enough to be visible from the air," Lori explained. "They're ruthless in their digging of ditches for their crude dam constructions, hauling in yards of plastic hose and irrigation equipment. Unless there's a random spotting by aerial search, the law is rarely ever close to finding them."

"If it's a big enough grow, we're talking thousands of plants raised during the season, worth anywhere up to 50 or 60 million dollars," Walter added. "I hate to say it, but the last thing these operators care for is human life."

"Then there's no time to wait on the authorities extricating Mia," I replied, regaining my composure. "Walter, Lori, where the hell do we start?"

Lori called her people. Walter called his. Everyone and anyone they thought might be of help. In turn, they asked their contacts to follow up with friends and neighbors of their own as to where Mia might have possibly been seen at some point in time. "We have a slim chance to find Mia," Lori said. "It's time to take a stand."

I was shaken to the core. "It is what it is, Maggie," Lori said, taking my arm. "Don't shy away from the truth. It's important that we all fully recognize what's going on here."

Walter was quick to call out the futility of confronting armed guards, the real and present dangers of the region's dark underworld. "There are all kinds of lunatics out there," he said. "Exploitation being the name of the game. It's an epidemic."

Lori and Walter agreed to cover ground together, by driving over to Trinity County in the east. They planned to check in with storekeepers and gas station attendants en route to Weaverville, a community hub and county seat in the far eastern reach of the Emerald Triangle.

"No telling how far into the forest Mia might be," Lori said. "Someone may have seen her. The only thing that makes sense is to spread out, cover all the bases we possibly can."

~

Marcus came up with a plan for he and I to head north along the Avenue of the Giants in Humboldt State Park and up to the town of Fortuna and out to Ferndale and the coast.

"You'd best extend your route and scour the redwood communities back down along the Ferndale Petrolia Road to the southern reach of the Lost Coast," Walter suggested, unearthing a crumpled, beer-stained paper map of the Redwood region from a pile of papers on a small desk wedged between the fridge and the wall oven. He smoothed it with his hands, flattening it out on the kitchen table. The four of us pored over it as I made an outline to weave our way up and back on down through the King's Range National Conservation Area.

It was arranged that Little Honey Momma would stay with a dog-friendly neighbor of Walter and Lori's while we were away. I felt bad for her, she'd gotten so comfortable in Walter's house, splayed out like the queen of Sheba on the cushion he'd placed for her by the stove. I hoped for the best, that she'd hang on to delivering her pups 'til we were back at Walter's with Mia, all of us safe and sound.

Deer scattered as we approached a tall, forged iron gate set into heavy-duty fencing. It was mid afternoon. A narrow driveway led to an A-Frame home fronted by an orchard of bare fruit trees. A pack of broad-winged turkey vultures hovered overhead.

Lori had set us up with a place to stay for the night in the home of her old friends, Lizzie and Jack. She'd described it as: "A Shangri-la of sorts, though times have changed. I'm not sure how much longer they'll stick it out up here. If anyone is able to help put word out, they will."

We found Lizzie and Jack to be a fit looking pair, slim and toned for their advancing years given the outdoor life and their necessary rounds of constant, daily labors.

Marcus had driven slowly and cautiously onto the couple's secluded property, located a half hour's drive along a dirt road up in the hills above the small, Gold-Rush era community of Myer's Flat in the heart of the Avenue of the Giants in Humboldt Redwoods State Park.

Four longhaired llamas munched at tall grasses that almost hid a herd of dwarf goats and some sort of small breed of fluffy sheep that were grazing in fenced pastures along the left side of the house. Dense wooded areas of Douglas firs, companion trees to the giant redwoods reached above the outer edges of the secluded homestead.

A fragrant scent of blue-green fir needles brought to mind the Christmas trees of my childhood. Each December the old man would cut down a suitable tree from the far reaches of the ranch and Bridget and I were given the job of decorating it with popcorn strings and childish homemade ornaments we'd made at school from corks and ribbon and hammered tin lids. These were some of the happier memories of my otherwise austere childhood.

Andres on the other hand, he'd hated the sticky residue of fir tree needles on a polished hardwood floor, depriving me, in turn of the simple aromatic pleasures of even the smallest of fresh evergreens. When he finally moved out, just as the holidays were approaching, I watched, somewhat bemused as he took with him a box containing the small, fake, tabletop tree he favored with its white lights and a monotone of matte silver baubles attached to the box in a clear plastic bag. Good riddance to that.

"Lori says you've been here a good long while," I ventured, after we made our introductions. "Your own slice of paradise," I said, focusing back in on the here and now. There'd be no shortage of fir trees to fell for a country Christmas on this property.

"Lizzie and me were among the first growers in the region," Jack replied. "Counted ourselves a part of the eco-conscious homesteader movement after migrating up here in the late 1960s." They were the embodiment of the Northern California cannabis pioneers we'd talked about with Bobby not an hour before his death.

There was no evidence in their place of peeling paint or any other signs of the dilapidation of the ramshackle McCleery homestead.

"We keep a large flock of heritage chickens and bees," Lizzie followed my gaze to the basket of fresh eggs with an assortment of soft colors, pale blue, green, reddish, brown and white she carried. "No use of pesticides here. Any fertilizers we employ are natural by-products of the farm."

Jack offered to take us on a tour. I was surprised by how upfront he was with us seeing as he had only just met us. "We consider this a way of life rather than a business," he explained. "At first, we snuck a few cannabis plants in behind the tomatoes at the back of the chicken house to make ourselves some much needed extra money. None of us had any idea how the industry would eventually monopolize."

Our hosts were of similar height and body type. If they hadn't at first, they'd grown to look alike as they lived and loved and toiled the depths of the redwood forest all those years, their kind, weathered faces inset with two pairs of same-colored, watery eyes, the shade of robin's eggs. They'd each tied their long white hair in the same efficient style of a pair of neat, thick braids that hung from the backs of their slim and sun-wrinkled necks.

"And is your grow organic?" I asked. Lizzie shook her head, explaining how they followed the concept of biodynamic growing over full-on organic. "Official government approved organic designation is not applicable to cannabis," Jack explained as they walked us over to the now dormant outdoor grow behind their home, his strong, bony hands fastened on narrow hips. "No matter the state and local laws, cannabis is still an illegal crop in the eyes of the Feds," he said.

Biodynamic cannabis, however, is grown outdoors, under the sun, throughout the full course of a natural growing season. "It's the biodynamic element that allows for the full flowering of the plant's healing properties," Jack concluded, evidently proud of his stance on growing the really good stuff. "This makes our crop suitable for medicinal use," he said.

As we turned back toward the house, he spoke of the new wave of growers who continue to arrive in the area to set up shop. "They're all about the business of hydroponics these days, employing grow lamps and plant food for fast turnaround — indoor grows."

Jack told us how these swelling numbers of indoor grow operations has heavily impacted their view of the night sky. "The glow," he said. "It's an abomination."

I felt for them, for Lizzie and Jack, their gentle way of life, pretty much over and from no wrongdoing on their part.

"Damn, that's a shame," Marcus said.

"Those who've moved in more recently with their fancy new trucks are more motivated by their winter vacations in Costa Rica than their neighbor's nighttime stargazing activities. And those are the good ones," he said.

Lizzie estimated at least a third of cannabis grown in the state of California is produced indoors, today. "Can you imagine the impact? This is nine percent of the state's electricity use we're talking about," she said.

"The green rush," Jack explained, looking out at the horizon of treetops: "as it surely should be known as, is a direct result of too many cannabis growers cashing in before it is fully legalized."

Lori had sent us to Lizzie and Jack as founding members of a group of concerned growers connected throughout the Emerald Triangle, known to be comfortable in taking matters into their own hands.

"We've heard of your service to your community," Marcus said, broaching the subject. "I'd imagine there is strength in numbers when you're dealing with such a changing landscape."

"The main mission of our grower's group is to encourage as many of the new arrivals as possible to grow a biodynamic crop, outdoors. For us, it's a moral issue," Jack replied.

"As a group, we've pooled our resources to help buy tanks to store water for the summer months," Lizzie added. "It's a big part of our conservation efforts."

Inside their wood paneled, art filled home, we sat over steaming mugs of lemon verbena tea and a plate of Lizzie's homemade oatmeal cookies, three of which Marcus inhaled in rapid succession.

"I learned to bake from necessity," Lizzie said, chuckling. "Sometimes we go for a couple of weeks between trips to the store."

I bit into one of Lizzie's delicious cookies and an image of Mia, malnourished, deprived of anything close to the comfortable room we were cozied up in ramped up a sense of urgency of what we were doing there. My throat tightened. I swallowed hard, discreetly wrapping the rest of my cookie in a napkin.

I looked at Marcus. His jaw dropped as he scanned the gentle craftsmanship of the spacious redwood cabin with its substantial, handcrafted beams, its neat doors and window frames. The touch and feel of Jack's artistry and expression in his carpentry was a calming tonic for the two of us. I understood how the beauty of the building's construction and its unassuming decor might appeal to Marcus on some quiet and profound level.

"Like it? I built it myself," Jack said, picking up on Marcus' appreciative gaze as the older man slipped his heavy cotton stocking feet from his work boots. He extracted a small knife from its sheath on his belt and placed it onto a narrow shelf on a wall by the table.

Lizzie went back to explaining how moving north had been a cultural shift for their hippie crowd who'd come up from the city together. "It was the first time since the original homesteaders staked claim in the region in the late eighteen hundreds that any ranch land had come on the market. The larger properties were carved up for subdivision into smaller parcels," she said.

"It was nothing to snap up a hundred acres, back then," Jack added. Marcus looked out of the window, dreamily.

"How did you meet?" I asked.

Jack said: "We were law students at Cal, both of us in our mid-twenties."

"Stewardship and conservation were part and parcel of the big shift north. We came here to raise our families, to leave it all behind. To live the good life," Lizzie added.

"Many of our early neighbors traveled to Mexico, Columbia and Jamaica, as far away as Afghanistan and Pakistan in the late sixties and seventies," Jack said. "These were the growers who smuggled much of the early marijuana strains into the States."

"I spent time in Iraq," Marcus shared. "Kind of ironic. A lot of guys I served with were pining for some good California weed."

Lizzie reached out and touched his forearm gently. "For us," she said, "the heyday was the era of these first breeder/growers in the region. Strains were crossed to yield and shorten the growing season."

"We took the ethos seriously and we did our own policing," Jack added. "Volunteer sentries were posted on hilltops, they still are, today, to let the community know via CB radio when there is a stranger at large."

"Most of the mom and pop grow operations such as ours are being forced to industrialize to compete with the corporations coming in and monopolizing the land," Lizzie said. "We're being crushed here by corporate takeover of the more remote, former timberland. Jack and me, we're at the age where we're close to being done with it. One or two more harvests, maybe, if we're lucky."

She talked of a honeymoon period if cannabis is ever fully legalized. "It's our last hope that the real deal, the biodynamic crops such as ours, that they might somehow be the ones to hold their own against the mass-produced commercial grows," she said, though the troubled expression on her face, I thought, belied the hopefulness of her sentiment.

"The same was said for the small, independently owned and farmed vineyards in the Napa and Sonoma Valleys," Jack said. "Truth is, eventually, most of the boutique labels have been swallowed up by the big wine conglomerates."

"Enough about us," Lizzie said. "It's time to talk about the real reason for your visit, your pressing need to find your niece."

It was hard for me to keep my voice from quavering. Marcus took my hand in his. These warm and hospitable people never even knew we existed until earlier that day — me, Marcus or Mia. And now here we were at their table, discussing the inconceivable and hideous danger Mia was in. There was no more time for niceties.

"As far as we know," I said: "Mia is being held against her will, degraded, forced into unspeakable acts."

Nobody spoke. We sipped tea for a minute or two more, our eyes lowered.

"The cartels have destroyed our safe haven," Lizzie broke the silence. "It's extremely dangerous here in the forest, Maggie. I'm so very sorry that your niece has been caught up in what sounds to be the worst of it," she said, reaching for my arm, touching it gently.

Jack circled back around to the subject of recounting their first few decades of farming in the days when a frontier-like attitude of independence had sufficed. "It's grown completely out of control," he said. "We're tired of it, of being robbed and of the raids, a collective blind eye turned toward the missing and worse."

"We're not suggesting that it's impossible to track Mia," Lizzie reassured. "But you must know that it's going to be extremely hard to find her given the circumstances."

Jack spoke, as Lori had, of trespass grows guarded by heavily armed goons. "It started with the Mexican cartels, but it could just as well be an Italian gang, Chinese, or Bulgarian that we're seeing around town in their striped leisure suits and heavy gold chains."

Ukranian crime syndicates have also been staking claims on swaths of forestland and vast tracts of private land we heard.

Lizzie laced her slim, bony fingers. She looked around the kitchen she so clearly loved. "Humboldt is no longer the nonviolent place we'd dreamed of," she said. "The powers that be, they have pretty much given up looking for all of the dead bodies buried out here in the wild."

"Truth is, we didn't fully grasp what we had started," Jack confessed. "Some might say our cult, if you will, of individualism, however indirectly, may have led to this whole scene of unlawfulness that spirals now so utterly out of control."

"That's a big statement," Lizzie intervened. "How could we have known?"

Marcus asked Lizzie how it was the cartels were able to set themselves up in the Emerald Triangle, given that the roads in and out are so remote and so incredibly hard to navigate.

"Think about it," she said. "An interstate network of highways connects the western states. These highways filter in and narrow down into a vast maze of wilderness that provides the perfect place to hide out."

"Is it OK if we talk about your trimmers?" I asked. I would need to get into Mia's head — to think like her if I was to find her.

"Lizzie and me, we take great care of our crews," Jack said. "Always have done. Each harvest season we set them up with tents, cots, clean sleeping bags, washroom facilities, fresh food, tea, coffee, wine, beer, musical instruments we've collected over the years, the regular evening highlight is a batch of Lizzie's cookies."

"Sounds good to me," Marcus said. I tried to picture him in a tent in the redwoods close to rock bottom, isolated, self-medicating, emotionally shutdown. It was hard to reconcile that man with this.

Jack and Lizzie talked of how they'd hired the same all-lesbian crew from Idaho each year for the past few seasons. "They're terrific workers," Lizzie said. "They drive here in their own bus. No trouble at all. Good people, the best."

"We've never hired off the street," she said. "It's not to be encouraged. It's not safe for anyone concerned. Your family has unfortunately discovered this."

"There is no smoking on the job," Jack said. "It was a deal breaker some seasons in the past, hence the reason why we treat our compliant all-women crew so well."

"Absolutely no meth, no heroin, no cocaine like you'll find on a lot of the farms these days," Lizzie added. "We don't stand for it."

They promised to call a meeting with their growing community the following morning to put urgent word out about Mia.

"Good news is, all sorts of folk other than the law are finally talking," Jack said. "Environmentalists and loggers are now working together on the same side of the fence, first time in the region's history in an all-out citizen-led effort to combat the cartels," he added.

None of this was making me feel any more hopeful. It only served to speed up my anxiety to get started in our physically scouring the forest for Mia.

"The obvious crooks, they're not the only ones who have to be stopped," Jack said, veering back around to his main beef — environmental impact. "We're looking for growers that clear-cut through the fauna, killing bears and deer and other animals for food, those who divert water and poison rodents and, in turn our region's raptors. It's an epidemic of destruction we're facing."

The owners of the region's larger land properties, Jack explained have started teaming up to track down cartel grows with the employment of private militia. "What they're looking for is the sorts of telltale signs of trespass grows — highly dangerous toxic mixes laying around in old Gatorade bottles, big volumes of debris and waste."

"Don't think for one minute the cartels are the only threat," Lizzie added. "We expect the same sorts of problems to creep into the environmental crisis when the mega box stores start selling large-scale cannabis."

After we'd helped clear the table of tea mugs and cookie crumbs, the two of them were back in the kitchen, readying a warming supper of Lizzie's spicy lentil soup and a loaf of home baked whole wheat bread with butter. What is it about the smell of freshly baked bread? It's surely the most universally best-loved aroma and Lizzie's loaf, still warm on the countertop, filled the entire house with the most wonderful sense of home. I made a mental note to someday start making my own bread if life ever settles into any sort of normalcy. Imagine?

"Make yourselves at home," Lizzie said, "go take a seat in the family room, relax for a few minutes, you'll be hitting the road early tomorrow morning, I assume."

Marcus had his eye on a vintage acoustic guitar propped on a metal stand in the corner of the room next to a faded, green velvet couch. We sat side by side, nestled among a set of needlework cushions depicting California wildflowers. Jack had noticed Marcus eyeing the guitar.

"Go ahead," he motioned. "You play?"

"Sort of. I learned a couple of songs during my time in Iraq," Marcus replied. "Never had the opportunity to play before joining up and I haven't had my hands on one since," he said, standing up from the couch and extracting the guitar from its stand as gently as if it was a small child. He sat himself down on a side chair, strumming and twisting his fingers on the chords, sliding his hand to the higher frets.

"The heaviness of the wood feels good in my hands," he said, wistfully. "Rosewood? Listen to these tones, man, they're so rich and full."

"Hey, not bad for a so-called beginner," I said, the melody of his guitar playing calming, almost hypnotic in the fading light of the early evening. He's a natural it appears.

Jack perched on the arm of the couch while Marcus sang along in a husky, slightly rusty rendition of Guthrie's California Stars. It was the Billy Bragg and Wilco mix version, he explained, after our applause.

"You sing, too!" I remarked. I was impressed. "Jeez, Marcus, you sounded pretty darn convincing there, any other talents you haven't told me about?"

"All will be revealed in time," he joked. "Though, seriously, this song was a big favorite of mine and a lot of the homesick Californian dudes. We all had plenty of practice."

"This here is a custom Martin guitar, out of Nazareth, Pennsylvania," Jack said, as Marcus handed back the instrument to its owner.

"Vintage, great surf guitar — I traded for it, wouldn't you know, back in the mid seventies?"

I helped Lizzie as she set the table for supper, all the while thinking how I'm going to have to get my hands on a guitar like that for Marcus, someday. We ate by candlelight at the small, round, kitchen table looking out over the stark shadows of the bare winter orchard. We ate heartily, Marcus and me, not knowing where the next cooked meal would come from.

"Thank you both so very much for your kind and generous hospitality," I said, spontaneously hugging each of our hosts as we readied for bed. We'd lingered at the supper table 'til late. "Please, don't mention it," Lizzie said. "It's been real quiet up here, with the storms. We're glad of the company, not least the chance to help you find Mia."

We were up and ready to take off soon after daybreak. There had been another storm during the night and yet, I woke only once in the wee hours when the wind that had whispered and cooed through the forest at bedtime reached its most violent peak, with rain slamming in heavy sheets against the bedroom window. I'd risen and peered out of the window into the dark, howling night, barely able to make out the limbs and branches of the trees that were closest to the house. They bent and braced against the storm like the supple fingers of a frightened child.

"I feel there's something wild and exhilarating about these winter storms so deep into the forest," Marcus shared from the comfort of the bed, dreamily. Later, after we'd drifted back to sleep, we awoke a second time to the smell of fried bacon wafting under the bedroom door and a double alarm in the form of a loud series of kak kak kacking — the unmistakable call of the peregrine falcon.

"Listen," Marcus whispered, placing two of his fingers on my lips. "This is the sound of the redwood forest, centuries of tree music in perfect tune with the bird kingdom and the whole rest of nature."

"Your natural habitat," I said, scooting closer under the covers to kiss his sleep-warm lips.

Marcus rolled out of bed and balanced on his crutch. He made his way over to the window and prized open its cast iron latch. As he flung it open to the elements, a flowery perfume scented the room with a thousand notes of wild, green, wintery vegetation. The essence of the Lost Coast mingled with the bracing air of the Pacific that blew across the treetops. The early morning mist shrouded the canopy and the ground below was thoroughly soaked.

A quick, hot water sponge bath removed the warm and sticky trace of our silent, late night lovemaking, laced with a lingering lavender scent of the soft linen bed sheets I'd stripped and set to launder in the washing machine.

We found Jack and Lizzie in the kitchen where he was busy making a pot of coffee. His mate stood at the range, frying bacon and eggs in a large, heavy skillet. We chatted over the freshly brewed coffee as Lizzie cracked an exotic, pastel blue colored egg on the edge of the iron skillet, its contents, a double yolk dropping neatly into the hot oil. Egg white hissed as it fried, the two, deep, dense, sunshine-colored yolks, sunny-side up, sizzled amidst the fast curling edges of the crispy white.

Jack seemed to want to talk more of how much things had changed. "Back in the day," he said, "we grew accustomed to pulling in up to 4,000 dollars a pound. On condition of there being no pesticides in our cannabis ever, no chemicals."

He described how they'd been able to get by for years on 20 to 30 pounds of sales each harvest season. "Now, we're selling at half that price," he said.

"If you don't mind me asking, how do you work around the federal issue, banking, that sort of thing?" Marcus asked. "I guess you can't pay taxes on it, even if you want to," he ventured.

"We have never declared the income from our crop, nobody does," Lizzie explained, with full transparency, I noted. "Pretty much every penny we make we put back both into the property and directly, as much as we're able, into our community."

By the time we left them, we were old friends, the four of us. We had Lori to thank and Walter, for Lori. I couldn't help but wish they were my parents and that I had them to run home to.

Marcus had warmed to them immediately and they to him. "I used to consider it a weakness, asking for help," he admitted, driving downhill on the weaving dirt road. Marcus was opening up to me a little more each day. He began to talk about how he'd always dreamed of building his own house, a home, like Jack and Lizzie's someday.

"Ever since we were real small, my brother and me," he confided, his voice now quavering slightly, "whenever we spent time with our grandpa in his workshop, we'd get to talking over some pretty darn big ideas for dream homes of our own."

I gently massaged the back of his neck with my left hand as he drove and reminisced. His grandpa had urged the boys to think big when it came to their future. "Not surprisingly, I guess," he said, "I lost sight of a lot of it after losing my brother and my grandmother, then him and, after the blast it was hard to see the point in anything to do with the future."

"You know Marcus, rebuilding a sense of inner security takes time. Don't beat yourself up, this is way more important than any material need we may have," I said. I should know.

"I'm not so sure that I'm any where near as smart as you make me sound," he replied, with a half smile. "I never thought I'd hear myself say this, Maggie, but it may be time for me to revisit the woodshop, start in on some new ideas."

Funny, but I've found in learning to want less of late, I've been able to let myself imagine so much more. Maybe it is the same for Marcus, I think so. He changed gear multiple times as he navigated flooded spots of deep, standing water as we headed deeper into the forest.

CHAPTER 23

MARCUS

Twilight falls in the month of February within the redwoods at around 6 p.m. This provided us with a good 11 hours on the road to stop off at campgrounds and visitor's centers into Humboldt Redwood State Park, headed northward on the highway and through the small communities of Redcrest, Pepperwood and Rio Dell. Maggie showed Mia's photo to a dozen or more convenience store workers, gas station attendants, tavern workers and the front desk staff of small inns and bed and breakfasts along the way.

It was my idea to spend a night or two in the truck so that we might cover more ground no matter how off the beaten track we veered. Not one person we spoke to remembered having seen Mia, specifically. This was no surprise given that there would've been so many young women her age passing through the region during harvest season. The fact that most of them took off after the trimming was done presented the slim chance of someone taking notice of her if she had managed to escape the compound at any point.

It was like we had the forest to ourselves. "For all its majesty, it sure is a creepy place come nightfall," Maggie said as we readied my truck under its camper shell for bedding down. It was not nearly as comfortable as the previous three beds we'd shared, but it served its purpose and we would keep one another warm.

I looked up into the canopy of the still and shrouded giants. "To think they've been here for centuries, these same trees, the oldest of them anyway," I said to myself. "Here they stand, listening, watching, whispering to one another as we, the humans of the world, go on making such a fucking mess of it all."

We'd picked up a rack of ribs in foil and a tub of potato salad from a country convenience store we'd come across with an industrial barbecue set up under a covered porch.

It was dry out that evening, a rare and welcome change, a real good thing considering we would have faced a few extra hours of hunkering down in the truck bed had it kept on pissing it down. I'd pulled off into a quiet spot on a forest service road a little ways off the main route. The emergency supplies we'd packed back at the ranch had come into use. We rolled out a foam mattress that fit the truck bed. Maggie pulled out a heavy flashlight, folding chairs and a portable camping stove with propane from the stash we'd found in the barn.

No sooner than we were settled, a set of vehicle lights rose and dipped on the service road, heading in our direction. We watched, intrigued as a battered Sprinter van pulled up alongside.

"Marcus," Maggie said, holding onto my arm. "Who the hell is this? Did someone follow us?"

I walked around the truck, popped the glove compartment and pocketed my knife. A weird looking, skinny, balding, middle-age-dude jumped out of his van. I'd been more concerned about a mountain lion or black bear wandering out of an early hibernation than anyone pulling up beside us.

"What's up?" I asked, keeping my distance. The dude was either a vigilante of some sort, desperate to make a connection or lost. "Howdy, man, how's it going," he replied, extending the opposite hand to the one that held a joint.

Maggie spoke: "You looking for someone?"

"No ma'am," he replied. "It's the cosmos I'm here for, would you just look up at them stars? It's been a while on account of the rains."

I could sense Maggie's hackles rising. It was a bold and intimidating move to pull into an occupied space with hundreds of thousands of acres of forestland to choose from. "So, that's cool," I replied. "Are you planning on taking in the cosmos from here?"

"Yes, sir," he answered. "This being one of my regular spots. I don't mean to crowd you out or nothing, though I sure do appreciate the company." With that, he rummaged around in his van for a minute or two and emerged with his own camp chair and a pile of blankets. "For sharing," he said, "Stargazing is way more satisfactory with other folk about."

Strange as he was, he offered Maggie one of his blankets. "For your shoulders, my dear," he said.

To my surprise, Maggie allowed him to drape the blanket over her. She sat herself down on her chair, her grip on the flashlight I figured would've served as a good weapon of self-defense as any should she have deemed it necessary.

We spent the next couple hours shooting the breeze with Charlie and drinking sweetened hot cocoa from packets stirred into water I boiled over the camp stove. He told us how he'd been on the road a while, looking for enlightenment, traveling solo through the redwoods.

I'm not sure why it was I felt he posed no threat, it's just one of those things you work out fast. "You'd be surprised," I said, after we'd split our supper three ways, "but I have an acute fear of the dark."

It was the blast that had made me most afraid of the unexpected, of exposure to whatever dangers might be lurking in the shadows.

Maggie moved her chair closer to mine. I didn't plan on blurting out any more on the subject of my battle with PTSD. It just came out of me.

"It's nothing new, your condition, dude, it's been around for centuries," Charlie replied, reading between the lines. "At least long as these redwoods have been on earth."

He launched into a long, informed monologue on the Trojan warriors of Greece and the soldiers led by the House of Plantagenet in the Hundreds Years' War no less. The more he smoked his spliff, the more he rattled on. He would've given Walter a run for his money as he touched on the tribal warriors in Africa, the soldiers of the Civil War and the troops who fought on both sides of the Spanish-American hostilities. "Let's not forget the folk who have battled and survived the atrocities of The Great War, World War II, the Korean War, the Vietnam War, men and women who served in the Persian Gulf, the War in Iraq, hundreds of thousands of battle survivors who share the same symptoms from combat stress and injury as you," he rattled on. It was an education and a half.

At the end of his long diatribe he came right out with asking how it felt to live with it day in and day out, the PTSD. "You want to know? It's a constant fight or flight feeling," I admitted. "Right now, this very minute, I can feel it in my muscular tissue, my heart, my lungs, my nerves, especially my brain."

The best way I'm able to describe my PTSD is how I experience sensitivity to light, to noise, to no light, to no noise, spending so much of my life in some sort of constant battle to control these sensations of mind and body.

I threw it out there, despite my not wishing to freak out Maggie any more than I figured I already had. Truth is, I've suffered these frequent feelings of dread, fear and occasional rage for so long now, it's almost commonplace. I've trained myself as best as I am able to resist the ratcheting up of the more violent feelings that may kick in at a moment's notice. "It was hanging out in the forest where I first trained myself to get a grip on this fear of the dark," I confessed.

I guess it was the peacefulness of the forest that moved me to be so brutally honest about this ever present, constant fight. I looked up into the stars and I let it all out. Tears ran down my face. Maggie, bless her heart, did not overreact and I was thankful for that. She sat real still and silent a while before announcing it time for she and me to call it a night, wishing Charlie a good sleep.

"Lock all the doors," she instructed, soon after we'd clambered into the covered truck bed and lain down fully dressed on top of the foam mattress, our sleeping bags unzipped over our bodies in a double layer of eiderdown with an extra blanket on top to keep out the chill.

"It's OK," I said, "he's not gonna pull any weird shit, other than already being way out there." I guessed he was ex-military himself with his historic war trove of information, though he never gave us any other clue as to who he was or where it was he'd come from. I figured he had established in his own min that I was not a man to mess with.

By the time we awoke, early, before dawn, Charlie was gone.

"Well that was an experience," Maggie said. "At least we're alive to tell the tale."

The ground was muddy and slick. I'd taken the risk of sleeping with my prosthetic still attached given the space logistics and lack of hot water and the off chance that Charlie may yet have posed a problem in the middle of the night.

We pressed on up to Fortuna, self-described 'friendly city', located in west central Humboldt, on the northeast shore of the Eel River. A sturdy and elderly waitress in a breakfast joint on Main Street enlightened us as to how it was the community had gotten its name: "Folks say it was a marketing tool cooked up by a local real estate agent and a minister back in the day," she said. "The two of 'em shrewdly petitioned to change it from its second known name of Springville, formerly Slide, so as to attract more folk to move on up here for the redwoods, the valley, its position on the river and proximity to the ocean." Unfortunately, she, like all the others, had no memory of having seen Mia in the area.

Our table was inlaid with vintage photos of local memorabilia, faded images of the old Depot Museum located in the former train station that was employed to transport lumber out of the area. I ordered four eggs, sunny-side up, a side of bacon and hot, buttered, sourdough toast with black coffee. Maggie ordered a Swiss cheese and mushroom omelet with fruit and an English breakfast tea before heading into the restroom to wash her face. I appreciate a woman with good hygiene and a healthy appetite. We pressed on, fueled by our morning meal, asking about Mia at random stores and gas stations, making our way north to connect to the Ferndale/Petrolia Road, later, heading southwest into the well-preserved Victorian downtown of the small city of Ferndale, settled in the Gold Rush era by Europeans for its location at the mouth of the Eel as it feeds into the Pacific.

"The entire town is registered as a historic landmark, Marcus," Maggie remarked, after we'd made a quick but thorough trek in and out of multiple brightly lit storefronts on Main Street. "And you know what, it was the dairy farming that led to all this lavish Victorian architecture back in the boom days," she added. "Same time the McCleerys settled south on the Sonoma Coast."

The only lead as to a possible sighting of Mia came from a server dude in a busy lunchette we'd stuck our head into. The kid said he might have seen her with another woman, older than her, a semi-regular who comes on in with her partner for the chicken noodle soup every now and again. It was fairly recent. "Can't be sure, but it could have been her," he said. "Haven't seen her since." He had no idea of the customer's name or where she lived. "Pays with cash, like most." he said.

It grew cold being close to the ocean and it was early evening by the time I swung the truck into the parking lot of the Old Six Mile House some miles south of Fortuna. Despondence was beginning to creep in. "What the hell are we doing, tooling around without any hope in hell of stumbling on Mia's whereabouts?" Maggie asked, her hands to her head. "This is all such a waste of time."

I parked under the expansive, leathery green canopy of a pungent bay laurel. Back when it was built, a remote saloon and stage stop such as this would have been reachable only by unpaved roads that were at best, treacherous and muddy for most of the year.

Even now with decent enough roads, conditions are tough. Maggie shivered, zipping her jacket against the chill. "I need a drink," she said, checking for cell phone reception as we made our way across a gravel parking lot into the warm light of the rustic roadhouse, its redwood paneled interior walls decked out with the usual taxidermy and rusty logging tools. A pile of old peanut shells crunched under foot.

"What is it with the goddamn shells?" she asked.

"Harkens back to Colonial days," I replied. "Peanuts make for a mightier thirst, plus, I'd wager the natural oils were an added benefit to a hard-worn wooden floor."

Maggie's phone lit up on initial contact with a cellular connection. She'd missed several calls during the hours we had been out of reach.

"Bridget's tried me three times," she said, with a degree of instant panic in her voice. A third message was from Lori. She replayed it on speakerphone so that we both were able to hear the recording. "Call me, Maggie, as soon as you can," Lori's message relayed. "I have news."

Maggie's hands were shaking, visibly.

"Now look here," I said, taking her hands in mine, "it's not necessarily bad news." I ordered drinks after we'd sat ourselves at the bar, a beer for me, a big ol' glass of pinot noir, as requested, for her.

Few in this neck of the woods appear to have much of a taste for the better wines on the bar list, for I noticed the unopened bottle was coated in dust when the bartender took it from the shelf.

Maggie swished the almost translucent, ruby colored wine in its clear glass globe, deliberately taking her time in suspending reality a few minutes more as she took herself a couple sips.

"Marcus, whoa, hold on a second," she said, reaching for my arm. "I've barely taken a sip and my vision's blurry all of a sudden. There's a fuzzy edge to those Latino guys in some sort of uniform hunched over the pool table over there."

I turned to take a look at two already empty pint glasses and a row of empty shot tumblers lining the shelf behind two postal workers and their half drunk beers.

A faceless dude in denim and a cowboy hat sauntered up and sat down beside me, nodding, undoubtedly confused as to what sort of drama was playing out with a couple of outsiders with the female one of the two of us growing increasingly distressed by the second.

Simon and Garfunkel belted out Cecilia from a beat-up juke box in one corner. I took Maggie's hand in mine after wiping the cold sweat from her palm with a paper napkin.

If I had laid my ear to her chest I believe I'd have been able to hear the thump, thump of her heart beating above the clink of the pool balls and the shuffling footsteps of the postal workers. She fixed her eyes on a working pot-bellied stove at the far end of the room, its smokestack built up into the ceiling. I pulled my stool closer as she rested her forehead on her fingers and thumbs, breathing deeply through her nose; a controlled effort, I figured to dispel an overwhelming sense of nausea and the smell of stale beer. There's no easy way to disguise a panic attack from someone like me.

I placed my arm around her shoulder. The unfortunate fact that she suffers from these occasional silent freak-outs makes me feel more a good deal less concerned about my own shortcomings. I placed my mouth by her ear and suggested that we step outside for some air. "Before you even think of returning that phone call," I added.

"I have to know what's happened," she gasped as she took in three or four more deep breaths, gripping the bar stool in an effort to steady herself. She raised her eyes and looked headlong into the concerned eyes of the bartender, a weathered looking chick with a beanie pulled low over a pair of scrawny pigtails. She was keeping her cool in assessing the situation, as well she should have. I'd wager she's seen a lot worse than Maggie's stress out session.

The bartender poured a tall glass of water over ice and slid it over the bar top in front of Maggie who, in turn, took herself a good, long, icy gulp. She pushed the barely touched glass of wine aside. I steadied her as she stood up from the stool, inhaling another round of long, slow breaths.

Maggie's phone vibrated on the bar. She picked it up, checked the caller ID and showed me the screen. It was Lori. By then everyone in the bar was staring at us. Ranch hands and Summer of Love Boomers gaped like they'd never seen a cell phone before. Had we stepped back into 1967? Maggie took the call. My heart lurched in time with hers.

"OK, I'm sitting down," she spoke into the phone, digging her nails into my wrist with her free hand and settling herself back on her stool. "Speak up, it's loud in here and please, just tell me."

I waited for her face to react. She kept her expression deadpan a minute more as she listened to what it was that Lori was telling her. "They've found her, Marcus, oh my God, I can't believe it," Maggie gripped my arm. She was sharing the news with me in the midst of Lori's call. "Lizzie's connections somehow came through it appears. Mia is alive and she's safe."

Maggie caught her breath as she attempted to let the news sink in. "Lori, wait," she urged, bursting into a flood of breathy tears, unsure whether to stand up or sit down, holding tight to the phone with Lori as messenger on the other end. She was trying to force a smile as her body shook.

I positioned my back to the prying eyes of those behind us, all of them still staring like we were from some other planet, wrapping a quieting Maggie in my arms and encircling her as she resumed the call.

"So sorry, Lori, I'm in crazy shock. I was so close to giving up. Are you still there?" she asked. "I'm confused. I mean, why? If she's somewhere safe, how is it she never reached out to Bridget to tell her what happened?"

Lori patiently explained how Mia was doing as well as could be expected considering the ordeal she'd been through. She described how Mia was ensconced in a safe and secure home for women and that it was not unusual for it to take considerable time for a victim to decompress.

So she was alive and she was free and she was being looked after. This was way better than any of us had been hoping to hear and yet, the disturbing part of it was that she had not let anyone know.

"Apparently we have to wait for Mia to give her permission before Bridget or myself are able to make direct contact," Maggie relayed to me Lori's strict instructions. "The most important thing is that she made it out, away from those fucking bastards who held her since September."

Lori was still on the line. I heard Walter's deep voice in the background. "Tell Maggie and Marcus to come on back to Garberville," he said, "tonight."

"We'll talk in more detail back at Walter's house," Lori said. "Drive safely you two, we'll expect you in an hour or so."

"Where is she?" I asked after Maggie ended the call. "Where is this safe place? Do we know?"

"Exactly where it's supposed to be . . . somewhere safe," Maggie replied.

The bar had filled up while we'd sat there awash in our potent blend of relief and semi-disbelief, doing our best to take in this sudden mixed bag of news. It was happy hour and the cash was flowing.

Maggie pulled out her credit card to pay for the drinks that neither of us drank. I slipped it back into her wallet, pulling bills from my pocket. "Credit card and cell phone shunning clientele," I said — "hey, you're keeping company with the cash kings, now, Maggie."

One of the postal workers had finished his beer and was walking haphazardly to the bar, his fingers full of empty glasses. A group of regulars stopped him in his tracks and they talked animatedly, laughing freely to the pulse of a reliable generator that would frequently be employed to keep the lights on in such a remote spot. I bet myself the postal workers were the only ones to pay taxes, seeing as they work for the government and therefore have no choice. Nobody much in these parts even registers to vote, it's the pioneer days here still, the general idea of minding your own business, far from the trappings of city and suburban life.

While I waited for the bartender to take her time in making change, my thoughts turned to Bobby and his crowd of regulars at the roadhouse. They'd be missing him real bad by now.

"If Mia had come to me in the first place," Maggie tried to express her rush of feelings, "I'd have told her, run, yes — but head to the city, to me, into my care for once. I would've looked after her, Marcus, helped her find a job, a space, for what it's worth, now."

"You don't know what she may have gotten into in San Francisco," I replied.

"True. But what if she doesn't want to go home?" Maggie asked. "What then?"

None of us had given that possibility a thought in our desperate race to find the girls.

"You'd best figure it all out with Mia, face to face," I told her. "All we need to know right now is that she's safe. The rest of it is up to her."

Maggie called Bridget from the sanctity of the truck while we still had wireless reach. What they shared in their conversation is private, as it should be when something as momentous as this is talked about between two sisters. Those two had endured far more than enough already.

Darkness engulfed the redwood forest and a light rain started up on the windshield. I drove south through the Avenue of the Giants, passing no one, not one single vehicle in either direction of the avenue's 31-mile span. In the summer months, tourists by the thousands flock to gape and wonder at the world's largest remaining stand of virgin redwoods. That evening we were totally alone, the two of us, heading into a starless indigo and violet tinged night.

"I can't believe it's over," Maggie said, leading to a several minute silence as she blew out air: "To be honest, I was scared to death these past few days that we were already way too late."

"It's not over, Maggie," I said. "None of it. Not by a long shot. We all expect a swift return to normalcy after bad things happen, but that's not how it works. Take it from me, you and Bridget and Mia will have your work cut out for a good while yet in figuring out which way is up. Some of it'll glue back together, you'll see and other parts may never truly fit right again. It's the nature of it and you have to learn to make the best of it is all."

CHAPTER 24

MIA

B y the time Christmas came, I had taken to rattling around the compound lighting candles in plastic cups during those darkest and most depressing of hours. This was my own small, if pathetic effort to remind myself of the season despite things having gone so deathly quiet on the top of that cold, lonely mountain. I'd been reduced to being sole exclusive slave, Jefe Hombre being the one remaining motherfucker on the compound.

The sick fuck was old enough to have daughters my age. He never talked about his family, though I caught sight of a faded photo that slipped from his wallet one time. From what I could see, he was stiffly posed with a woman and a bunch of small kids, all of them dressed up in their Sunday best. I would not have been surprised if the bastard had been taking them to church.

After the others left, he refused to leave me unattended during his long round trip journeys into town and back, and so, rather than lock me up, he took to bringing me along.

After my bullshit punishment in the barn, tying me up like a goddamn animal, shaving my head, keeping me from Jazmin, I never made one single wrong move insofar that he saw. I knew full well that my timing had to be perfect for me to make it out alive. I also had to figure on getting out without putting Jazmin at risk. No one would be able to know I was gone.

He'd warned me, the night they dragged me into the barn, he was a man who was capable of far worse than the nightmare treatment I had already undergone at his hands. Every tiny atom inside of me yearned to be unleashed, to kick the shit out of him, to bite and spit and scratch and scream. If there were any way that I could have shed my skin, I would have; it crawled so bad I could hardly stand it. He and his crew of animals had stolen my strength, my dignity, worst of all, my soul sister, my sweet Jazmin. I plotted away inside my head, day and night, hour by hour, minute by minute, gradually building any ounce of courage I could muster. I readied myself to roar.

I went on stoking this mounting fire through the end of December and all the way into January, my anger building by the minute. He thought he had me at his mercy, subdued, tamed. Men like him, I've learned the worst way, they think they know women, they're so sure they're stronger than us, that they're the dominant sex. They're wrong.

Who knows where I found the strength I needed, but I did and I kept it together. I'd made up my mind when I was shackled like a beast in the barn, if he should let me live through that, oh man, I would make him pay. Full price. No returns.

The key was to convince him otherwise. I surrendered to his every need and demand, a sick game, but essential in that I pandered to every single one of his sadistic, narcissistic needs.

Fuck, I had nothing to lose but to set the stage for the fight of all fights. I promised myself I would risk it all when the moment was right.

After I was left there alone with him, there was no more creeping back to my bunk at night. I stuck on a mask of fake surrender as I tried my best to imagine being with a guy my own age, someone I was with willingly.

I forced myself to lie still beside him each time he was done with me, though my shoulder muscles would tense and my back set rigid. And I worked to maintain the slightest skin contact so he that began to figure I was warming to him. It was effective and I learned to play him like a fool.

In my head I stuck to my games of make-believe. I'd cycle through the one same reassuring story line, over and over, picturing myself lying in bed, in my own apartment, Jazmin in the next room, studying. I fantasized about the pictures I would put on the wall, which classes I would take that day, the cool outfits I'd soon have hanging in my closet. I even thought about the tasty food I'd stack in the refrigerator, pesto, cream, butter, good cheese, all the stuff I missed so bad it made my stomach hurt.

I somehow perfected this trick of looking outward in suspending my reality, half way convincing even myself that the body of the small, fat, hairy middle-age man splayed there beside me was not a monster but my boyfriend. Even I was surprised at how good I'd become at gaslighting myself — you know, twisting reality. Self-preservation baby.

I'd been tasked with cooking and other daily drudgery, doing his laundry and cleaning the place after the others had gone. It gave me something to do that wasn't directly tending to him. I trained my mind to drift off in thoughts of the wild animals of the forest around me, the birds of prey, the ones that were free to roam and fly and feast on the rotting corpses of the less fortunate captives of this murderous place. I was on constant alert as I formulated a plan to get myself out of there, away from him, forever, alive and breathing, free from his horrible hands.

I was, in equal turns, afraid for my life and for Jazmin's life if I messed up, desperately lonely and totally bored out of my brain. Jefe Hombre appeared to have little purpose during the day other than to patrol the property, fix fences, shore up trailers against the storms that had come in with a relentless cycle of wet weather.

The more the rain fell, the colder it was on that isolated mountain-top and the earlier in the evening he'd make his nasty demands on my attentions.

My hair had begun to grow back. I had regained a little of the weight I'd lost, though not through any solid nourishment.

I'm pretty sure he had worked out what was going on with me, physically. It was becoming impossible to hide. We barely spoke, in part due to the language barrier of my Spanish not being as good as it should be and also, because, why the hell would we? Still, I detected small efforts on his part to behave in a slightly less rough and abrupt way with me when he was in one of his more affectionate moods. It felt even more sickening to be treated nice than not. What sort of monster figures someone they're forcing into something this disgusting would ever come to care for them? I've heard there's a name for that. Well, it did not apply to me, even if he thought it did.

I went on faking it as best as I could. I hoped that Jazmin was doing the same that is if she hadn't made a run for it already. How I prayed she was free and would send someone to come find me. I never would have guessed it would be me who bust out first and by a couple weeks at least. I like to think we were mentally connected, the two of us, on the timing.

Truth is, he knew and I knew, if he should have decided to do away with me at any given time, not a soul would have any idea, other than Jazmin, that is. She would have known.

The alternatives were equally grim — what if I was still there when the baby came? What if he got rid of it and kept me or, less likely, I thought, killed me and kept the kid?

It was my worst fear that he would do something unspeakable to the one living thing other than Jazmin I cared for more than myself. A light bulb had come on along with my growing condition and it kicked my ass into gear.

An inner protective instinct to nurture, I guess you'd say, surfaced from someplace deep I never knew existed. I was shocked at the strength of feelings I had inside of me. This was after I'd come through weeks of total self-denial. I guess it's not surprising to want to pretend something like this is not happening and yet it grew impossible for me to ignore the signs. An innocent human being was taking root inside of me and the shock of the realization of this being real, gave way to a whole set of new and even more unexpected emotions. Instinctively, all I wanted to do was to wrap my arms around it, hide it from him, protect it and keep it warm and safe and, most importantly, growing. I started stashing towels and blankets, scraps of material, obsessing on how I'd take care of it.

I willed myself to keep on exhibiting my restrained acceptance toward him in bed and out, for the sake of survival, for the baby and for Jazmin mostly.

I took to looking him straight in the eyes, those ice-cold, dark brown almost black mirrors of his wicked soul, unblinking. I felt my power grow as I drew the fucker further in.

The last time we'd headed into town for supplies, he had made the mistake of letting me sit beside him with my hands and feet untied. I was still not allowed to wear shoes. Plastic bags served as protective footwear over a pair of ugly pink, fluffy socks he'd given me as some sort of concession from the dirty white athletic socks I'd worn for months.

It had been a first, me sitting up front beside him. Though I'd given him no real cause for concern since it had come down to him and me and he was growing more accustomed to my company in and out of his bed.

This time, I kept a close eye on his facial expressions as he took to the wheel, crooning along in his low, rough voice to the same dire tracks of the number one Latin pop compilation I'd suffered through during previous road trips into town and back.

I tapped my feet and rocked my head to and fro in rhythm to the music, faking like I was getting into it, waiting for the songs he liked best, the ones I knew he would rattle his piggish hands on the dashboard to. The asshole sang along to his favorite parts as rain lashed at the windshield, the wipers swishing back and forth in time, a kind of percussion to the sickly beat of the song.

He took his eyes off the road and turned to look at me, full on, grinning like a sucker. It turned him on big time, to think that I was somehow the hell into it all, the music, the ride into town, being with him. His sleazebag gaze traveled back and forth from the road ahead and up and down my body.

It was now or never. I knew it. I'd waited for this moment long enough, endured way more than enough for any one person. Still, I was nervous as all hell. Go for it, Mia, I told myself, don't stop to think, girl. You've got him right where you want him. I knew I may have gotten myself badly hurt in the process, killed even, but I took this calculated risk.

I forced a seductive glance, biggest come-on of my life, almost theatrical — batting my eyelashes and widening my eyes, all the essential bullshit that it would take to slay the stupid fucker for once and for all. Oh yes, a super confusing sensation came over him, I could see it, a blatant invitation, a first, from me to him and not the other way around and on the open road, of all places.

"Qué pasa?" Jefe Hombre, oh, how he smiled, the glint of the gold teeth at the back of his mouth reflecting on the windshield. He was falling for it, hook, line and sinker, I was sure of it. Steering with his left hand he draped his right arm over my shoulders. The dumb fool completely forgot himself. He was off to town with a pocketful of cash and for once, his teenage sex slave who was fully coming on to him.

Excited by his prospects, Jefe Hombre turned up the music right at the crucial point where we were fast approaching the river, a tricky, winding part of the route, thick with the scent of damp redwood trees and fallen branches. He opened his and my side windows half way, letting in air, inhaling, greedily and as he leaned back in his seat, he pulled me closer to him.

I took my chance and slid my left hand up and over his as he rested his disgusting fingers on my right shoulder. Still, I inched his fingers down toward my chest. He cupped my breast as I caressed the back of his hand, digging my nails in tantalizingly. He let out a gasp followed by a low moan and I watched as his eyes widened in wonderment of his sheer dumb fucking luck.

Slowly, I slid my left hand onto his thigh. Each move I made was slight, precise, given that, if I failed, I was done for. Who the hell was this? I listened to his breathing growing slower and heavier.

Bingo. He shot me a heavy-lidded, lust-filled, sideways leer as he attempted to maintain a half focus in navigating the slick road. It was the look I'd been waiting for, he was so close to pleading, if not begging for more.

I knew I had him exactly where I needed him. Don't ask me how I came to be this good in as deadly a manipulating move as this. It was all his doing, months of forcing me into the hideous role I was now more than ready to play to the full.

This was survival.

I took my time unbuckling his thick leather belt, slipping my hand down the front of his jeans to ready him for what he was after. He groaned with pleasure as I unzipped his fly, leaning back in his seat, slowing the speed of the truck until he was only barely in control. I released my seatbelt, twisted my torso toward him and lowered my head.

All I'm gonna say is that he thought that he was getting what he wanted, one last time. Oh yes, he was beside himself and having as good a time as he'd ever had until I bit down on him, hard, so fucking hard my teeth broke skin. He bolted up from his seat in reaction to the sudden, sharp piercing of flesh, the shock and unexpected horror of it, a potent cocktail of pain that threw him instantly off course.

My head shot up hard into the steering wheel. What happened next was a violent blur of several distorted seconds as I somehow managed to lift myself upright in my seat. He was lashing out, throwing his arms around, flailing, letting go of the steering wheel, wild, desperate to do something, anything to ease his throbbing pain. I can't shake the image of the veins of his neck thickening in the mayhem as he lost control of the truck.

Looking back, it's a wonder we never rolled or hit a tree head on. The hulking vehicle careened through a clearing in the trees and down to the riverbank in a manic zigzagging motion through mud and brush. A life-passing-before-your-eyes, slow-motion next move dropped us directly into the fast flowing river below.

Instinctively, I held on tight to the grab handle, or the 'Oh Shit Handle' as I've heard my mom refer to it more than a few times. The truck floated for about 30 seconds, before taking a nose-down position into the water and abruptly tipping driver side down as my brain frantically figured what the hell to do to get out.

Frigid brown water gushed in through the partially open windows. I hadn't planned for anything near as frightening and grotesque as this. A strange calm came over me and I waited for sufficient water to fill the vehicle. Electronics were disabled so a brief attempt to fully open my window failed. I wasn't strong enough to force open the door. I had zero choice but to hold my breath and head first, I managed, by some miracle to slither my way through the half open window and into the river as the truck began to turn turtle onto its back. One thing my mom taught me in rainy season was that if I was ever in a situation like this, I'd have about a minute to get out. I never thought it would happen to me.

Jefe Hombre — well, he was not so fortunate.

My last sight of him and one I will never forget for the rest of my life was his veins popping on his forehead, his mean, cold eyes — wide open, bulging, utterly panicked as he tried, desperately and failed to keep a hold of the leg of my soaked jeans.

It was sheer self-preservation strength at that point, not just for me, for the kid I'm carrying around inside of me.

I pushed on up to the surface, gasping for air as I splashed through the cold, murky, swirling water that had encapsulated the truck. My head dunked under again and again as I struggled. I kept my mouth shut so as not to suck in a shitload of dirty river water. I thrashed about and raised my head above the waterline. Fixing my eyes on the sky, rain fell like steel poles pounding through the surface of the river. Thick mist rolled through the trees beyond. I'd gotten this far, there was no way my adrenaline would allow me to succumb to the roiling water, to fucking drown. The river was surprisingly deep. I slid across a sand bank to rest up as I caught my breath. It was bitter cold in the water and out. I was shaking like crazy by the time I plunged forward and threw myself on to the riverbank.

I dared not stop. All I could think of was if Jefe Hombre had somehow made it out of the submerged truck, he'd have grabbed my legs and dragged me down surely into the dark, brown, muddy depths of hell that lay beneath the flow.

I wasted no time when I reached shore, clawing at reeds, bushes, anything I could get my hands on to haul myself out. I stumbled up the riverbank to the side of the road, ripping off the one torn and sodden sock that made it out of the water. I threw it to the side of the bank and climbed up through the undergrowth barefoot and soaked to the skin.

There was nothing to do but push on along the deserted river road, shivering, sobbing, running off and on as I caught my breath, terrified my captor might emerge at any moment, chase after me and pounce like a creature from the swamp. Somewhere in the distance, I heard music.

My feet were ice cold, cut up and bloody when I came across a man and a woman sitting outside a camper van that was parked in a clearing in the redwoods. Folk music played from a portable speaker. It was weird how the familiar sound of home made for a feeling of safety and refuge. I'd spent so much time talking shit about my mom's taste in music. Suddenly it was the best thing I'd ever heard.

Smoke came from a camp stove sheltered under a pullout canopy off the side of the van. The distinctive smell of sausages hit me in the gut and I stopped short of collapsing at their feet.

"My goodness," the woman gasped, springing to her feet and immediately wrapping me up in a knitted blanket she shook from her lap. "Where on earth did you come from out of the blue, honey? Heavens, you're soaking wet and freezing, let's get you warm and dry and off those poor feet," she said.

"River — accident," I spit out, between sobs. It was the same level of utter shock and horror I'd experienced after the violent branding that had seared the flesh on the back of my neck. This time, I was chilled to the bone, drenched, shaking uncontrollably. It all happened so frickin' fast I could barely process my escape. And I was still too terrified to feel much sense of relief.

"I'm Marybeth," she said, taking me by the arm and gently bundling me into the van. She shut the door softly as her husband, Malcolm, stepped aside to give us some privacy. Marybeth rummaged around inside for dry clothes. I shivered wildly as she peeled off my wet layers and dried me briskly with a towel.

"This will do," Marybeth said as she dressed me, hurriedly in several layers of random clothing including warm sweats and a pair of her husband's socks that had been drying from a clothesline hung across the narrow width of the van. It was surreal. I had no choice other than to surrender myself to their mercy, whoever the heck they were.

Malcolm passed a sausage sandwich through an open window. I devoured it despite my stomach lurching at the first bite. Marybeth poured warm tea down my throat, urging me to "eat slowly." Soon after, the retching started. My tummy, like my brain, was unable to process the shock and the shaking just wouldn't stop.

Malcolm sensed my fear and he made himself scarce for a bit. "Are you alone, honey? Is there someone else who needs our help?"

Marybeth asked, after Malcolm eventually figured it was okay to knock on the door and step in. He took his phone from his pocket. I thrust my hand out on instinct to grab it from him. He looked startled.

"No. Don't . . . " I screamed. They both froze. "I'm sorry," I sputtered, holding on tight to his phone. Marybeth looked at her husband, then at me. "We're not about to do anything to hurt you, sweetie," she said. "You tell us what we need to know in order for us to help you."

I pulled myself together enough to give them the basics, leaving out the part about the monster I'd left to drown in the river. I told them I'd escaped from the compound in a truck that I'd accidentally crashed into the water: "I'm in a lot of trouble," I confessed, blabbing on about the trimming and my being on the run from the cartel.

Marybeth assured me in her soft toned way of talking that I was safe with them and that whatever had happened was behind me. "We won't abandon you," she promised. "We're on our way from our place over the Oregon border to visit Malcolm's folks in Southern California — in fact, we met here in Humboldt when we were trimmers, ourselves, back in the day."

The couple had a lot of old friends in the area, they claimed. "Things were way less dangerous back then," Malcolm remarked. "We're going to take you to the safest place we know."

He packed up and drove the camper van as Marybeth sat with me in back, her arm around my shoulders to steady my constant shaking. After a fairly short drive, we pulled up outside of a small cabin somewhere to the south. I'd seen no other signs of habitation on the side road they took and I wondered who the heck would want to live in such a place, all alone?

"Julia grows the real deal," Marybeth said. "Some of the best weed on the market." She explained to me, in short, how she and Malcolm had trimmed for the now retired social worker on her farm for several harvest seasons back when they were students at Humboldt State. "We've stayed in touch," Marybeth said. "Julia's the salt of the earth and she's sure to have all the right contacts to get you where you need to be for now."

Julia was pretty old and super heavily wrinkled and she had the knowing eyes of a wise woman. She took me in without question and after she sent Marybeth and Malcolm into the kitchen to make us all some tea, she drew me a warm, oil-scented bath. Though at first the water stung the cuts on the soles of my torn-up feet, the sheer sight of a bathtub was a comfort, the first actual tub I'd seen since I'd left the ranch.

The wood paneled bathroom looked more like a family room with its potted ferns and a funny looking collection of paintings of fairies and wood sprites scattered about the walls in heavy, gilt frames. I've never seen a bathroom decked out like this. It's strange how when you're in a wigged-out frame of mind you take more notice of your surrounds than you normally would. I remember every small, funky detail of Julia's peculiar but at the same time way cool bathroom.

The thought of putting my head in the water freaked me out all over again. I panicked and clutched the sides of the bath 'til my knuckles turned white. "Here," Julia said, padding into the room softly in an old pair of sheepskin slipper boots like the ones I'd left at the ranch. It was as if she had known full well I would need her help. "Lean back into my arm, honey and let me wash your hair."

I concentrated on a small, scented candle in a flowery china saucer on a shelf on the other side of the room. Its small flame was flickering in the drafty cabin, but still it burned. The warm light it gave off, along with the hushed tone of the old woman's voice helped me to breathe easier.

Saying nothing, she ran one forefinger gently over the sign of the cross that will be forever there on the back of my neck. Afterwards, she helped me out of the bath and wrapped me in a warm towel, a second, she tied in a turban around my head and sat me on the toilet seat. She sat on a stool to treat the soles of my feet with a soothing, natural balm and cotton bandages. By the look in her eyes, though she never said anything, I knew she'd figured the shape I was in from my protruding belly. Marybeth had seen it too. Naked, there was no way to hide it. I like to think of Julia as kind of an awesome white witch of the forest when I remember that first night of freedom. I was sure for the first time in months that I'm gonna get through this. She sat me by the fireplace and fed me buttered toast and mushroom soup from a small bowl, served on a wooden tray, inlaid with abalone shells and set with a mug of warm milk and a vase containing three eagle feathers.

CHAPTER 25

MAGGIE

I t started with my offer to help Walter with a little in-home organization. Who knew how long we were to be holed up in Garberville waiting for me to be given the green light to see Mia. Might as well do something helpful, productive, I decided, as I rolled up my sleeves to hunt out the empty boxes stashed in Walter's bottomless pit of a garage.

"My Connie would have a conniption if she walked in right now and saw the state of the place," Walter said in response to my asking, as delicately as I could, if he would be okay with me doing some tidying up.

"You don't have to dump any of it," I said. "We'll simply box it up, make more room for you to move around and breathe come summer. It'll feel good, I promise."

For two days, I poured my nervous energy into sorting through years of Walter's mounting detritus, old newspapers, seed catalogs, plastic food containers from take-outs he claimed he intended to re use some day as propagating vessels. I cleaned out kitchen cabinets, tossing mugs with broken handles, emptying aging condiment shelves and washing the bins in the boxy, old, mustard-colored refrigerator. It was invigorating and it took my mind off everything, Mia, Bobby, Bridget . . . and, not least, whatever it was that Marcus and me were doing with each other.

Walter followed me around like a puppy for the first couple of hours, shaking or nodding his head when I held up items I retrieved from under the bed, behind doors, crammed into the spare room closet. After the first half a day of it, he and Marcus left me to it, the pair of them instead worked together to clear the veggie beds of the last of the previous year's withered tomato plants.

We'd all approved the idea of Walter defrosting a pack of wild boar stewing meat from the freezer in the garage. "Ooh, man, I'm partial to the flavor," Marcus said, patting his stomach. "Wild boar, slowly braised — as good as it gets."

"I have a couple vacuum packs of dried porcini mushrooms in my pantry," Walter replied. "Reconstitute the beauties and throw in some garlic, onion, olive oil, fresh sage and rosemary from the yard, tomato paste, salt and pepper and we're good to go. First things first," he said, "after the meat's done thawing, I'll braise it in a bottle of my best reserve."

Walter's wine cellar was a small cupboard in the garage. "Most of what you see here has sat in the dark since Connie passed," he said, pulling out a couple of dusty old bottles that had been stored on their sides. "She was the wine gal, I prefer a beer. My Connie, bless her soul, she sure liked to get her hands on a good Cab."

He handed me two identical bottles of Parducci Reserve Cabernet Sauvignon. "Oldest winery in Mendocino County," he said. "Her favorite. One for the marinade, one for the table."

"This is a tad extravagant for a marinade, don't you think?" I asked. I was thinking I would way rather savor each last drop from a wine glass than watch it swirl down the sink as a meat tenderizer. "Don't you have something less special for the meat?"

"Life's too short for bad wine," Walter laughed. "And anyway, aren't we celebrating in our own way? Your girl getting the hell out of these damn woods."

"A tad too soon to throw caution to the wind," I said. "Still, we've gotta eat and I for one am working up one hell of an appetite with all this spring cleaning."

"That's a girl," Walter said.

It was the following evening, just before the big boar supper and during a walk-through inspection of my completed work when my phone rang. I was to see Mia the next day, at noon.

"Good thing we planned on a substantial supper this evening," Marcus said. "You're gonna have a big day tomorrow, Maggie."

The stew was every bit as delicious as promised. Walter had concocted a tasty base of minced pancetta, onion and carrots, mustard seed, cloves, a cinnamon stick, paprika and juniper berries with the fresh ingredients he'd sent Marcus to pick up at the grocery store. I'd sorted through his cache of dried herbs and spices in my whirlwind cleanup of the kitchen, clearing out a bunch of near empty containers. "Gotta love a guy with such an astute sense of seasoning, Walter," I quipped, flattering his ego. The wild boar was soft and subtly infused by the wine, the fresh rosemary and sage. We mopped our bowls with fresh chunks of a hearty fresh baked rosemary loaf and butter that Marcus had brought back from the store.

It was my first taste of wine since the mere sip of the glass I'd pushed aside in the roadhouse. This time, it went down fast and smooth, like a cherry liquor, flavors of exotic spices exploded in my mouth. I felt my muscles fully relax by the time I was half way into my second glass.

"Maybe go steady," Marcus said, shooting me a look that instinctively served to piss me off and in one hot second. I know my limits. Where was this coming from, I wondered? Hadn't he been the one tempted by the pills back at the shelter, that terrible night? My enjoying two or three glasses of damn good wine was hardly a comparison.

"I'm a grown up, Marcus, thank you," I snapped. "I'm enjoying Walter's hospitality here, is all, lighten up won't you? It's been tense enough these past few days."

Marcus wisely opted not to respond as I promptly divided the remains of the bottle between Walter's glass and my own. He stood, clearing our empty bowls from the table.

"I'll take care of the dishes," Marcus said, his back to Walter and me as he filled a bowl with hot water and bubbles, looking out of the window above the sink into the darkened yard.

Small talk with Walter gave way to a queasy feeling, a dangerous mixture of one too many glasses of wine combined with the rich ingredients of the stew. Roiled up emotions also played a part in this undesirable cocktail I'd shaken up for myself.

"You know," I said to Marcus, after I'd made it across the kitchen without hurling the contents of my stomach to stand beside him at the sink. "You can't truly know someone, start to love someone, until you've learned them inside out. The good and the not so good."

What the hell? Why had I mentioned the love word? As soon as it was out of my mouth, I flinched. I was acting like an idiot making a statement as intense as this so early on, despite our inexplicable attraction and rushing headlong into such a physically intense relationship the way we had. As if this wasn't enough to send him hightailing through the redwoods back to Point Reyes.

"It's not about judgment, it's about sharing stuff, small joys, sorrows, all the shit that life throws in our way," still I continued with my tipsy rant.

"Who's judging?" Marcus replied, deadpan, calmly drying the inside of the Dutch oven with an old dish towel. "I guess we're on a crash course, you and me," he joked.

"Maybe it's all too much for a fucked-up person like me to ask for," I cried, tears springing from my eyes.

"I would not categorize you as fucked-up, Maggie," Marcus said, turning to hold my arm at the elbow. "And it's not what we've had to face along the way, nor what might happen in the future," he added, "it's how we deal with it all going forward that counts."

"I need to pee real bad," I said, breaking the tension. I made it halfway across the kitchen before tripping over one of the piles of boxes I'd stacked that afternoon. A head thumping, heart racing, queasy feeling came over me as I leaned forward on the rug between boxes and promptly threw up the contents of my stomach in front of Walter and Marcus both. They looked at me like neither of them had seen this coming on this fast though I sure had. I felt too wretched to set about cleaning it up.

"Time to make my excuses," Walter said, leaving the room as I attempted to compose myself. "Marcus, see that the lady is taken care of, won't you?"

The rest of the night was an unfortunate blur except for my being aware of Marcus lifting me up from the floor, taking me to the bathroom, feeding me water, holding up my hair and washing my face.

It must have been Marcus who cleaned the patch on the rug, as, much to my relief and any further humiliation the following morning, there was no material sign of the damage I'd done.

I was up and about before Marcus awoke. He had placed his truck keys neatly on the kitchen table with a note that let me know he was planning on sleeping in an extra hour or two. Clearly, giving me some room to exit gracefully. His note wished me luck with reuniting with Mia. "Drive safely," he'd written. "Love, Marcus xo."

Crap, my cheeks flushed, what a complete fool I had made of myself. And yet, no one had forced him to leave me his truck keys, or to sign off with the L word, I noted. I hoped to God the guy had enough humility about him to let it go, my first messing up around him. If he'd been gone when I returned, I wouldn't have blamed him.

CHAPTER 26

MIA

The two women I came to know and trust as Jo and Kate drove me to their place that very same night of my bath and fireside meal in Julia's cabin. The inside of their mud encrusted SUV smelled of a curious mix of pine needles and vanilla. It was the most pimped out vehicle interior I have ever traveled in, all soft sheepskin seat covers, a pile of fluffy blankets on the back seat, a sparkly crystal dangling on a dark pink ribbon that swung from the rear view mirror. I found a box of tissues and a tin of mints in the pocket behind the driver seat. I was wired enough by this point to take it all in.

I'd listened to the three women speak in hushed tones after Julia had greeted them at the door. It did not appear as if they knew each other, though Julia had a quick, quiet manner that put us all at ease. She told them about Marybeth and Malcolm and how they had taken off on their way south soon after they'd delivered me into her care. The two younger women gave me a sort of emergency run-down as to what they were all about, what they do for girls like me. They'd asked if I was OK with them driving me to their house right away. I never said so much to anyone but I was deathly afraid of Jefe Hombre having somehow survived. I'd have willingly traveled to the end of the frickin' earth with these two clearly capable, in charge women. I wished Jazmin was with me, I had zero way of knowing that she was yet to make her move and my worst fear was that she would pay the price for what I'd done.

Anyway, I was in no fit state to take care of myself. I was going nowhere on my own, barefoot, for God's sakes, except for a pair of chunky, hand knitted socks Julia had slipped over my thick, bandaged feet. I was totally helpless, dependent on the goodness of a string of strangers.

I'm not about to recount the route we took that night. Nobody needs to know where we were headed, or where Grace Place is located, that's the whole point of it, you see. The secret part is what keeps women, girls like me who wind up there, safe, protected.

It was pitch-black and so dense with redwoods not a single star shone through. I closed my eyes and imagined myself being ferried through a long, dark tunnel to someplace light and bright and peaceful where no one would be able to touch me let alone hurt me ever again.

The women were talking in soft, low voices up front. Their lilting conversation seemed to me as if it was a whole new language, like it was taking place on a different planet from the silent hellhole I had escaped from.

The SUV pulled to a stop at the end of a winding driveway after we'd passed over a rickety wooden bridge into an unlit, heavily wooded property. I barely detected the outline of a house as I squinted through the tinted window. Talk about hidden. It filled me with relief to figure any random passersby would be hard pushed to stumble on this place, day or night.

From the outside, the silhouette of the house in the trees made me think of the small, wooded cottage in the Hansel and Gretel story. I remembered it as pictured in a faded color print in a tattered, old, fairy tale book, one of the few permanent books at the ranch when I was a kid. I'd carried home all kinds of books to read from the mobile library that trundled along the coast every couple of weeks, though I don't remember any of the stories as well as I do the dark, scary Brothers Grimm tales: Rumpelstiltskin; Snow White; Cinderella; Rapunzel — and not the Disney versions, neither. The book had been my aunt Maggie's when she was a kid. I know this because she'd scribbled her name inside of the cover in crayon. Had she been as scared of those stories and as thrilled by them as I was and who had read them to her, I wondered?

This real house, on closer inspection appeared to glow, softly, lit from inside with a lamp in each of the front windows. It still looked like a fairy tale cottage to me, but a safe and cozy one — a full-size cuckoo clock a bit like the one back at the ranch. I couldn't get inside the front door fast enough.

You'd think accustomed as I was to being in the middle of nowhere, I'd have been on fresh alert, but this was different. I swear my muscles began to relax the second I set eyes on the place.

"As you'll see, when the rains start up again in all seriousness, these roads turn to mud," Kate said. "Four-wheel drive's the only option. Rest assured, we're not accessible in any ordinary vehicle, or otherwise."

She opened the door, holding out her hand to guide me out of the vehicle. "Put these on first," she said, slipping my thick-socked feet into a pair of rain boots she'd pulled from the trunk. My legs had turned to jelly. I could barely walk. I was in need of physical support. All I wanted was to lay my head down, somewhere, anywhere on the inside of that door, to curl up in a warm spot and sleep.

Inside, Grace Place is as every bit welcoming as it looks from the outside, thick walls of exposed wood, a reddish-colored paneling with thick, overhead beams and those old-fashioned light fixtures. It's hard to put my finger on it, other than to say it's like someone has figured out how to stop time and to bar any bad stuff from the modern world seeping in through its walls.

A stag head hangs over the large stone fireplace, its big, old antlers intact. I looked at him that first time and he looked back at me, the pair of us, transfixed. "We're safe now," he seemed to be saying, you and me, the both of us here in this secret, hidden place. Whatever had happened, that was then and this was now.

Last remnants of the evening's wood fire crackled in the hearth. The parlor, as I've come to know it, was warm and toasty. Still, I kept the blanket Marybeth had given me wrapped around my body like it was a shield, or a cocoon.

One of them, Kate, suggested we sit a while in a pair of high-backed, leather armchairs positioned on either side of the fireplace. Another two saggy, low-backed chairs faced inward toward the fireplace, a colorful braided-rug in between. I felt like I had stepped into one of those old-fashioned Christmas cards as I sank into one of the chairs closest to the fire.

Kate sat across from me, curling her legs up beside her while Jo went into the kitchen to make us some tea. Kate's wavy, chestnut hair is cut to shoulder-length. It glowed in the firelight that night. I felt a spark of envy since my own hair had been hacked off so brutally. She sat without speaking for a while. I watched her closely as she tucked her hair into a neat ball on the back of her head with a band she'd slipped off her wrist. It was all so normal, so freakishly painless I half expected something bad to happen. It took my breath away to the point of feeling faint. Still, I was quickly at ease with Kate. I find her company comforting, reassuring, motherly almost, but not in a bossy way and nothing at all like being around my own mother.

Jo, on the other hand, she has a strength about her that makes everyone around her feel safe and strong, like she's not taking any shit from anyone, in a good way. The way she carried herself across the room that night, I figured she was the practical, no-nonsense one of the pair, her short, blonde hair framing a friendly, open, freckled face.

They way they looked at one another, lovingly, the way they talked to each other, touching arms and squeezing hands, it was clear from the offset that they were together.

I drank tea while Jo started in on telling me more about the place. "You'll meet the others in the morning," she said. "It's a bit of a maze on first impression, but don't worry, you'll soon find your way around." Floorboards creaked underfoot. I remember how I inhaled the scent of polished wood and cedar candles. It smelled like home. Not the ranch, but home as in how I'd like it to be.

"After we took it on, Grace Place," Kate explained: "we added four bedrooms and a bathroom to the early footprint of the house. You'll meet your housemates in the morning."

"Enough of that for now," Jo said. "There's plenty of time for you to get to know the place and all of us, Mia. As for tonight, what you need now is sleep."

The two of them ushered me through a spacious kitchen. A polished wooden dining table filled a good portion of the room. It was set for breakfast. The seats of a set of carved-back chairs were tied with padded blue and white plaid cushions, the type I've seen on television sitcoms and in magazines but not in real life. We never had anything close to a decorative chair cushion for God's sake, back at the ranch. This new scene appeared in crazy contrast from the stark, cold, commando kitchen at the compound, that's for sure. Was it too good to be true? I rubbed my eyes in a mixture of exhaustion and disbelief, half expecting to wake from a dream.

Dried herbs hung from a heavy beam that looked like a converted log, wedged above the stove. I did a double take at several big bunches of rosemary and thyme, neatly tied with twine and hanging within reach of the big pots and pans stacked on a shelf above the range top.

Back at Bruce and Bonnie's place a million years ago, I'd helped hang heavy clusters of cannabis buds to shrink to half their size. We had hung weed from washing lines strung in the drying sheds. I learned how to place the buds in paper bags to cure, after they'd dried. By the time the weed was ready for trimming it was all crispy on the outside, still slightly moist on the inside.

"Culinary herbs," Jo said, smiling. She had noticed my gaze as it lingered on a big bunch of dried rosemary. "We are completely substance free here at Grace Place, just so you know."

I nodded. The last thing I needed was another godforsaken raid in the middle of the night.

"The predecessor of this old stove was a wood burner," Kate added.

I wanted nothing more to do with the outside world. If they'd told me to curl up in the corner on the kitchen floor that night, like little Cinderella herself, hell, I'd have been more than content to do so. I was warm, I was fed and I was done in — almost, but not entirely. It was only as they readied to leave me in my room that I dared tell them about Jazmin. "She's out there, somewhere, I don't know where. I can't give up on her. I won't rest until I see her again."

The women exchanged a concerned look. "You are welcome to tell us however much more you are ready to share in the morning, Mia." Kate said, "but for now, try to get some rest." The bedside lamp cast a reassuring glow as she closed the door softly and left me to my thoughts, completely alone as I lay in the narrow bed in the small, snug room, unsure what to make of it all. Deep yellow and cherry-red checkered drapes that matched the bedspread were pulled across a narrow window set high into the buttery yellow wall. I stayed perfectly still for some time as I fixed my gaze on the door, not daring to move for fear that I would break the spell. My head began to spin. My feet hurt. I was suspended in place, pinned to the bed, my mind in one moment back at the compound, in the truck and plunged into the river with the brown sludge waters of hell gushing in around me, a pair of bulging eyes staring back.

I pinched my arms and tried desperately to conjure a picture of myself back at the ranch, eating supper at the kitchen counter. I couldn't see my face in that familiar scene. That night it came to me that it was another me, a new Mia I'm gonna have to insert into the picture. The old Mia is gone and she isn't ever coming back.

It's not that I don't want to see my mom, to have her give me one of her big, annoying bear hugs I'd squirmed away from over the past few, awkward years. My biggest fear is that when I do see her, this hard shell I've built up will crack open and I will lose it completely.

I had no idea this sort of place existed. No matter how much I'd thought I hated it, the dead end of it all, I'm fully and painfully aware by now of how sheltered and protected my childhood had been on the ranch.

How clueless I was. Now, I'm one of these girls, these women, the ones with the stories many never get the chance to tell. Well, I've had no choice but to spill the beans, confess the most part of what went down, though it has taken me some time to open up and talk about it. I have others to think about. Jazmin and the kid inside of me for starters, the two of them are worth way more to me than my guilt and humiliation multiplied by a thousand.

Anyway, I am not so ashamed, despite of it all. I owe that to Grace Place, not just Kate and Jo, but all of the others here like me. Girl power. You better believe it. There is nothing that women cannot do.

It was dark when I woke up. Rain. So much fucking rain, it seemed like it would never stop. It took me a while to gather my bearings. Waking up and my being aware that I was alone in a room that was light years from the compound was almost impossible to believe. I snuggled up under my protective stack of covers. If I could have, I would have stayed in that position for days.

It was frickin' insane good luck my having run into Marybeth and Malcolm out at the river. I do believe I would have frozen to death out there, if not, freaked-out and soaking, my bare feet all bloody, unable to carry me much farther beyond the stretch of road I'd found them at, minding their own business, listening to Peter, Paul and Mary for God's sakes in the middle of the redwoods as they'd sat there grilling sausages in the open air.

Someone up there was looking out for me for sure. Maybe I'd been punished enough for my stupidity. The universe works in mysterious ways, right? Just when you think you're the biggest loser in the world, you get a break and you'd better fucking grab it.

My only hope was that Jazmin had made it to as safe a place as this — I prayed her good karma had come through, I guess I was willing it on her, unbeknown to me just as she was laying the groundwork to get herself out. I vowed I would never ask for anything more for the rest of my life.

Someone had placed a giant, fluffy blue robe at the foot of my bed while I'd slept. I must have fully been out for the count, or I'd have surely jumped in fear of being tracked down.

I rolled out of bed and slipped the thick robe over a fresh pair of flannel pajamas Kate had handed me the night before. They were lemon scented, like heaven, pressed and neatly folded, along with a pair of terry cloth, one-size-fits-all slider slippers she'd taken from the top dresser drawer. I knew it was real, what had happened, seeing as the messed-up soles of my feet were hurting like hell beneath the bandages, though they healed way faster than I thought, in the days and weeks that followed.

Voices sounded from the kitchen. Laughter. When was the last time I'd heard anyone laugh? I really could not remember. Then, it came to me, Jefe Hombre had enjoyed his evil chortle the time he'd found my stack of precious handicrafts — the small things I'd taken to making from recycled materials to keep myself from breaking down.

I had hungrily fantasized night after night especially come December about the foods I was missing most, Bobby's ravioli with meat sauce, our favorite 'family' dish he'd make from scratch on Christmas Eve.

How my heart had ached, a mixture of guilt and sadness to think of the Christmas stocking with my name embroidered on the front that Mom dug out from the one, small holiday box she kept in the barn with its mess of old tinsel and lights back from when she was a kid.

I looked around me. I didn't have one thing in my possession I could call my own, aside from Marybeth's blanket. I thought of all the little things I'd taken for granted, the small gifts my mom stuffed into that old felt stocking — the lip-gloss and silly socks and pens and notebooks and gum and fun, cheap, but cute and thoughtful shit she'd pick out from the discount store in Petaluma during the weeks between Thanksgiving and Christmas.

As the worst Christmas in my life was approaching, I'd acted on a deep urge to use my hands to make something meaningful for my family. Even though there aren't very many of us and we're a pretty odd bunch, they're all I have and I had decided there in the compound, as captive, I was going to make it up to them, one day, to show them I really did love them in my own messed up way despite what I'd gone and done.

Searching around for inspiration, I'd stumbled on a stash of old plastic juice bottles and a bag of metal pull-tops. And whenever my jailer was out on his rounds around the compound, I'd sat myself down at one of the foldout tables in the kitchen and worked a half hour or so at a time on my stupid little dolls.

First I punctured the bottle tops with a knife, tying string into knots of hair that either I trimmed or braided depending on if it was a guy or a girl. I gathered twigs and leaves and moss and bark and fashioned them into small items of clothing. I took a marker pen that was used for identifying dried weed strains on bags and carefully painted their faces to suit the personalities I'd made up in my head.

By the time I was done, I'd produced a dozen plastic bottle wood sprites. It was the closest I'd come to feeling anything remotely like happiness or contentment in months. After I grew bored with making dolls, I moved on to crafting a bunch of bracelets, necklaces and key rings from the metal ring pulls and a ball of brown string.

It may sound silly and childish but it took my mind off my miserable existence, gave me a focus on something constructive while I figured how to get the hell out of there. I've never been much into arts and crafting and all that maker stuff, but this sparked something in me that brought out a side of myself I'd never known existed. It felt good. It still does. I like making things and growing things. I've learned that about myself.

Jefe Hombre was as quick as an eagle in swooping down on a bracelet I'd accidentally dropped under the table. He made fun of my work, scouring the kitchen 'til he came across the stash of my pull-top jewelry and dolls.

My stomach ached afresh as I focused on the bare surface of the small dresser across from the end of the bed. He'd laughed his head off as he dumped my handiwork out of its hiding place in a cardboard box under the sink and onto the folding tabletop. I leapt forward to stop him but I was too late. He swept my creations to the floor with the side of his hand, followed by a cruel-ass show of stomping all over it as he flattened the plastic bottle dolls with the bottom of his boot 'til their faces were sad and distorted.

Why did he have to do that? Destroyed the one innocent thing that I'd been able to do for myself, my sanity? Later that same evening, he'd taken great pains in his preparations to cook — his version of a chocolate mole sauce with shredded chicken and rice — only time I'd ever seen him at the stove. Didn't I know, it was Christmas Eve, he asked? "Wipe your tears, bitch," he barked. I knew enough Spanish to scrape by with a basic understanding but I never let on how much.

I watched him take a can of tomatoes, chicken stock, chili, garlic, onion, peanuts, raisins, peppercorns, sesame seeds, cinnamon, sugar and almonds from a brown paper sack of ingredients he'd bought the previous evening. It had been the first trip he had taken me on into town. He'd locked me in the back of the truck, my hands and feet tied, after dark, sufficient blocks from the main drag for me remain unnoticed. All he'd had to do was mention Jazmin. He still assumed at that point there was no way I was going to run while he was alive and breathing and threatening to retaliate. He'd watched me clean up the mess of my crushed handicrafts as he settled in to preparing his holiday feast. I ate what little he deemed my portion as I held back my tears.

My tummy rumbled loudly at the thought of food. I was back in the here and now at Grace Place. I wasn't yet anywhere near ready to tell them all of what went down in the compound. The smell of coffee wafted down the corridor and in through the open door to my room. I've never been much of a coffee drinker and I can't stomach coffee in my condition.

I checked myself out in the small mirror on the wall above the dresser, barely recognizing the gaunt looking chick with the short hair and the protruding belly. There'd been no mirrors in the compound, yet another way to dehumanize us.

~

Three girls ranging from around my age into their late twenties sat around the table in the kitchen, dressed and ready for the day wearing what looked like a uniform of jeans, dark green hooded sweatshirts and sturdy work boots.

Rachel, the oldest looking of the three, smiled, a surprisingly big, broad beamer for such a thin, pale face. She held out her hand to introduce herself. She'd read my thoughts. "I know, it looks a bit weird, all of us in the same getup, but there's little use for being dolled up here," she said.

I was to go find my own set of jeans, tees and sweatshirts, plus underwear and socks, stacked, she told me, in the linen closet down the hall.

"You'll find sneakers and outdoor boots on a rack by the back door," Rachel said. "Pick out two of each item of clothing to fit and footwear your size, that's all you're going to need for now."

"Meet Carla and Sandra," Rachel added, indicating who was who. "Don't worry, it's not a cult," she laughed — "we dress alike and eat as a family but that's about where the similarity ends."

I reached out and nodded my head at each of them. Carla was short and round, Sandra tall and heavy set. They both looked like they'd been through the ringer and still only in their early twenties at most. Rachel motioned me over to the stovetop where a big pot of oatmeal as good as any my mom ever made bubbled away beside a stack of bowls.

"Help yourself," she said. "We soak the oats overnight. I'm on breakfast shift this week," she explained. "It'll be your turn soon enough."

The oatmeal was thick and creamy. Heaven. It warmed and filled the ever-hungry hollow in my tummy, topped with a more than generous helping of brown sugar, cinnamon, sliced bananas and walnuts.

I'd woken feeling faint and nauseous, my new normal, though I was ravenous by the time I stepped into the kitchen. The first time I'd felt it wash over me, it took me to my knees, I had no idea what the whole nastiness of morning sickness was about. I had zero knowledge of any of this before it happened to me, how would I? Despite the name, take it from me, morning sickness strikes at any time during the day or night during the first weeks.

It had taken me missing my period twice and throwing up at multiple, random times for a few weeks to catch a clue. I soon learned to keep something in my stomach at all times, even if it had meant stealing a supply of dry crackers for my pockets, whatever I could get my hands on.

I was relieved to spot a clear glass canister filled with granola bars on a shelf above the sink where the girls washed and dried the breakfast dishes. Emergency snacks.

Still, I had said nothing to no one, not even Jazmin, though I was sure she had figured it out. It was classic denial on my part and who wouldn't do the same given my circumstances? I'd willed it to go away but that didn't work and by the time I figured out what was really happening, I found myself feeling sorry for the poor little thing, attached, responsible.

I was the last one at the table. I shoveled in spoonful after spoonful of the delicious, sugary oats, best thing I'd tasted in I don't know how long, reminding myself, as I have since I accepted what was really happening to my body, that none of this is the baby's fault. I mean, how does a girl my age, someone who had never even gotten close to doing the business with someone she actually liked, wind up getting herself impregnated in the worst possible way? At 18 this shit happened to me.

One of the girls asked me if I was finished with my breakfast, "Not yet," I said, wanting my first feast of freedom to last forever. "I'll wash my dish myself, thank you."

My statement was met with a glare and a swift and assertive: "We do things in shifts around here, keeps it fair and efficient."

I scraped up the last of the oatmeal and dutifully handed over my bowl. By my calculations, I was somewhere around 16 weeks. The same pair of jeans I'd worn since I left home had suffered some serious stretch around the middle, even with the button and zipper undone. I rummaged through the closet after breakfast and found a pair of jeans that looked big enough to pull over my belly.

Rachel figured it out in seconds, though she said nothing. I could tell by the way she kept darting a look at my stomach, quickly sliding her eyes away. She'd disappeared for a few minutes but popped her head back into the hallway.

"Kate will be in shortly," she said. "She'll meet you in the kitchen after you've washed and dressed. It's okay to take your time today, Mia."

The girls chatted and laughed as they put on their rain gear and headed outside to various parts of the property for their preassigned rotational work duties. It was Carla's lunch shift.

She reached for a waterproof jacket from a coat rack by the door. "Rich pickings in the winter garden," she said. "Wait 'til you see what we have going on out there. It's great."

Rachel was off to the barn to help work on what she described as a random mess of old farming equipment. "We're fixing up a beater truck this week," she said, which explained why her fingernails were so grimy. Jo was the resident self-taught mechanic and, in her words, she was as happy as a pig in mud when up to her arms in overalls and grease, taking engines apart and making them work again.

Sandra was on laundry and dinner duty that day. "Come see the art studio before you get started. That's also where we dry the sheets," she said.

It felt weird wearing boots for the first time in months. It was a bit like walking on the moon. I was forced to remove the bandages from under my socks in order to squeeze my feet into their tight, leather confines. Small bolts of pain rose up through my legs from the cuts on the soles of my feet. I hobbled along as I followed Sandra outside and into the white painted interior of the barn. My eyes were immediately drawn to a kiln. "Most of the pottery we make here is sold in a gallery up in Ferndale," Sandra said, catching my interest. "The money goes back into our art program for supplies."

I experienced a ping of something strangely exciting and familiar as I ran my hand over the surface of the kiln. It was the same feeling I'd had when I'd made my ring pull jewelry and the ill-fated doll collection. I couldn't wait to get my hands on a pile of clay.

Back in the kitchen, Kate took off her rain jacket and hung it to dry by the stove. She made us a big brown pot of yet more lemon ginger tea, these women drink it by the gallon, I swear. She launched into a second short account of the history of Grace Place, this time, how she and Jo had come to be here.

The place was in her family since her grandparents' generation. Kate's grandfather was a lawyer in San Francisco. I liked hearing how he'd traveled north to hunt and fish and to get the hell out of the city for a couple of weeks at a time, longer in the summer months. I have only ever spent the odd day here and there in San Francisco, my whole life. I have no idea what it's like to live in a big city. I'm gonna have to start small when it's time for me to get back out into the world.

"My mom, his only child, she kept the house as it was," Kate said. "She rented it out to a fishing family for years."

Her mom passed and she left the house to Kate. "It hadn't been lived in for a while. It needed work," she said. "A lot of work."

Kate was a lawyer, like her grandfather before her. Smart. She met Jo in her job at one of the tech companies in Silicon Valley.

"We connected through our dislike of the vast moneymaking mentality and the constant hustle and bustle, the endless work days and constant high pressure," she explained. I knew nothing of that world, but I nodded my head, anyway.

Jo was raised on the Oregon Coast. When Kate brought her out to the Lost Coast to visit the closed up house she'd inherited, Jo was blown away by the beauty and peace of the place and the similarity to the house where she herself was born.

"It was Jo who named it Grace Place," Kate said. "We set about making it our permanent home soon after."

I loved hearing their story. What came out of this kind, unintimidating woman's mouth next, stopped me in my tracks. Kate told me point-blank how she'd been raped when she was my age. He was a college jock and they were at a frat party that got out of control.

She was calm as anything when she told me this. I sat back in my chair with wide eyes and said nothing. I didn't know what to say.

Kate took a minute. She reached out and touched my arm. "There is zero pressure for you to share any details you wish to keep to yourself with regard to what happened to you in the compound, Mia," she said.

"When you feel the time is right to talk, I'll be here. Just to listen, mind you. The rest is up to you."

She never said a word about my bump. No one did, at first.

Kate switched back to explaining how she'd taken a leave of absence from the legal world to oversee the fixing up of Grace Place and make it livable. It was during that time she'd trained in crisis support counseling for women.

"Jo urged our move to Grace Place and it all made sense," Kate said. "In the past two years, we've welcomed 15 girls and women into our fledgling program." She told me I was the sixteenth. It made my heart hurt to think of all the others.

Most women stay six months, some longer. It was a huge comfort to learn that I'd be welcome to stay here a while, a massive load off my mind. I knew there was no way I was anywhere near ready for the outside world or the isolation of the ranch and my mother's questions.

"However long it takes," Kate said. "When you're ready to leave, you'll know it."

I was placed in rotating work duty doing my part in keeping Grace Place going with hot meals, laundry and gardening, which has turned out to be my absolute favorite thing, after playing with clay, when the rains finally stopped. I've learned new and practical skills in

Jo's basic engineering program and to make pottery during art therapy time over in the art barn.

Was I on board with all of this, she asked? "Yes, please, ma'am" I said, my first real smile forming in months. If I could have figured out how best to say it, I would have blurted out how I'd rather have curled up and died than leave.

I tucked my hands under the small mound of my belly. How I had craved even the smallest feelings of safety and security and I willed my relief to pass through to the baby.

The other girls are nice and all. We'd all been through some crazy shit or other. It makes for a strange bunch of sister chicks, but I like them well enough and there is strength in numbers, for sure. I was hesitant to be overly trusting at first, restless and forever looking over my shoulder, but the constant reassurance I feel in their presence is the best thing for me and I can't help but start to feel safer by the day.

If I think about it too much, why I'm here, what I've escaped, I freak myself out. It was hard to get any of it out of my mind those first few weeks. Kate and Jo, they are the ones who keep us from ourselves, steering us away from reliving whatever trauma we've gone through, keeping us occupied, talk being the best therapy, I now know. They pour so much into this place, so much of themselves, it's amazing. It makes me want to be as good as them, no matter the mess I've made. I'm making my peace with myself, but it's taking time.

A week into my being hidden away in the safe haven of Grace Place, Jo handed me a pair of baggy overalls for my first shift working on the engine in the barn.

We tinkered around in the cold for a couple of hours. "Put on some extra layers next time, Mia," she said. I could see my breath when I stepped outside. Though I still prefer to work in the garden, I do like learning how to handle the various tools, the feel of oil and grease on my fingers. It's empowering to handle the sorts of greasy spanners and spark plugs that I'd never in a million years have thought of picking up. I have the capability now of looking after my own truck or car engine thanks to Jo and that old fixer. I can't even drive, yet I'll never need a guy to change a wheel for me. Jo put her tools down and stood there, looking at me across the open hood.

"Be sure you wash up well, Mia," she said. "Scrub those hands." Then, simply, glancing at my midsection: "Especially in your condition."

So they all knew, they'd known since the first, of course they did. I kind of thought it would come out as a hushed and awkward "are you pregnant?" sort of whispered inquiry after dinner one evening, by the fire. Instead, I figured this was Jo's way of telling me that I was in charge of my baby and me. She wiped her hands with an oily rag.

"I haven't said the words out loud to anyone," I sputtered. "I haven't had my period in four months." It was impossible to hide it, physically, anyway, so there was little point denying the truth.

"Well, hon," Jo said, completely unfazed. "Let's talk to Kate. You're in your second trimester by your calculations. Best she sets you up with a doctor's visit sooner than later, Mia — and then you'll know for sure."

Marybeth and Malcolm had wanted to take me to a doctor the afternoon of the accident and my escape. I'd said no way, for fear of being touched so soon, interrogated, prodded and pushed around against my will. If I wanted to stay put at Grace Place a while yet, I had no choice but to face up to things and cooperate. And it was only fair to the kid.

We continued with our tinkering a while longer. Neither of us spoke another word on the subject until later on. Kate met us in the kitchen and we three talked it over in our indoor voices before the rest of the girls came in for their supper.

CHAPTER 27

JAZMIN

It was back in early December when Jose Luis drove me, blind-folded, out of the compound and down from the mountaintop, warning me over and over that Jefe Hombre would chop the head off my stupid fucking girlfriend if either of us so much as made a wrong move. If I'd known it was gonna be the middle of February before I would finally muster the courage to escape I would have had an even harder time making it through those long, miserable weeks without Mia.

The hairs on my arm stood on end as he'd brushed my cheek with the back of his hand. "Hey, don't worry chica," he said, his voice cloying. "You are the smart one. You know what's good for you."

Jose Luis took deposited me in a new spot that was over an hour's drive from where I was forced to leave Mia. I was to wait out the winter there, he told me, matter-of-fact. Meantime, the cold fucker informed me he was headed home to Mexico for Christmas.

"But don't you worry, I'll be back," he promised, taking my two hands in his and kissing them as a departing gesture. As if I was going to miss a second of the sadistic bastard's company.

I'd scrawled a desperate, hurried, handwritten note for Mia as soon as I'd learned I was leaving. They'd kept us apart even then. Valeria sneaked it to her, the stub of a pencil hidden in her pocket. Mia wrote back: "Bide your time, J, then RUN. Don't stop. Don't worry about me and don't look back. I WILL find you."

The smaller compound in the lower elevation consisted of a cluster of crappy old portable cabins, located closer to the ocean. I never saw the waves for the trees, but I could smell the proximity of the surf, the Pacific. I was one step closer to home. Each night I dreamed of my parents, the little ones, of Miguel. I was made painfully aware of a series of deadly booby trap explosives on the property having been told that trip wires would trigger a blast if I so much as tried to make a run for it.

A growly old German shepherd dog lay in the doorway day and night, keeping watch, always with at least one eye half open, even when he was fast asleep.

This time there were no other girls to keep me company in my imprisonment on a southern slope of a steep hillside, surrounded by brush. I cooked up cauldron after cauldron of rice and beans on the propane stove. Jose Luis had made it clear to the handful of mostly younger guys who were to stay there with me over the winter, that I was not to be touched.

As far as they were concerned, I was his property and his alone. His nephew, Mario, a pimply-faced, unschooled kid younger than me, was put in charge of keeping a personal watch.

"Best not forget," Jose Luis reminded me as he'd prepared to leave. "You run, she, your little friend, she dies."

Still, I figured if I did get out I would have to make it to the cops before he got news of it. Lead them to where Mia was at before he took me up on his word.

If I were to rewind a CCTV recording of the weeks I was there, it would make for pretty boring viewing. I played the innocent, attended to my domestic duties without complaint. Slowly, over the days and weeks that passed, I made more of an effort to clean myself up. I washed and brushed my hair, pinched my cheeks and left the smallish flannel shirt I'd found there unbuttoned just low enough to tease, to give him a preview, Mario. Poor kid, he could not fail to notice. What would you expect out there in the middle of nowhere? If I were pig ugly, it would've been a no-brainer. I mean, if you place a young dude with raging hormones in a restricted zone with a girl around his age, the chances are something's gonna happen. I was the only female in miles. Still, he looked at me not like I was a possession, more like I was Ariana Grande herself.

The more time went by with me keeping up with my subtle flirting, the more he let his guard down. Earliest sign I was making headway came in the form of a pair of cheap white sneakers he brought back from his trip into town, first pair of shoes I'd put on my feet in months and new ones at that. He even figured out the right size. The next week he produced some cheap-ass bottle of drugstore cologne. It was powdery, musky, something about the sweet smell of the fur at the back of a kitten's neck in the product description on the back label. I almost felt bad for the dude he was so misty-eyed.

On the long days and nights when it was his turn to drive bags of weed to the Bay Area, I forced myself to stay awake. I waited up for him, late into the night, watched over by the mean dog and at least one other young kid. Constant rainstorms and mudslides made driving dicey and exhausting and he was flattered that I seemed to care about his safety enough to await his return.

The dude sampled enough of his own stash it was clouding his head. Conveniently for me, he wasn't thinking with his brain. He'd been told in no uncertain terms that no one was to touch me and he'd been a man of his word, though he was hardly a man and he was very obviously growing sweeter on me by the minute. His foolish crush was my golden opportunity. I was careful to nurture it.

It was February, the rains relentless. I continued to worry myself sick for Mia, her expecting and all. I forced myself to eat to keep my strength. One rainy night, after Mario returned to the compound to sit beside me and smoke a joint, I told him that I'd missed him. "Take me with you next time," I said, moving toward him, brushing his lips with the slightest hint of tongue. It was all he could do to pull away, his expression at once all excited, confused, frustrated, pained. "What, you like that?" I whispered. "There's more where that came from, baby, but we can't be seen together, not here."

I'd figured the only way for me to save Mia was to make my move someplace outside of the compound. I had no idea she was already in hiding by then. With Mario and his virginal hard-on behind the wheel, I knew I had a chance to pull it off, my one big escape act. It had better be good.

He was a terrible driver, self-taught, like me, I guessed, though he was soon to find out how much better a driver I was. We were headed south on the Redwood Highway a few days after I had progressed into sticking my entire tongue in his mouth. He could barely contain himself. His plan was to drive to San Francisco, make the delivery and head on back, an eight or nine hour round trip, more given that we would be dodging rivers of mud on the road every few miles. If I was to die doing this, I figured it would have been worth it just to know that after all that I'd been through it was me who had the fucking balls, not them. It gave him an erection just to think of the moment he would pull over some place private and secluded enough to do the deed with me.

The boy was so darn smitten he pretty much straight away started showing off his macho skills behind the wheel, stupid bravado kicking in. He kept on weaving over and back across the centerline, talking up some bullshit or another, cracking jokes, doing his best to impress me. I smiled as sweet as pie as he took up the middle of the highway like he owned the road.

I about choked when a goddamn law enforcement officer played right into my plan, cruising up to the rear and pulling us over, flashing lights and all. The two of us were sitting on 30 pounds of market ready pot stashed in turkey bags under the floor of the flatbed. I kept my cool. It was perfect.

Mario, he was all of a panic. The cop stepped out of his vehicle and walked over to the window, real slow. Before I could open my mouth, the dumb kid leapt out of the truck, took an instant swing at the officer dude and knocked him clean onto the rain-slick road.

I stayed where I was, calming myself, thinking fast. "Shit," I said, "Mario, drag him down the riverbank, tie him to a tree."

I wasn't sure how far Mario would go. "Don't even think of doing him in," I yelled. "You're no cop killer." Mario had no idea that I could drive. Don't suppose it ever crossed his mind.

Dumb ass did as I said, thank God. And he left the keys in the ignition. The second they were out of sight and I was sure he had dragged the unconscious cop all the way down the riverbank, I slid over into the driver's seat, chill as could be and I stepped on it, peeling out of there like a bat out of hell.

I passed no more than two or three vehicles that were heading in the opposite direction and, like a bat out of hell, I stopped for no one 'til I got to Ukiah, first port of civilization where I found myself a police station and fell to the floor.

I turned myself in — not exactly home free. I have a shitload of explaining to do. Still, I'm past being disgraced, done worrying. All I can to do for myself, for Mia and the baby, is talk.

CHAPTER 28

MIA

K ate piled me into her SUV and drove me up the winding coast
road into the small city of Ferndale, my thin disguise, a beanie,
scarf and sunglasses. "Little chance we'll run into anyone problematic,
Mia," she said, "but let's think of it as an undercover mission,
anyway."

It was the first time I'd set foot in Ferndale with its ornate storefronts and big, old, fancy ass homes. It's a real nice place, a postcard
Victorian town and so way off the main route to anywhere it was no
surprise I'd never been there before. We parked as a good-looking
contractor dude helped a cute Aussie shepherd dog into the back of a
pickup truck. I watched as a heavily pregnant woman who must have
been his wife or his girlfriend emerge from a small grocery store, her
arms full of packed brown bags. For a minute or two, I almost forgot
why we were there.

On the way into town, Kate asked me if there was anything more
I wanted to share before we met with the doctor. It was hard to know
where to start on all the shit I could have told her. I mean, who had I
ever confided a single word to of a personal nature my whole life to
aside from Jazmin?

She kept her eyes on the road while I did my best to give her a
brief but brutal enough outline of the bastard who'd held me captive.
She'd seen the branding on the back of my neck, they all had, my hair
being what is and yet, I still could not speak the word out loud when it
came to the nightly torture, the —OK, let's face it, rape. That's the
truth of it and I had been forced to endure it frequently more than

once a night. I knew how bad it was. Kate knew it. Everyone at Grace Place probably knew it. Now, at least it was over.

Kate, especially, never pushes for more than I am willing to tell.

I left the drive to the river out of it, especially the part where I'd left the fucker to his watery grave. At least I hope he is dead. For all I know he might have made it out, somehow. I would like to know once and for all, for peace of mind, but I don't want to get Kate and Jo into any trouble, so I'm saying nothing. It's my secret. I earned it.

It was a woman doctor who was waiting for me when we walked in. "Would you like for Kate to stay, Mia?" she asked. I appreciated the fact that she did not seem the type to judge me as one of those sad, tragic cases who must come her way. I know all doctors are supposed to be this way, nonjudgmental, but it's not always been my experience. Seeing as my mom and me had been without health insurance when I was a kid, we, my mom mostly, grew accustomed to being lectured on how irresponsible it is to live without it. She finally got it, thank God, when the Affordable Care Act she talked about kicked in. If that hadn't happened, she'd probably be dead by now.

The doctor, a tiny Indian woman in a pale green and pink sari, her big, black eyeglasses filling her face, smeared some clear sticky gel stuff on my tummy as she explained to me what an ultrasound is.

"Your baby is as big as an avocado," she said. "Look . . . "

Kate squeezed my hand. I was way too scared to look at the screen, not sure of what I'd see.

"Take a look, Mia," she urged.

I was nervous and having trouble prying my eyes from a painting of yellow sunflowers in a vase on the beige wall above the screen. The doctor readjusted her latex glove with a curt snap. She asked me if I wanted to know the sex of the baby. She'd obviously been told the basics of my being there. I also guessed she was careful to not come across overly enthusiastic. For all she knew I might not have wanted a single thing to do with this kid that was growing inside of me.

I nodded, wordless, daring myself a sneak peek. Though I'd found it hard to picture the real, mini human being growing behind the bump, whatever it was, whoever it was, he or she was a part of me and I was a part of it and it was all I'd had to hold on to.

"Look, here . . . " the doctor pointed out the outline of the baby's neck and head and backbone and . . . "here," she said, to my astonishment, "your baby is a boy, Mia."

I swallowed. I hadn't really allowed myself to think of him as a real person, not while I wasn't sure I'd be alive to give birth to him, but sitting in that doctor's office it hit me hard. He'd already learned to turn his head and his heart was pumping away on the screen for all to see.

"His liver is performing its digestive function," the doctor explained. "Kidneys, bladder, they are every bit as active as we like to see at this stage of his development."

The baby, she said, was readying for a rapid stage of growth that would make my pregnancy more noticeable on the outside. I burst into tears. Kate held my hand. I was terrified of what was about to happen to my body, to me, to this poor little avocado-size kid who never asked to be here.

"It was nice to meet you, Mia," the doctor said. She shook my hand firmly, leaving Kate and me alone in the small room. It was all so suddenly, freakishly real. I'd never been to see a doctor without my mom with me. Now, here I was, seeing an obstetrician of all things with someone I barely knew by my side, a baby in my belly, really, truly, frickin' pregnant.

Kate announced she had a plan for lunch and that we could talk it over if I'd like. She drove me to her and Jo's favorite diner on Main Street for a bowl of chunky chicken noodle soup with an extra serving of fresh veggies. "Best ever," she said, this being their regular pit stop when they're running errands in town.

"We'd best pick out a couple pairs of maternity jeans while we're near to the stores," she said. "You're going to need them."

I asked her after a couple mouthfuls of the comforting soup, how she'd feel if she was the one who was pregnant. I didn't think about it being rude to ask; Kate was in her forties, I guessed, Jo around the same age, maybe they didn't want kids, maybe they were happy as they were, the two of them, taking care of the likes of me.

She said straight out that she and Jo both hoped some day soon they'd be in a position to raise a child or two of their own. "When the time is right," she said.

We picked out jeans and a bottle of prenatal pills in a funky old department store that looked like something out of a '70s movie. I guess Amazon hasn't made too much of an impact up on the Lost Coast as yet.

Kate talked about my having options as she drove us back to Grace Place. "You're over 18, Mia," she said. "It's entirely your decision when you're ready to make your mind up as to what you want to do going forward."

She asked about my family. "Your mother," she said. "Are you ready to let her know that you're safe?"

I know it was wrong of me but after being so mad at my mom for being sick and helpless last summer and mad at myself for being so hella stupid and selfish since, I confessed that I wouldn't know where to start in trying to talk to her. "She can't find out about the baby, yet, Kate," I said. "She just can't."

It all came tumbling out of me in a jumble of strangled words and tears, me staring out of the windshield as Kate kept her eyes on the road. "I was a stupid, spoiled brat, in many respects," I admitted. "Not that we had anything much at all as far as material things. It's more that I made things tough for my mom and her boyfriend Bobby for years. I ruled the roost. I was a little bitch, when I think about it now, getting away with whatever shit I could."

"And your dad?" Kate asked, gently nudging me into one of my most difficult subject matters.

Not in the picture. I explained how Bobby had showed up when I was at an age where what I needed most was my mom to set me straight. For the most part, as I'd grown into my teens, they'd left me to my own devices, at home, alone, while they were at work.

"Don't get me wrong. There wasn't any mistreatment, nothing like that. It was just that they never had time for me," I explained. "I never asked for that life, trapped out there in the wind and the fog and the mud, just another nobody, going nowhere."

I've been thinking more than ever about my mom and how hard it must have been raising a child on her own.

"History repeats itself," I said, wiping away the tears with tissues from a small pack Kate dug out of her purse with one hand on the wheel. "Isn't that what they say?"

Kate thought on it a while, her eyes on the road. "We all have the power to take charge of our future, Mia," she said. "You and your mom are two different people. You don't have to be defined by her path, or anyone's for that matter."

Another seven days went by in a suspended haze. Jo and Kate tried their best to leave me to my business, to let me settle into my own head while at the same time, stick to my schedule of chores set out on a whiteboard in the back hallway. I was confused for sure, but otherwise, I felt good, at least physically better than I had in months. I stopped throwing up in the mornings. I was back to the weight I'd been when I'd left the ranch. I looked for changes in the mirror each morning. My boobs were already too big for the bra I'd picked out when I arrived. I sorted through the box of spare underwear and found a larger one that fit.

What was the sense in hiding out and putting off my facing reality? I had a brand new human being to consider. I'm putting it out there and saying out loud for the world to hear, I know it sounds crazy, but I have never felt anything but love for this little guy from the first. Thing is, I know deep down inside that he isn't really mine. I don't deserve him and if I can't yet take care of myself, how am I supposed to take care of him after he's born? It's hard to explain without sounding like I don't want him. I do, I want something way better for him. After that day in the doctor's office when I saw him for the first time, I've thought of nothing else.

One evening, after dinner when the dishes were washed and stacked to dry and the other girls had left the table to shower and tend to their evening activities, reading, drawing, writing, I made up my mind. I'd been thinking about it for days and I finally decided on it. I sat myself by the fireside with Kate and Jo as we warmed ourselves by the flickering flames.

"I've thought about it and what I want is to give you two my baby," I said, straight out, unblinking, no point in my beating around the bush. I turned first to Kate and then to Jo. "If you'll take him." It all made perfect sense.

"Mia," Jo gasped, sitting back in her chair, her eyes widening. "My goodness, sweetie, that's a mighty big decision to be making all on your own."

I told them I had thought of little else. "Let's face it," I said. "I'm a kid. He's a kid, there's no way for me to raise him like he deserves. I want this. I was pretty sure you'd want this, too."

In my mind, it was meant to be. Why else had I landed here like this? This baby was meant to come their way. They deserved to be parents. Kate had said they wanted kids. I couldn't think of any two people more worthy.

Fat tears welled in Jo's eyes. Kate held herself very still, lightly gripping the arms of her chair. She was keeping it together as best she could. "There's no need to make such a hasty plan, Mia," she said, reaching out for my arm. "We're honored, of course, but honey, you have a family, it would be wrong for us to take this any further right now. You'll want to talk it over with your mom when you're ready."

Jo nodded. She stood, walked over and stroked my back, gently. "There's plenty of time to figure things out with regard to the baby Mia," she said. "You'll be surprised at how you feel when you see him. Best not make promises you might not be able to keep."

My boy, I daydream of him as a tiny newborn and a toddler and later, after he starts kindergarten, decked out in a set of Little League clothes. I fell asleep that night picturing what he'll look like when I meet him for the first time, his face, his eyes, his hair, his small, chubby hands and tiny little feet.

I'll be 19 when he's born. I'm way too young and clueless for all of this and I'm an only child with zero experience of kids. My mom would most likely take us in if I asked but who am I to do that to her after what she's been through?

Heck, I had no idea if she was even through with her cancer treatments. No, it was time to let them tell her I was safe and when I'm ready, I'll tell my mom the whole truth, face to face, starting with how I've found the perfect parents for my boy.

The next afternoon I walked in from the cold of the winter garden for a sit-down with a mug of tea and a granola bar in the warmth of the kitchen. I heard Jo and Kate taking a group phone call in the next room. It was a community elder in their network.

"I've been asked to confirm your whereabouts, Mia, to verify that you are safe," Jo announced after the two of them found me sitting in the kitchen, listening to their end of the conversation. "Your family deserves to be informed, if you give your permission. We think it's time."

"You're under no obligation to see anyone in person, Mia," Kate assured me. "Not until you decide you are ready. Your aunt Maggie has been up in the redwoods searching for you. The sheriff's department is looking for you. And, what's more, your aunt has good news of Jazmin, Mia — she wants you to know that she's spoken to her, Jazmin is safe and well and desperate to know that you are too."

My heart folded inwards, flipped upside down, inside out. I thought I was going to throw up, pass out. I held on to the edge of the table and closed my eyes to steady myself. Jo sat down beside me: "Your aunt is here in Humboldt, Mia, she's waiting to hear that you're OK."

I thought I'd puke for sure, but I didn't. My head raced with thoughts of Jazmin. I'd barely dared hold on to the smallest hope these few past few weeks, but in my heart I had known all along that she would figure it out. Sweet, tough, badass Jazmin — after all we'd been through, she and me both, it was over and we'd gotten out.

I was euphoric. First time in my life I have cause to use a big, powerful word to describe my own darn feelings. I shook and cried and shook and cried some more. Kate sat beside me, holding my hand. "This is good, Mia," she said, over and over. "Let it out, honey, let it out."

Next thing that filled my mind after a sense of overwhelming relief started to sink in was a mix of surprise and confusion in that it was Maggie who was up here in the redwoods looking for me and not my mom.

"My aunt barely had anything to do with me growing up," I explained.

"People change, circumstances change," Kate replied. "In my experience, an aunt generally makes for a good, solid buffer between a young woman and her mother. I'll bet she's a smart one with plenty of wisdom to share."

"I'm not going back to the ranch," I declared, gripping Kate's arm. "What if she tries to make me leave with her?"

"No one is suggesting that so soon," Jo assured me. "Maggie will see how well you are doing here. And, you are an adult, Mia, you get to choose what happens next."

"Does she know about the baby?" I asked, suddenly feeling weighted down by the prospect of being judged. I was nervous, scared.

"Not yet. That's for you to talk about, together, in person." Jo replied.

I'd gotten used to opening up and wearing my heart on my sleeve around these two. They'd gone about it in all the right ways, Kate asking me little things about my home life as we worked side by side tending the winter garden. We'd covered a whole load of ground in our chats while we were out there getting our hands dirty, digging onions, trimming kale and winter cabbage in the cool, moist air.

We'd talked about my mom getting sick, how I felt about it, even so far as to why it was I felt that way. No one had ever asked me what it meant to me. I told her how I had lost what little interest I had in school.

"Anyway, what incentive did I have for even thinking of getting into a four-year school?" Nobody gave a shit if I did well in class. "There was no talk of going on with school and no way to get there or to pay for it," I said.

"Truth is, I felt ambushed."

I was mad with my mom and with Bobby and Kate heard a whole lot more about it.

"Please don't tell anyone I told you this," I said. "I did something stupid at the end. It's so embarrassing. It was plain dumb and worse still, mean."

"What did you do, Mia? It's OK to tell me, that's what I'm here for," Kate stopped digging and laid her shovel on the ground. She touched my arm, reassuringly.

"Looking back on it, I was mad as hell at my mom for making our lives miserable," I confessed. "I know that's a terrible thing to admit, but it's true. It was immature and selfish. Still, I don't know what came over me that one night last summer. I guess it was attention I was after, any would do. I just wanted someone to notice me for once."

"Attention from your stepdad?" Kate asked.

"Please don't pass judgment," I replied, nodding, my face turning red despite the cold. "He's not technically my stepdad. Anyway, I did it to hurt her, my mom, I guess. I sort of hit on him, I suppose . . . it was a total shithead move."

"How did he react?"

"He pushed me away like the stupid asshole kid I was. It was late. My mom was in bed, upstairs. It was hot for once, one of the few nights of the year when it was too warm for wearing nightclothes."

I explained how I had stepped out of the shower just minutes before Bobby returned from working the evening shift at the roadhouse.

"My hair was wet and it needed to dry. I was lonely, bored out of my brain and I'd taken a hit of one of my mom's doobies she'd left laying around. I don't know why, as I fucking hate the way weed makes me feel, like I'm not in control of myself. Jazmin and me were the only ones who weren't lit all last summer. Anyways, I was sprawled out on the couch with a towel wrapped around me, stoned, music blasting from my mom's record player."

Bobby had been earlier than usual in coming home from work. It wasn't premeditated on my part.

"He stood in the doorway. I watched him watching me. It went on a second or two longer than it ought have. He never said a word." I remember how sad and tired he looked.

"I could tell he was all flustered by my flaunting myself like that, half naked. I acted on some dumb ass, stoner impulse is all I can say."

A woodpecker flew into the bird feeding station across from us, Kate's face expressionless as I told my torrid tale. I watched the woodpecker as it pecked around for seed. We try our best to encourage insectivorous birds into the garden here to help keep the grubs and bugs at bay.

"I slid off the couch, stood and the towel dropped," I said, cringing at the thought of it. "Honest to God, I never thought it through, never planned it or nothing. I just stood there, waiting to see what he would do. It disgusts me to think, the first guy to see me like that was my own mother's boyfriend."

"What happened next, Mia?" Kate asked.

"I walked over to him as he stood there frozen in the shadow of the doorway. I threw my arms around his neck and pressed myself against him. I've tried to blank that part out these past few months, but it won't go away."

Bobby never did an intentional mean thing to my mom or me.

"The look in his eyes," I remembered. "Shock, confusion, disappointment. He turned me around by the shoulders and shoved me away from him. I slipped and hit the floor. He walked over to where I'd dropped the towel, picked it up and threw it on top of me. I'd best not ever make a move like that again, he said, or I'd break my mother's heart."

Without another word, he legged it up the stairs. I knew full well he'd not tell my mom what a fucked-up kid she had. I left the ranch the following week.

That's when Jo said: "There's something else you need to know, Mia, "We'd planned on waiting for your aunt to break the sad news, but I think it's time for me to talk to you about what she's told us with regards to Bobby . . ."

CHAPTER 29

MAGGIE

Kate greeted me in the driveway, minutes before Mia came to the door. She gave me a funny look as if to say I was not how Mia had likely described me. I was not the wannabe San Francisco socialite she'd probably expected to show up. I'd tucked one of Marcus' plaid flannel shirts into my jeans and my face was devoid of any trace of makeup that would've certainly helped perk up my appearance after my unfortunate drinking binge the night before. A little woodpecker had been tapping inside my brain since I'd awoken that morning.

I sensed an unexpected camaraderie, some warmth and humility in this stranger's first embrace and I began to get an idea the kind of vital lifeline I would be expected to provide for Mia to be able to move forward and reconnect with her past.

"It's best to curb the emotions in circumstances such as these," Kate urged, shaking hands in greeting.

Mia, now almost nineteen, was certainly not the same girl I'd last seen from the photo in Lori's files. She was wearing baggy overalls and work boots. Jo, I learned, had done her best to shape and tidy her hair. She was much changed, a schoolgirl no more and what was most apparent was that she was clearly with child.

"Oh God," I asked myself. "Where's the good aunt instruction manual when I need it?"

"Come on in, Auntie Maggie," Mia kept her distance, avoiding my eyes as well as any physical contact as she motioned for me to meet Jo. I shook hands again and the four of us walked on into the kitchen where mugs and a plate of chocolate chip cookies sat waiting on the table.

"Mia baked these herself earlier this morning," Kate said.

I sat stiffly beside Kate as Mia set about making tea. Kate took my hand in hers: "We're so pleased you're here," she said, breaking the awkward silence. Mia nervously handed out mugs of tea, sloshing a few drops onto the polished tabletop. I shook out a cloth napkin from a neat pile and soaked up the spill.

"Why don't you sit across from us, Mia, next to Jo?" Kate suggested, "That way your aunt may see how well you are."

"Are those my earrings?" Mia asked. I reached for the small, hammered silver hoops in my ears.

"Oh yes, I clear forgot about these. I hope you don't mind, Mia, I stayed in your room at the ranch for a couple of nights. I switched them out for some silly diamond studs for safekeeping. You can have them back, now, if you'd like." I raised my hand in a motion to remove the hoop from my right ear.

"No, you keep them," Mia said, her ears were bare. She wore no jewelry that I could see.

"I've lost count of how many 'family reunions' we've presided over at this kitchen table in the years we've run Grace Place," Jo said, breezily. Hardly what I'd describe as joyful experiences I thought to myself, smiling politely, though any willing reconciliation must have its positive aspects.

Another sliver of silence passed as Mia pushed her chair from the table, placing just enough distance between us to prevent my reaching over to take her hands. Despite Kate having asked me to keep our reunion as low-key as possible, I couldn't help myself. I proceeded to deliver a bungled "thank God you're alive" roughly pre-rehearsed speech that didn't quite come out the way I'd planned.

Mia balked. I burst into tears. I was the one who was the bigger mess. Kate slid a box of tissues around the table.

"Oh God, I'm sorry," I said. "I'll stop. I know that me showing up and bawling is the last thing you need. It's just that it's been such a relief, Mia, I can't tell you. Your mom and me, we've been beside ourselves."

"It's okay Maggie." Mia said, dropping the auntie bit. All she really wanted was to hear news of Jazmin, how she had managed to get away from her captors, where she was. "I have to see her, Maggie," she begged. They had shared the same trauma. It was cruel for the authorities on Jazmin's side to delay their reunion.

"She's in a safe place, like you, though it's more recent for her than it is for you, Mia. It took her longer than you to get to safety it appears and it's a different sort of set up than this," I tried my best to reassure her that a phone call was in the works. They would see one another as soon as it was deemed possible. "The important thing is that she is out of danger, you both are," I said, my hands spread out on the table before me. "Unfortunately, Jazmin is not allowed to leave her location until her state-appointed attorney is able to sort out the legal proceedings," I explained. "Very soon, the two of you will be able to speak in private, by phone."

My eyes rested on Mia's protruding belly, fully evident despite her baggy overalls.

"As you can see, I have something to tell you, too" Mia said, placing her hands protectively across her midriff. "It's a boy. Don't go getting ahead of yourself, Maggie, telling Mom. I'm not keeping him. What I want is for Kate and Jo to adopt him."

I shot up onto my feet running my hands through my hair, my stomach flipped at Mia's additional news like I was the one who was expecting. I glared at Jo before shooting an accusing look at Kate.

"What is this?" I demanded, my eyes narrowing. "A baby racket? Sounds like a done deal? She has a family, you know. Mia has me and she has her mother, she's in no way destitute." Kate sat me down and assured me that nothing had been decided.

Mia raised her voice: "This was my idea and one I've come to on my own, Maggie, I don't see how it is any of your business, anyway."

Jo jumped in to calm things down. "In all honesty, we're amenable to making this one of Mia's options," she explained, "though we've absolutely no intention of pressuring her into making any decision concerning her baby's future until after he's born and after she's had time to discuss the situation thoroughly with her mother."

Kate spoke up, gently backing up her partner, insistent that there would be plenty of time for Mia and her mother to visit, to talk and to listen as she makes up her mind as to what is best both for her baby and for herself.

"Your niece is in a safe place here, Maggie," Jo explained, kindly, but firmly, re-establishing the ground rules, I wagered. I kept my cool as best I could. "Mia is working on herself and processing her path forward as a focused and mature young woman."

"Your niece is an adult," Kate added. "It may be hard to accept that as her aunt, especially after all you've been through as a family, Maggie, but acceptance and respect are important first steps for all in the reconnection process."

"What the hell will I tell Bridget?" I asked, flabbergasted, addressing Kate, Jo, Mia, each in turn. Who could blame me for flying off the handle? I had never anticipated any of this.

"I want you to tell my mom I'm not coming home. Not yet. One day, when I'm ready," Mia said, looking down at her hands. "Tell her I love her and that I'm sorry and I'm ok, I'm really more than ok and it's up to me to sort myself out."

After we sat there, silently, drinking our tea, Jo suggested that Mia take me on a tour of the property, just the two of us.

By the time I readied to leave, I sensed Mia growing a little more relaxed in my company. We agreed that I would come visit once every four weeks for the next few months and Bridget would come with me only when Mia was ready to see her.

"And Bobby?" Mia asked, tears welling. "Whatever will Mom do without him?"

I assured her that I was back in the picture. "I won't let your mother do this alone," I said.

After a difficult goodbye with Mia at the door, Kate walked me to my truck. A light wind brushed our faces.

"Where the hell do we go from here, Kate?" I asked. "I feel so powerless, so clueless, what do I know?"

"The details are for Mia to tell in her own time," Kate explained. "Suffice to say, your niece is a tough cookie. She's survived a harrowing time."

"I don't fully understand. Are we not to talk about what happened with her?"

"I'm not suggesting we turn a blind eye to Mia's experiences," Kate replied as I opened the door to the truck. She reached for my arm. "It's important for all of us to be on the same page in order to help her as she heals," she said. "I've been constant in my counseling of Mia," Kate assured. "I'm thankful that she's beginning to understand that she's in no way deserving of any of the bad things that have happened to her or anyone in your family."

When we'd first talked by phone, she'd told me how it is all too common for women who've been victims of kidnapping and sexual assault to blame themselves. Kate and Jo's goal in working with Mia and the other women is to help them learn how to fully forgive themselves and to recognize the wrongdoings done to them in order to start the healing process.

The focus at Grace Place is on fully transitioning Mia back into the world. It can't have been an easy option for these two women, choosing this life. Their underground operation is a labor of love. It was all the more humbling to find out they're not publicly funded in any way.

I know how it takes time and trust to peel back the layers of hurt and distrust. Bringing in each new girl is a daunting task for these women, emotionally intense for all involved and as far as Kate and Jo see it, there's sadly no end to it.

"And if she decides to leave the baby with you, when the time comes, what then?" I asked as I started the engine. I was struggling with this idea, seemingly more so than the pregnancy itself and all of its many implications for my niece. Most girls her age, any age, given the circumstances, would not have hesitated to get rid of it. To carry it to term was something else.

One more question, I asked. "I need to know. Tell me this is not some pro-life situation where Mia has been forced into going through with it?"

"No. This is entirely her decision and hers alone," Kate replied. "Besides, she was already considerably far along when she wound up here. We'll have lots of time to talk this through over the next few months."

My mind returned to Marcus. Hadn't he just seen the worst of me? I hoped he'd forgiven me for being such a lush the previous evening and for all that I'd said. I rolled down the window and extended my hand.

Kate said: "Go back to the ranch, Maggie, spend time with your sister, break this news as gently as possible. I can't emphasize enough how important your role will be in you being there for them as a steadying influence on Mia and her mother, considering the extent of suffering they've been through."

I let my guard down. "Thanks for the vote of confidence," I said, releasing my arm and taking the steering wheel, "I hope you're right about me."

"Oh, I believe so," she said. "You're strong, Maggie, you're a good role model for Mia. Trust me, I'm a great judge of character."

CHAPTER 30

MIA AND JAZMIN'S TELEPHONE CALL

"Hello."

"Mia?"

"Jaz? Is that really you?"

"For real. Oh my God, I can't believe it. I'm sorry . . . hold on a sec, I can't get my words out, I'm trying not to lose it . . . wait."

"Jesus . . . we did it, we made it, Jaz, like we said we would, we got the fuck out, alive, you and me, babe, the both of us . . . it's OK, let it out, I'm here."

"I can't breathe, I'm bawling so hard . . ."

"Same . . . take it easy, breathe deep, wipe your tears, we've got all the time in the world to catch up, to talk about what happened, after."

"I wanna see you like crazy, Mia . . . they won't let me leave 'til things are figured out."

"What things?"

"Oh, like getting me out of serving time in juvenile hall . . . or worse, they could try to deport me."

"Juvie? For what?"

"Long story. I did what I had to do. There's this kid, a guy they had running weed. I screwed him over in order for me to get the hell outa there . . . to find you."

"Do not be feeling sorry for one second for any of those fuckers after what they did."

"Ha! Don't worry, I'm not sorry . . . there's talk of a plea bargain or something since I'm gonna be of some use to the law. I've boatload of information they're interested in."

"Hell no, that's way too risky . . . what if any of the others come after you, me, us?"

"I don't see as I have much choice."

"Where are you Jaz? Are you OK?"

"I'm someplace safe, yeah — there's a ton of good food at least, yummy fresh fruit, hot water, clean clothes, heck, even a pair of skate shoes, Vans, my size they brought in today, shampoo and conditioner, body wash, frickin' organic deodorant from Sephora for God's sake. There's a bunch of nice caseworkers milling around, a therapist woman and some crime witness chick who keeps on coming in to talk. So far they're low-keying it, don't wanna freak me out, I guess. And you, where the hell are you, babe?"

"Same. Sorta, but with work boots instead of Vans!"

"What sorta work? You sleeping?"

"Planting, pulling weeds, mostly in the garden. Hey, I learned to do an oil change. Yes and no to the sleeping part. You?"

"Not much. The flashbacks, they come at night."

"It's the feeling like I'm still fenced in that freaks me out."

"What happened? After they took me away?"

"Oh, you don't wanna know . . ."

"Shit, Mia, I do and I wanna see you so so bad."

"We've gotta stay strong and see it through, Jaz, you and me . . . I feel so damn guilty. I wouldn't blame you if you hated me for all I've put you through . . ."

"It's not your fault."

"It is my fault. I dragged you into it."

"I'm a big girl, I agreed. Anyway I'm OK, for real."

"How can you be OK?"

"Dunno, somehow. All I know was I was sure as hell getting out of that shit show if it killed me. Getting you out safe was all I could think of. And see, you got yourself out."

"How long, Jaz, 'til they let me see you?"

"Who knows? I'll make it happen, whatever it takes. Believe me."

"There's one thing I have to tell you but don't ever tell a single soul. Promise? He's finished — the fucker, Jefe Hombre."

"What do you mean finished?"

"Just that."

"Okay. Sure but not sure."

"Don't ask."

"I never heard nothing."

"Far as you know I stole his truck, wrecked it crashing into the river."

"Is that true?"

"Look, Jaz, we're gonna have to stick to that part of my story is all."

"What else are you not telling me?"

"I think you know."

"About the baby?"

"Yes. July."

"Jesus . . ."

"Well, he's a boy, but I'm pretty sure that's not what I'll be naming him!"

"You sure never lost your sense of humor, girl."

"I don't wanna go into it now, J, it's complicated. We'll talk about it later."

"If you say so . . . but I'm gonna be there for you, babe, both of you."

"Hey, you gotta stay strong, Jaz, for all of us."

"Try to stop me."

"Will they let us talk again soon?"

"I think so. My caseworker is making faces through the glass window in the door, I think she wants me to hang up."

"I love you. What a total fucking badass, Jazmin, I always knew it."

"It's gonna be alright, Mia, soon. I promise. I love you too . . . look out for the two of you."

CHAPTER 31

MARCUS

Little Honey delivered her pups the day Maggie drove my truck over the border and up into Mendocino County. She never did tell me the whereabouts, being sworn to secrecy on the location where Mia is being taken care of.

I walked back to Walter's place with a big ol' bag of groceries, directly tipping a portion of dry kibble into Little Honey's bowl and expecting her to scarf it down. She was having none of it, scurrying off behind an overstuffed armchair, pulling a blanket between her teeth. I watched her as she dragged it into the corner.

Walter strode in and took one look at her. "She's ready," he declared, as plumes of smoke from a freshly lit joint filled the air. "See, she's nesting. Time to make her up a birthing box and best leave her to it for a few hours."

He at least appeared to know what the hell he was talking about. I found an empty cardboard box in the surplus from Maggie's big cleanup. It was about the right size for little Honey to stretch out in. I lined it with towels and slid the box behind the armchair where the dog had settled in the corner of the room. She'd been restless for a good hour before her contractions became noticeable. Walter brought in a laundry basket with a second folded towel inside. A lingering smell of weed infused with the rich aroma of a robust brand of coffee that sat, stewing in the pot I'd brewed earlier.

"Take the pups from her as they come out, one at a time," Walter instructed. "Place them in the laundry basket, so she can see them." He chuckled, looking at my face. "You've never done this before?"

"My first time," I said.

"I figured," he replied.

"How the hell did I get here, sitting in your front room with you, Walter, the two of us waiting on a dog to birth?"

Who was this? I barely recognized myself as the willing caretaker.

"It takes a whole load of wrong turns to make the right one," Walter answered. "I try not to over question the universe, buddy, fate, life whatever it is that pushes open doors we're meant to walk through."

Little Honey Momma groaned. "Don't touch her," Walter said.

I sat there, keeping a watch on Little Honey Momma in her time of need thinking how, through so many years of denying myself the simple truth of it, I was fairly aching for some kind of a normal life. Your normal is not necessarily my normal. For me it's the ordinary, regular, everyday pleasures of companionship I am coming around to as much as the mad attraction that I feel for Maggie. I'd lived without it for too long, a good, honest, solid relationship of any kind, except for what I had with Bobby. Ever since I lost my brother, I guess, I'd been dead afraid of any form of attachment for fear of unbearable loss. I've put my heart back on the line for this one. She says I'm mad to take her on, but I'm not so sure it is not the reverse, that she's more than a little crazy to be falling for me. All I know is I will not let her down.

Four pups. Little Honey crouched down in a squatting position and out they slithered, one by one. The whole birthing episode stretched out over an hour and a half.

I watched the whole process, fascinated, in awe. She knew just what to do. Each of the pups was born back end first, which Walter duly informed me was breech. It did not appear to trouble their momma none. Nor did the delivery of a slippery placenta apiece.

Once they were all out and we were sure there was no more of 'em coming, I did what Walter said and placed these slick little space creatures back into the birthing box alongside Little Honey. I recounted the litter to make sure I had the same number as those I'd placed in the laundry basket.

After they'd each taken their first breath, Little Honey licked her babies good and clean, washing off the membranes that coated them in their delivery. I took a closer look at them, all so sleek and lean and alive. The pups had arrived into the world with their eyes closed. Walter said: "It's best not to handle them for too long, or we'll make their momma anxious."

It was nothing short of astonishing, uplifting, plain beautiful to witness a multiple birthing with, thank God, not a darn thing going wrong. I've seen way too much death. Walter warned there might yet be complications. I thought of my brother, of Nick, my womb mate. The tears came fast and free. I wiped them away with the cuff of my shirt.

"What kind of dog do you reckon the father was?" Walter deflected, a diversion tactic to save my pride. I sniffed a couple times, before answering: "I'm not really sure, they're so small."

"My money's on Chihuahua," he said, flashing his big ol' grin.

Three of the pups looked to share the same coloring as their momma, the fourth was as black as night.

Walter said the pups would take a good six weeks to wean. "Lori and me will gladly take care of this little family while you and Maggie sort things out back at the ranch," he said.

Though I was grateful for the offer, it was hard to fathom leaving behind what I had taken to so surprisingly well in my and Maggie's responsibility, our new "found" family.

Walter read my mind. "Timing's right for you to take your Maggie home," he said. "Settle things with her sister. Talk about the gal. When all's said and done, the two of you head back up here for Little Honey and her pups, though if you don't mind, I'd like to keep one of these cuties myself."

I offered him the pick of the litter. "Except for the black one," I said. "He's mine."

As soon as she set her eyes on him, Maggie was all for keeping the exact same pup I'd picked out. "We'll get supermom fixed after the weaning is done," she said, bending down to look over a tired but content Little Honey Momma.

Maggie barely said another word all evening, other than cooing over the puppies as she sat cross-legged on the floor. I figured she was working out which parts of Mia's story to tell to Bridget and which parts to hold back.

A sense of peace descended on Walter's house, humans and animals all. Once Maggie crashed out for the count, sober as a judge, I'll add, I took a notion to have a wander around Walter's winter garden in the moonlight. He joined me, outdoors, a blanket wrapped around his shoulders. "Keeps me busy in the warmer months," he said, breathing in the night scent of damp redwood and earth. "Gives me a good enough reason for sticking around, I guess." Walter explained how the money from his produce sales comes in handy in supplementing his fixed retirement income. "The weed I grow myself I sell to a local collective," he said, pinching off a sprig of winter mint and rolling it between finger and thumb. "Whatever I don't save and cure for my own personal use, that is."

Walter has gotten to know all sorts through his garden. Aside from the many multigenerational townsfolk he has befriended over the years, a whole bunch of colorful characters populate his neighborhood — folk, who, like me, and Maggie, I guess, have for the most part, sought to escape the ass-busting financial grind of a more conventional way of life.

"I'm on friendly terms with everyone — the law, for all its worth, out on the rounds, all the old hippies such as myself, many of them musicians who've hung up their hats from a life on the road," he explained.

All sorts, Walter said. One day it might be a German tourist, backpacking off the beaten path and the next a noisy, new wave family with a gaggle of dirty-faced kids attempting to live off the grid. "I've had the occasional run-in with thieving travelers, snarling mutts in tow," Walter said, as we listened to the rustling sound of a nocturnal creature somewhere in the shadows. "There are plenty of shady characters who don't feel the need to pay for a bag of tomatoes."

It was a rash of violent break-ins by drifters in the neighborhood that led to Walter acquiring his first full-size, service pistol, the one he'd revealed to Maggie and me on our eventful drive north together. "I took up regular rounds of tin can target practice in the forest in order to perfect my shot," he explained.

I crept real quiet into bed beside a deep sleeping Maggie, drifting off to the call of a great horned owl. We awoke together at the same time the following morning to the welcome sight of a blue sky and an orchestra of birds outside of the bedroom window.

~

Lori stopped by with news a half hour after Maggie and me were up and about. Her face was ashen. "What is it, Sugar?" Walter asked, padding around the kitchen barefoot, making a pot of his extra strong coffee to see us off.

"I just heard, two bodies have been found in a shallow grave on ranchland way up on the Humboldt/Trinity border," Lori announced.

"Word is that they were teenagers — girls — most likely Latino given their clothing, hair color and other distinctive evidence," she said. The only additional information the authorities had released was that their bodies had been in the ground for two to three months.

"Thank God it's not our girls, Maggie," Lori said, giving each of us a bear hug, in turn. She smelled of patchouli. "Though Lord knows, it breaks my heart to think that they were some poor mother's precious daughters."

She never said so, there was no need, yet I couldn't help but think that after two or three months, their young bodies would have been reduced to mere skeletal remains. Creepy crawlies and creatures of the forest work take their job seriously in returning the dead to the sanctity of the earth. It's nature's way and their remains would be hard to identify, though I kept these tragic thoughts of justice un-served to myself.

CHAPTER 32

MAGGIE

B ridget anxiously awaited our return to the ranch. My sister held out her frail hands to me and I could see that she'd bitten what was left of her fingernails down to the quick. We hugged. We cried. We hugged again. Aside from in the emergency shelter at the Veterans Building, this was the most prolonged physical contact we'd shared in years.

Marcus headed out to walk the property on the semi-pretense of checking the fence line for any further storm damage. Luna busied herself scraping playdough off the kitchen table, picking up Legos from the floor. Her kids were still in school at that hour. They'd been sleeping at the ranch with their mother so that Bridget was never alone in her hours of grief. Bobby's caps and jackets hung by the door as if he might saunter back in at any moment.

"You've seen her?" Bridget asked, nervously. She looked like she hadn't showered in days, her freshly sprouting hair, uncovered, unwashed.

"Yes."

"But she's not comin' home?"

"Not for a while." After I sat my sister down I made tea for the three of us women. I think it was Virginia Woolf who wrote of the shelter of a common femininity. It came to mind.

"I'll leave you two to talk," Luna said, standing beside my sister, her arms full with the box of toys. Bridget took her by the elbow and urged her to stay. "Sit here a while longer, Luna," she said. "You and the kids, you're a part of this family now."

We looked around the table at one another, three women facing an unknown future. It was difficult to know where to begin. "There's so much I have to tell you, Bridget," I said.

I described Grace Place, without giving away any details of its location, keeping my word. "Mia's safe and she's well cared for," I said. "Don't freak out, Bridget, but you need to know that she's pregnant. Mia's expecting a baby, a boy. She's due four months from now — July."

"Mia? Pregnant. No, this can't be happenin'," Bridget cried. "Jesus Christ, can things get any worse for us? All of it, it's my fault, I pushed her away, I failed her," she sobbed. "My baby girl."

"Hush, now, Bridget," I urged. "Mia's surprisingly strong, she's in good hands. She's alive. It's where we go from here that's going to matter."

"A baby's not a death sentence, Bridget," Luna reassured, smoothing the colorful dress she wore over a pair of black leggings, a pair of big, blue Doc Martens boots on her feet. "Look at us, single mothers both. It happens."

"Not like this," Bridget said. "My teenage daughter. Raped." I kept calm and made more tea, picturing Mia as I had seen her, in control of herself, protective of her child. I followed her lead.

"We're all here for her," I said. "That's more than either of you had when your babies were born." It was time to introduce the concept of a possible adoption. An open adoption. Bridget raised her arms in the air and flew into a fit.

"Am I not her mother? Jesus Christ. I get to have a say in this."

"She wants to see you soon, Bridget, not immediately, but soon. There's much to work out. The good thing is that Mia has support and options. Nothing will be decided until you've talked it all through. We'll press on through this together, I promise."

Luna said her goodbyes as she left for school. She packed the trunk of her car with a bag full of her family's clothing. They were headed back to their cute little cottage rental on the ranch they'd made their home. Bridget started telling me how she had begun to figure out Bobby's immediate affairs.

"Isn't it a bit soon?" I asked.

"Someone has to do it," she said. "Might as well be now."

"And?"

"Unbeknownst to me," she explained, "Bobby kept a handwritten will in the safe at the roadhouse. Angelina came to see me. Turns out he had some family money tied up, not much, but it's enough for my basic needs."

Bridget described how Bobby had squirreled away a small inheritance from his family's property.

"Angelina, she hid it for him as an investment in the roadhouse so his ex wouldn't get wind of it. I don't suppose he'd ever have asked Angelina to buy him out," she said. "The roadhouse was his livelihood, mine too for a long time."

"Is she okay to pay you out?" I asked.

"She didn't have to tell me, Maggie," Bridget said. "Who would have known? Angelina's a good soul, she and his brother are as honest as anyone. She handed me Bobby's will and offered up the money in long-term payments."

At least one of us had taken it upon ourselves to have the good sense to stash some cash. I had a new respect for Bobby and his simple ways. Bridget took a breath. "It's enough for me to be able to leave here, Maggie. The ranch. I'm done. It's your turn, now."

I choked on my second mug of tea. "What the fuck? Slow down. Let's talk about this in a month or two, Bridget. Where on earth would you go?"

"Someplace in town, I'm not fussy, closer to the dispensary," she replied, she had it all figured out. "I don't need much and with Bobby's money I'll be able to afford to rent a small apartment plus a share workspace in a commercial kitchen. It's what I want to do, what I need to do."

"Wow," I said, lost for words. "That's a whole lot of thinking you've done this past week."

"All I ask is you make room for Mia."

"Of course," I said. "This is her place, too." I fixed us a small supper of chicken quesadillas from a bunch of Luna's leftovers in the fridge. Marcus was a reassuring presence at the table. The three of us sat together in the dwindling light. Bridget was spent. Her voice was wrung of its old spirit, her eyes glazed over. She nibbled at her food, excused herself and slwly made her way upstairs to bed.

"Bridget — would you believe, thinks it's time for me to take over this downtrodden old place," I told Marcus, when I was sure my sister was asleep. "What's left of it, that is."

"And you, what do you want?" Marcus asked. He was sitting beside me on the couch. "Do you see yourself staying on here, Maggie?"

"It has some potential, you said as much yourself — the barn at least." I smiled, pinching his forearm. "Besides, I've got no place else to go."

Marcus leaned in closer, tracing the lines of my wrist with his finger as he'd done the morning after we'd first made love. "Don't make that your reason to stay," he said. "If you take it on, weather-beaten as it is, the mildew and rot, you're gonna have to embrace it with your whole heart, make something of it, breathe new life into this tough, ol' McCleery legacy."

Bridget was clearly done with the past, the present and the future of this damp and lonesome place. I could hardly blame her, could I? Where did that leave me?

"Grab a jacket," Marcus said. We walked out under the stars of a clear and peaceful night sky and into the old milking barn where he settled himself on the edge of the cold remnant of a concrete milking stall, motioning for me to sit beside him. He is comfortable here on the ranch and it's evident. Together, under the one remaining flickering florescent overhead light, we attempted to absorb the scope and potential of the space and more indirectly, each other. Bat wings flapped in the shadows of the high rafters.

"It's coming, Maggie, whether people like it or not, the end of cannabis prohibition," Marcus said. "If you don't seize the opportunity to do it right, then others surely will."

"Isn't that jumping on the bandwagon?" I asked. "I'm tired of the latest and greatest."

"Think about it," he said. "First it was potatoes, then it was wheat, eggs, dairy and later on, grapevines . . . if you follow the path of progress out here on the Pacific ranchlands you'll put your stake in the ground. If you do it by the books and you are smart and educated and experienced enough to do so, you have every right to stand shoulder to shoulder with those who've fought to make growing cannabis legal in this county."

He spoke of the pros and the cons of capitalizing the property given that we have an abundance of groundwater out here on the ranch, an essential commodity for any environmentally ethical medical cannabis production.

"Water is king," Marcus said, sharing some of his basic geological knowledge of underground water learned from his years of working outdoors. "There's a ton of water stored here in the cracks and spaces of soil, sand and rock," he explained. "What you have here on the ranch is known as aquifers," he said. "Basically — liquid gold. You can't go into an enterprise like this without water."

"If we were to plant more of the high-grade, boutique weed that Bridget cooks with, then I'll have to get up to speed in learning how to breed and crossbreed plants," I said.

"We're at a turning point in modern medicinal history, Maggie," Marcus continued. "The county is in the process of rolling out its permitting rules. We're talking best land management practices, legal compliance — it's your family's land, Maggie, your water, it's agriculturally zoned, it sits on more than ten acres and you have no neighbors close enough to be impacted. You do as you see best, but this is a viable option for sure if you decide to give it a go."

"But don't you think we've had more than enough of what can go so badly wrong?" I asked. "I mean, look at the state of us, my family, all that's happened this past six months?"

"It's the black market that legalization and zoning will eventually do away with, ideally," he replied. "No more raids, no more trafficking, it's time to figure out how to curtail the mayhem."

I'm thinking it through. It remains to be seen what will transpire over time. It certainly would be a hell of a decision for me to go down this wild, crazy, still largely uncharted road, even if it is legal. I'm going to have to do a lot of research and sit down to discuss it with my sister when the time's right, Mia, too — there's no way I'm about to go full throttle with an idea like this without their consent. It's equal part their ranch, when all's said and done. And who's to say how long this crazy green rush will last?

"Aside from all that, first things first, please say your work will let you stick around long enough to help me haul the bulk of the crappy old furniture outdoors and into the barn?" I begged. "If Bridget chooses to take any of it with her after she finds a place, she's more than welcome to sort through it and I'll gladly get rid of the rest."

I was more than a little giddy at the thought of liberating the old place, stripping it of its heavy haul of relics, finally releasing its ghosts. I'm happy that my sister gets to reinvent herself after all those years of self-sacrifice. If I'm to live here, I will have to make peace with the place, turn it into my idea of a home for Little Honey Momma and me. Maybe, if things work out like I hope they will, Marcus and the new puppy will move in with us, give living together a shot. Together, we'd set about stripping the house to its bare bones, inside and out, slowly, over time. I guess what I do have is nothing but time right now and an evolving picture in my mind of how I might transform the place, carefully and thoughtfully. It will have to be a frugal effort at the start.

Later that evening, I slipped my hand beneath the layers of clothing in Mia's dresser. I found what I was looking for, the small, velvet pouch that held my platinum wedding band and diamond engagement ring, the pair of diamond stud earrings I'd switched out for Mia's silver hoops and the Rolex watch Andres had gifted me in what felt like entirely different life. I figured these last remaining material fragments of my marital legacy would, hopefully, afford me at least the basic materials for the most urgent of renovations. It's amazing what a coat of white paint can do to a place. I can't wait to rip out the smelly old rugs and curling linoleum, to sand and refinish the original hardwood floors I know are under there somewhere. I'm thinking modern country farmhouse, paired down, sunny and light filled. Mia won't recognize the place and I think that's a good thing — when she's good and ready that is. And who knows, she may never want to move back in. I hope now that she understands how important she is to me and to her mom, to our family such that it is and she may then allow us to help her make her own best choice of what comes next in her life.

~

Marcus volunteered to help Bridget pack up Bobby's clothes and modest possessions before it was time for him to head back to his work after an extended hiatus cleared by his boss given the circumstances of his best friend's sudden death. "Save Bridget the added sorrow of doing it alone," he said as we stood together, arm in arm looking out into the darkness of the empty ranchland, its possibilities and its never-ending needs. To think it was all so late in the game. I'd given up on the idea of happiness and home and then there was this. I'm taking it day by day. I don't dare to do otherwise.

I flung open the windows and doors to a greet second day of clear, impossibly blue, cloudless sky, the clean scent of freshly laundered sheets, the first of my efforts, carried outside to hang on a clothesline Marcus had rigged up at my request between two of the old eucalyptus trees. Spring would follow soon. I could almost smell its bounty of wildflowers and whispers of warmer days ahead.

I thought of the city, of how it hummed on, endlessly as it went about its usual business, it's bright lights and all of its promise and potential and noise continuing on without me. Do we miss each other, the city and me, the modern world? I think not. Barefaced and hopeful, I hung the blue dress I'd yet to wear in the open door frame to air in the ocean breeze.

"Where to start?" I wondered as I took it all in, the peeling wallpaper, worn rugs . . . I rolled up my sleeves and made a start with removing the cuckoo clock from the kitchen wall.

Here we are, Marcus and me, two of the most unlikely people to connect and yet each of us seeing something worth loving in the other. It's OK for life to be messy, as he said and I'm finally learning.

"Are you in?" I asked, "as in making this home?" What do I have to offer him except a falling down farmhouse, two dogs and the reclaimed wreck of myself?

Without a second's pause, he stood behind me, wrapped his arms around me and, after turning me around, he looked me in the eyes and replied: "Hell yes. I'm in. I've been in from the start. But first we'll have to fix that roof."

AUTHOR'S NOTE

Big Green Country is a work of fiction with its strong sense of place being one of the main characters. I hope through my writing, to take you by the hand and lead you through this lesser traveled part of Northern California so that you may experience the redwoods and rugged coastal terrain as we explore the importance of family, how bonds can be lost and found and what endures. Many of the locations within this story do exist, though others are fictional creations set within the geography of the region. The McCleery farmhouse, for example, is a reimagined Victorian ranch home based on multiple historic structures that have survived along the seacoast of Sonoma and Marin counties. Many of its architectural details I derived from original photographs viewed in the Sonoma County History Archives. The Daniel Boone Roadhouse was modeled, in part, on Marin County's oldest saloon, The William Tell House. A Bloom of One's Own is a fictional blend of contemporary dispensaries located throughout the United States, though this one is firmly rooted in Sonoma County with its Victorian architectural heritage, succulent-filled front porch and West Country vibe. The Russian River Resort Cabins and Cottage is an imagined redwood oasis in the forest based on several rustic places I have stayed in along the California coast. All of the homes and the compounds I describe throughout this story are fictional places, including Grace Place. Old Six Mile House, the roadhouse outside of Fortuna exists only in my mind, though readers may recognize many aspects of this Western watering hole in any number of old-time saloons.

All of the characters and incidents in this story are imaginary and scenes such as the one in the evacuation center at the real Veteran's

Memorial Building in Santa Rosa I made up. Any similarity between them and living or deceased people or real incidents is unintentional and coincidental. And, no, none of the characters in this story are me or based on anyone I know. Any inaccuracies in specifics of health, plant, production, operation and safety processes are my own. It only takes around six inches of water to sweep a person off his/her feet and a mere one to two feet of water to float a vehicle off its wheels. Drivers must always heed warnings about low water crossings and never make an attempt to cross a flooded highway. Wearing seat belts increases the chance of surviving a vehicular crash into water. Drivers are advised to research and rehearse emergency escape and survival procedures according to vehicle make and model and have rescue/escape tools readily available to self-extricate before a vehicle begins to sink.

Human trafficking is an epidemic of modern-day slavery. It takes the form of any sort of commercial sex act or labor or services brought about through force, fraud or coercion, whether or not the victim is moved from one place or another. Those who traffic humans do not exclusively target young women like Mia and Jazmin. Men, women and children of all ages are victims of this heinous crime in its many forms. Self-designated, self-funded programs such as the one depicted at fictional Grace Place provide round-the-clock access to safety geared specifically to women like the ones in this story. Sadly, there are not nearly enough regional emergency and transitional housing options for victims such as Mia and Jazmin, those who escape the hidden horrors of captivity in Northern California and other rural outposts. Farming environments hide the highest number of victims of human trafficking, with unpermitted cannabis farming leading the pack. Most federally funded resources for victims of human trafficking are funneled into large, urban areas, big cities. More must be done. Though dedicated people such as fictional characters Kate and Jo are taking great strides to help women like Mia and Jazmin access services after initial rehabilitation through networks of social service organizations, it's not enough. For more information on this crisis and how to be better informed, see humantrafficking.org. If you suspect someone is a victim of human trafficking call the National Human Trafficking Hotline 1 (888) 373-7888.

Though Marcus, as with all of the characters in this story, is not based on any one specific military veteran, many thousands of wounded warriors throughout the United States share his very real struggles. The Veterans Crisis Line is a free, confidential resource available to anyone, even if they're not registered with VA or enrolled in VA health care. The caring, qualified responders at the Veterans Crisis Line are specially trained and experienced in helping Veterans of all ages and circumstances. Since its launch in 2007, the Veterans Crisis Line has answered more than 3.5 million calls and initiated the dispatch of emergency services to callers in crisis nearly 100,000 times. In November 2011, the Veterans Crisis Line introduced a text messaging service to provide another way for veterans to connect with confidential, round-the-clock support, and since then has responded to nearly 98,000 texts. If you or someone you know is a veteran in crisis and need to speak to someone urgently, call 1 800 273 8255.

ACKNOWLEDGEMENTS

Thank you to Rocco Rivetti for patiently imparting your wisdom and talent in detailed concept editing of the first two drafts of Big Green Country. Your keen instinct and insight into the human condition, gentle nudging and general all-round backing and faith in my work has taught me how to open all the drawers with more abandon, pull it all out and turn it upside down, peek into the glove box, populate the minutiae, dig for buried motivations in order to reveal the underlying feelings of my characters and the land they live in.

No manuscript of mine is ever complete without a round of expert treatment by book midwife Elaine Silver, who helped me to pick up the pacing two-years in. Thank you for speaking up for those who needed to be given a louder voice. And for your unstoppable scratching beneath the surface of this love affair of mine with regards to the lesser-known and more remote aspects of a region that I will never exhaust in my writing.

Michelle Wellington, for sharing the rich details of your teenage musical influences as a Northern California native. Though we've found so many common references between us in discussing the music of our transatlantic youth, the soundtrack of Bridget and Maggie's coming of age is largely thanks to your invaluable insight and passion for the music of the '80s.

Thank you to early readers, Lesley McCullaugh, Kerry Parnell, Lindsey Chadwick and Dana Weitzenberg. Releasing this complex tale to the world was made so much easier after your insightful feedback and suggestions.

When I tasked proofreader Brenda Bellinger with the job
through this story with a fine toothcomb and employing ar
eagle eye in identifying my many subtle Britishisms, ne
imagined how many had stubbornly hung in there, hopir
exposure. In that vein, any bloopers, words or phrases that s
British than American are the sneaky survivors of a long pro

Friends and family and my extended reader/writer commu
me constantly and enthusiastically through more than thre
of writing and editing, revising and figuring out my path to
with this, my first work of fiction. You all know wh
Together, we've gone through some wild times in Sono
over the past few years and we're ever stronger together.

Morning walks with my rescue dog Rosie kept me sane an
fit during this extended writing process. It was sweet, patier
accompanied me on my location scouting/research trips int
County and faithfully sat by my writing desk for hours at a

My three wonderful sons, Rocco, Luc and Dominic are
inspiration as I pursue my passion for asking deeper que
world. I love you guys and thank you for making my life
rewarding. Thank you, Dom for capturing my author hea
Green Country under an ancient oak in our backyard. Fo
me, Mr. Motivator, my husband is my biggest fan. Ultim
to Timo for encouraging and cajoling me all the way to t
steepest writing hill yet. Many hundreds of mugs of
graciously delivered to my desk have had a lot to do with i

Translating contemporary culture into fiction has allow
share stories of those who don't ordinarily have much of
modern society in order to expose the cracks in the sy
dangers posed to the more vulnerable among us. I ho
makes a difference.

Last but not least, if you've enjoyed Big Green Country,
a few minutes to give it a brief review online. Good, ge
are golden and so, big thanks to any reader who fe
warrants a few positive words to share with the world at l

 CPSIA information can be obtained
at www.ICGtesting.com
Printed in the USA
LVHW040742310520
656912LV00003B/348

ACKNOWLEDGEMENTS

Thank you to Rocco Rivetti for patiently imparting your wisdom and talent in detailed concept editing of the first two drafts of Big Green Country. Your keen instinct and insight into the human condition, gentle nudging and general all-round backing and faith in my work has taught me how to open all the drawers with more abandon, pull it all out and turn it upside down, peek into the glove box, populate the minutiae, dig for buried motivations in order to reveal the underlying feelings of my characters and the land they live in.

No manuscript of mine is ever complete without a round of expert treatment by book midwife Elaine Silver, who helped me to pick up the pacing two-years in. Thank you for speaking up for those who needed to be given a louder voice. And for your unstoppable scratching beneath the surface of this love affair of mine with regards to the lesser-known and more remote aspects of a region that I will never exhaust in my writing.

Michelle Wellington, for sharing the rich details of your teenage musical influences as a Northern California native. Though we've found so many common references between us in discussing the music of our transatlantic youth, the soundtrack of Bridget and Maggie's coming of age is largely thanks to your invaluable insight and passion for the music of the '80s.

Thank you to early readers, Lesley McCullaugh, Kerry Parnell, Lindsey Chadwick and Dana Weitzenberg. Releasing this complex tale to the world was made so much easier after your insightful feedback and suggestions.

When I tasked proofreader Brenda Bellinger with the job of poring through this story with a fine toothcomb and employing an especially eagle eye in identifying my many subtle Britishisms, neither of us imagined how many had stubbornly hung in there, hoping to avoid exposure. In that vein, any bloopers, words or phrases that sound more British than American are the sneaky survivors of a long process!

Friends and family and my extended reader/writer community rallied me constantly and enthusiastically through more than three long years of writing and editing, revising and figuring out my path to publishing with this, my first work of fiction. You all know who you are. Together, we've gone through some wild times in Sonoma County over the past few years and we're ever stronger together.

Morning walks with my rescue dog Rosie kept me sane and somewhat fit during this extended writing process. It was sweet, patient Rosie who accompanied me on my location scouting/research trips into Humboldt County and faithfully sat by my writing desk for hours at a time.

My three wonderful sons, Rocco, Luc and Dominic are my joy and inspiration as I pursue my passion for asking deeper questions of the world. I love you guys and thank you for making my life as a Mom so rewarding. Thank you, Dom for capturing my author headshot for Big Green Country under an ancient oak in our backyard. Fortunately, for me, Mr. Motivator, my husband is my biggest fan. Ultimate kudos go to Timo for encouraging and cajoling me all the way to the top of my steepest writing hill yet. Many hundreds of mugs of P.G.Tips tea graciously delivered to my desk have had a lot to do with it.

Translating contemporary culture into fiction has allowed me to the share stories of those who don't ordinarily have much of a voice in our modern society in order to expose the cracks in the system and the dangers posed to the more vulnerable among us. I hope this book makes a difference.

Last but not least, if you've enjoyed Big Green Country, please do take a few minutes to give it a brief review online. Good, genuine reviews are golden and so, big thanks to any reader who feels this story warrants a few positive words to share with the world at large.

9 780990 492122